HELLBOY AND THE BUREAU FOR PARANORMAL RESEARCH AND DEFENSE

THE BEAST OF VARGU AND OTHERS

Created by MIKE MIGNOLA

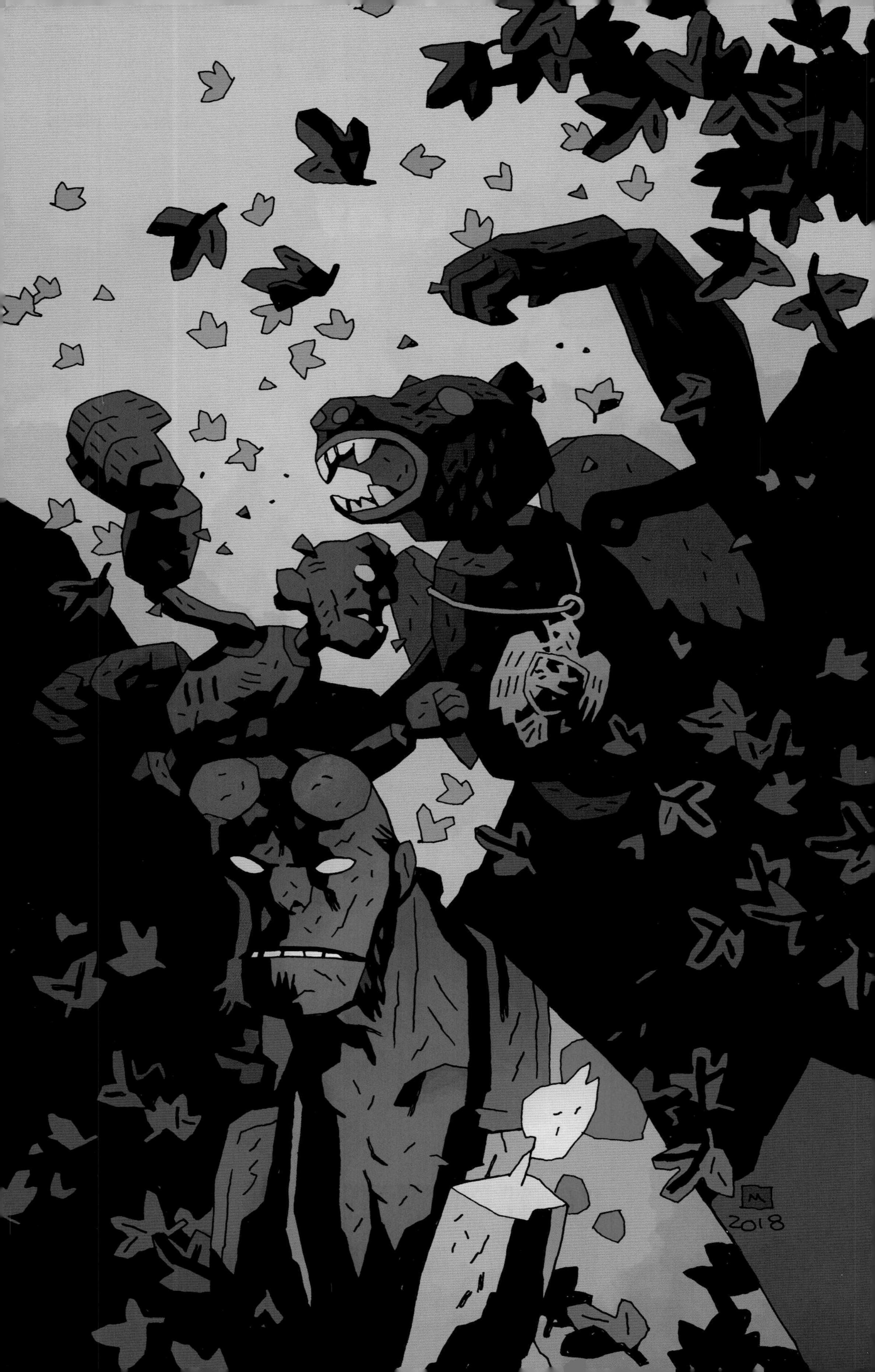
2018

MIKE MIGNOLA'S

HELLBOY™ AND THE B.P.R.D.

THE BEAST OF VARGU AND OTHERS

THE BEAST OF VARGU

Story by MIKE MIGNOLA

Art by DUNCAN FEGREDO • *Colors by* DAVE STEWART

✠

SATURN RETURNS

Story by MIKE MIGNOLA *and* SCOTT ALLIE

Art by CHRISTOPHER MITTEN • *Colors by* BRENNAN WAGNER

✠

KRAMPUSNACHT

Story by MIKE MIGNOLA

Art and colors by ADAM HUGHES

✠

RETURN OF THE LAMBTON WORM

Story by MIKE MIGNOLA

Art by BEN STENBECK • *Colors by* DAVE STEWART

✠

Letters by CLEM ROBINS

Cover by ADAM HUGHES

Publisher MIKE RICHARDSON ✠ *Editor* KATII O'BRIEN ✠ *Assistant Editor* JENNY BLENK

Collection Designer PATRICK SATTERFIELD ✠ *Digital Art Technician* ANN GRAY

DARK HORSE BOOKS

Published by Dark Horse Books
A division of Dark Horse Comics LLC
10956 SE Main Street • Milwaukie, OR 97222

DarkHorse.com
Facebook.com/DarkHorseComics
Twitter.com/DarkHorseComics

Advertising Sales: (503) 905-2315 • Comic Shop Locator Service: ComicShopLocator.com

First edition: June 2020
ISBN 978-1-50671-130-0

1 3 5 7 9 10 8 6 4 2
Printed in China

Hellboy and the B.P.R.D.: The Beast of Vargu and Others

This book collects *Hellboy: Krampusnacht*, *Hellboy: Return of the Lambton Worm*, *Hellboy and the B.P.R.D.: Saturn Returns #1–#3*,
and *Hellboy and the B.P.R.D.: The Beast of Vargu*.

Library of Congress Cataloging-in-Publication Data

Names: Mignola, Mike, author. | Fegredo, Duncan, artist. | Stewart, Dave,
colourist. | Allie, Scott, author. | Mitten, Christopher (Christopher
J.), artist. | Wagner, Brennan, colourist. | Hughes, Adam, artist. |
Stenbeck, Ben, artist. | Robins, Clem, letterer.
Title: Hellboy and the B.P.R.D. : the Beast of Vargu and others / Mike
Mignola, Duncan Fegredo, Dave Stewart, Scott Allie, Christopher Mitten,
Brennan Wagner, Adam Hughes, Ben Stenbeck, Clem Robins.
Description: First edition. | Milwaukie, OR : Dark Horse Books, 2020. |
"This book collects Hellboy: Krampusnacht, Hellboy: Return of the
Lambton Worm, Hellboy and the B.P.R.D.: Saturn Returns #1-#3, andHellboy
and the B.P.R.D.: The Beast of Vargu." | Summary: "A wide variety of new
dangers lie in wait for you in this Hellboy story collection! Face the
mysterious Lambton Worm, track down an ancient corpse collector in the
untamed wilderness, and more in this series of monster meet-ups! Some of
Hellboy's most notorious exploits, including the story of Eisner
Award-winning one-shot Hellboy: Krampusnacht and fan-favorite Hellboy:
The Beast of Vargu await in this new short story collection! Mike
Mignola and Scott Allie are joined by veteran Hellboy artists Duncan
Fegredo, Adam Hughes, Christopher Mitten, and Ben Stenbeck to present
stories collected for the first time in paperback, complete with bonus
sketchbook section"-- Provided by publisher.
Identifiers: LCCN 2020002509 (print) | LCCN 2020002510 (ebook) | ISBN
9781506711300 (paperback) | ISBN 9781506711317 (ebook)
Subjects: LCSH: Comic books, strips, etc.
Classification: LCC PN6728.H3838 M299 2020 (print) | LCC PN6728.H3838
(ebook) | DDC 741.5/973--dc23
LC record available at https://lccn.loc.gov/2020002509
LC ebook record available at https://lccn.loc.gov/2020002510

THE BEAST OF VARGU

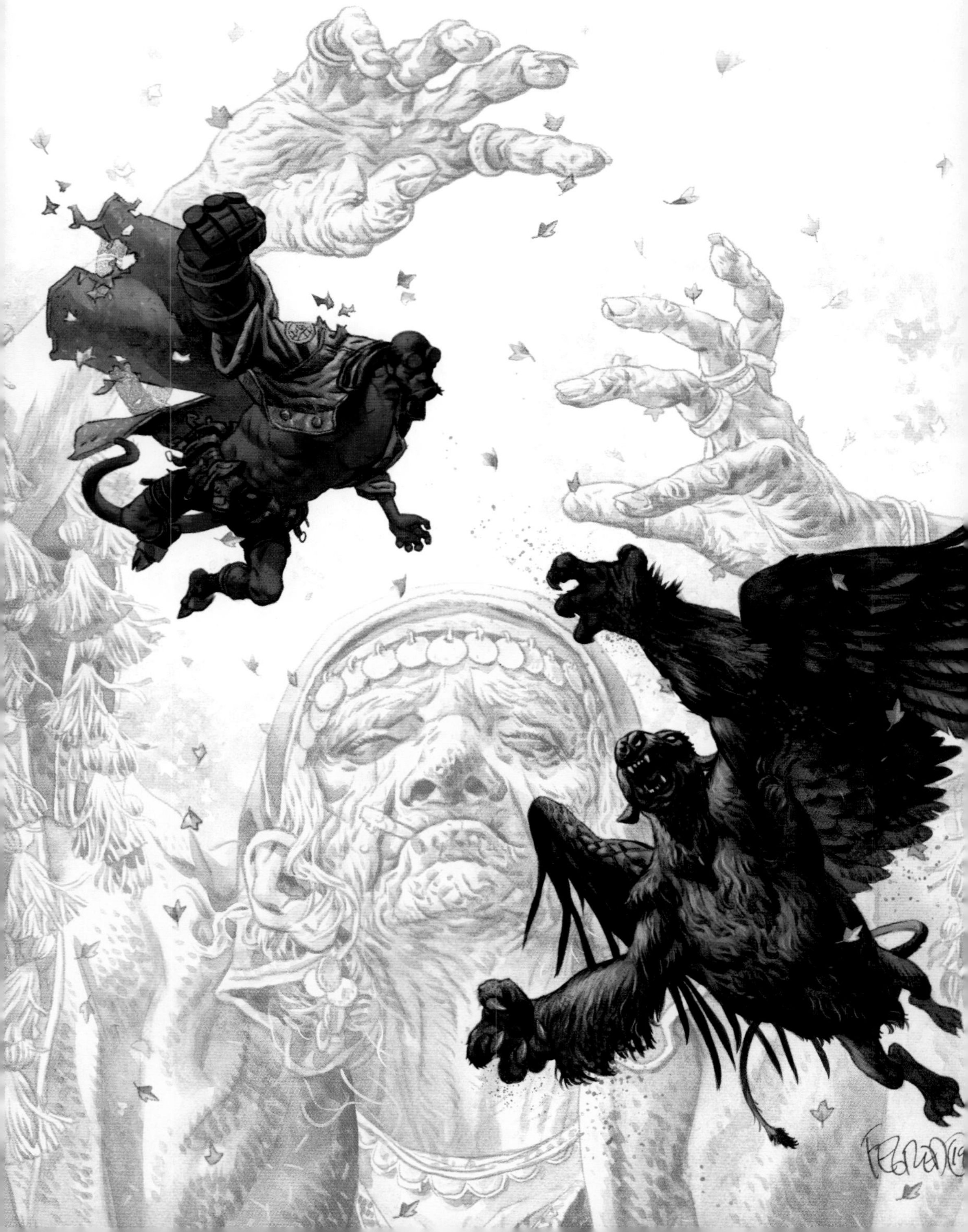

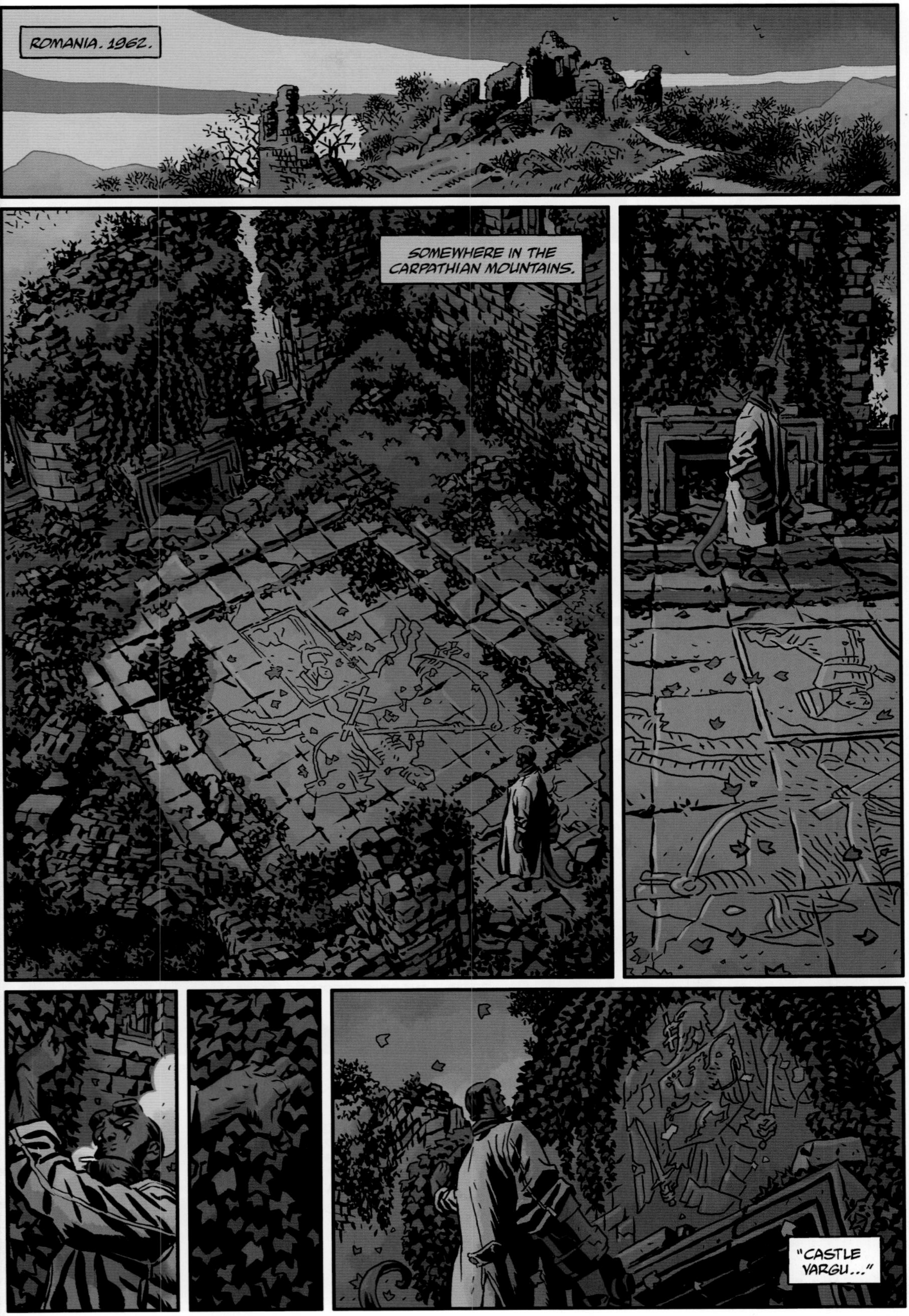
ROMANIA. 1962.
SOMEWHERE IN THE CARPATHIAN MOUNTAINS.
"CASTLE VARGU..."

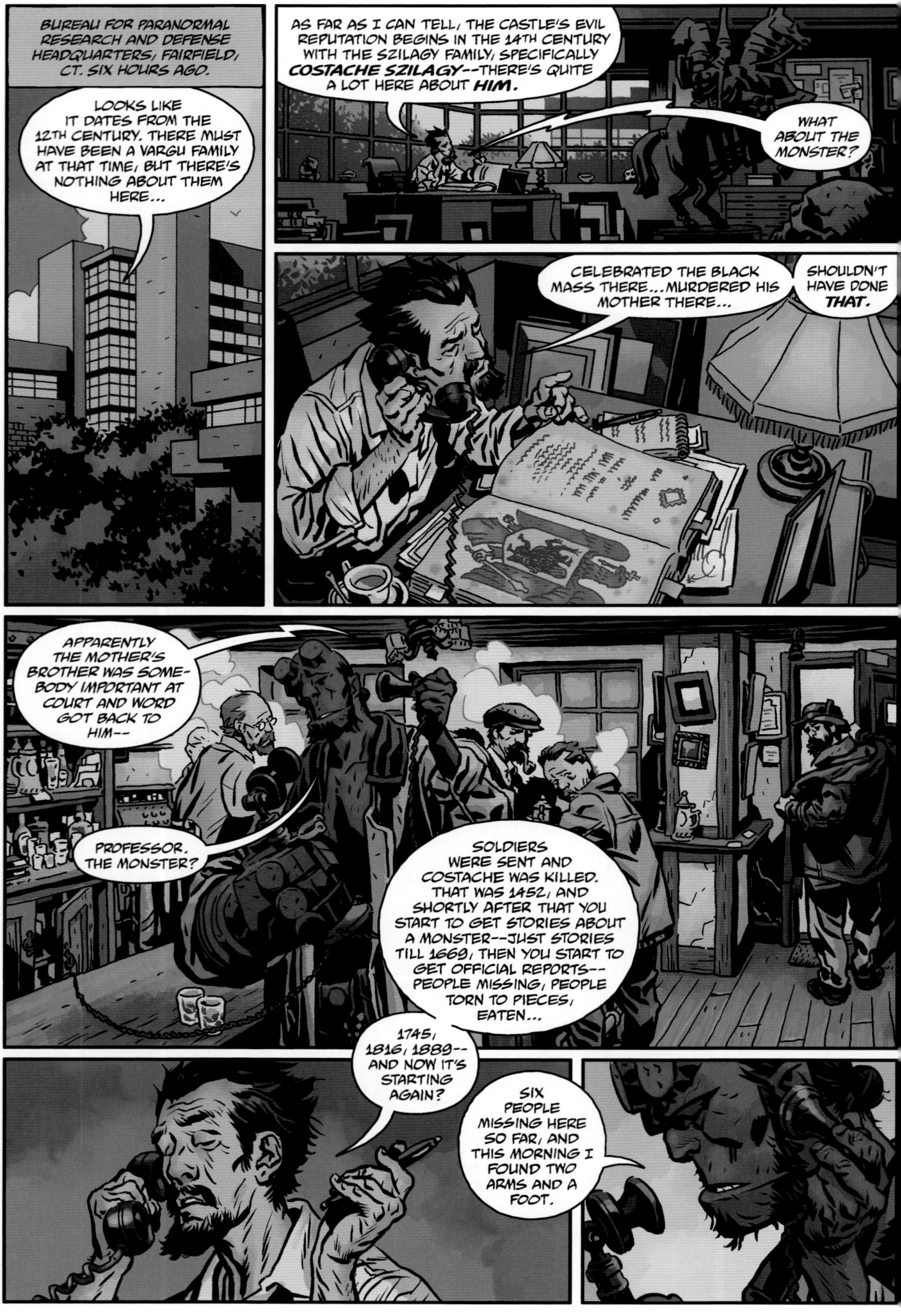
BUREAU FOR PARANORMAL RESEARCH AND DEFENSE HEADQUARTERS, FAIRFIELD, CT. SIX HOURS AGO.
LOOKS LIKE IT DATES FROM THE 12TH CENTURY. THERE MUST HAVE BEEN A VARGU FAMILY AT THAT TIME, BUT THERE'S NOTHING ABOUT THEM HERE...
AS FAR AS I CAN TELL, THE CASTLE'S EVIL REPUTATION BEGINS IN THE 14TH CENTURY WITH THE SZILAGY FAMILY, SPECIFICALLY **COSTACHE SZILAGY**--THERE'S QUITE A LOT HERE ABOUT **HIM.**
WHAT ABOUT THE MONSTER?
CELEBRATED THE BLACK MASS THERE...MURDERED HIS MOTHER THERE...
SHOULDN'T HAVE DONE **THAT.**
APPARENTLY THE MOTHER'S BROTHER WAS SOMEBODY IMPORTANT AT COURT AND WORD GOT BACK TO HIM--
PROFESSOR. THE MONSTER?
SOLDIERS WERE SENT AND COSTACHE WAS KILLED. THAT WAS 1452, AND SHORTLY AFTER THAT YOU START TO GET STORIES ABOUT A MONSTER--JUST STORIES TILL 1669, THEN YOU START TO GET OFFICIAL REPORTS--PEOPLE MISSING, PEOPLE TORN TO PIECES, EATEN...
1745, 1816, 1889--AND NOW IT'S STARTING AGAIN?
SIX PEOPLE MISSING HERE SO FAR, AND THIS MORNING I FOUND TWO ARMS AND A FOOT.

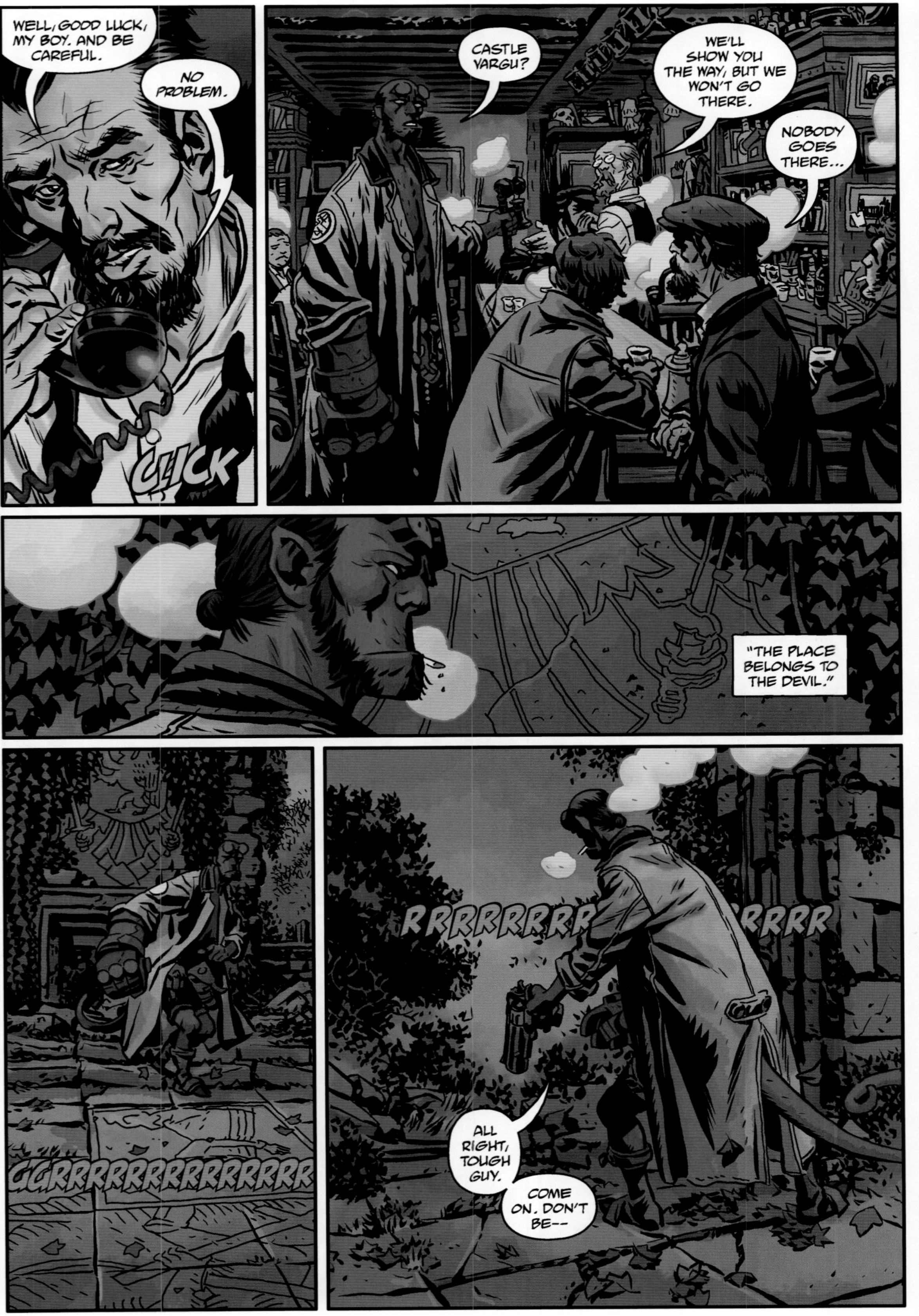
WELL, GOOD LUCK, MY BOY. AND BE CAREFUL.
NO PROBLEM.
CLICK
CASTLE VARGU?
WE'LL SHOW YOU THE WAY, BUT WE WON'T GO THERE.
NOBODY GOES THERE...
"THE PLACE BELONGS TO THE DEVIL."
GGRRRRRRRRRRRRRRR
RRRRRRRRR
RRRRR
ALL RIGHT, TOUGH GUY.
COME ON. DON'T BE--

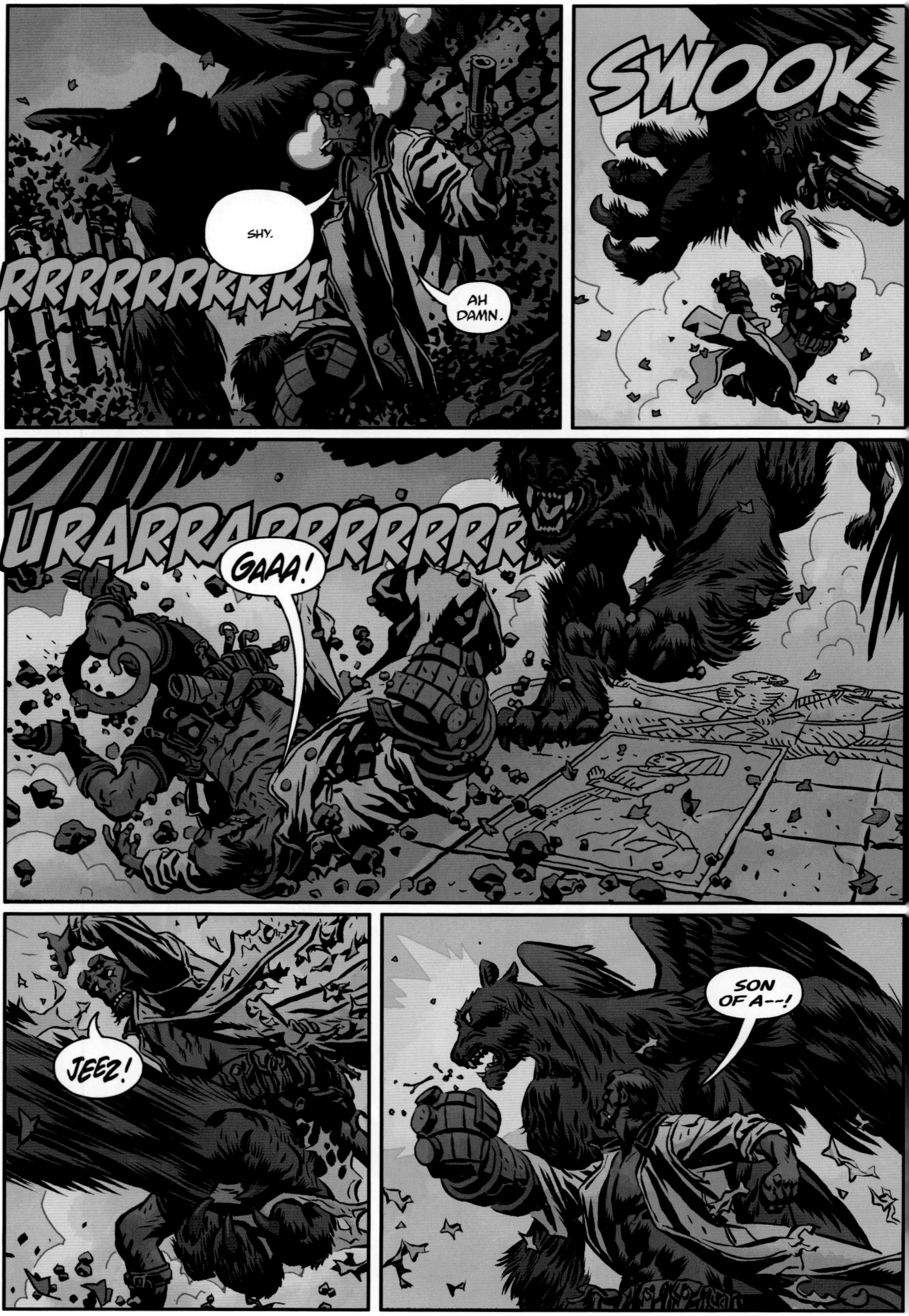
SHY.
RRRRRRRRRR
AH DAMN.
SWOOK
URARRARRRRRRRR
GAAA!
JEEZ!
SON OF A--!

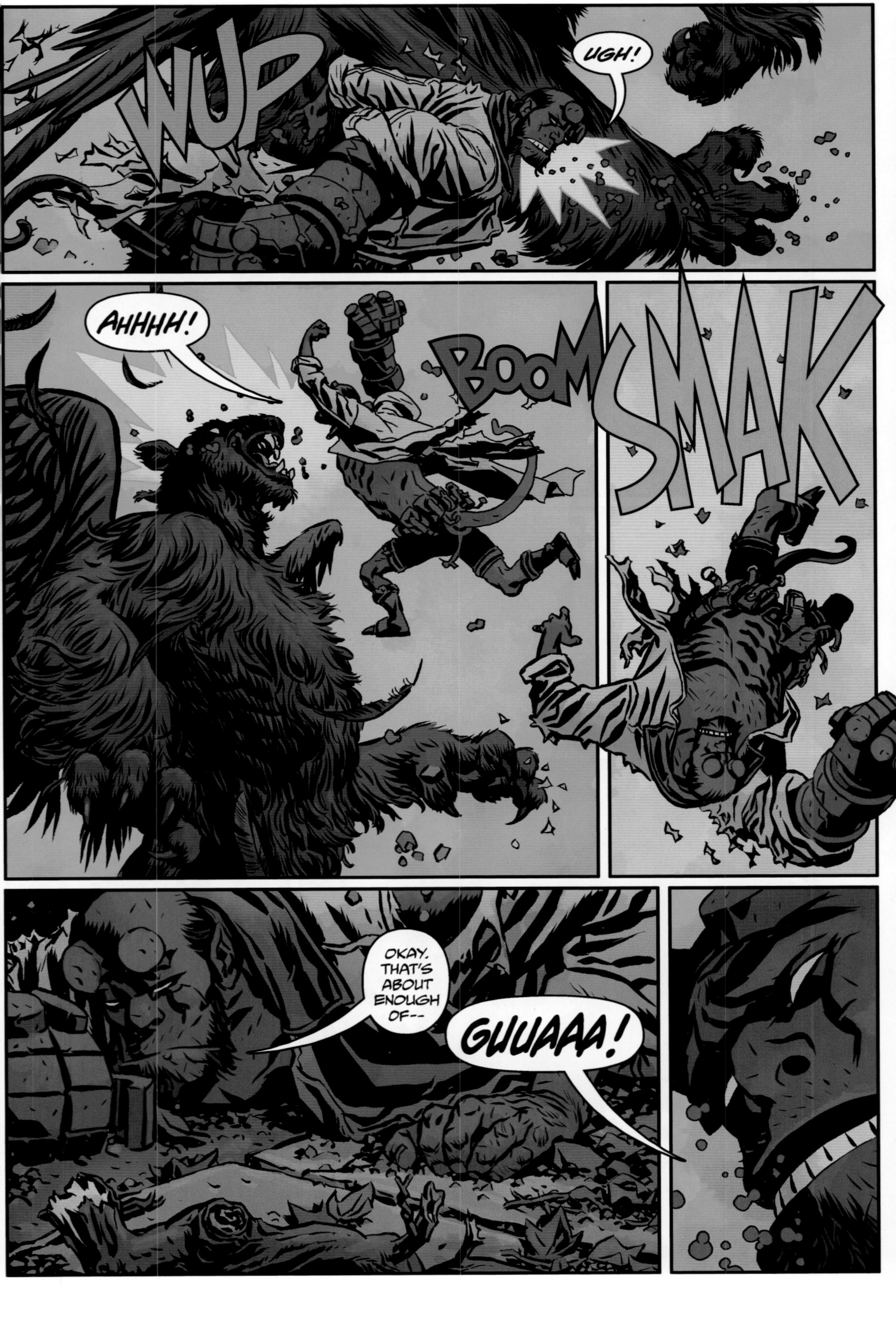
WUP
UGH!
AHHHH!
BOOM
SMAK
OKAY. THAT'S ABOUT ENOUGH OF--
GUUAAA!

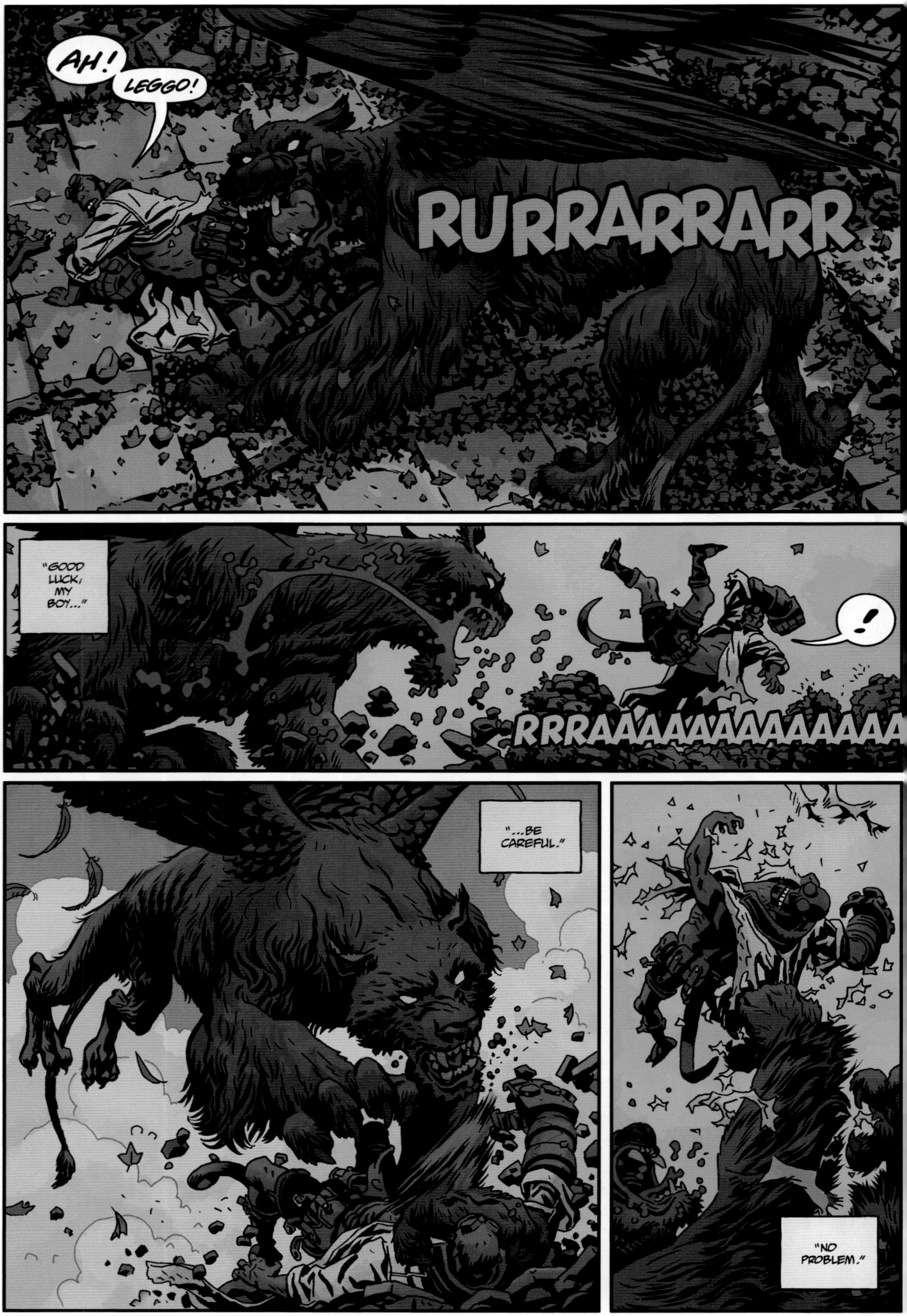
AH!
LEGGO!
RURRARRARR
"GOOD LUCK, MY BOY..."
!
RRRAAAAAAAAAAAAA
"...BE CAREFUL."
"NO PROBLEM."

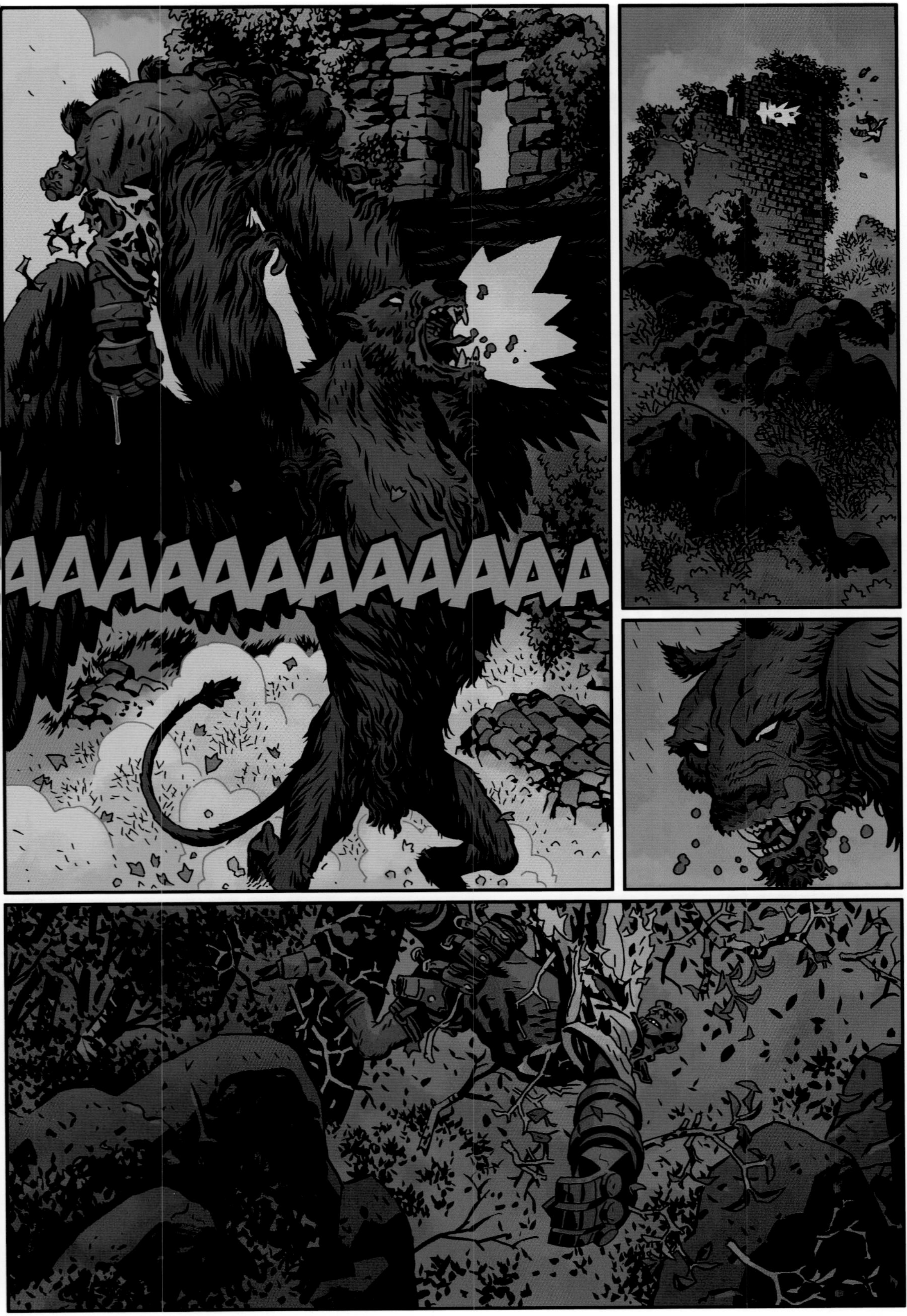
AAAAAAAAAAAAA

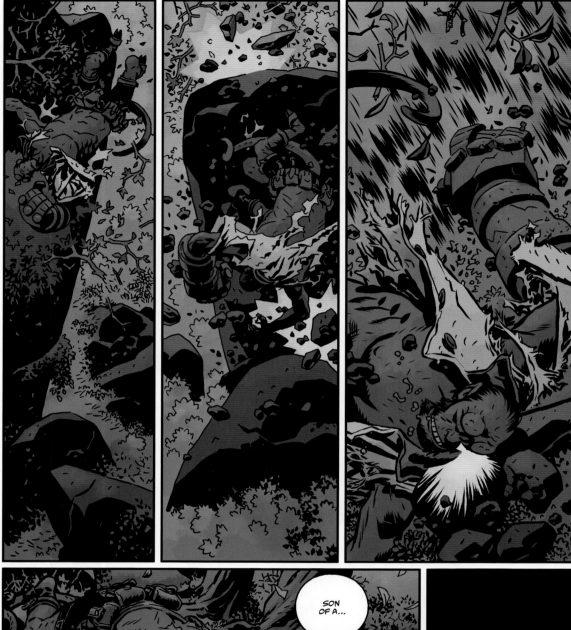

SON
OF A...

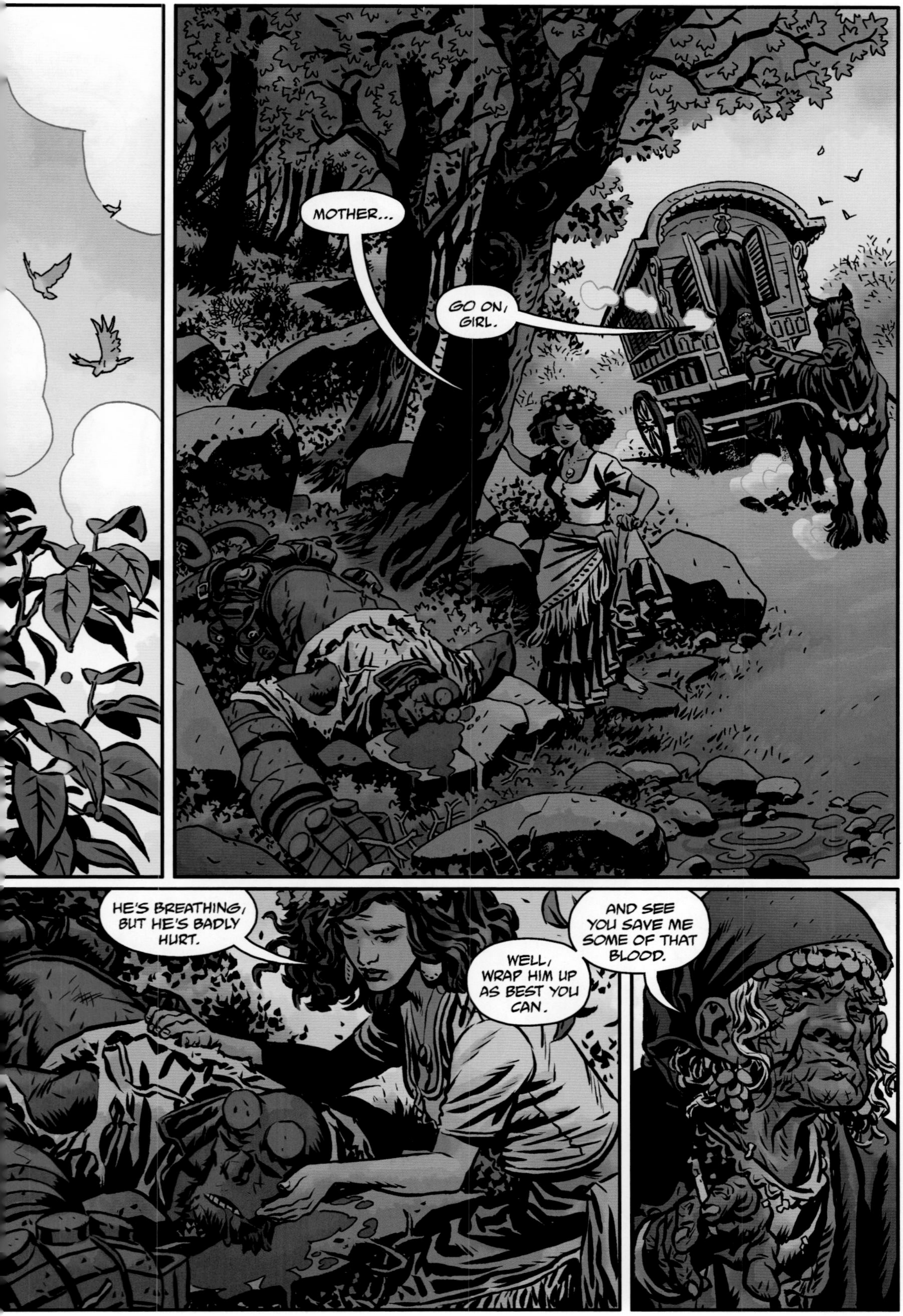
MOTHER...
GO ON, GIRL.
HE'S BREATHING, BUT HE'S BADLY HURT.
WELL, WRAP HIM UP AS BEST YOU CAN.
AND SEE YOU SAVE ME SOME OF THAT BLOOD.

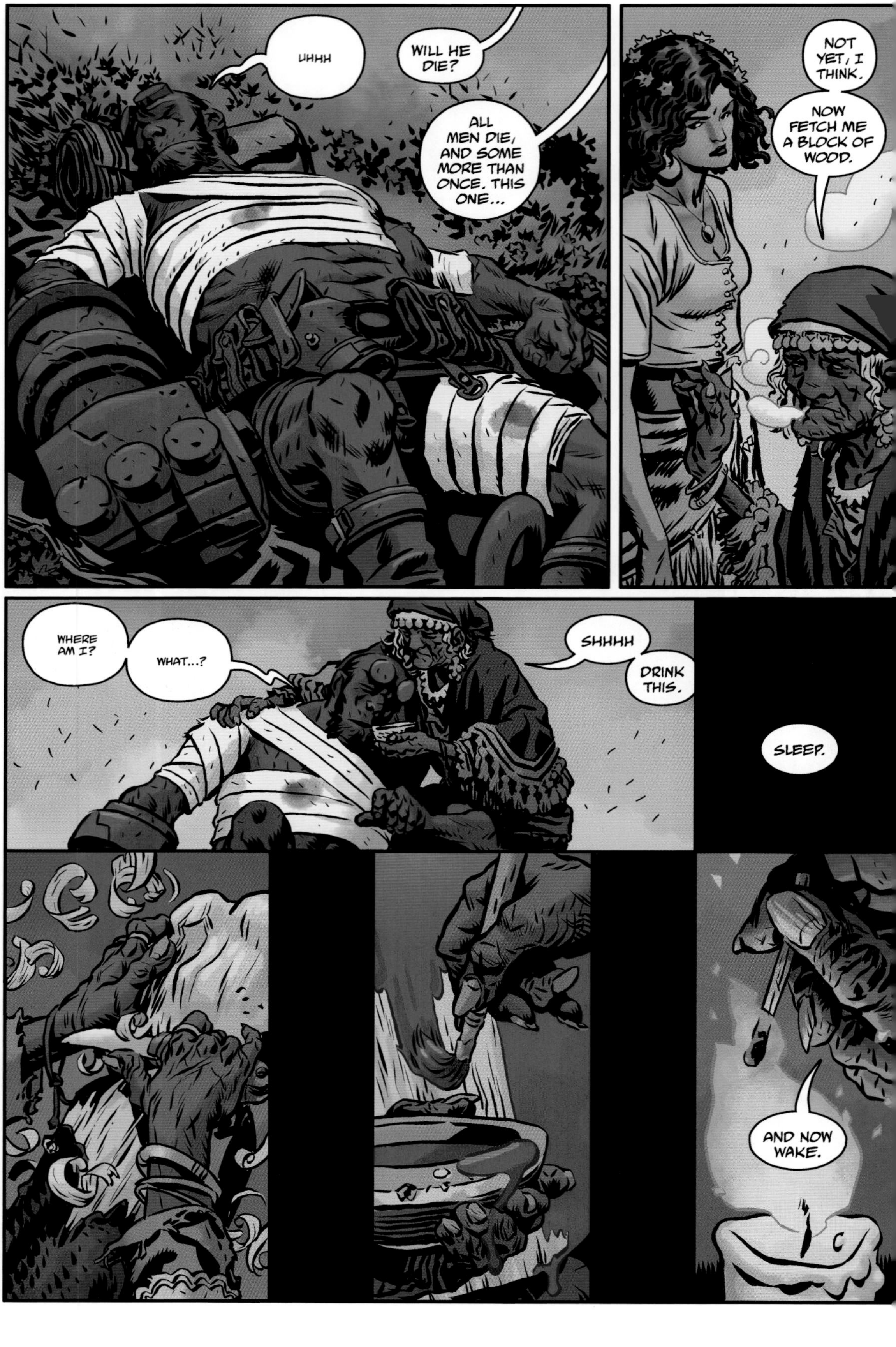
UHHH
WILL HE DIE?
ALL MEN DIE, AND SOME MORE THAN ONCE. THIS ONE...
NOT YET, I THINK.
NOW FETCH ME A BLOCK OF WOOD.
WHERE AM I?
WHAT...?
SHHHH
DRINK THIS.
SLEEP.
AND NOW WAKE.

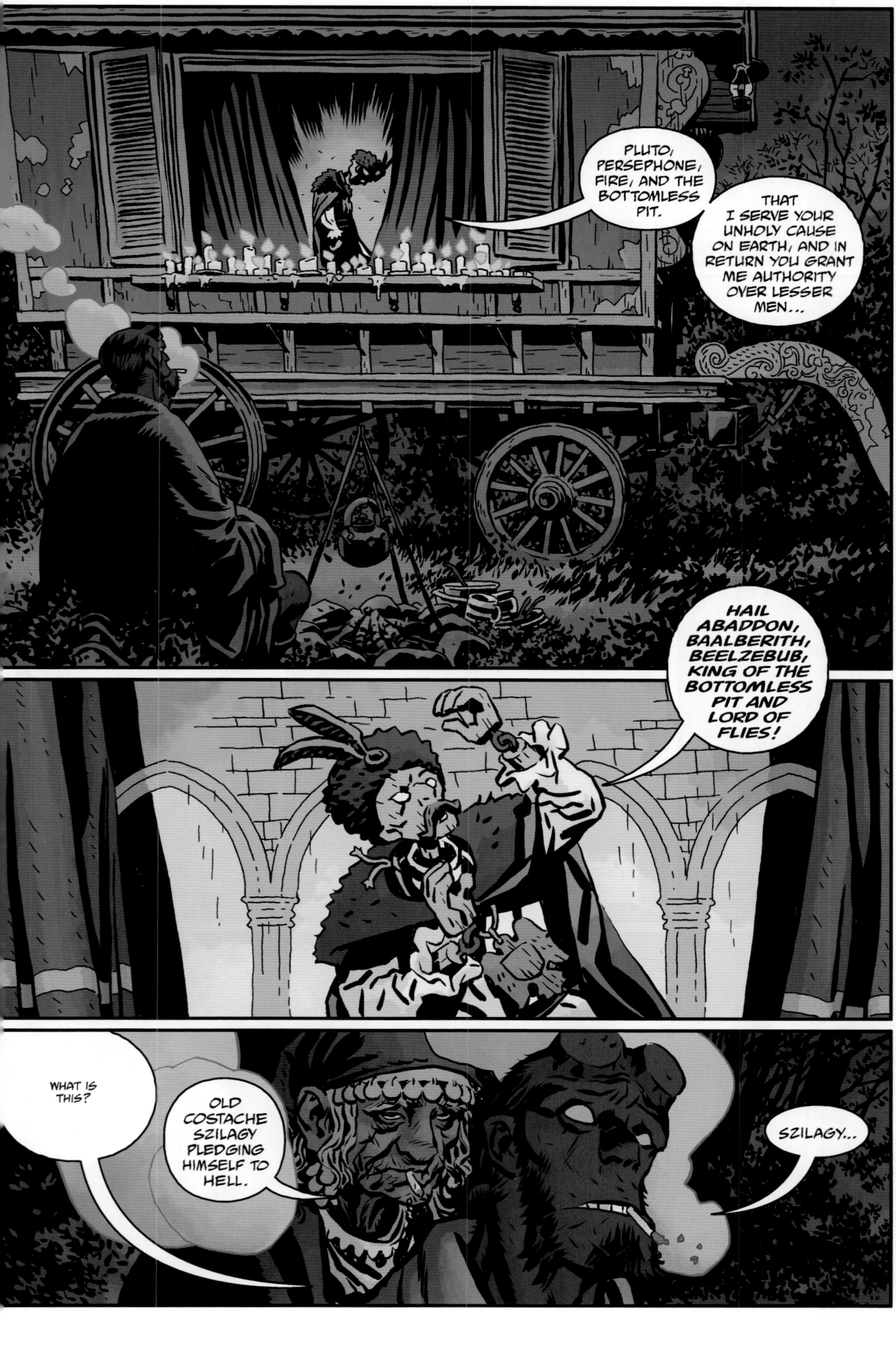
PLUTO, PERSEPHONE, FIRE, AND THE BOTTOMLESS PIT.
THAT I SERVE YOUR UNHOLY CAUSE ON EARTH, AND IN RETURN YOU GRANT ME AUTHORITY OVER LESSER MEN...
HAIL ABADDON, BAALBERITH, BEELZEBUB, KING OF THE BOTTOMLESS PIT AND LORD OF FLIES!
WHAT IS THIS?
OLD COSTACHE SZILAGY PLEDGING HIMSELF TO HELL.
SZILAGY...

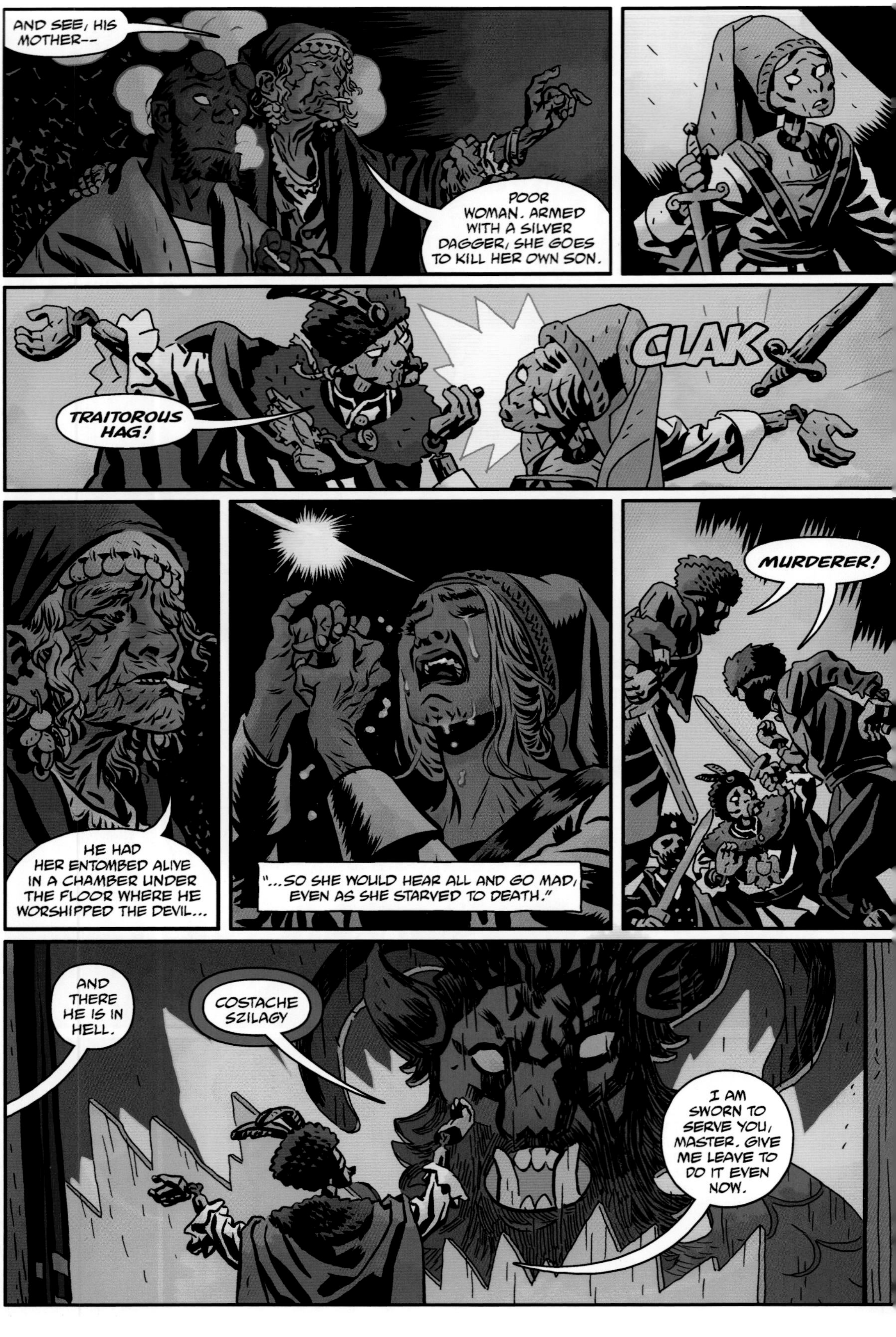
AND SEE, HIS MOTHER--
POOR WOMAN. ARMED WITH A SILVER DAGGER, SHE GOES TO KILL HER OWN SON.
TRAITOROUS HAG!
CLAK
HE HAD HER ENTOMBED ALIVE IN A CHAMBER UNDER THE FLOOR WHERE HE WORSHIPPED THE DEVIL...
"...SO SHE WOULD HEAR ALL AND GO MAD, EVEN AS SHE STARVED TO DEATH."
MURDERER!
AND THERE HE IS IN HELL.
COSTACHE SZILAGY
I AM SWORN TO SERVE YOU, MASTER. GIVE ME LEAVE TO DO IT EVEN NOW.

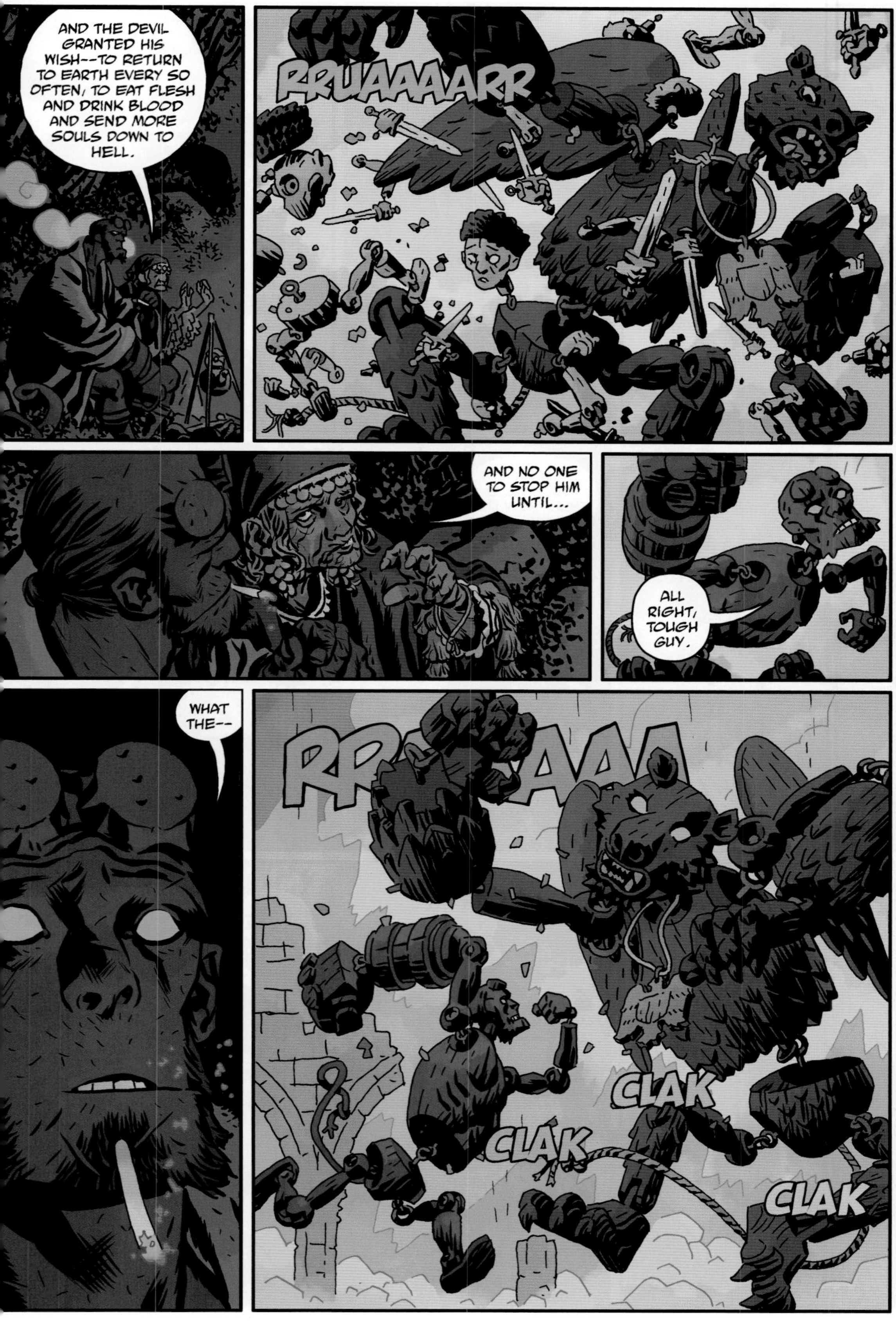
AND THE DEVIL GRANTED HIS WISH--TO RETURN TO EARTH EVERY SO OFTEN, TO EAT FLESH AND DRINK BLOOD AND SEND MORE SOULS DOWN TO HELL.
RRUAAAAARR
AND NO ONE TO STOP HIM UNTIL...
ALL RIGHT, TOUGH GUY.
WHAT THE--
CLAK
CLAK
CLAK

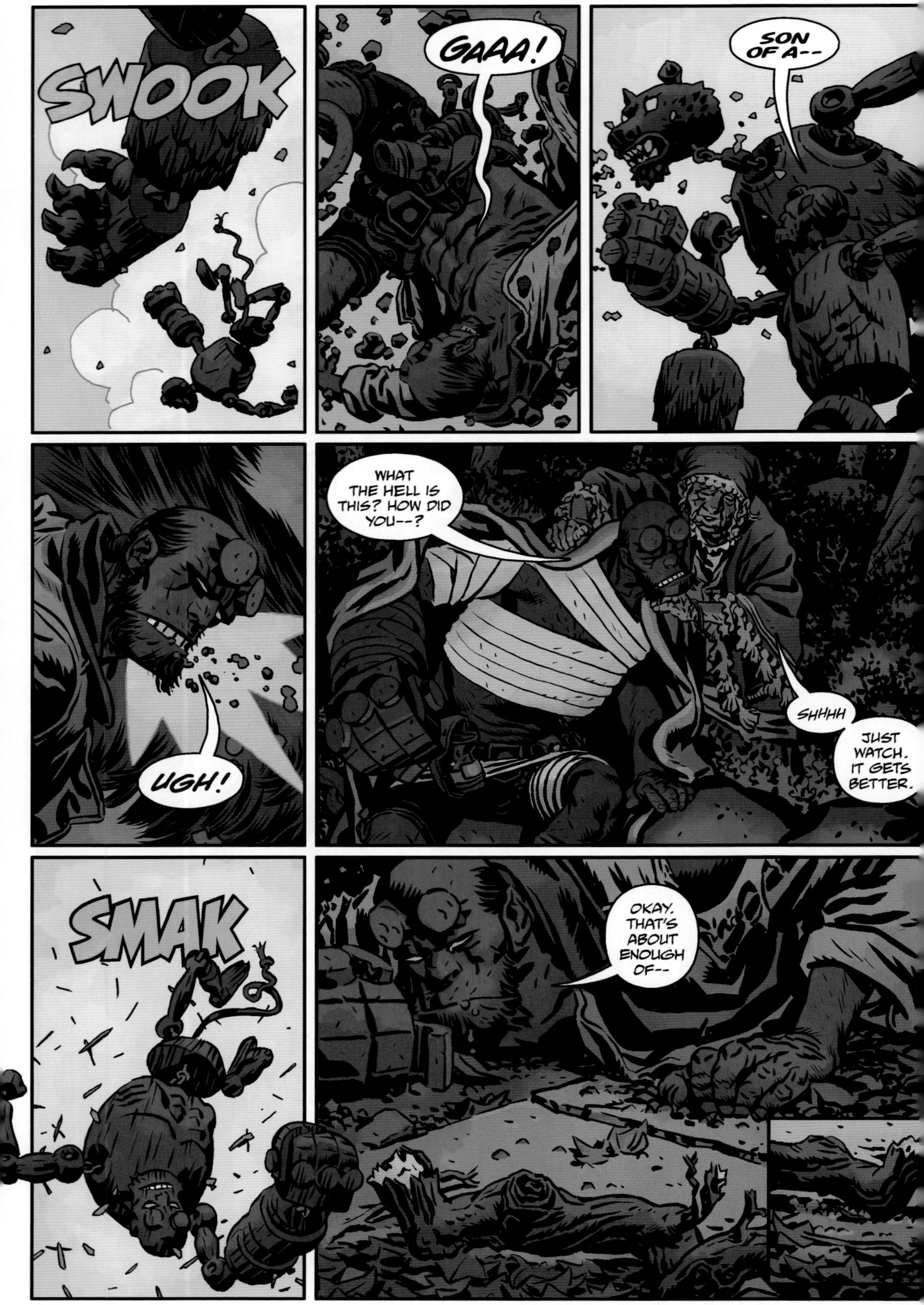
SWOOK
GAAA!
SON OF A--
UGH!
WHAT THE HELL IS THIS? HOW DID YOU--?
SHHHH
JUST WATCH. IT GETS BETTER.
SMAK
OKAY. THAT'S ABOUT ENOUGH OF--

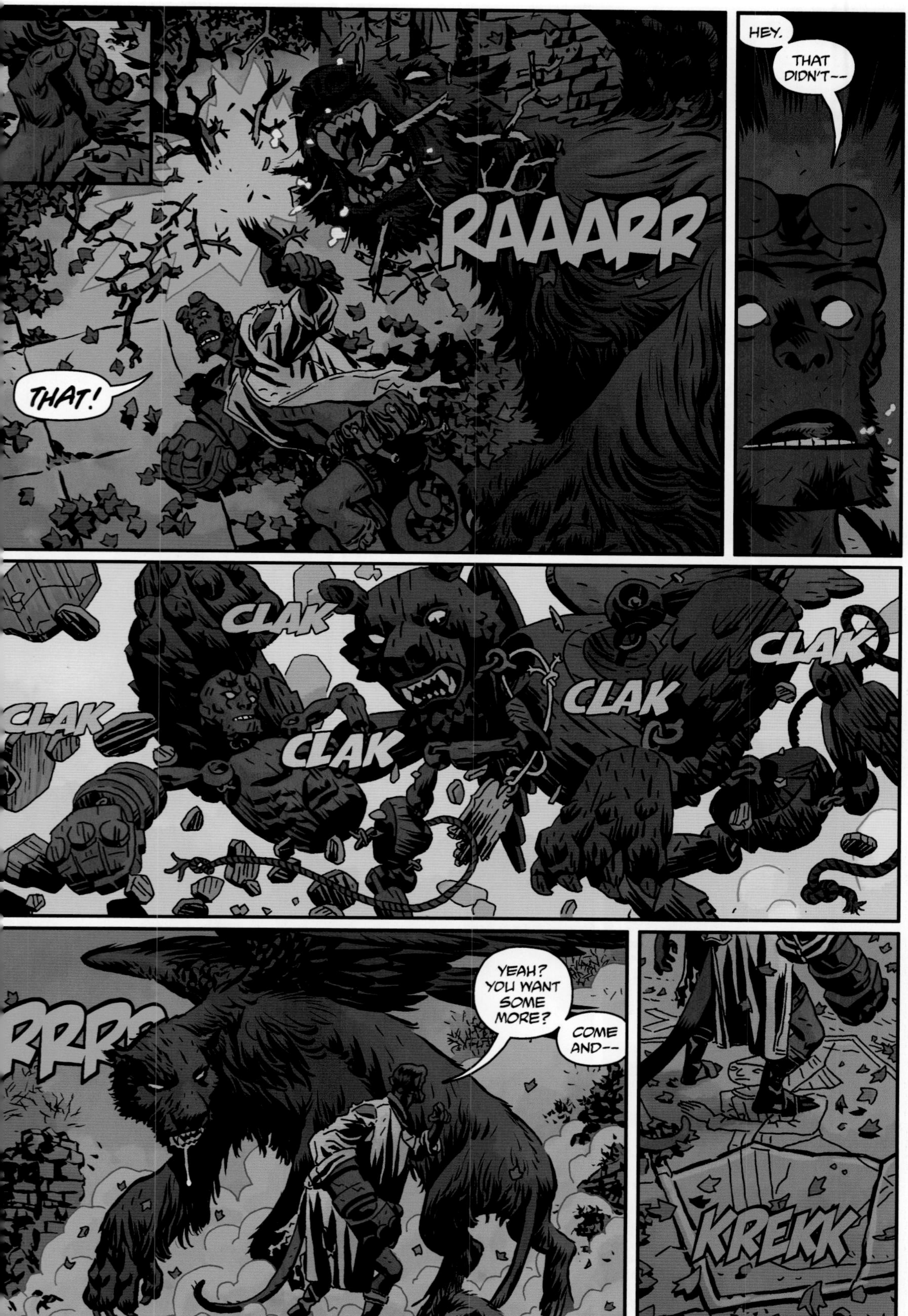
RAAARR
THAT!
HEY.
THAT DIDN'T--
CLAK
CLAK
CLAK
CLAK
CLAK
YEAH? YOU WANT SOME MORE?
COME AND--
KREKK

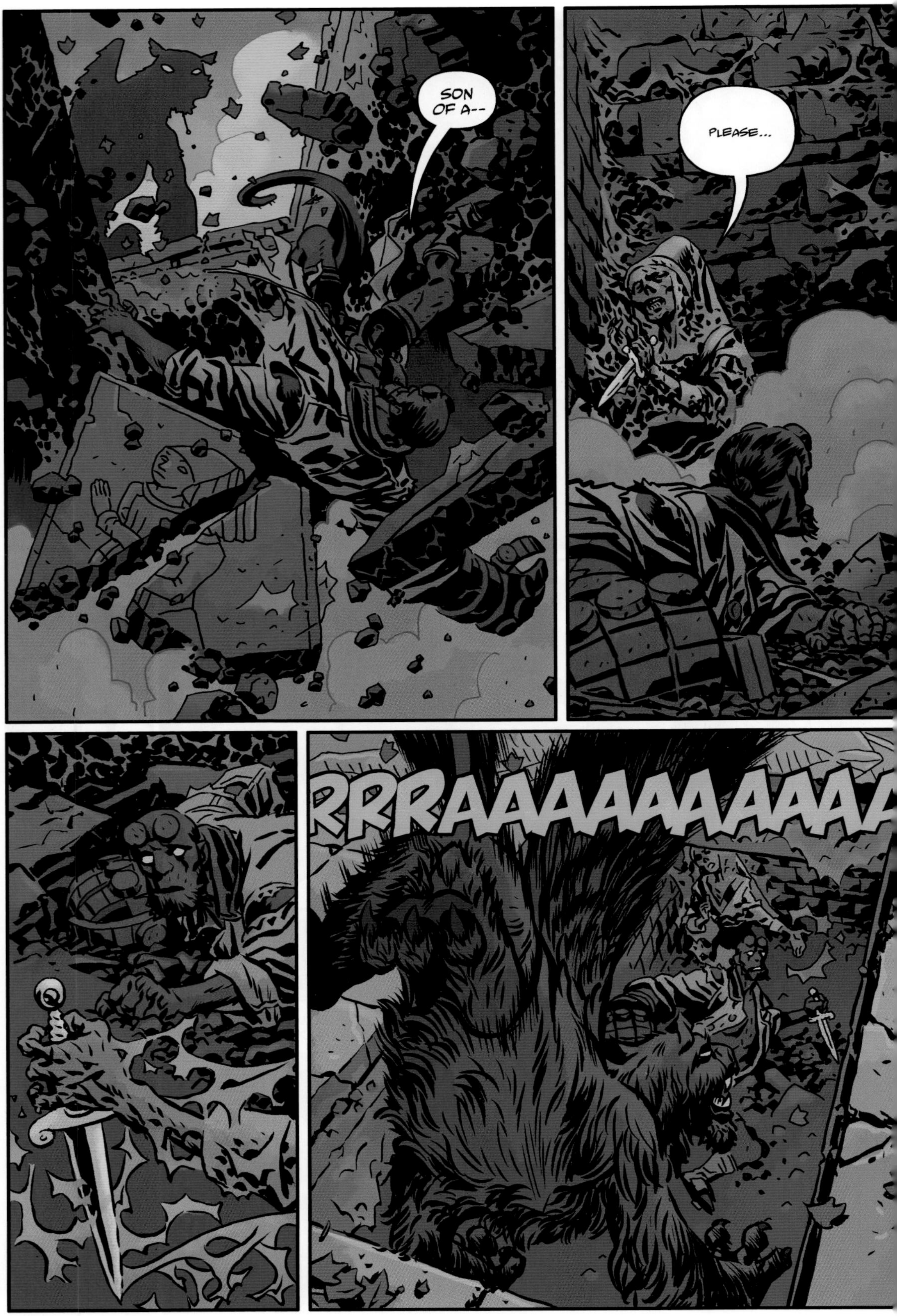
SON OF A--
PLEASE...
RRRAAAAAAAAAAA

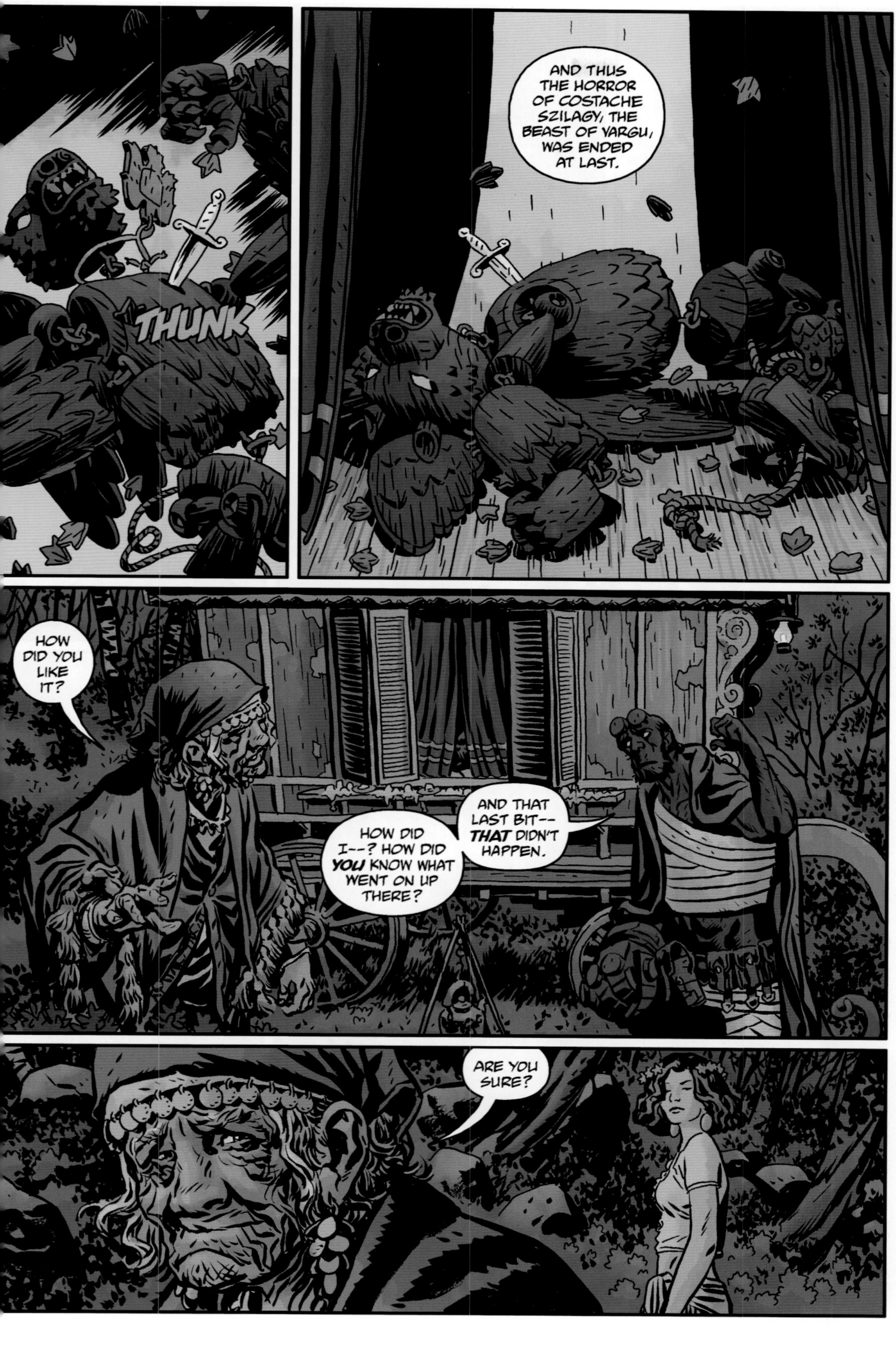
THUNK
AND THUS THE HORROR OF COSTACHE SZILAGY, THE BEAST OF VARGU, WAS ENDED AT LAST.
HOW DID YOU LIKE IT?
AND THAT LAST BIT-- *THAT* DIDN'T HAPPEN.
HOW DID I--? HOW DID *YOU* KNOW WHAT WENT ON UP THERE?
ARE YOU SURE?

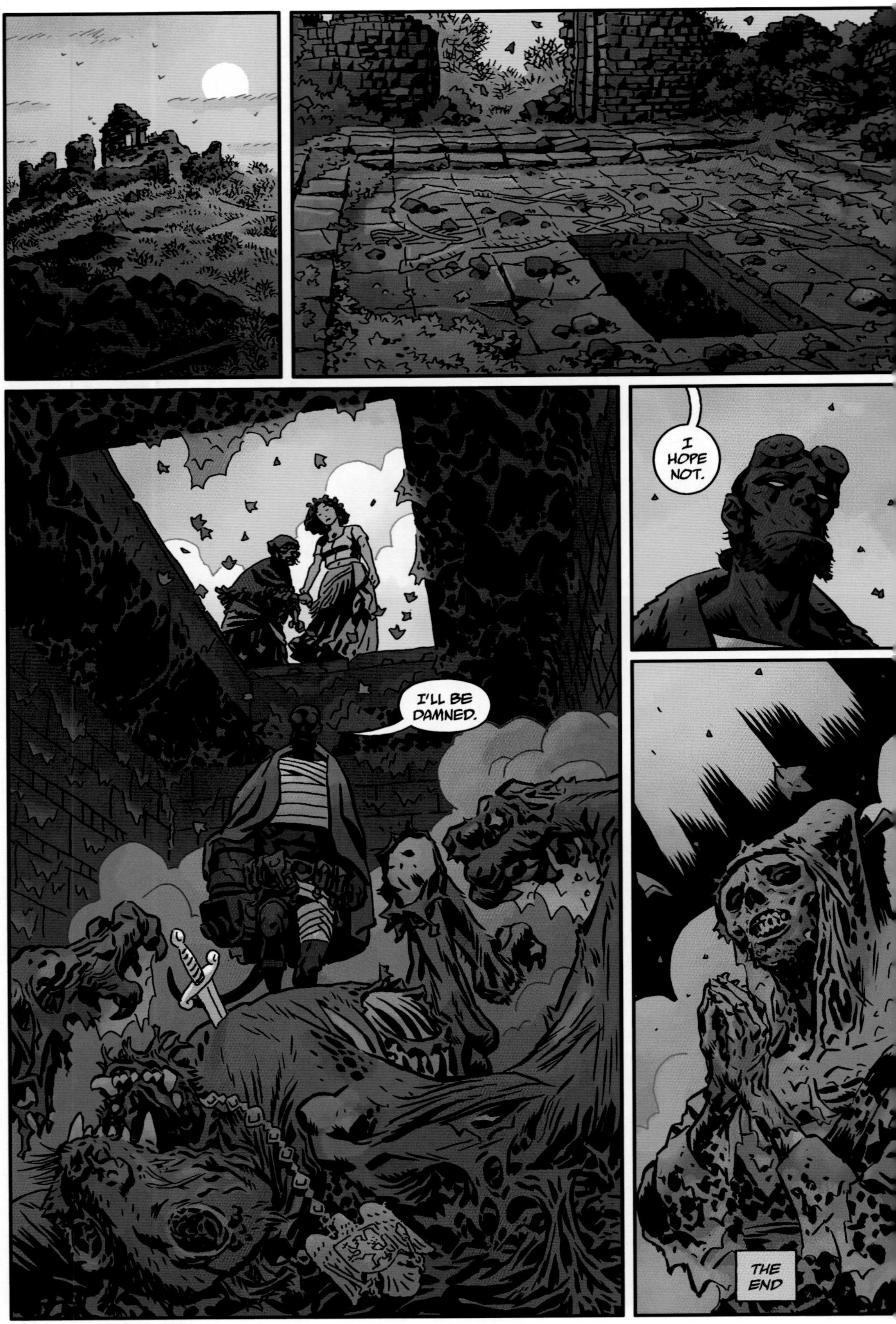
I'LL BE DAMNED.
I HOPE NOT.
THE END

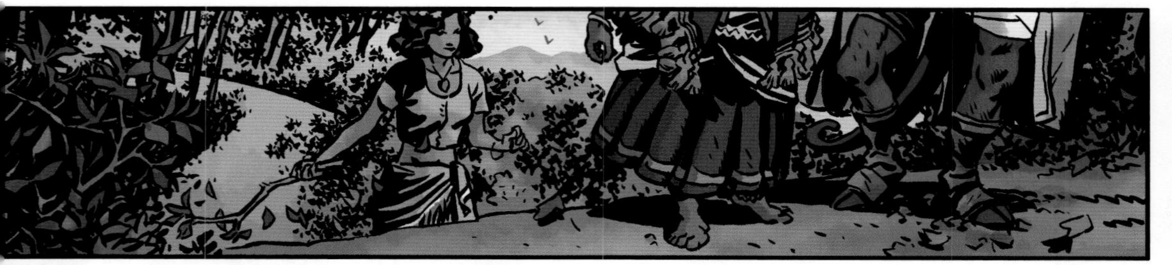

The Secret God of the Roma

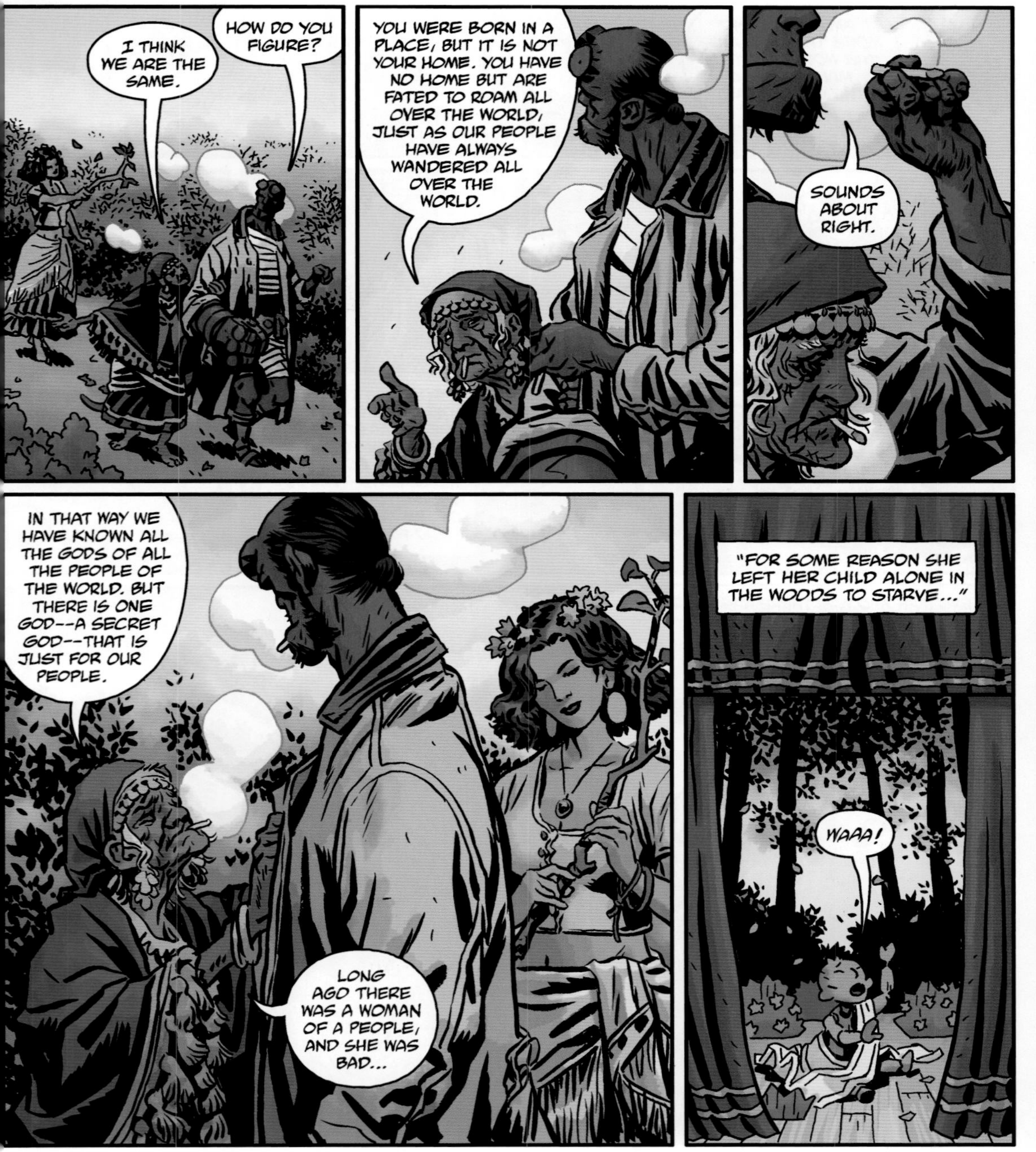
I THINK WE ARE THE SAME.
HOW DO YOU FIGURE?
YOU WERE BORN IN A PLACE, BUT IT IS NOT YOUR HOME. YOU HAVE NO HOME BUT ARE FATED TO ROAM ALL OVER THE WORLD, JUST AS OUR PEOPLE HAVE ALWAYS WANDERED ALL OVER THE WORLD.
SOUNDS ABOUT RIGHT.
IN THAT WAY WE HAVE KNOWN ALL THE GODS OF ALL THE PEOPLE OF THE WORLD. BUT THERE IS ONE GOD--A SECRET GOD--THAT IS JUST FOR OUR PEOPLE.
LONG AGO THERE WAS A WOMAN OF A PEOPLE, AND SHE WAS BAD...
"FOR SOME REASON SHE LEFT HER CHILD ALONE IN THE WOODS TO STARVE..."
WAAA!

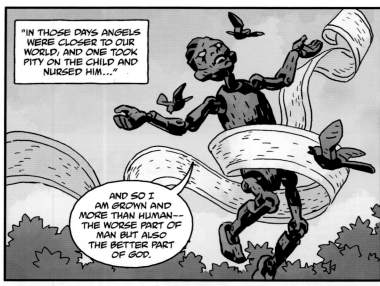

"IN THOSE DAYS ANGELS WERE CLOSER TO OUR WORLD, AND ONE TOOK PITY ON THE CHILD AND NURSED HIM..."

AND SO I AM GROWN AND MORE THAN HUMAN-- THE WORSE PART OF MAN BUT ALSO THE BETTER PART OF GOD.

"THE ANGEL TOLD HIM THAT ON ALL DAYS BUT FRIDAY HE MUST BE VERY GOOD, BUT ON FRIDAYS HE MIGHT DO AS HE PLEASED..."

"SO ONE FRIDAY HE DECIDED TO HAVE A GREAT FEAST. HE HAD MANY DIFFERENT KINDS OF FOOD FOR HIS GUESTS--ALL BUT FISH, FOR THE PART OF HIM THAT WAS BAD HAD FORGOTTEN..."

"AN EVIL MAN WHO WAS THERE WAS OUTRAGED..."

I AM OFFENDED!

"EMBARRASSED, THE MAN-GOD WENT TO THE RIVER AND CALLED TO THE FISH, AND THEY FLEW AT ONCE RIGHT INTO HIS COOKING FIRE..."

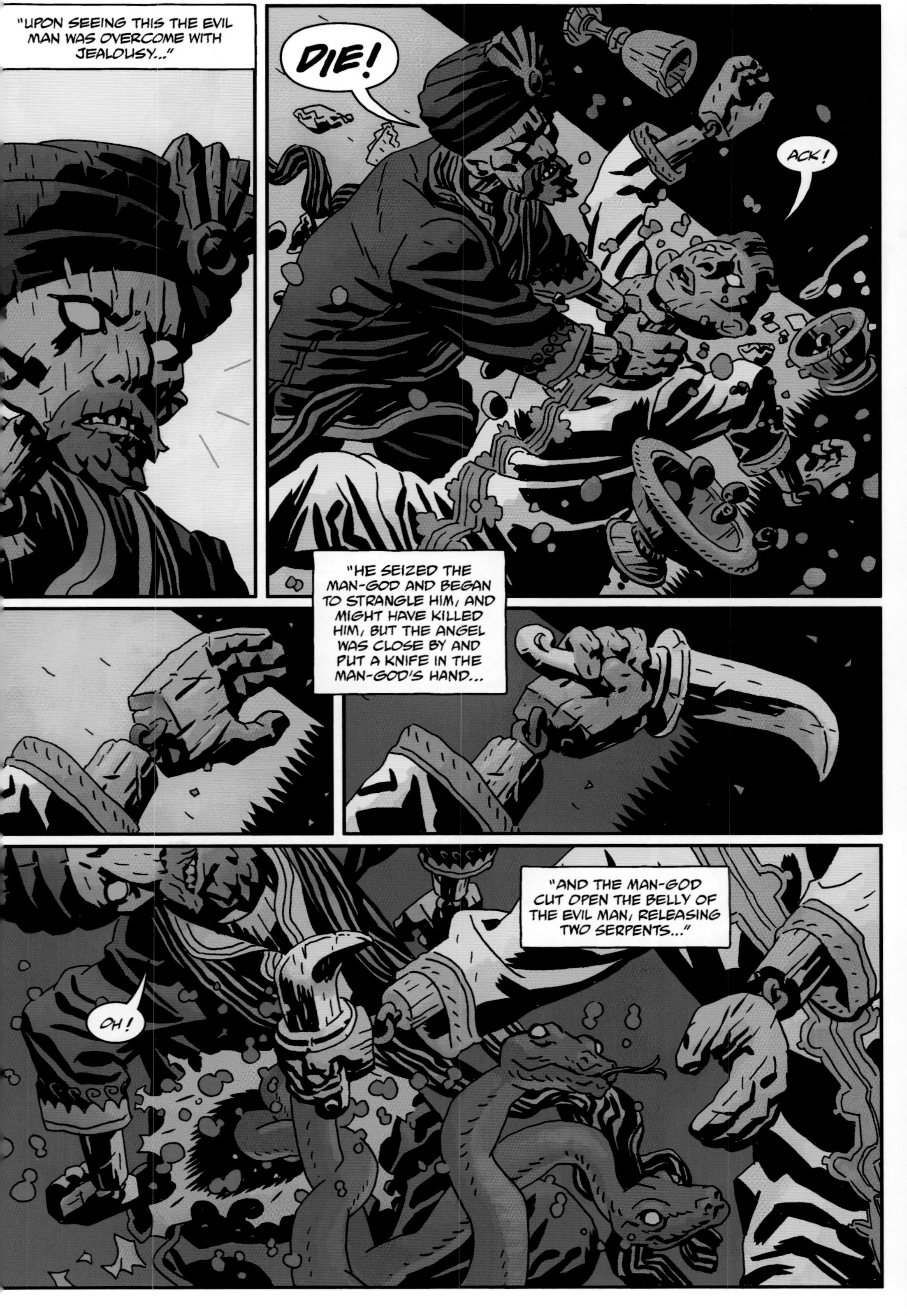
"UPON SEEING THIS THE EVIL MAN WAS OVERCOME WITH JEALOUSY..."
DIE!
ACK!
"HE SEIZED THE MAN-GOD AND BEGAN TO STRANGLE HIM, AND MIGHT HAVE KILLED HIM, BUT THE ANGEL WAS CLOSE BY AND PUT A KNIFE IN THE MAN-GOD'S HAND...
"AND THE MAN-GOD CUT OPEN THE BELLY OF THE EVIL MAN, RELEASING TWO SERPENTS..."
OH!

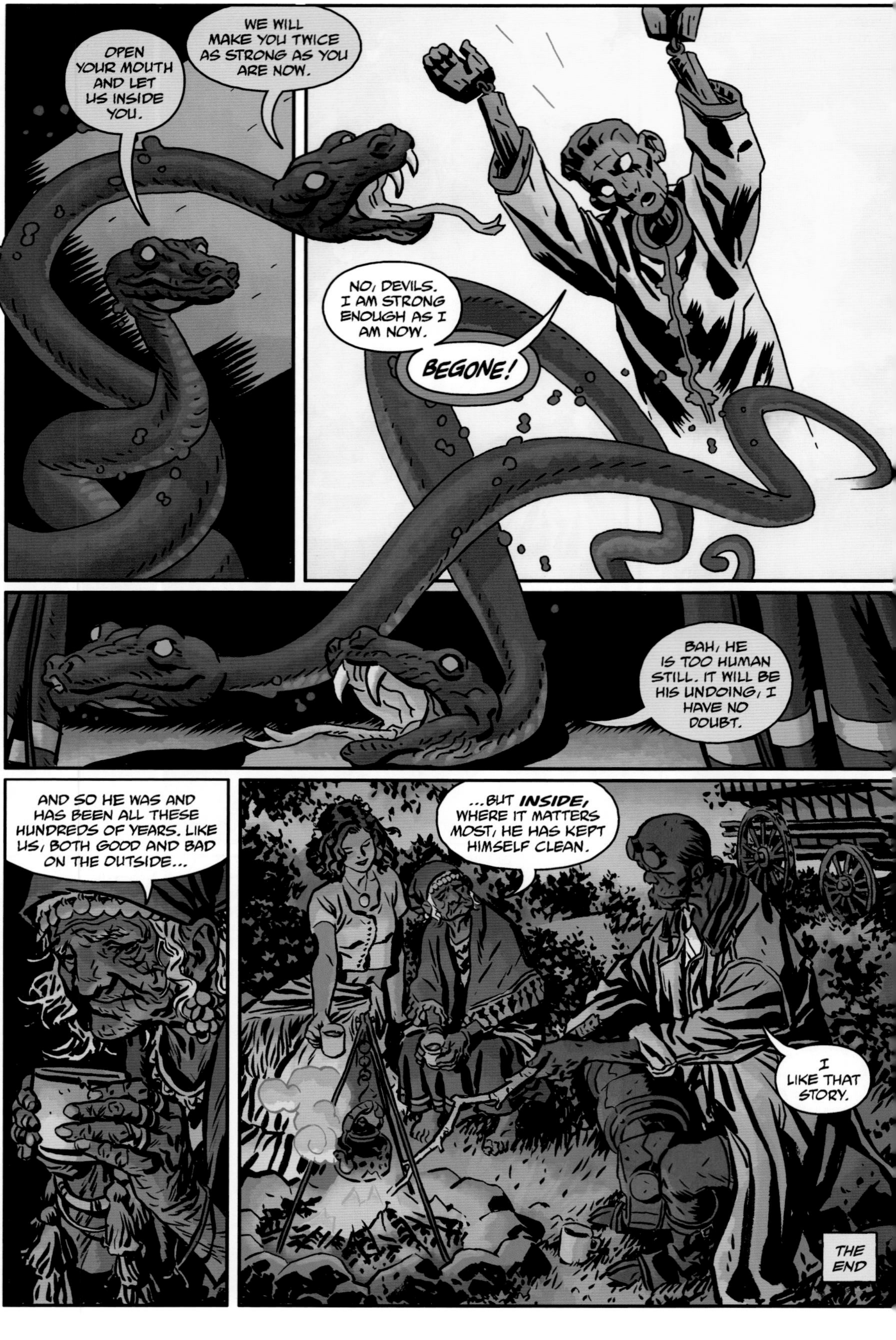
OPEN YOUR MOUTH AND LET US INSIDE YOU.
WE WILL MAKE YOU TWICE AS STRONG AS YOU ARE NOW.
NO, DEVILS. I AM STRONG ENOUGH AS I AM NOW.
BEGONE!
BAH, HE IS TOO HUMAN STILL. IT WILL BE HIS UNDOING, I HAVE NO DOUBT.
AND SO HE WAS AND HAS BEEN ALL THESE HUNDREDS OF YEARS. LIKE US, BOTH GOOD AND BAD ON THE OUTSIDE...
...BUT INSIDE, WHERE IT MATTERS MOST, HE HAS KEPT HIMSELF CLEAN.
I LIKE THAT STORY.
THE END

SATURN RETURNS

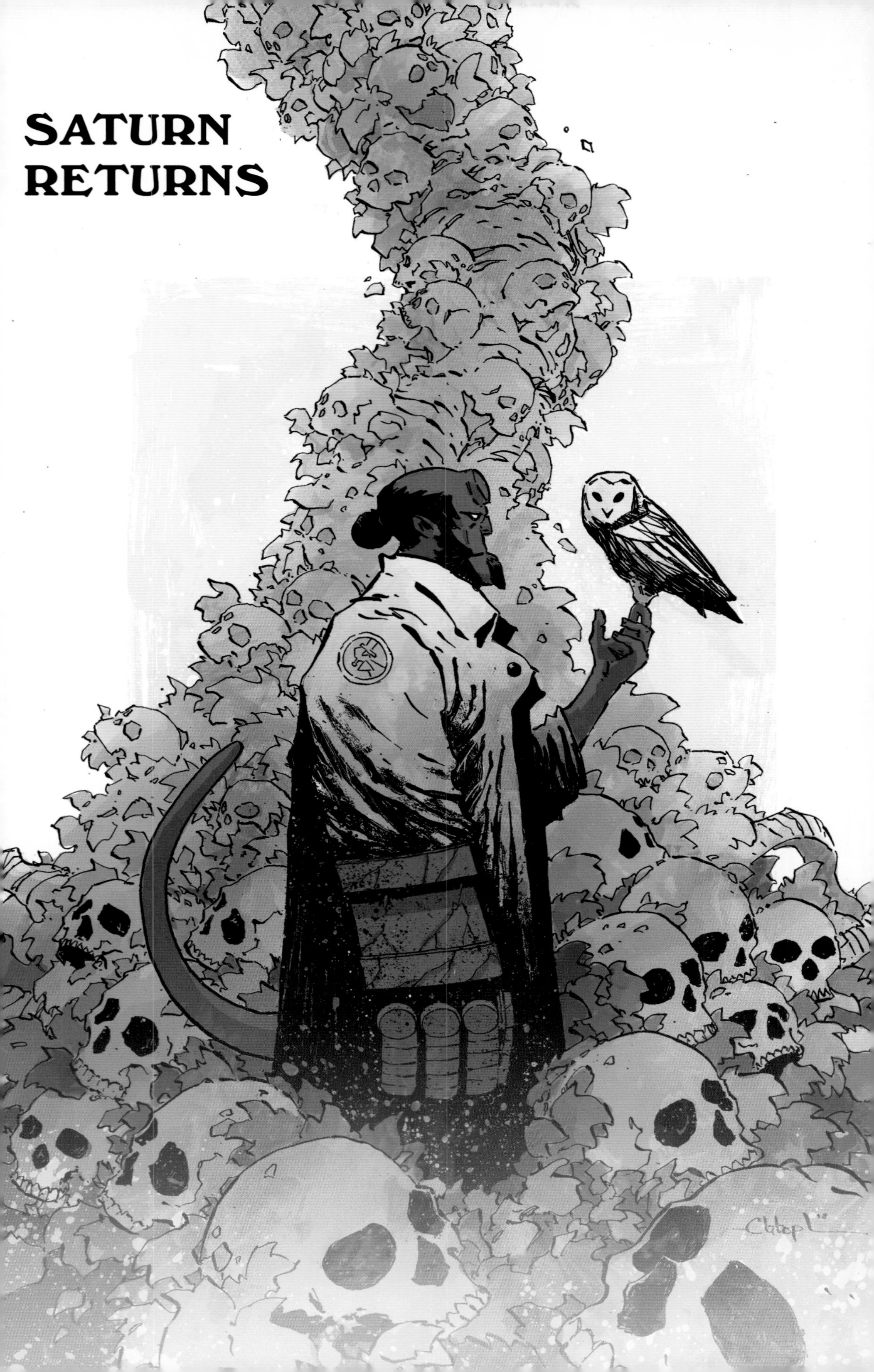

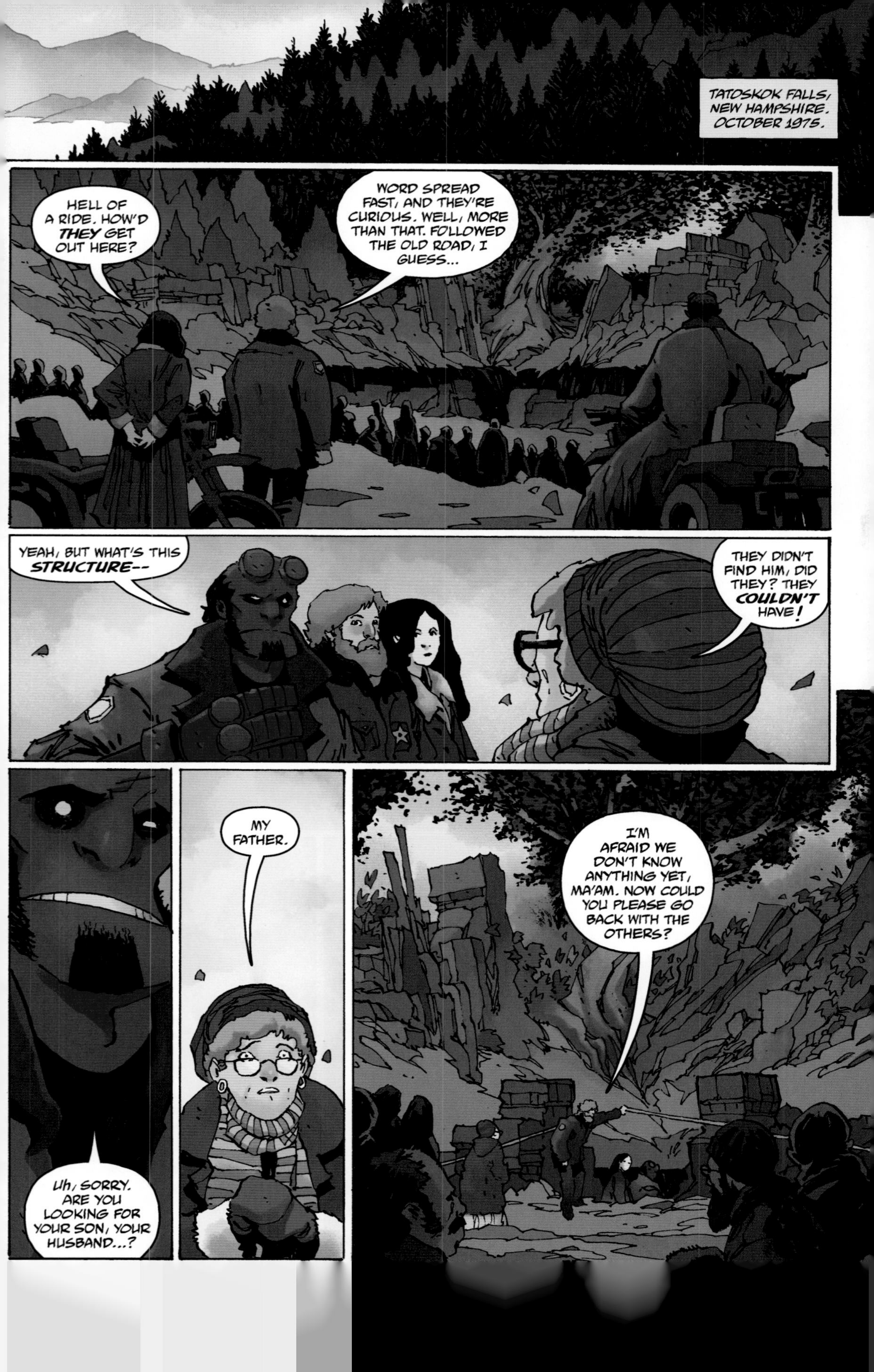
TATOSKOK FALLS, NEW HAMPSHIRE. OCTOBER 1975.
HELL OF A RIDE. HOW'D THEY GET OUT HERE?
WORD SPREAD FAST, AND THEY'RE CURIOUS. WELL, MORE THAN THAT. FOLLOWED THE OLD ROAD, I GUESS...
YEAH, BUT WHAT'S THIS STRUCTURE--
THEY DIDN'T FIND HIM, DID THEY? THEY COULDN'T HAVE!
UH, SORRY. ARE YOU LOOKING FOR YOUR SON, YOUR HUSBAND...?
MY FATHER.
I'M AFRAID WE DON'T KNOW ANYTHING YET, MA'AM. NOW COULD YOU PLEASE GO BACK WITH THE OTHERS?

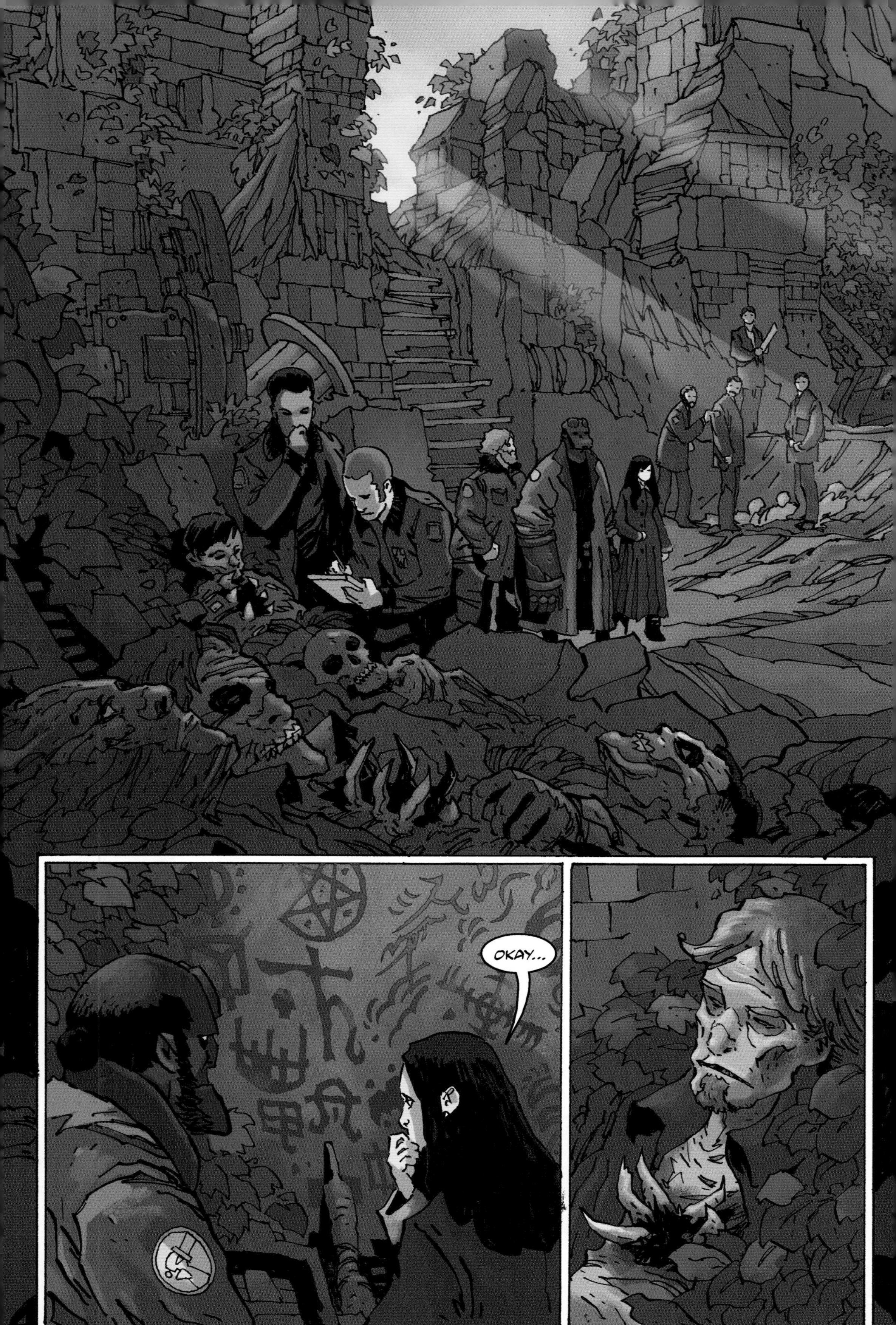
OKAY...

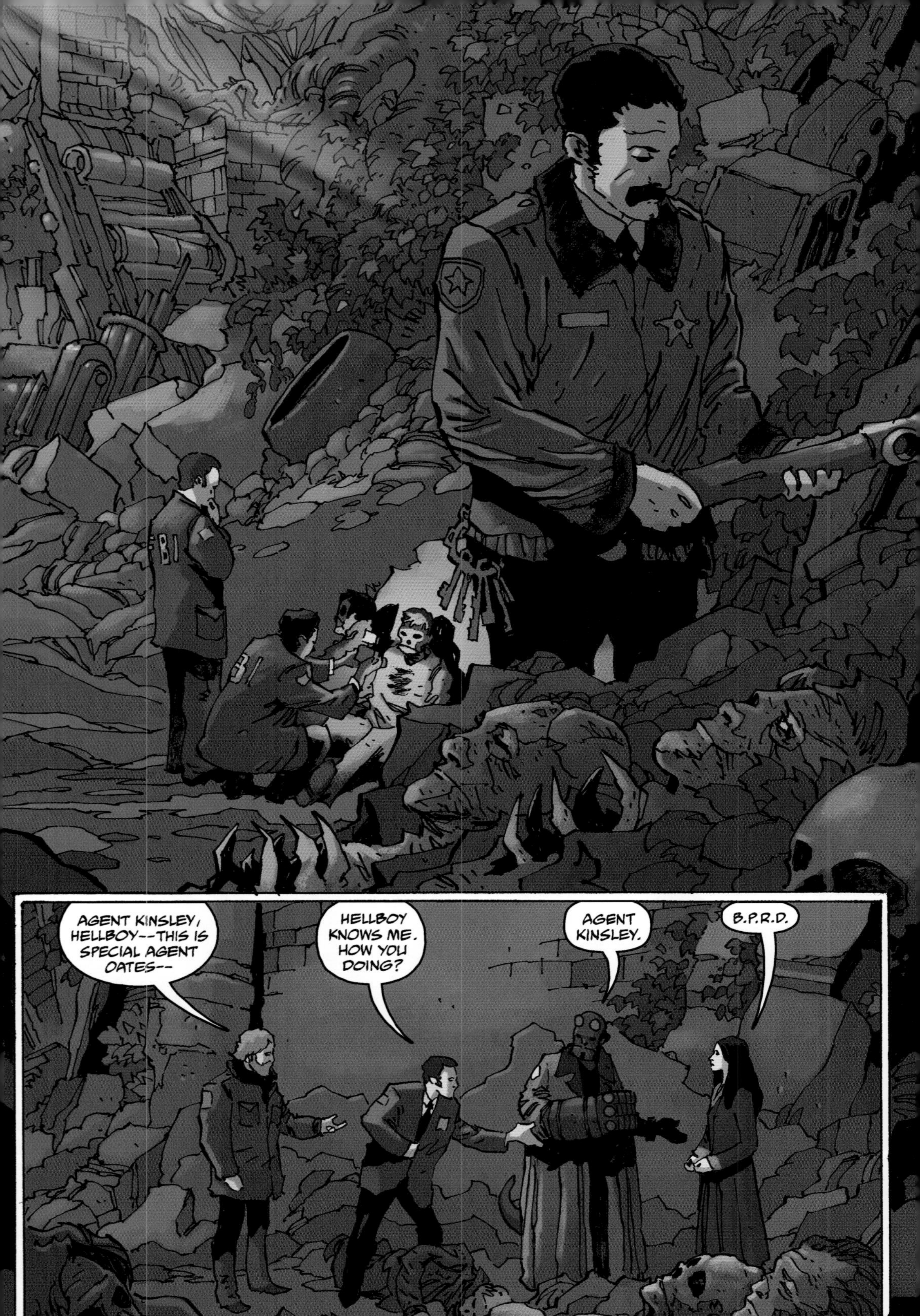
AGENT KINSLEY, HELLBOY--THIS IS SPECIAL AGENT OATES--
HELLBOY KNOWS ME. HOW YOU DOING?
AGENT KINSLEY.
B.P.R.D.

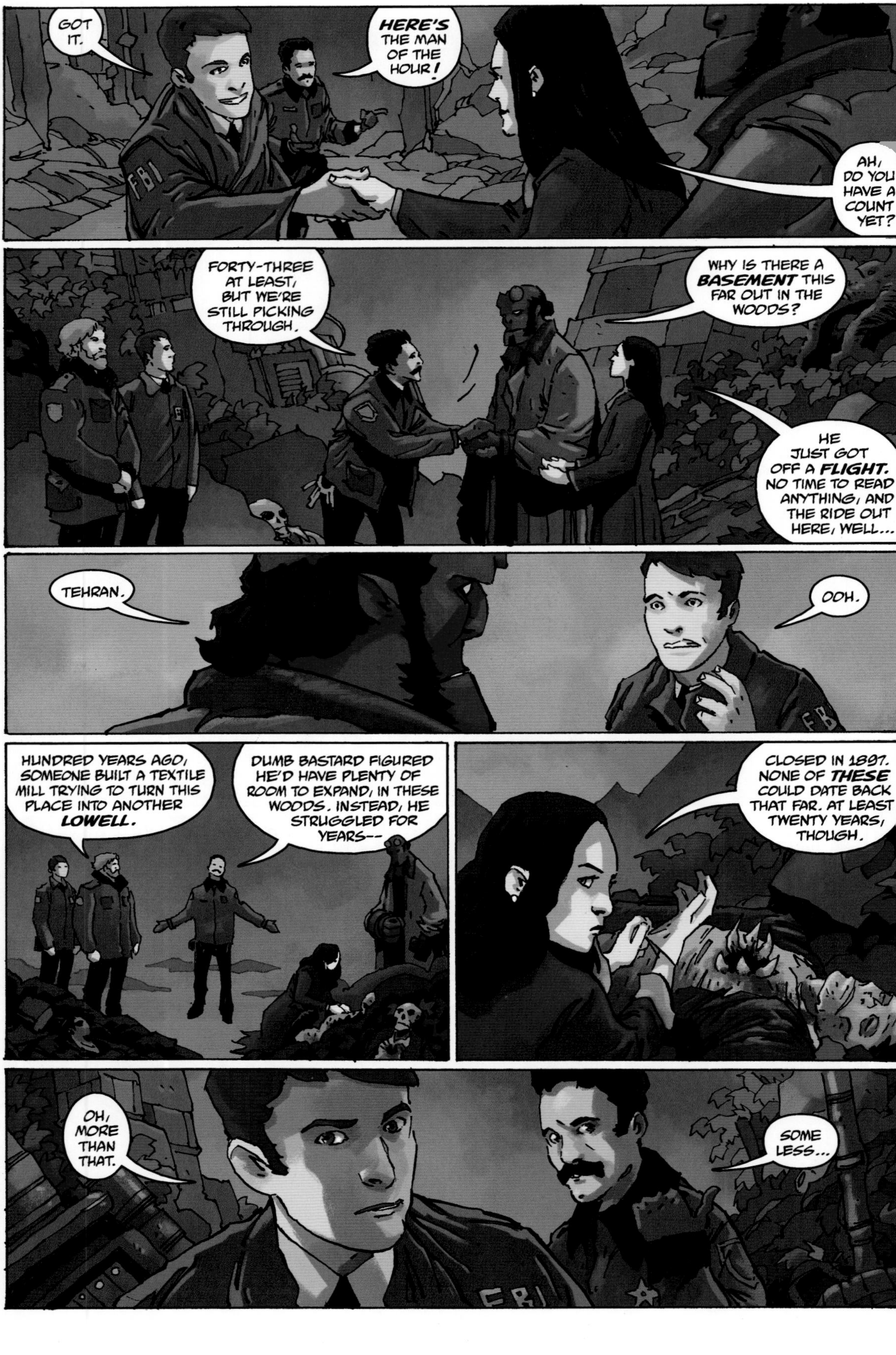
GOT IT.
HERE'S THE MAN OF THE HOUR!
AH, DO YOU HAVE A COUNT YET?
FORTY-THREE AT LEAST, BUT WE'RE STILL PICKING THROUGH.
WHY IS THERE A BASEMENT THIS FAR OUT IN THE WOODS?
HE JUST GOT OFF A FLIGHT. NO TIME TO READ ANYTHING, AND THE RIDE OUT HERE, WELL...
TEHRAN.
OOH.
HUNDRED YEARS AGO, SOMEONE BUILT A TEXTILE MILL TRYING TO TURN THIS PLACE INTO ANOTHER LOWELL.
DUMB BASTARD FIGURED HE'D HAVE PLENTY OF ROOM TO EXPAND, IN THESE WOODS. INSTEAD, HE STRUGGLED FOR YEARS--
CLOSED IN 1897. NONE OF THESE COULD DATE BACK THAT FAR. AT LEAST TWENTY YEARS, THOUGH.
OH, MORE THAN THAT.
SOME LESS...

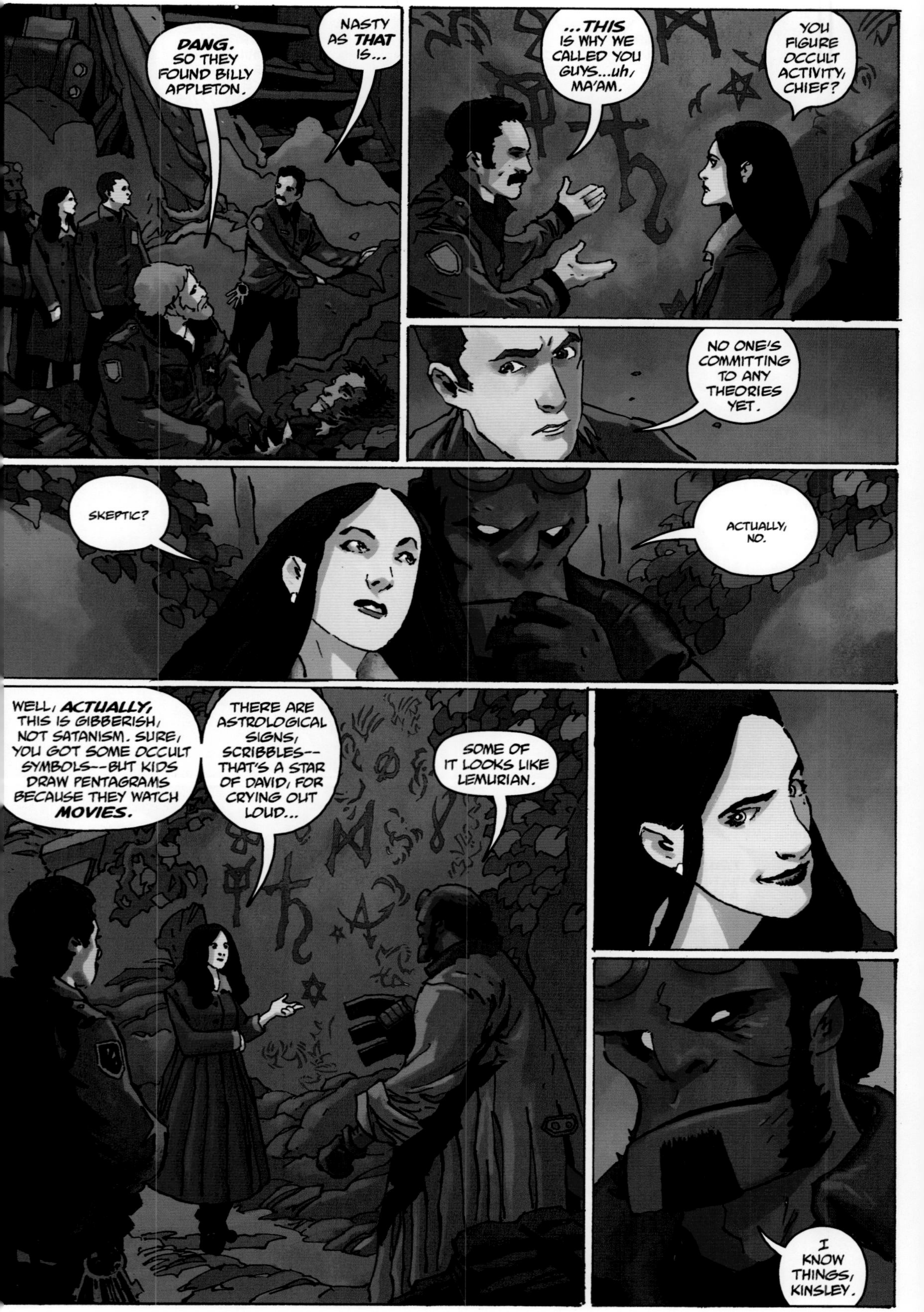
DANG. SO THEY FOUND BILLY APPLETON.
NASTY AS THAT IS...
...THIS IS WHY WE CALLED YOU GUYS...uh, MA'AM.
YOU FIGURE OCCULT ACTIVITY, CHIEF?
NO ONE'S COMMITTING TO ANY THEORIES YET.
SKEPTIC?
ACTUALLY, NO.
WELL, ACTUALLY, THIS IS GIBBERISH, NOT SATANISM. SURE, YOU GOT SOME OCCULT SYMBOLS--BUT KIDS DRAW PENTAGRAMS BECAUSE THEY WATCH MOVIES.
THERE ARE ASTROLOGICAL SIGNS, SCRIBBLES--THAT'S A STAR OF DAVID, FOR CRYING OUT LOUD...
SOME OF IT LOOKS LIKE LEMURIAN.
I KNOW THINGS, KINSLEY.

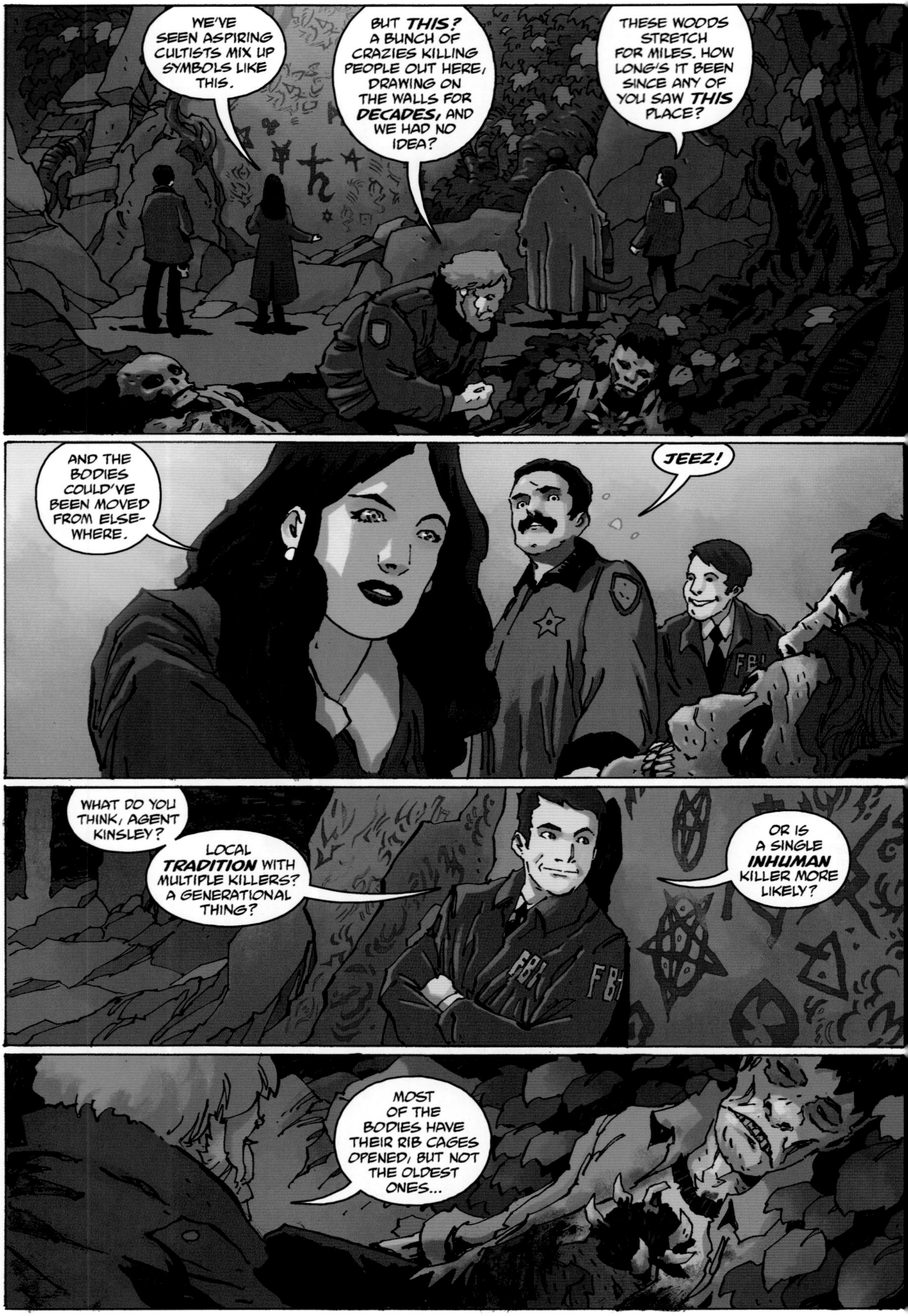
WE'VE SEEN ASPIRING CULTISTS MIX UP SYMBOLS LIKE THIS.
BUT THIS? A BUNCH OF CRAZIES KILLING PEOPLE OUT HERE, DRAWING ON THE WALLS FOR DECADES, AND WE HAD NO IDEA?
THESE WOODS STRETCH FOR MILES. HOW LONG'S IT BEEN SINCE ANY OF YOU SAW THIS PLACE?
AND THE BODIES COULD'VE BEEN MOVED FROM ELSE-WHERE.
JEEZ!
FBI
WHAT DO YOU THINK, AGENT KINSLEY?
LOCAL TRADITION WITH MULTIPLE KILLERS? A GENERATIONAL THING?
OR IS A SINGLE INHUMAN KILLER MORE LIKELY?
FBI
FBI
MOST OF THE BODIES HAVE THEIR RIB CAGES OPENED, BUT NOT THE OLDEST ONES...

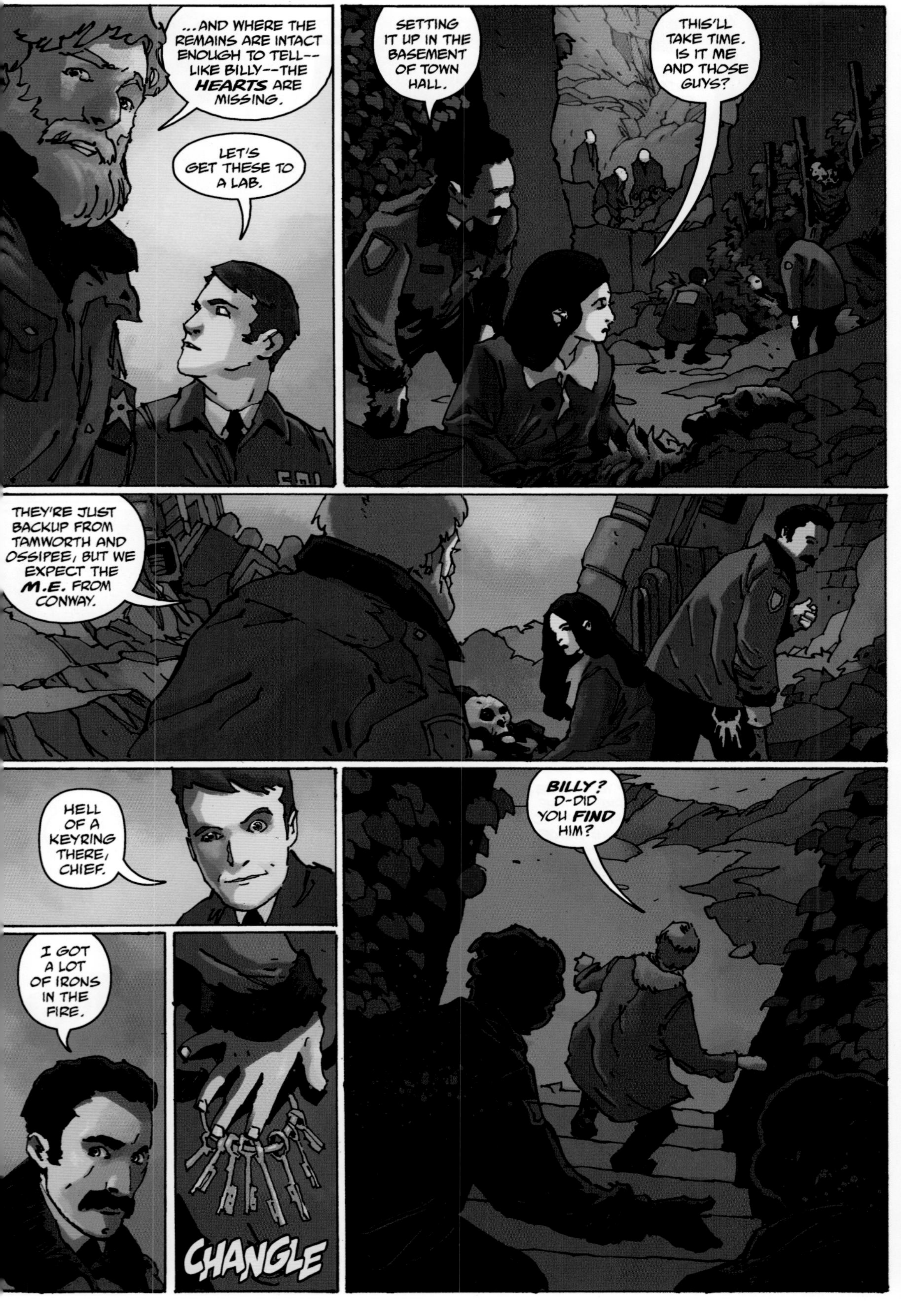
...AND WHERE THE REMAINS ARE INTACT ENOUGH TO TELL-- LIKE BILLY--THE HEARTS ARE MISSING.
LET'S GET THESE TO A LAB.
SETTING IT UP IN THE BASEMENT OF TOWN HALL.
THIS'LL TAKE TIME. IS IT ME AND THOSE GUYS?
THEY'RE JUST BACKUP FROM TAMWORTH AND OSSIPEE, BUT WE EXPECT THE M.E. FROM CONWAY.
HELL OF A KEYRING THERE, CHIEF.
I GOT A LOT OF IRONS IN THE FIRE.
CHANGLE
BILLY? D-DID YOU FIND HIM?

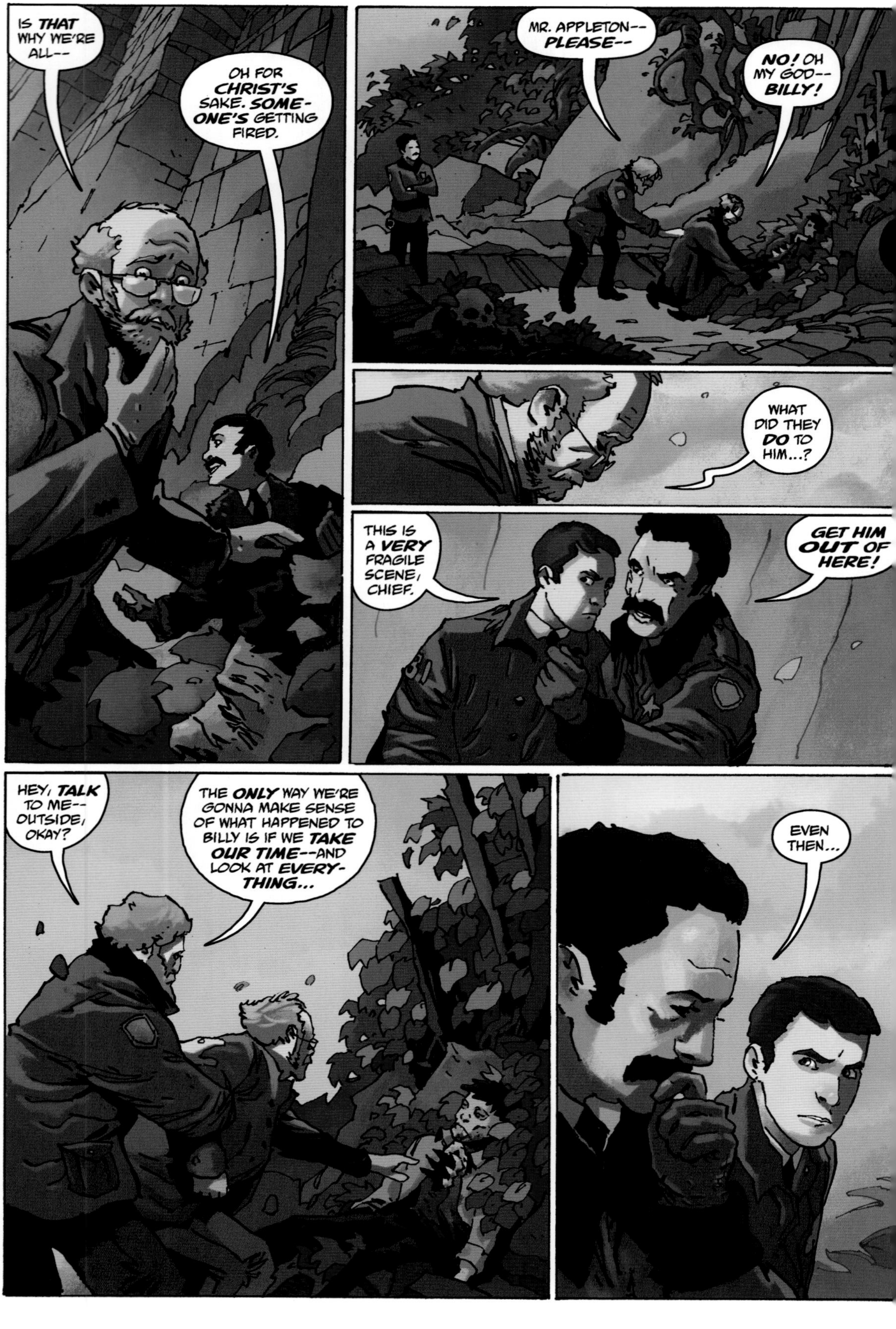
IS THAT WHY WE'RE ALL--
OH FOR CHRIST'S SAKE. SOME-ONE'S GETTING FIRED.
MR. APPLETON-- PLEASE--
NO! OH MY GOD-- BILLY!
WHAT DID THEY DO TO HIM...?
THIS IS A VERY FRAGILE SCENE, CHIEF.
GET HIM OUT OF HERE!
HEY, TALK TO ME-- OUTSIDE, OKAY?
THE ONLY WAY WE'RE GONNA MAKE SENSE OF WHAT HAPPENED TO BILLY IS IF WE TAKE OUR TIME--AND LOOK AT EVERY-THING...
EVEN THEN...

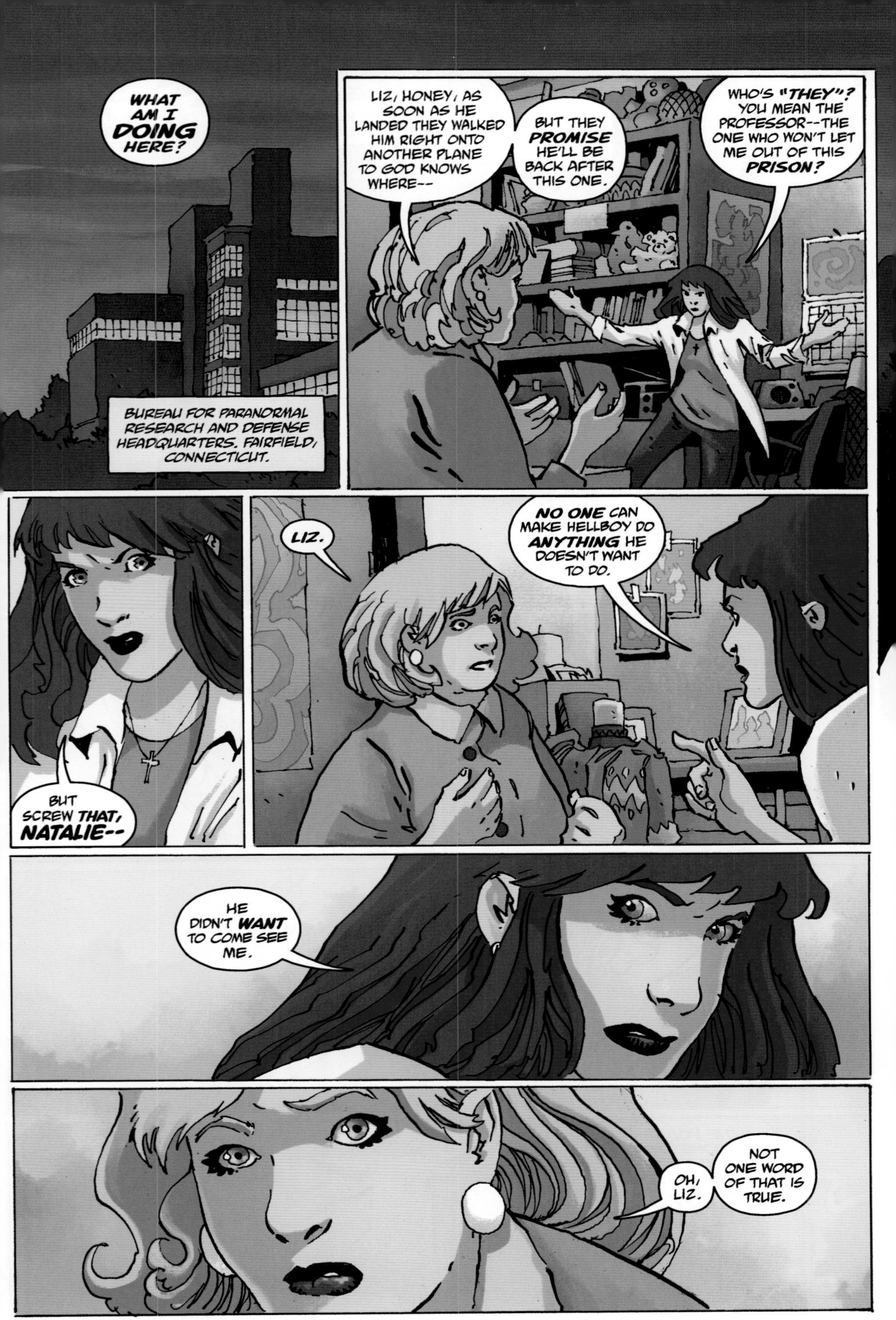
WHAT AM I DOING HERE?
BUREAU FOR PARANORMAL RESEARCH AND DEFENSE HEADQUARTERS. FAIRFIELD, CONNECTICUT.
LIZ, HONEY, AS SOON AS HE LANDED THEY WALKED HIM RIGHT ONTO ANOTHER PLANE TO GOD KNOWS WHERE--
BUT THEY PROMISE HE'LL BE BACK AFTER THIS ONE.
WHO'S "THEY"? YOU MEAN THE PROFESSOR--THE ONE WHO WON'T LET ME OUT OF THIS PRISON?
BUT SCREW THAT, NATALIE--
LIZ.
NO ONE CAN MAKE HELLBOY DO ANYTHING HE DOESN'T WANT TO DO.
HE DIDN'T WANT TO COME SEE ME.
OH, LIZ.
NOT ONE WORD OF THAT IS TRUE.

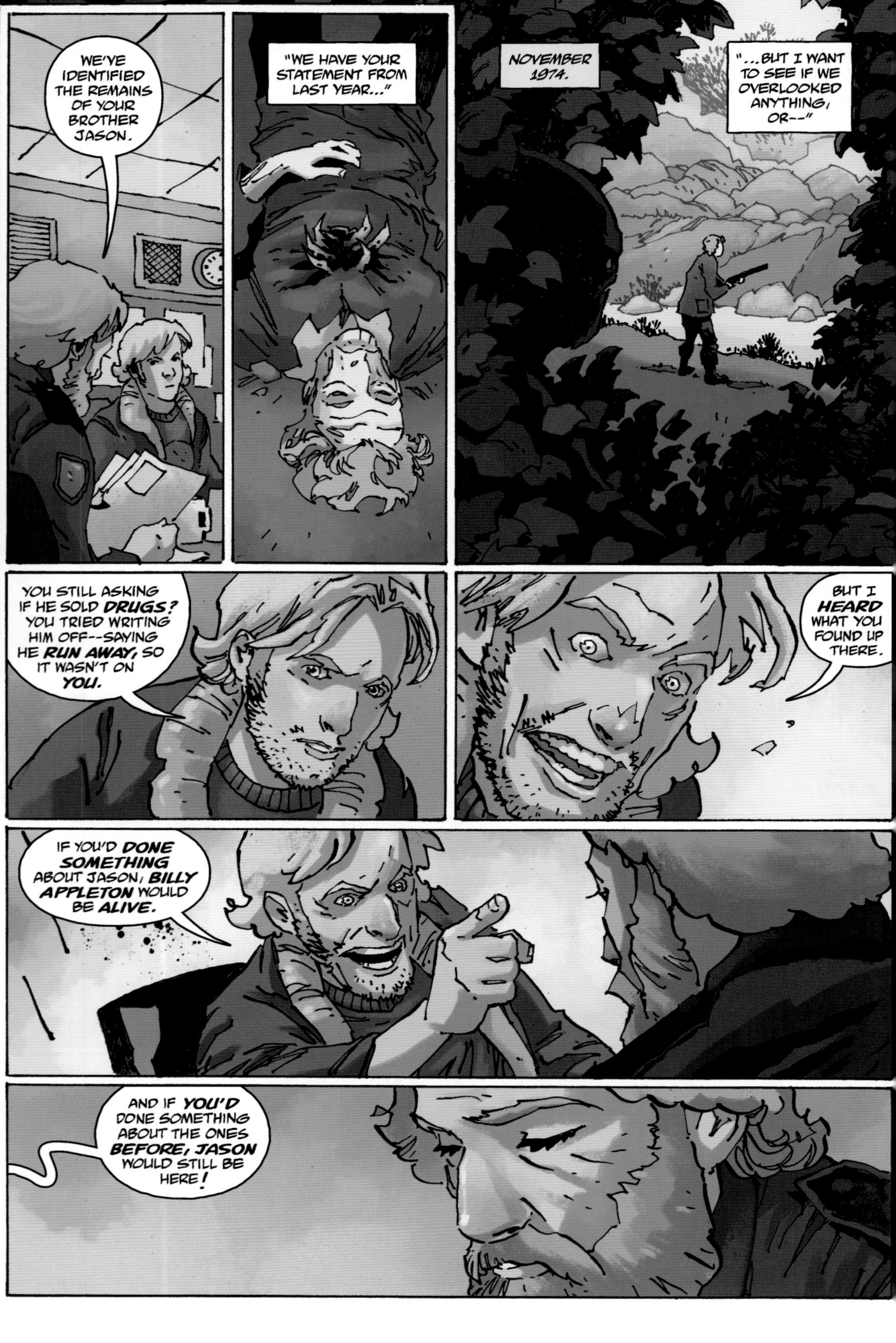
WE'VE IDENTIFIED THE REMAINS OF YOUR BROTHER JASON.
"WE HAVE YOUR STATEMENT FROM LAST YEAR..."
NOVEMBER 1974.
"...BUT I WANT TO SEE IF WE OVERLOOKED ANYTHING, OR--"
YOU STILL ASKING IF HE SOLD DRUGS? YOU TRIED WRITING HIM OFF--SAYING HE RUN AWAY, SO IT WASN'T ON YOU.
BUT I HEARD WHAT YOU FOUND UP THERE.
IF YOU'D DONE SOMETHING ABOUT JASON, BILLY APPLETON WOULD BE ALIVE.
AND IF YOU'D DONE SOMETHING ABOUT THE ONES BEFORE, JASON WOULD STILL BE HERE!

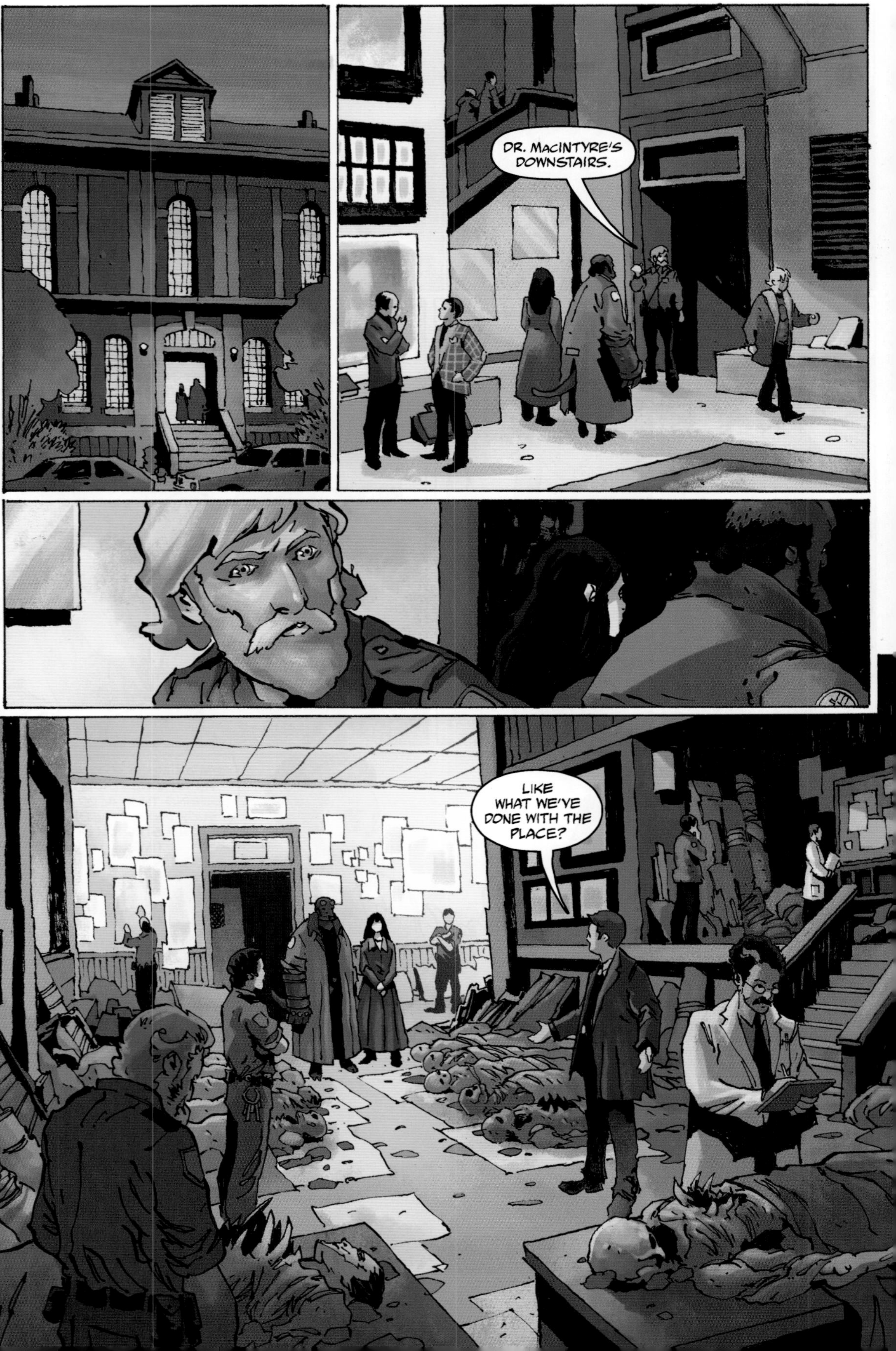
DR. MACINTYRE'S DOWNSTAIRS.
LIKE WHAT WE'VE DONE WITH THE PLACE?

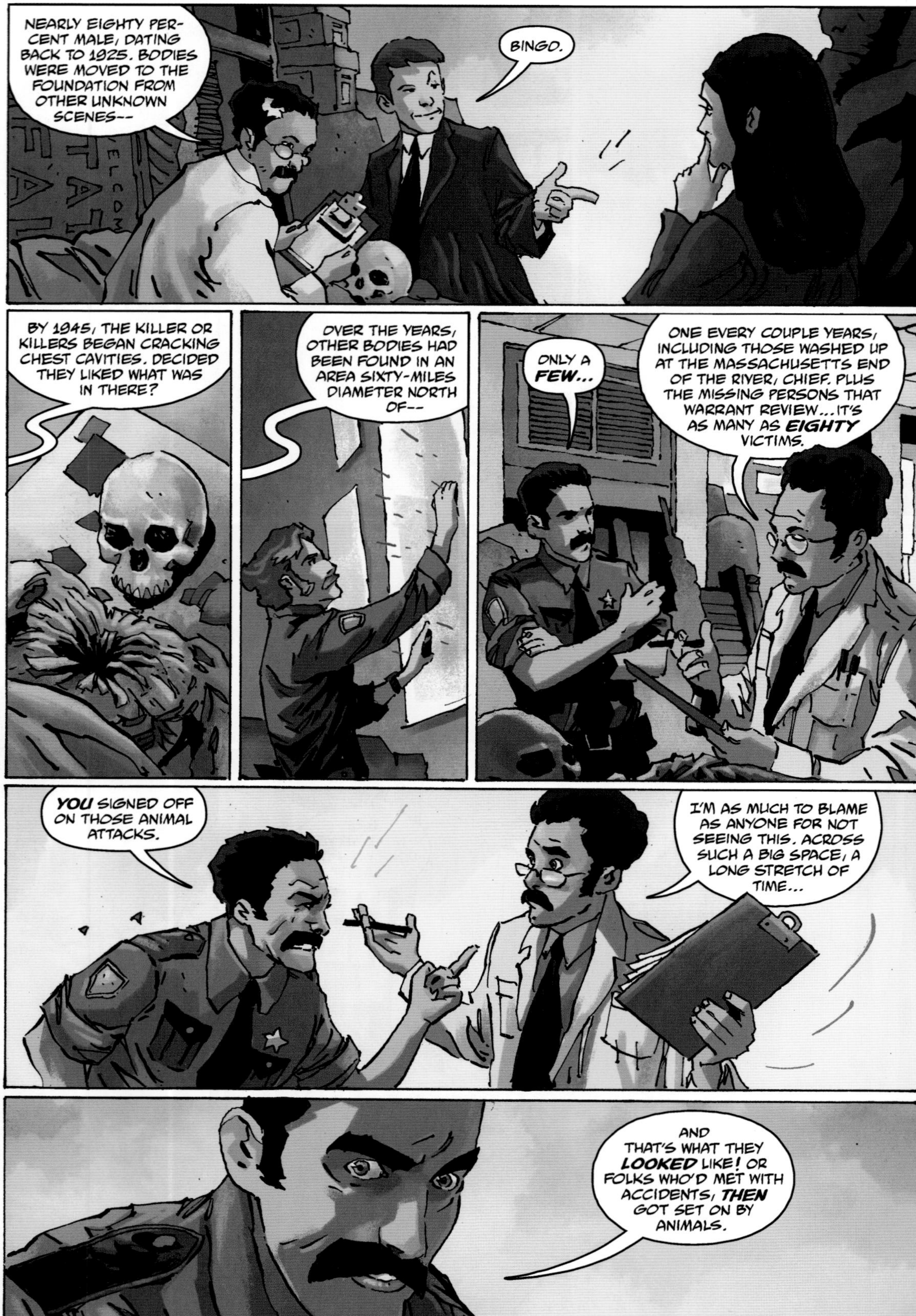
NEARLY EIGHTY PERCENT MALE, DATING BACK TO 1925. BODIES WERE MOVED TO THE FOUNDATION FROM OTHER UNKNOWN SCENES--
BINGO.
BY 1945, THE KILLER OR KILLERS BEGAN CRACKING CHEST CAVITIES. DECIDED THEY LIKED WHAT WAS IN THERE?
OVER THE YEARS, OTHER BODIES HAD BEEN FOUND IN AN AREA SIXTY-MILES DIAMETER NORTH OF--
ONLY A FEW...
ONE EVERY COUPLE YEARS, INCLUDING THOSE WASHED UP AT THE MASSACHUSETTS END OF THE RIVER, CHIEF. PLUS THE MISSING PERSONS THAT WARRANT REVIEW... IT'S AS MANY AS EIGHTY VICTIMS.
YOU SIGNED OFF ON THOSE ANIMAL ATTACKS.
I'M AS MUCH TO BLAME AS ANYONE FOR NOT SEEING THIS. ACROSS SUCH A BIG SPACE, A LONG STRETCH OF TIME...
AND THAT'S WHAT THEY LOOKED LIKE! OR FOLKS WHO'D MET WITH ACCIDENTS, THEN GOT SET ON BY ANIMALS.

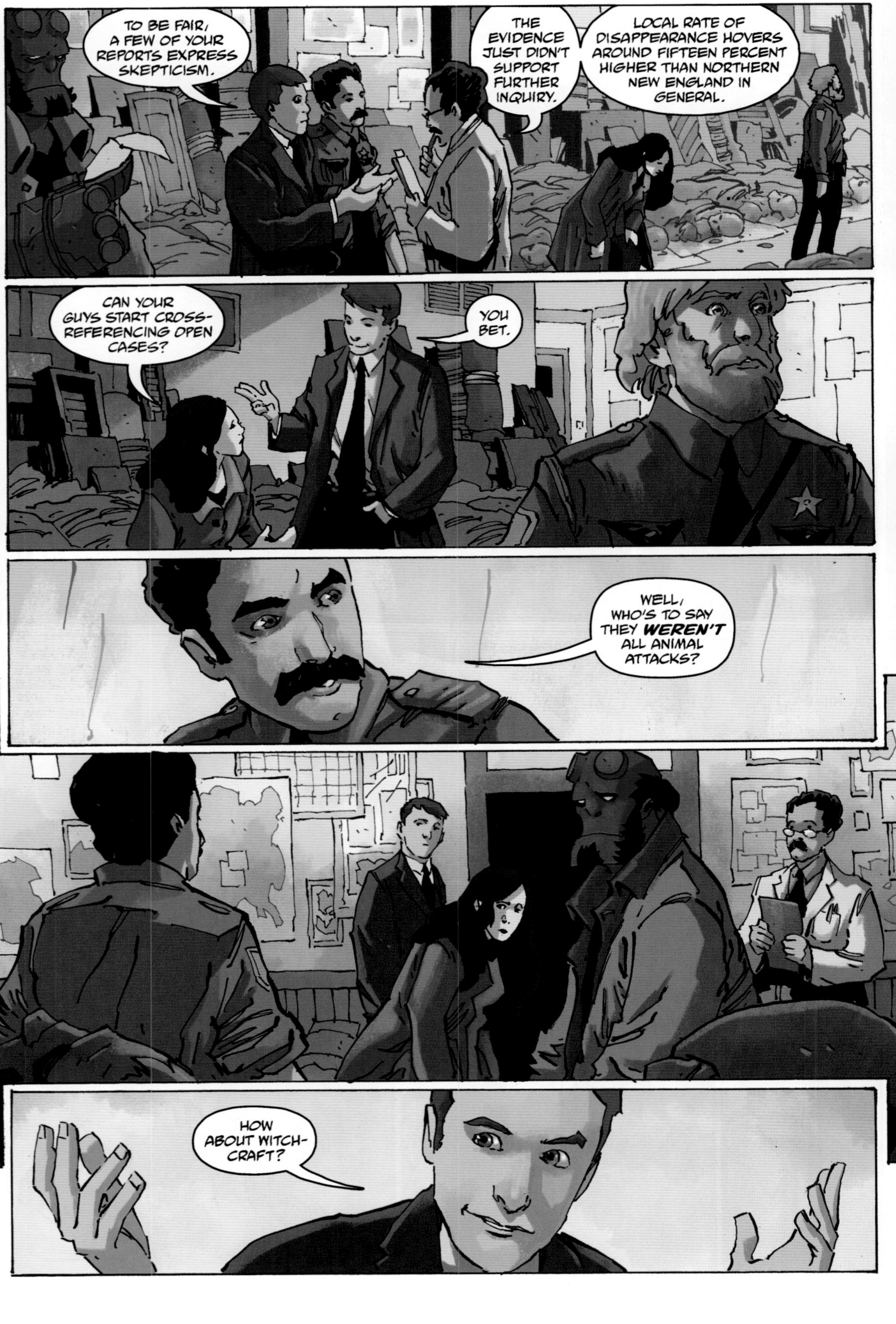
TO BE FAIR, A FEW OF YOUR REPORTS EXPRESS SKEPTICISM.
THE EVIDENCE JUST DIDN'T SUPPORT FURTHER INQUIRY.
LOCAL RATE OF DISAPPEARANCE HOVERS AROUND FIFTEEN PERCENT HIGHER THAN NORTHERN NEW ENGLAND IN GENERAL.
CAN YOUR GUYS START CROSS-REFERENCING OPEN CASES?
YOU BET.
WELL, WHO'S TO SAY THEY **WEREN'T** ALL ANIMAL ATTACKS?
HOW ABOUT WITCH-CRAFT?

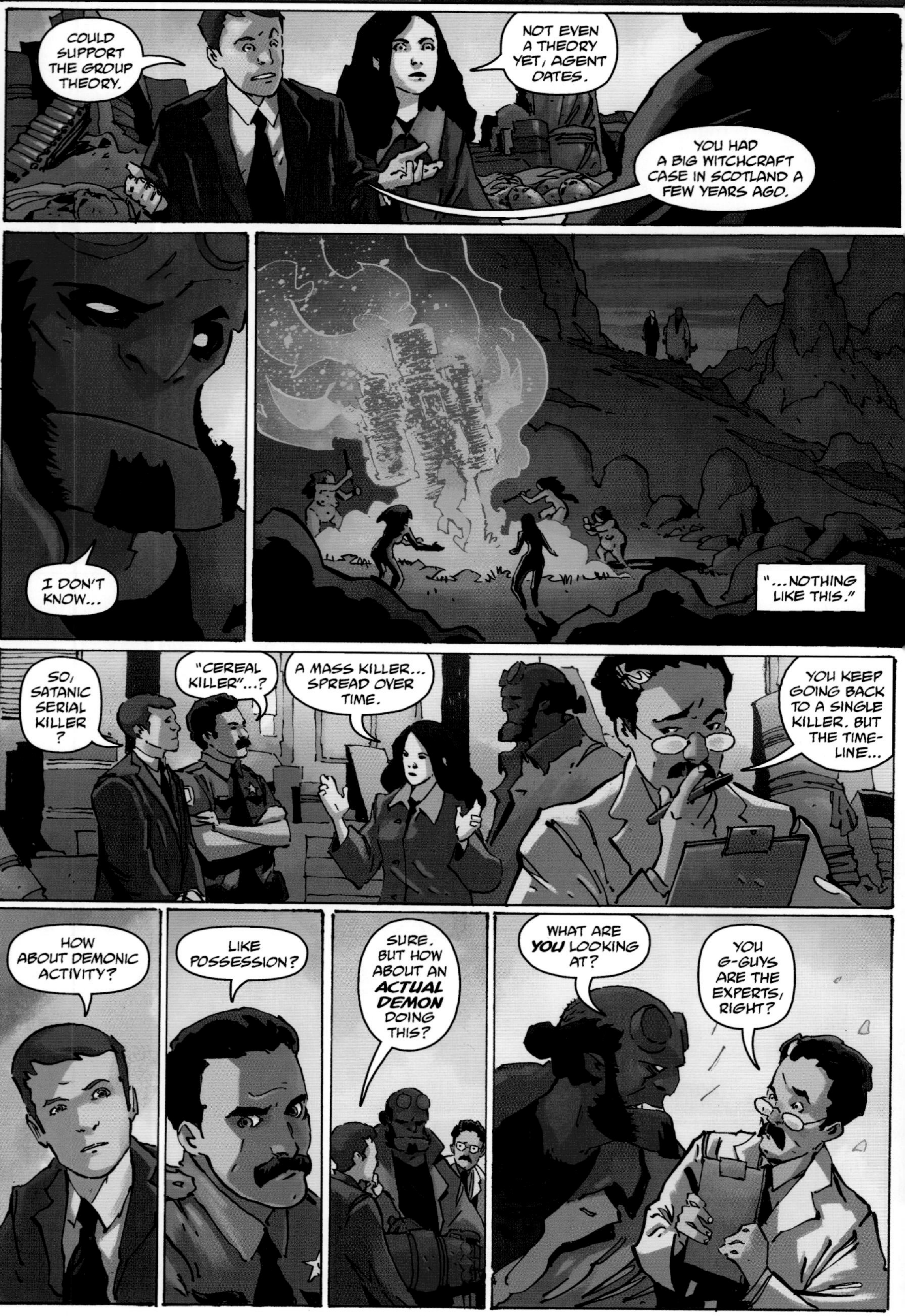
COULD SUPPORT THE GROUP THEORY.
NOT EVEN A THEORY YET, AGENT OATES.
YOU HAD A BIG WITCHCRAFT CASE IN SCOTLAND A FEW YEARS AGO.
I DON'T KNOW...
"...NOTHING LIKE THIS."
SO, SATANIC SERIAL KILLER?
"CEREAL KILLER"...?
A MASS KILLER... SPREAD OVER TIME.
YOU KEEP GOING BACK TO A SINGLE KILLER. BUT THE TIME-LINE...
HOW ABOUT DEMONIC ACTIVITY?
LIKE POSSESSION?
SURE. BUT HOW ABOUT AN **ACTUAL DEMON** DOING THIS?
WHAT ARE **YOU** LOOKING AT?
YOU G-GUYS ARE THE EXPERTS, RIGHT?

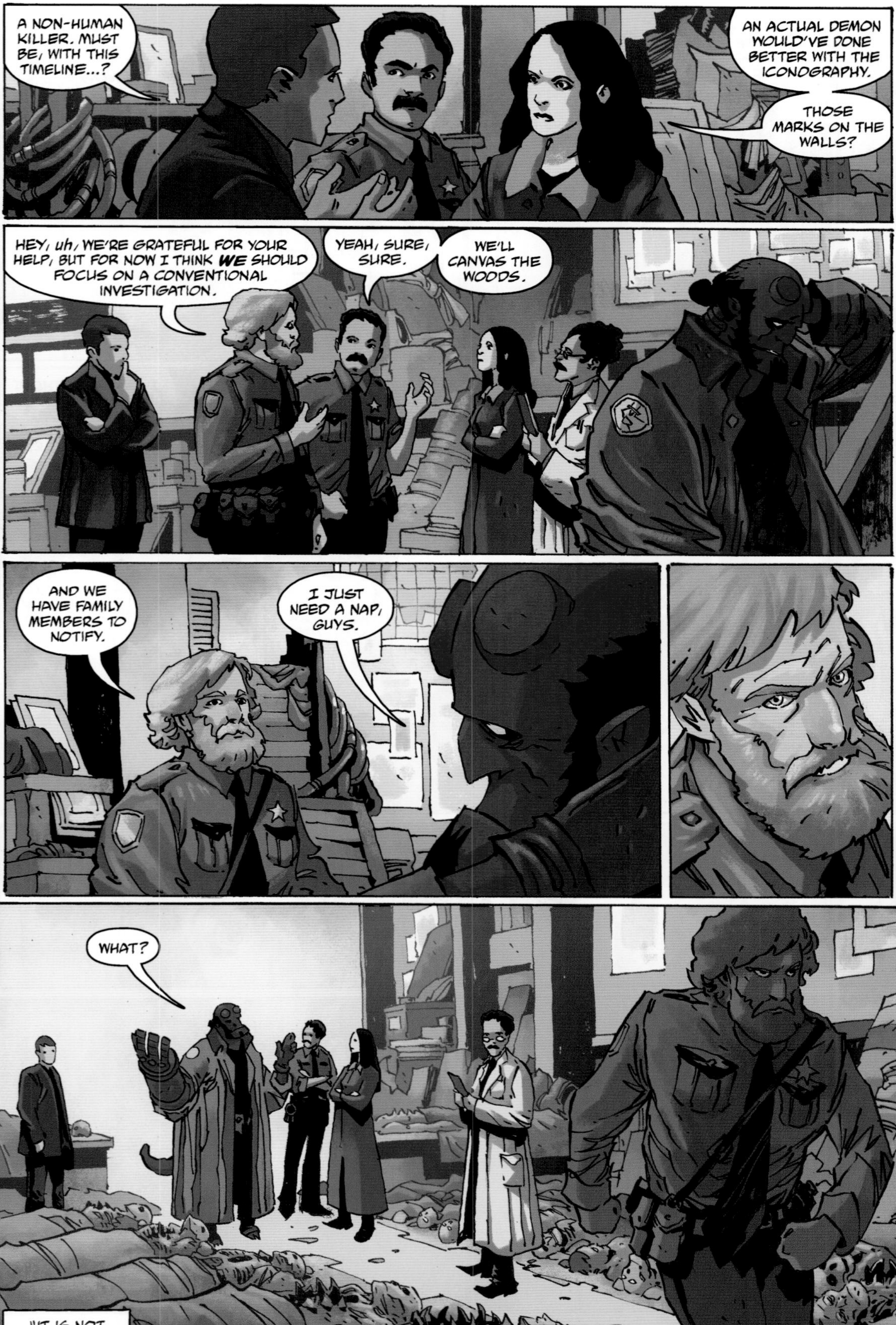
A NON-HUMAN KILLER. MUST BE, WITH THIS TIMELINE...?
AN ACTUAL DEMON WOULD'VE DONE BETTER WITH THE ICONOGRAPHY.
THOSE MARKS ON THE WALLS?
HEY, *uh*, WE'RE GRATEFUL FOR YOUR HELP, BUT FOR NOW I THINK **WE** SHOULD FOCUS ON A CONVENTIONAL INVESTIGATION.
YEAH, SURE, SURE.
WE'LL CANVAS THE WOODS.
AND WE HAVE FAMILY MEMBERS TO NOTIFY.
I JUST NEED A NAP, GUYS.
WHAT?
"IT IS NOT ***'GOSSIP'***..."

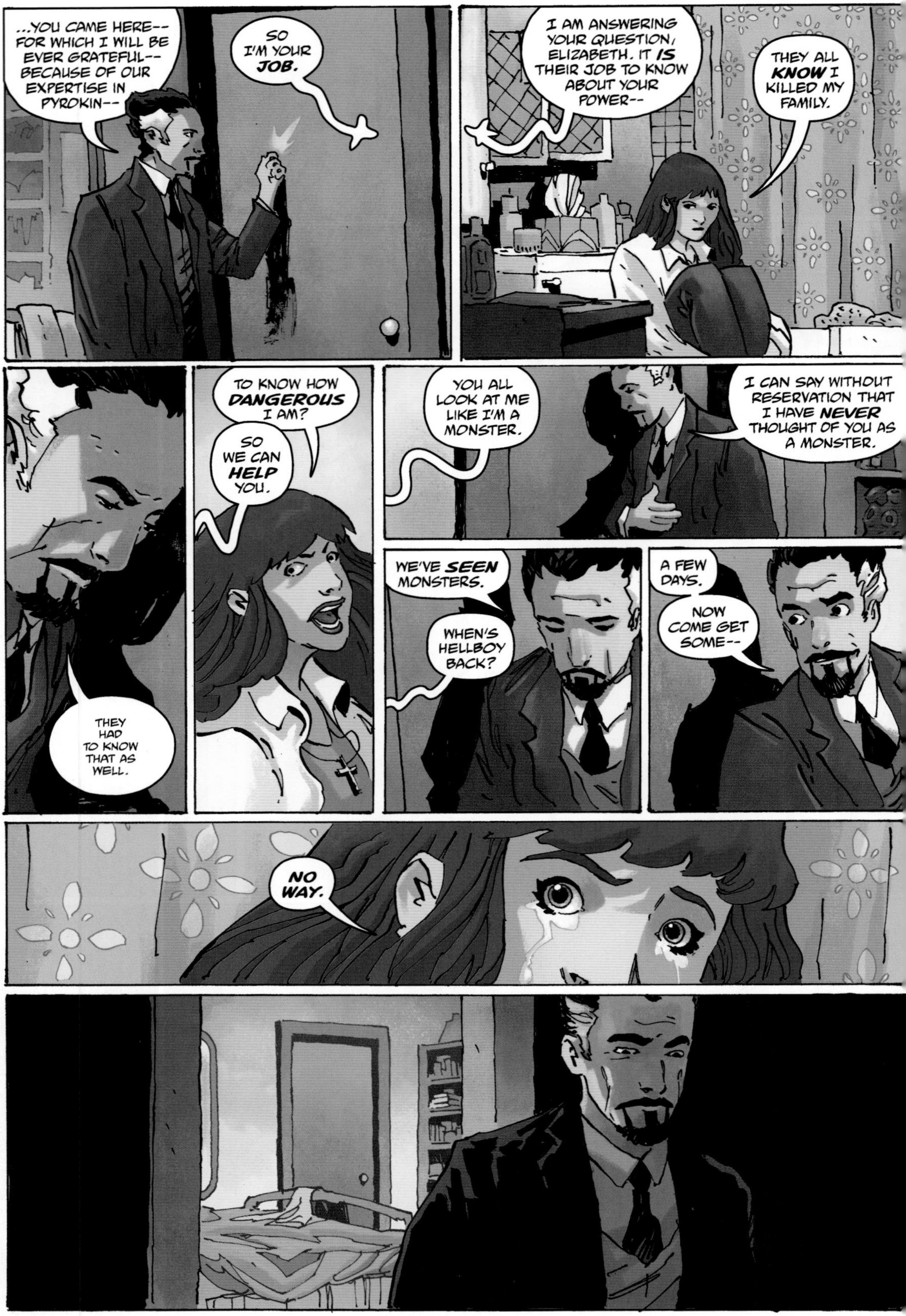
...YOU CAME HERE-- FOR WHICH I WILL BE EVER GRATEFUL-- BECAUSE OF OUR EXPERTISE IN PYROKIN--
SO I'M YOUR JOB.
I AM ANSWERING YOUR QUESTION, ELIZABETH. IT IS THEIR JOB TO KNOW ABOUT YOUR POWER--
THEY ALL KNOW I KILLED MY FAMILY.
THEY HAD TO KNOW THAT AS WELL.
TO KNOW HOW DANGEROUS I AM?
SO WE CAN HELP YOU.
YOU ALL LOOK AT ME LIKE I'M A MONSTER.
I CAN SAY WITHOUT RESERVATION THAT I HAVE NEVER THOUGHT OF YOU AS A MONSTER.
WE'VE SEEN MONSTERS.
WHEN'S HELLBOY BACK?
A FEW DAYS.
NOW COME GET SOME--
NO WAY.

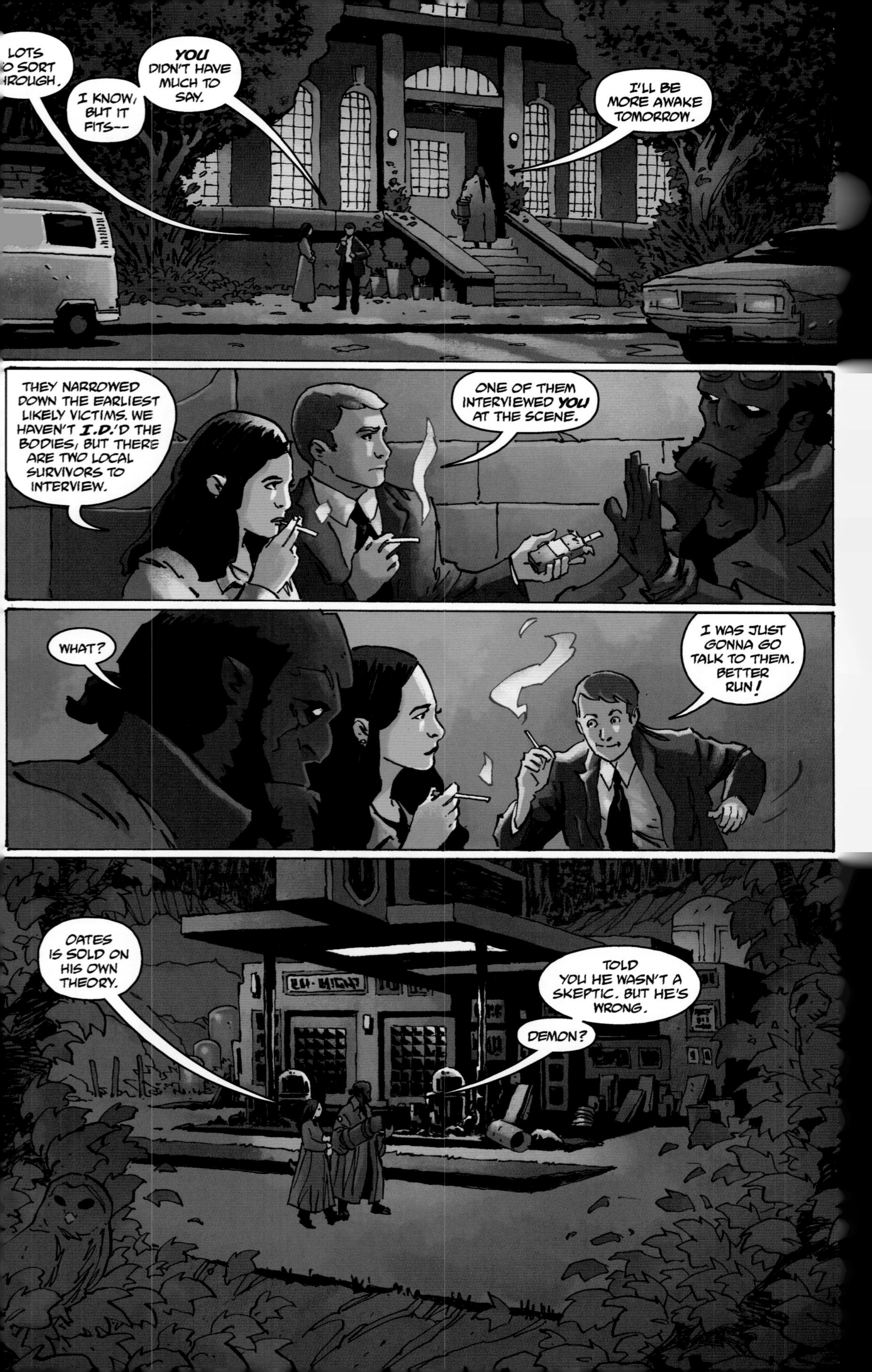
LOTS
O SORT
HROUGH.
I KNOW, BUT IT FITS--
YOU DIDN'T HAVE MUCH TO SAY.
I'LL BE MORE AWAKE TOMORROW.
THEY NARROWED DOWN THE EARLIEST LIKELY VICTIMS. WE HAVEN'T I.D.'D THE BODIES, BUT THERE ARE TWO LOCAL SURVIVORS TO INTERVIEW.
ONE OF THEM INTERVIEWED YOU AT THE SCENE.
WHAT?
I WAS JUST GONNA GO TALK TO THEM. BETTER RUN!
OATES IS SOLD ON HIS OWN THEORY.
TOLD YOU HE WASN'T A SKEPTIC. BUT HE'S WRONG.
DEMON?

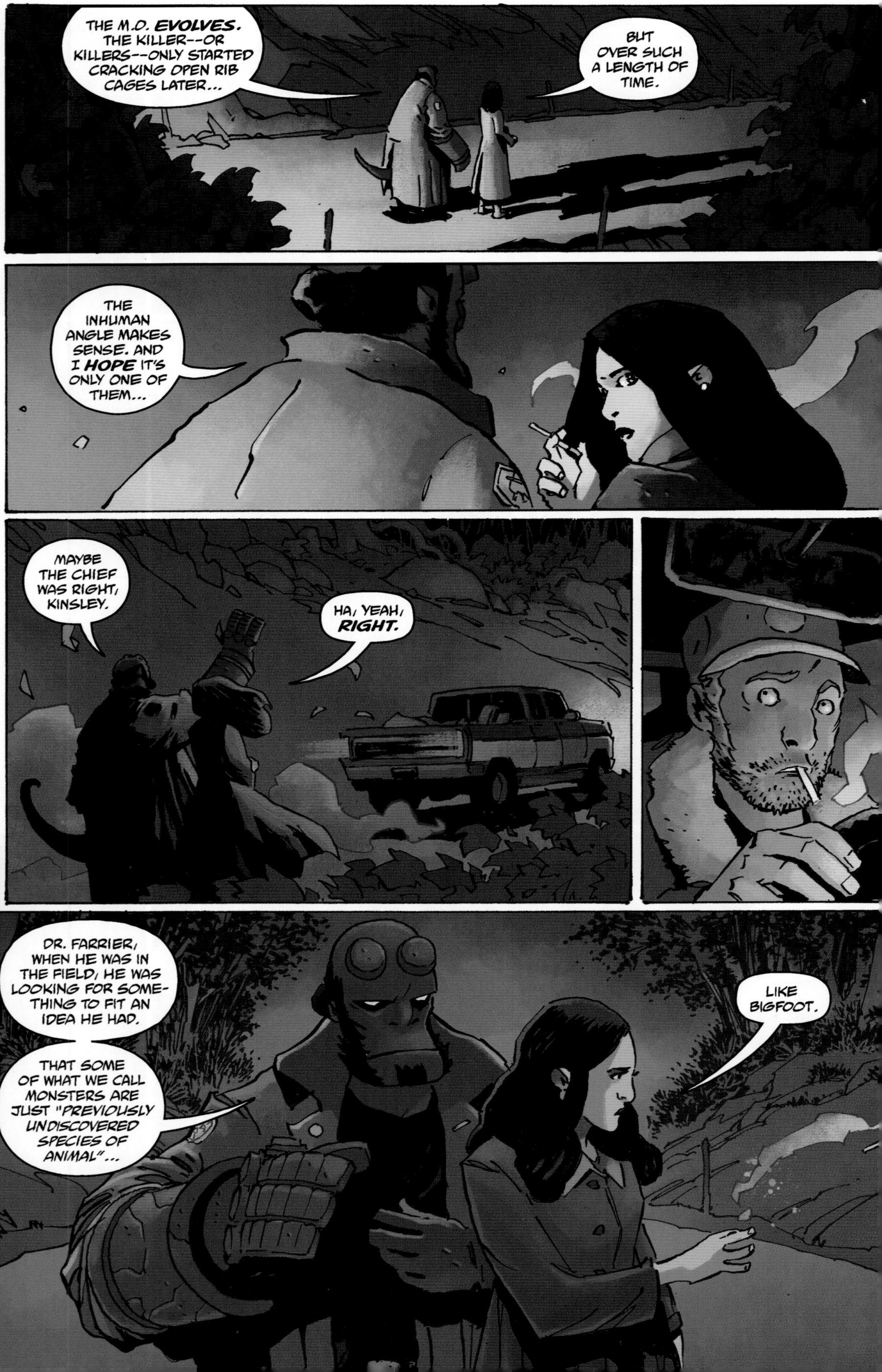
THE M.D. EVOLVES. THE KILLER--OR KILLERS--ONLY STARTED CRACKING OPEN RIB CAGES LATER...
BUT OVER SUCH A LENGTH OF TIME.
THE INHUMAN ANGLE MAKES SENSE. AND I HOPE IT'S ONLY ONE OF THEM...
MAYBE THE CHIEF WAS RIGHT, KINSLEY.
HA, YEAH, RIGHT.
DR. FARRIER, WHEN HE WAS IN THE FIELD, HE WAS LOOKING FOR SOME-THING TO FIT AN IDEA HE HAD.
THAT SOME OF WHAT WE CALL MONSTERS ARE JUST "PREVIOUSLY UNDISCOVERED SPECIES OF ANIMAL"...
LIKE BIGFOOT.

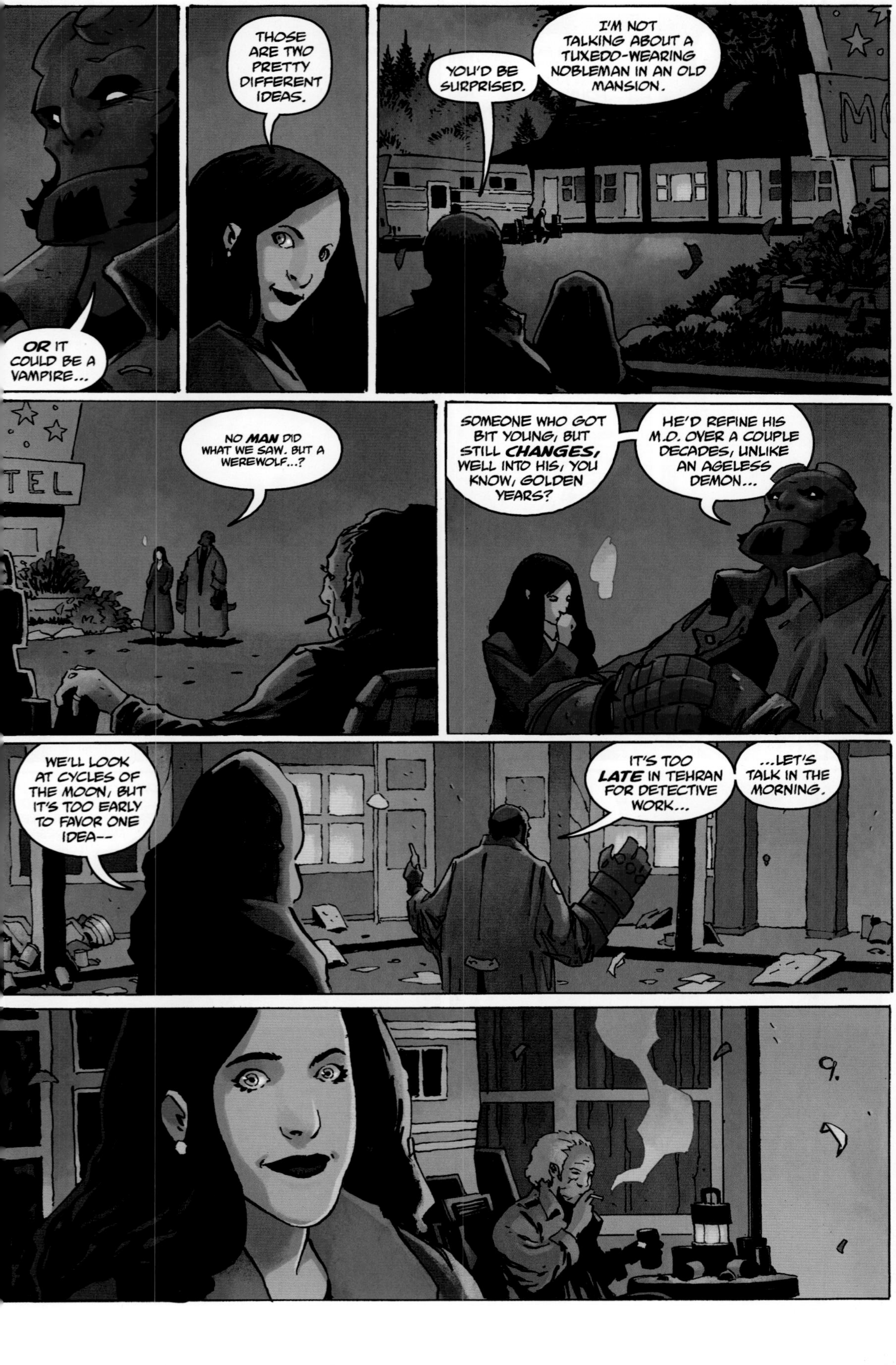
OR IT COULD BE A VAMPIRE...
THOSE ARE TWO PRETTY DIFFERENT IDEAS.
YOU'D BE SURPRISED.
I'M NOT TALKING ABOUT A TUXEDO-WEARING NOBLEMAN IN AN OLD MANSION.
NO MAN DID WHAT WE SAW. BUT A WEREWOLF...?
SOMEONE WHO GOT BIT YOUNG, BUT STILL CHANGES, WELL INTO HIS, YOU KNOW, GOLDEN YEARS?
HE'D REFINE HIS M.O. OVER A COUPLE DECADES, UNLIKE AN AGELESS DEMON...
WE'LL LOOK AT CYCLES OF THE MOON, BUT IT'S TOO EARLY TO FAVOR ONE IDEA--
IT'S TOO LATE IN TEHRAN FOR DETECTIVE WORK...
...LET'S TALK IN THE MORNING.

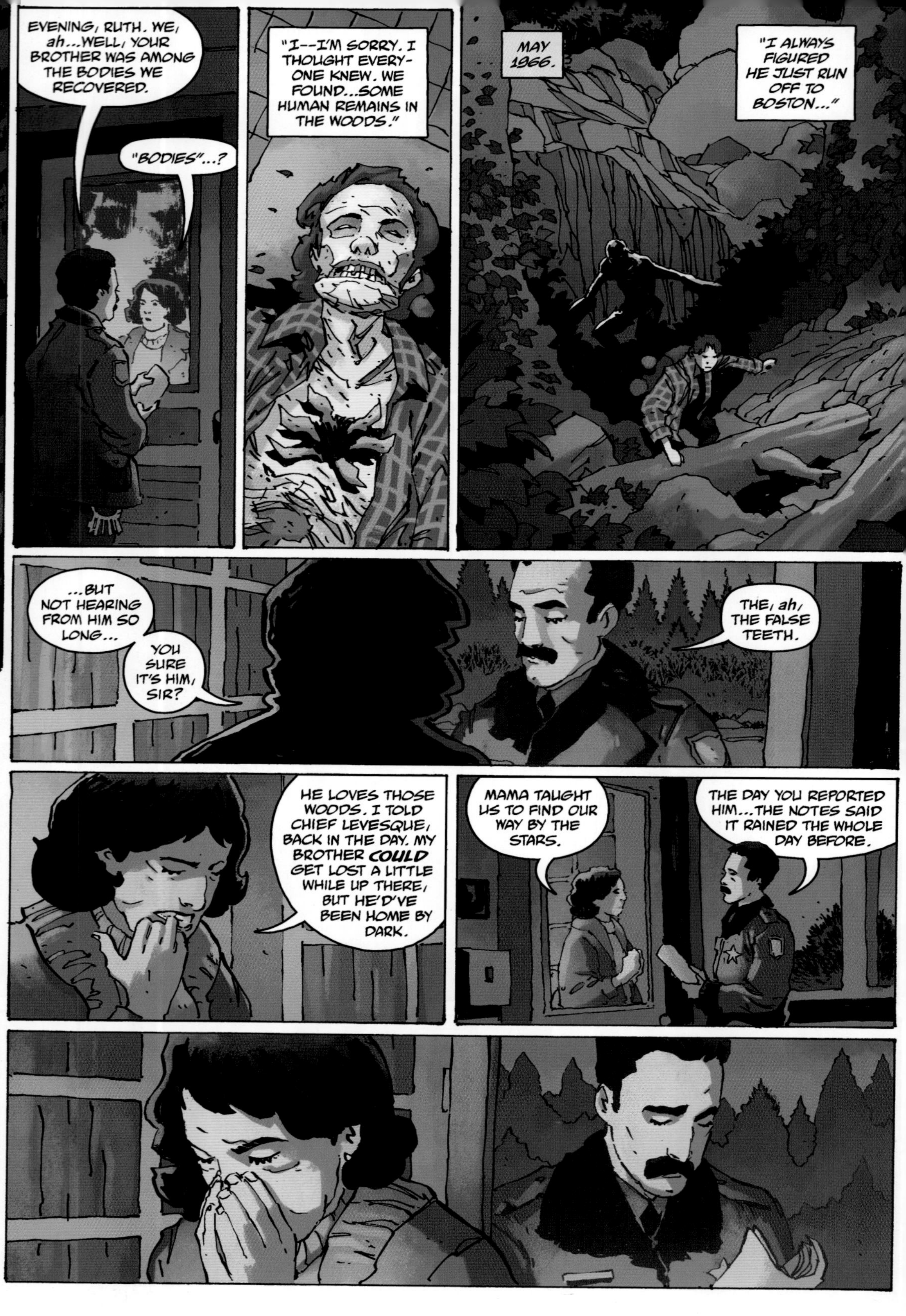
EVENING, RUTH. WE, ah...WELL, YOUR BROTHER WAS AMONG THE BODIES WE RECOVERED.
"BODIES"...?
"I--I'M SORRY. I THOUGHT EVERY-ONE KNEW. WE FOUND...SOME HUMAN REMAINS IN THE WOODS."
MAY 1966.
"I ALWAYS FIGURED HE JUST RUN OFF TO BOSTON..."
...BUT NOT HEARING FROM HIM SO LONG...
YOU SURE IT'S HIM, SIR?
THE, ah, THE FALSE TEETH.
HE LOVES THOSE WOODS. I TOLD CHIEF LEVESQUE, BACK IN THE DAY. MY BROTHER COULD GET LOST A LITTLE WHILE UP THERE, BUT HE'D'VE BEEN HOME BY DARK.
MAMA TAUGHT US TO FIND OUR WAY BY THE STARS.
THE DAY YOU REPORTED HIM...THE NOTES SAID IT RAINED THE WHOLE DAY BEFORE.

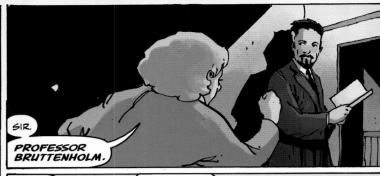

SIR.

PROFESSOR BRUTTENHOLM.

DID YOU SPEAK TO LIZ?

YOU **ASKED** ME TO SPEAK TO HER, NATALIE. I'M SORRY IF MY EFFORT--

NO, I DIDN'T MEAN--

DID SHE EVER COME TO DINNER?

KNOCK

KNOCK

KNOCK

PLEASE OPEN THE DOOR.

ELIZABETH?

FAIRFIELD, CONNECTICUT.

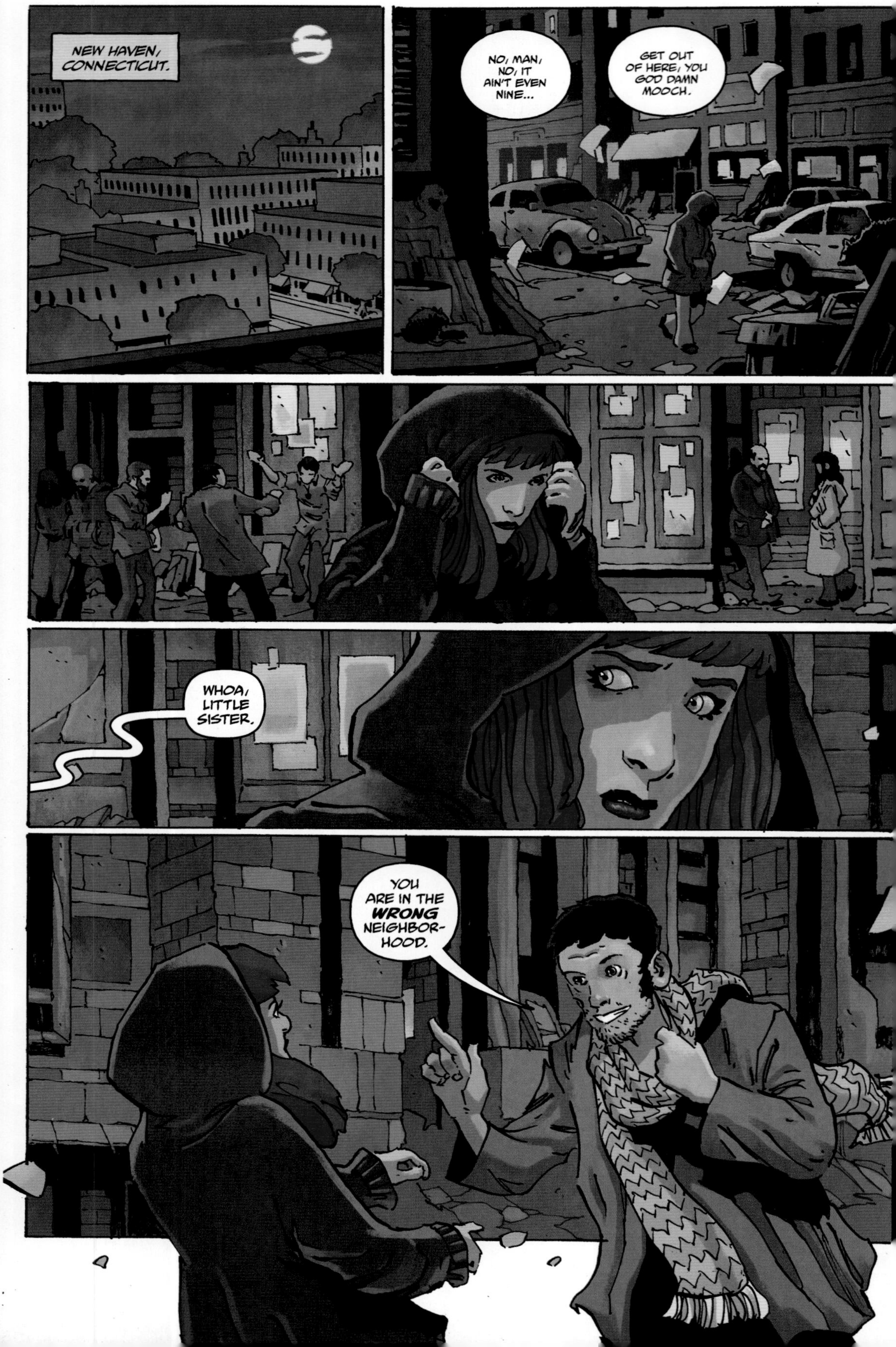
NEW HAVEN, CONNECTICUT.
NO, MAN, NO, IT AIN'T EVEN NINE...
GET OUT OF HERE, YOU GOD DAMN MOOCH.
WHOA, LITTLE SISTER.
YOU ARE IN THE WRONG NEIGHBOR-HOOD.

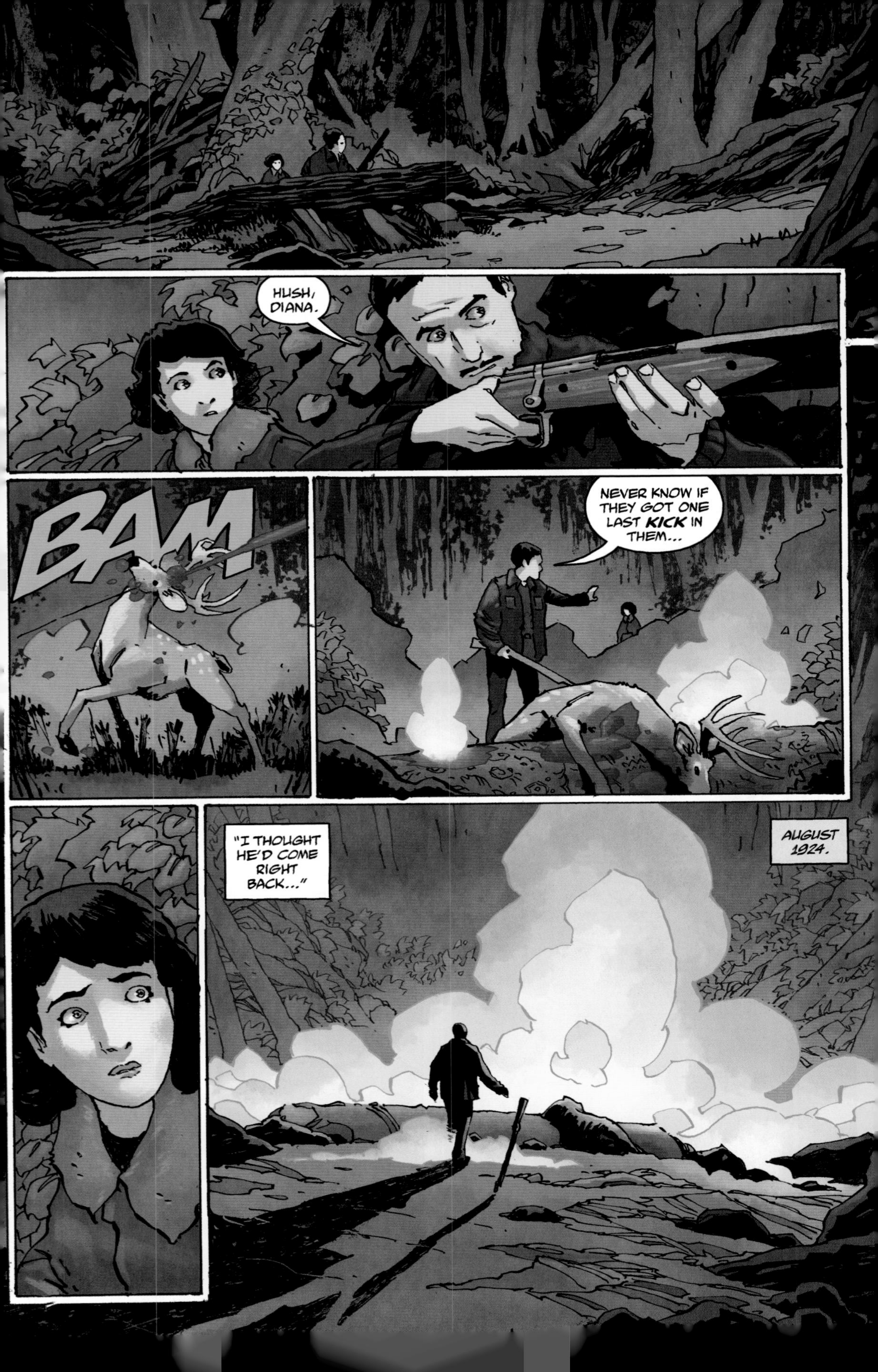
HUSH, DIANA.
BAM
NEVER KNOW IF THEY GOT ONE LAST KICK IN THEM...
"I THOUGHT HE'D COME RIGHT BACK..."
AUGUST 1924.

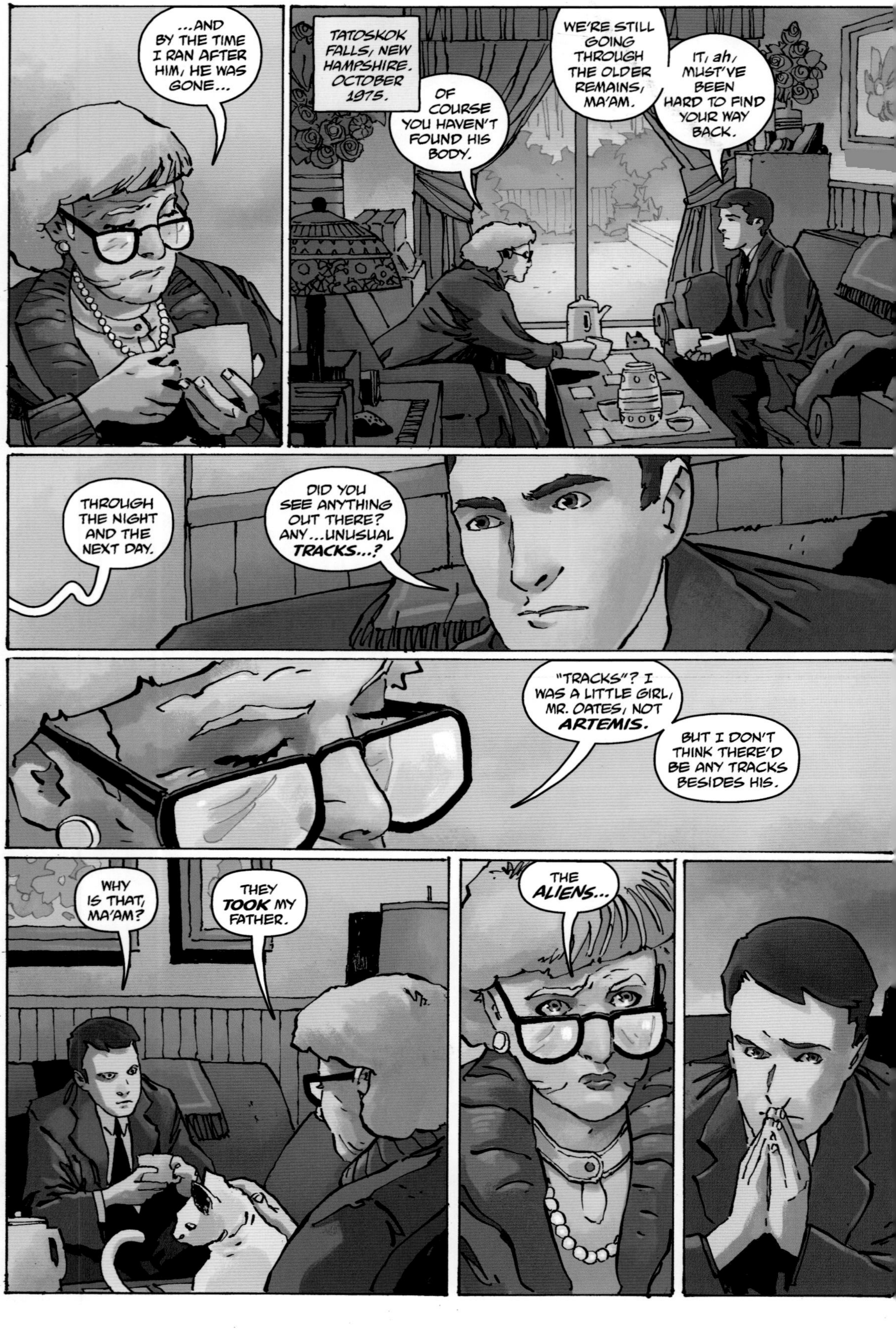
...AND BY THE TIME I RAN AFTER HIM, HE WAS GONE...
TATOSKOK FALLS, NEW HAMPSHIRE. OCTOBER 1975.
OF COURSE YOU HAVEN'T FOUND HIS BODY.
WE'RE STILL GOING THROUGH THE OLDER REMAINS, MA'AM.
IT, ah, MUST'VE BEEN HARD TO FIND YOUR WAY BACK.
THROUGH THE NIGHT AND THE NEXT DAY.
DID YOU SEE ANYTHING OUT THERE? ANY...UNUSUAL TRACKS...?
"TRACKS"? I WAS A LITTLE GIRL, MR. OATES, NOT ARTEMIS.
BUT I DON'T THINK THERE'D BE ANY TRACKS BESIDES HIS.
WHY IS THAT, MA'AM?
THEY TOOK MY FATHER.
THE ALIENS...

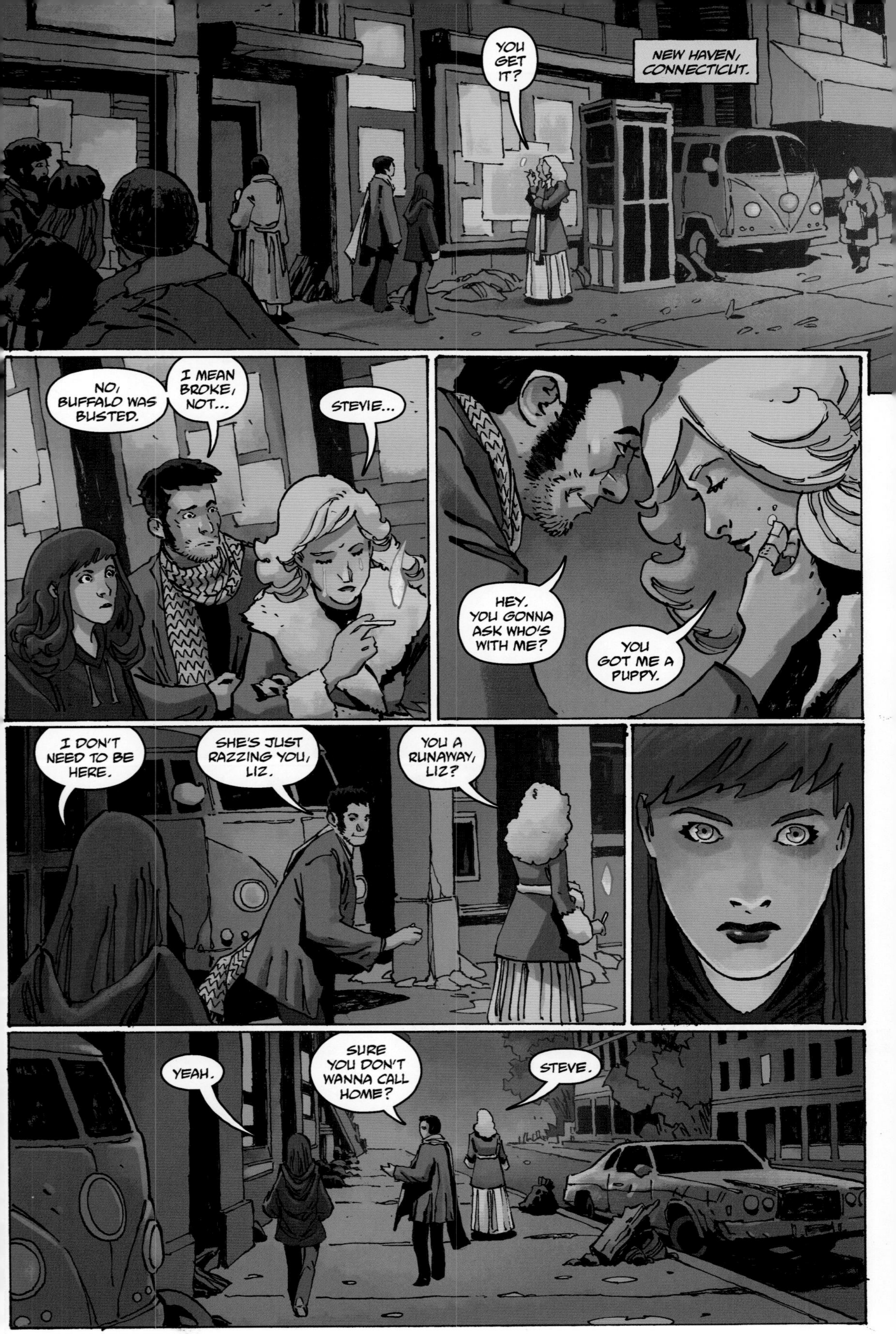

NEW HAVEN, CONNECTICUT.
YOU GET IT?
NO, BUFFALO WAS BUSTED.
I MEAN BROKE, NOT...
STEVIE...
HEY. YOU GONNA ASK WHO'S WITH ME?
YOU GOT ME A PUPPY.
I DON'T NEED TO BE HERE.
SHE'S JUST RAZZING YOU, LIZ.
YOU A RUNAWAY, LIZ?
YEAH.
SURE YOU DON'T WANNA CALL HOME?
STEVE.

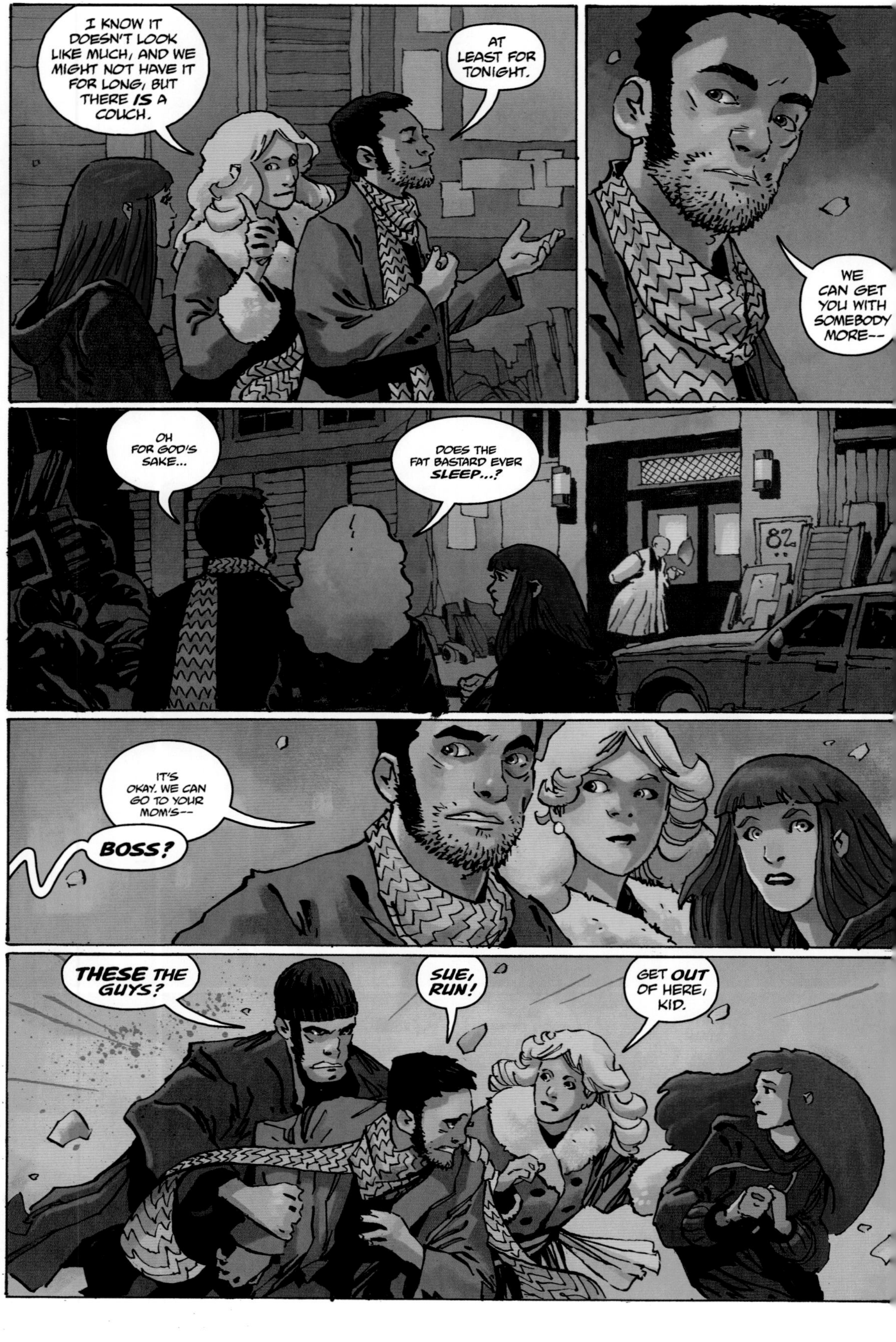
I KNOW IT DOESN'T LOOK LIKE MUCH, AND WE MIGHT NOT HAVE IT FOR LONG, BUT THERE IS A COUCH.
AT LEAST FOR TONIGHT.
WE CAN GET YOU WITH SOMEBODY MORE--
OH FOR GOD'S SAKE...
DOES THE FAT BASTARD EVER SLEEP...?
82
IT'S OKAY. WE CAN GO TO YOUR MOM'S--
BOSS?
THESE THE GUYS?
SUE, RUN!
GET OUT OF HERE, KID.

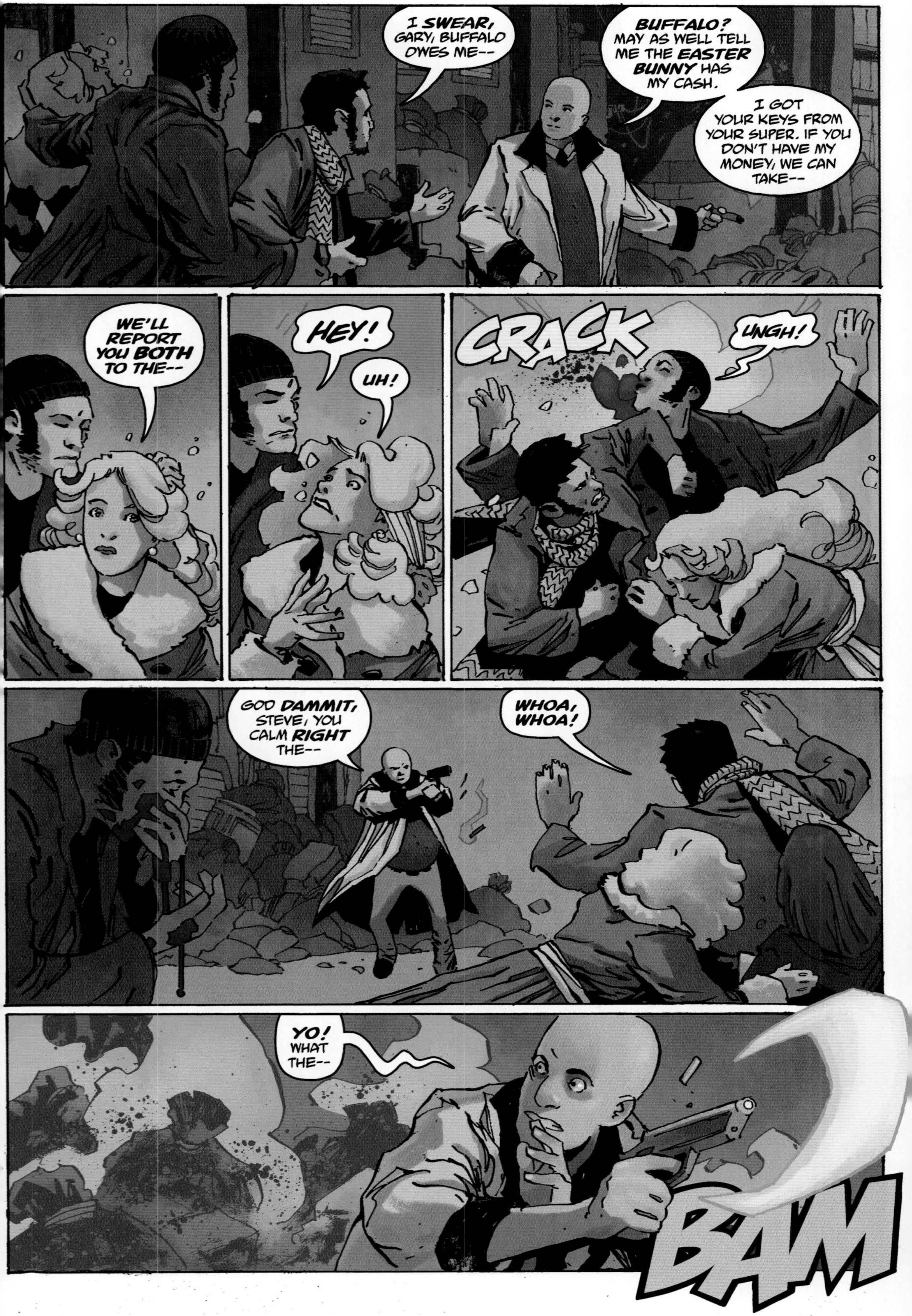
I SWEAR, GARY, BUFFALO OWES ME--
BUFFALO? MAY AS WELL TELL ME THE EASTER BUNNY HAS MY CASH.
I GOT YOUR KEYS FROM YOUR SUPER. IF YOU DON'T HAVE MY MONEY, WE CAN TAKE--
WE'LL REPORT YOU BOTH TO THE--
HEY!
UH!
CRACK
UNGH!
GOD DAMMIT, STEVE, YOU CALM RIGHT THE--
WHOA, WHOA!
YO! WHAT THE--
BAM

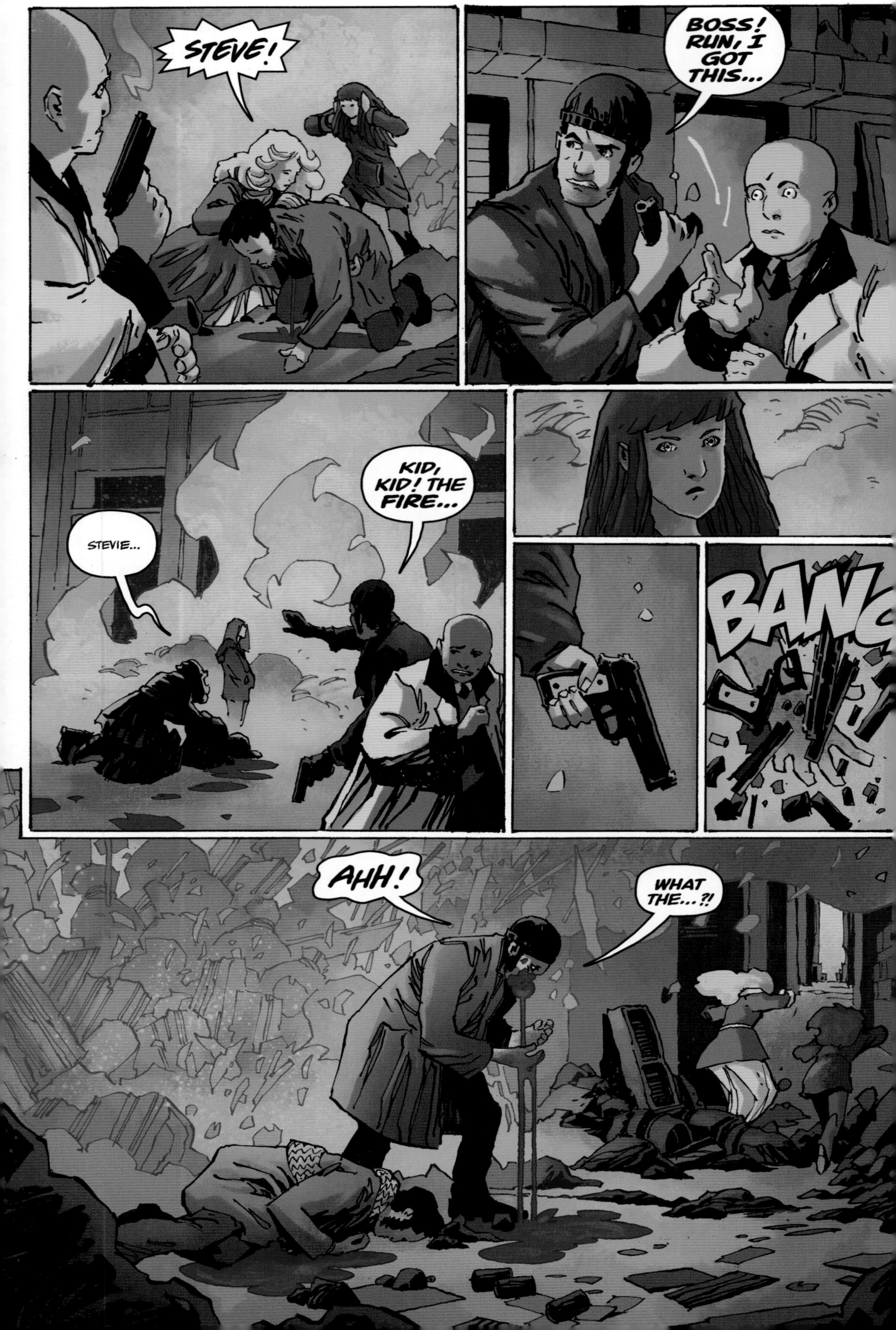
STEVE!
BOSS! RUN, I GOT THIS...
STEVIE...
KID, KID! THE FIRE...
BANG
AHH!
WHAT THE...?!

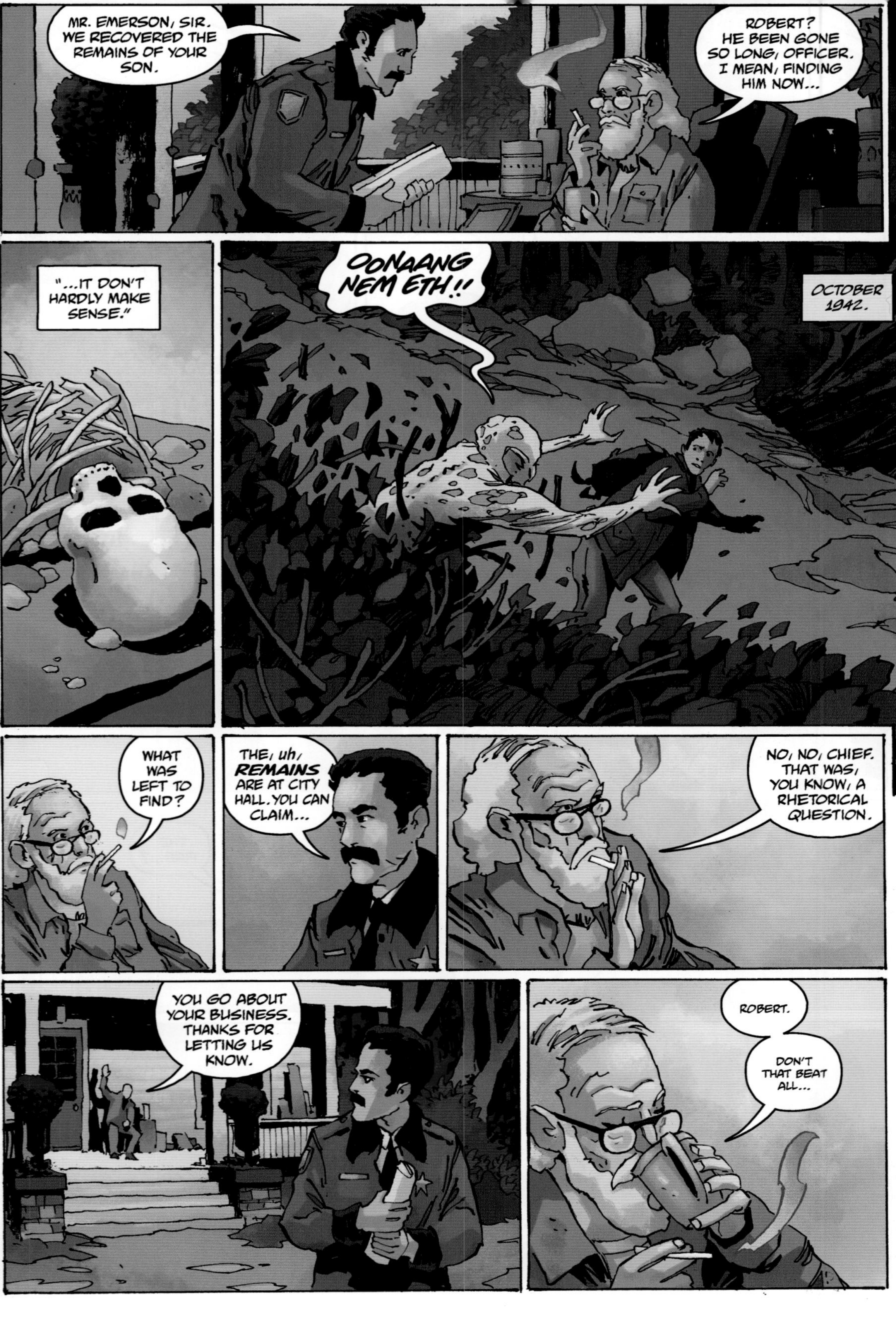
MR. EMERSON, SIR. WE RECOVERED THE REMAINS OF YOUR SON.
ROBERT? HE BEEN GONE SO LONG, OFFICER. I MEAN, FINDING HIM NOW...
"...IT DON'T HARDLY MAKE SENSE."
OONAANG NEM ETH!!
OCTOBER 1942.
WHAT WAS LEFT TO FIND?
THE, uh, REMAINS ARE AT CITY HALL. YOU CAN CLAIM...
NO, NO, CHIEF. THAT WAS, YOU KNOW, A RHETORICAL QUESTION.
YOU GO ABOUT YOUR BUSINESS. THANKS FOR LETTING US KNOW.
ROBERT.
DON'T THAT BEAT ALL...

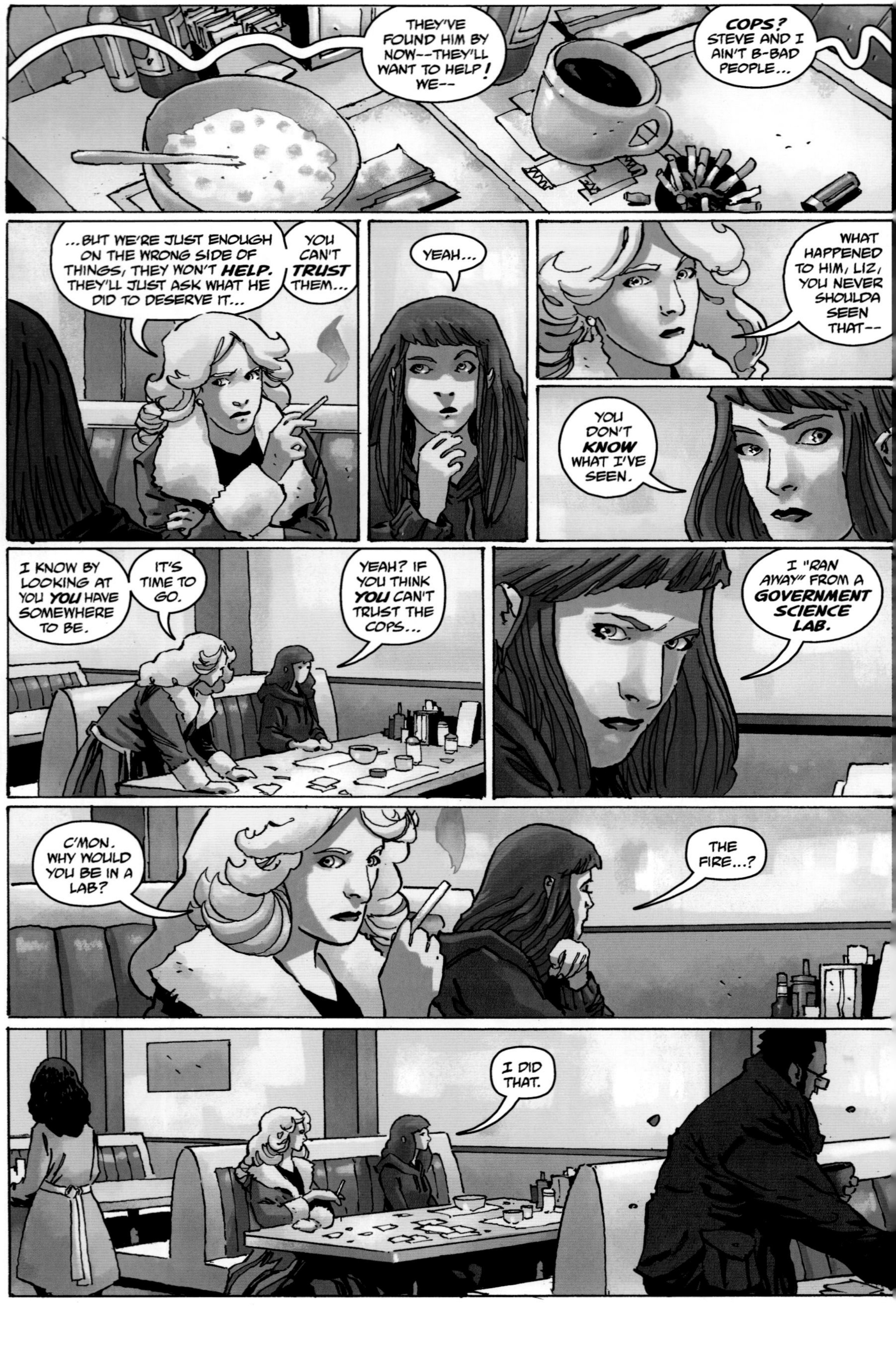
THEY'VE FOUND HIM BY NOW--THEY'LL WANT TO HELP! WE--
COPS? STEVE AND I AIN'T B-BAD PEOPLE...
...BUT WE'RE JUST ENOUGH ON THE WRONG SIDE OF THINGS, THEY WON'T HELP. THEY'LL JUST ASK WHAT HE DID TO DESERVE IT...
YOU CAN'T TRUST THEM...
YEAH...
WHAT HAPPENED TO HIM, LIZ, YOU NEVER SHOULDA SEEN THAT--
YOU DON'T KNOW WHAT I'VE SEEN.
I KNOW BY LOOKING AT YOU YOU HAVE SOMEWHERE TO BE.
IT'S TIME TO GO.
YEAH? IF YOU THINK YOU CAN'T TRUST THE COPS...
I "RAN AWAY" FROM A GOVERNMENT SCIENCE LAB.
C'MON. WHY WOULD YOU BE IN A LAB?
THE FIRE...?
I DID THAT.

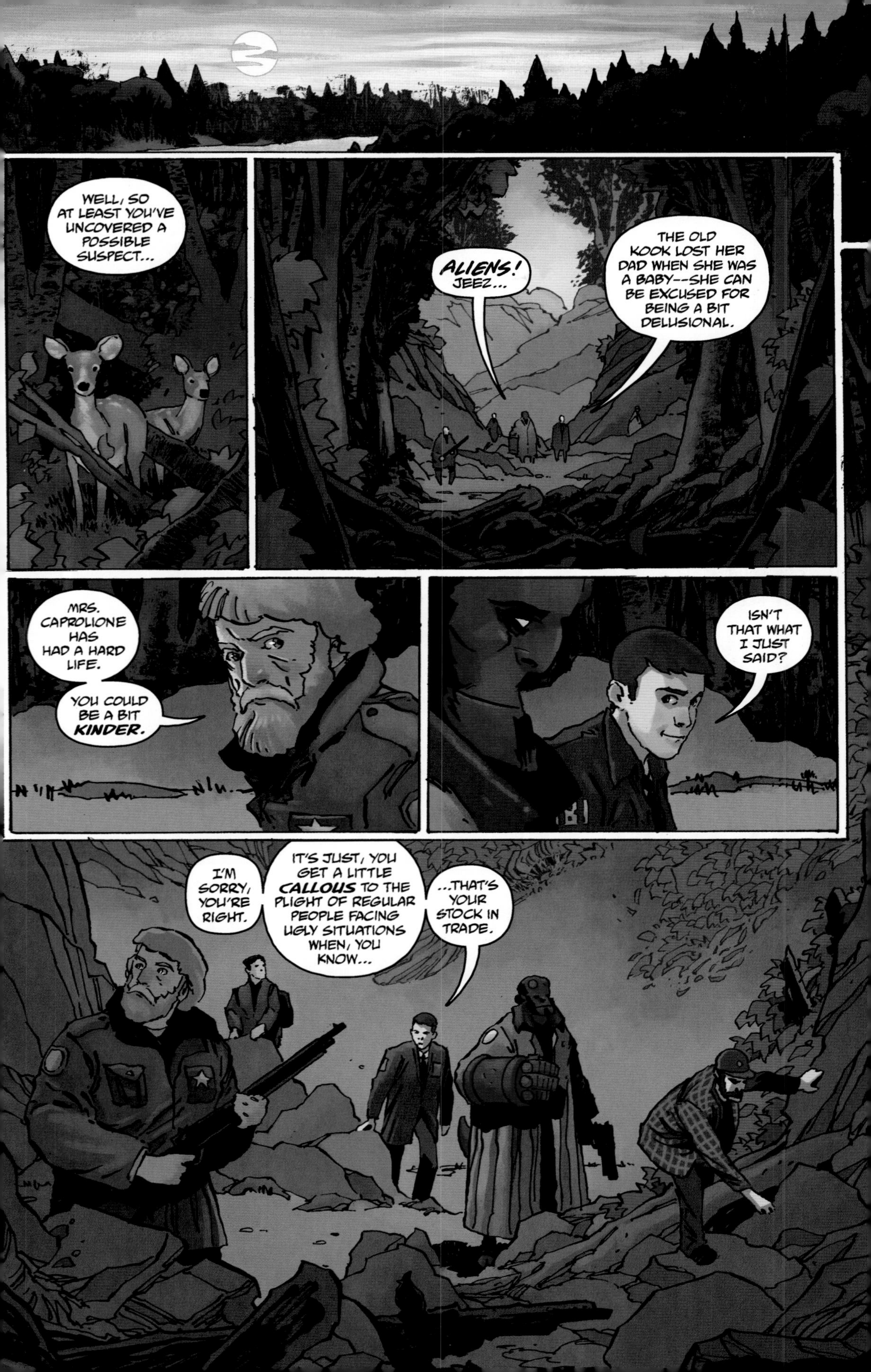
WELL, SO AT LEAST YOU'VE UNCOVERED A POSSIBLE SUSPECT...
ALIENS! JEEZ...
THE OLD KOOK LOST HER DAD WHEN SHE WAS A BABY--SHE CAN BE EXCUSED FOR BEING A BIT DELUSIONAL.
MRS. CAPROLIONE HAS HAD A HARD LIFE.
YOU COULD BE A BIT KINDER.
ISN'T THAT WHAT I JUST SAID?
I'M SORRY, YOU'RE RIGHT.
IT'S JUST, YOU GET A LITTLE CALLOUS TO THE PLIGHT OF REGULAR PEOPLE FACING UGLY SITUATIONS WHEN, YOU KNOW...
...THAT'S YOUR STOCK IN TRADE.

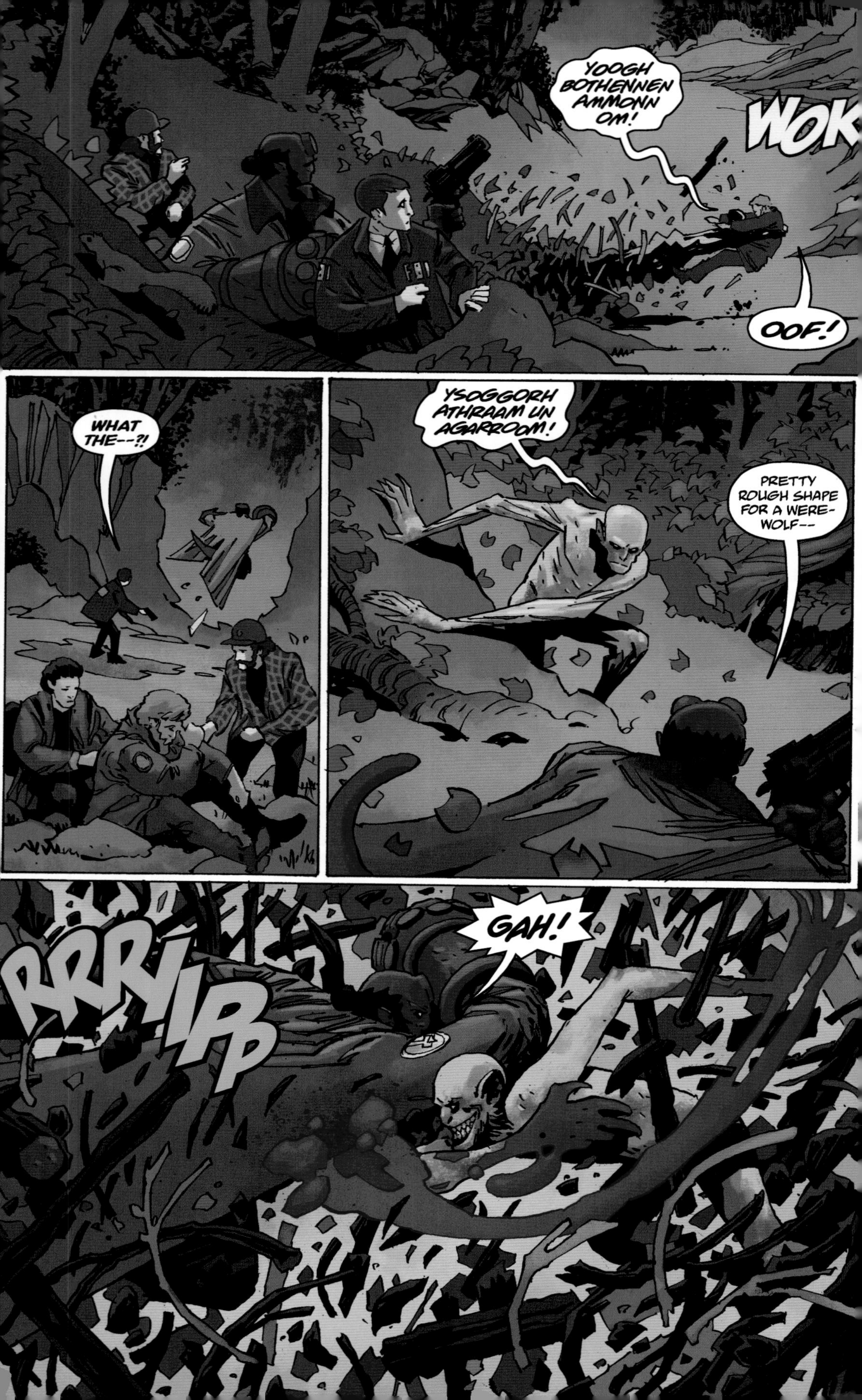
YOOGH BOTHENNEN AMMONN OM!
WOK
OOF!
WHAT THE--?!
YSOGGORH ATHRAAM UN AGARROOM!
PRETTY ROUGH SHAPE FOR A WERE-WOLF--
GAH!
RRRIPP

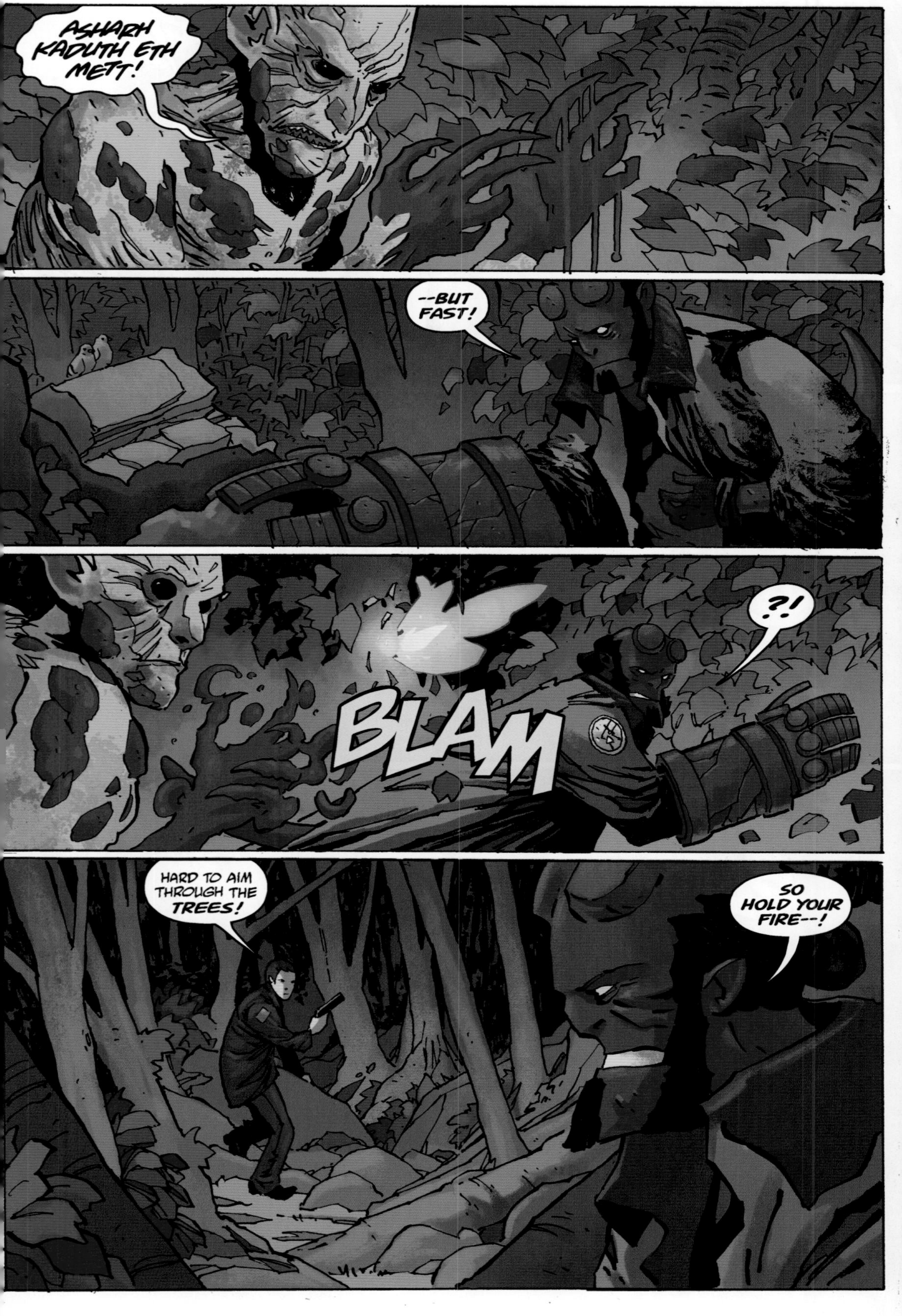
ASHARH KADUTH ETH METT!
--BUT FAST!
?!
BLAM
HARD TO AIM THROUGH THE TREES!
SO HOLD YOUR FIRE--!

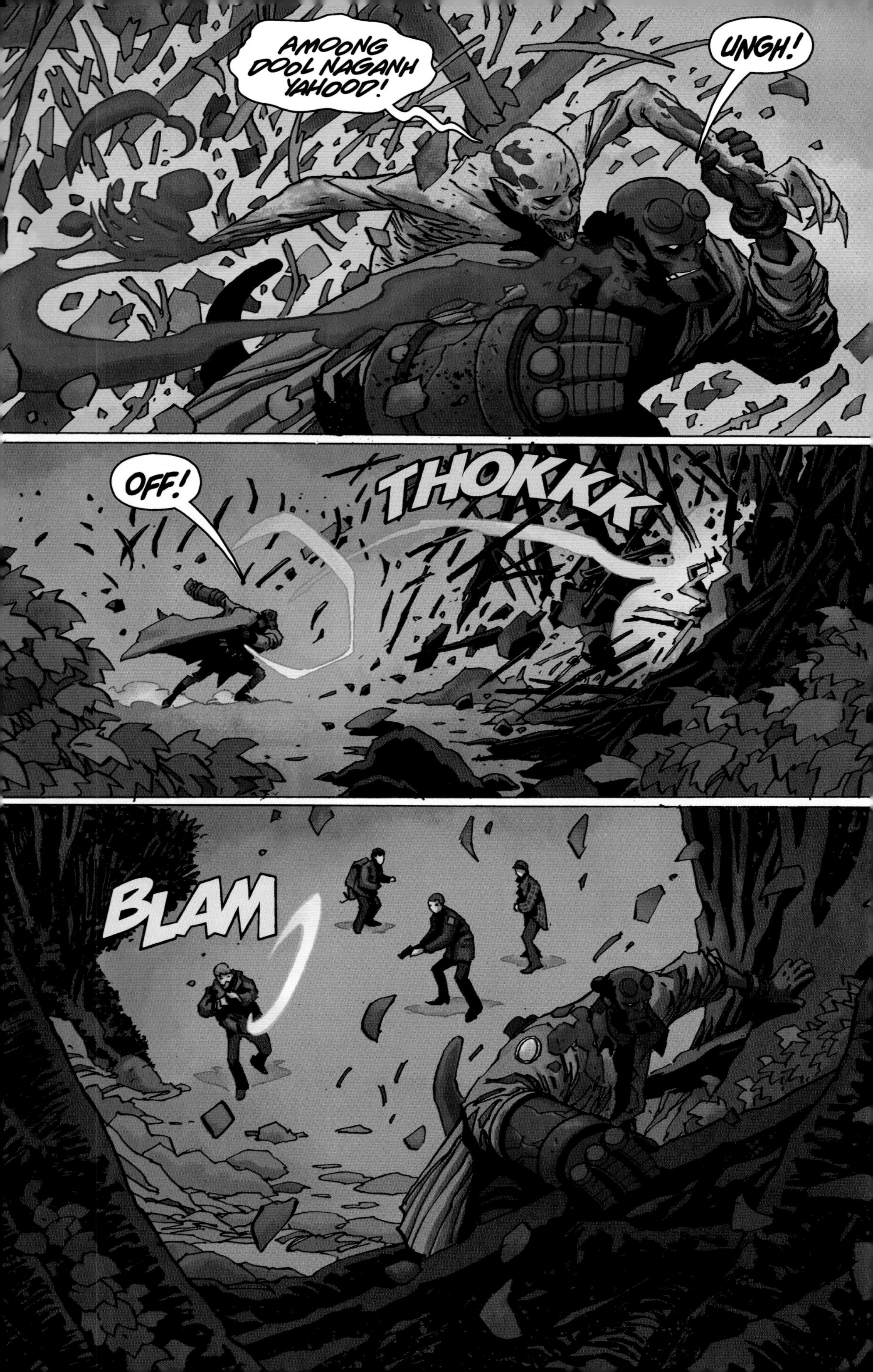
AMOONG DOOL NAGANH YAHOOD!
UNGH!
OFF!
THOKKK
BLAM

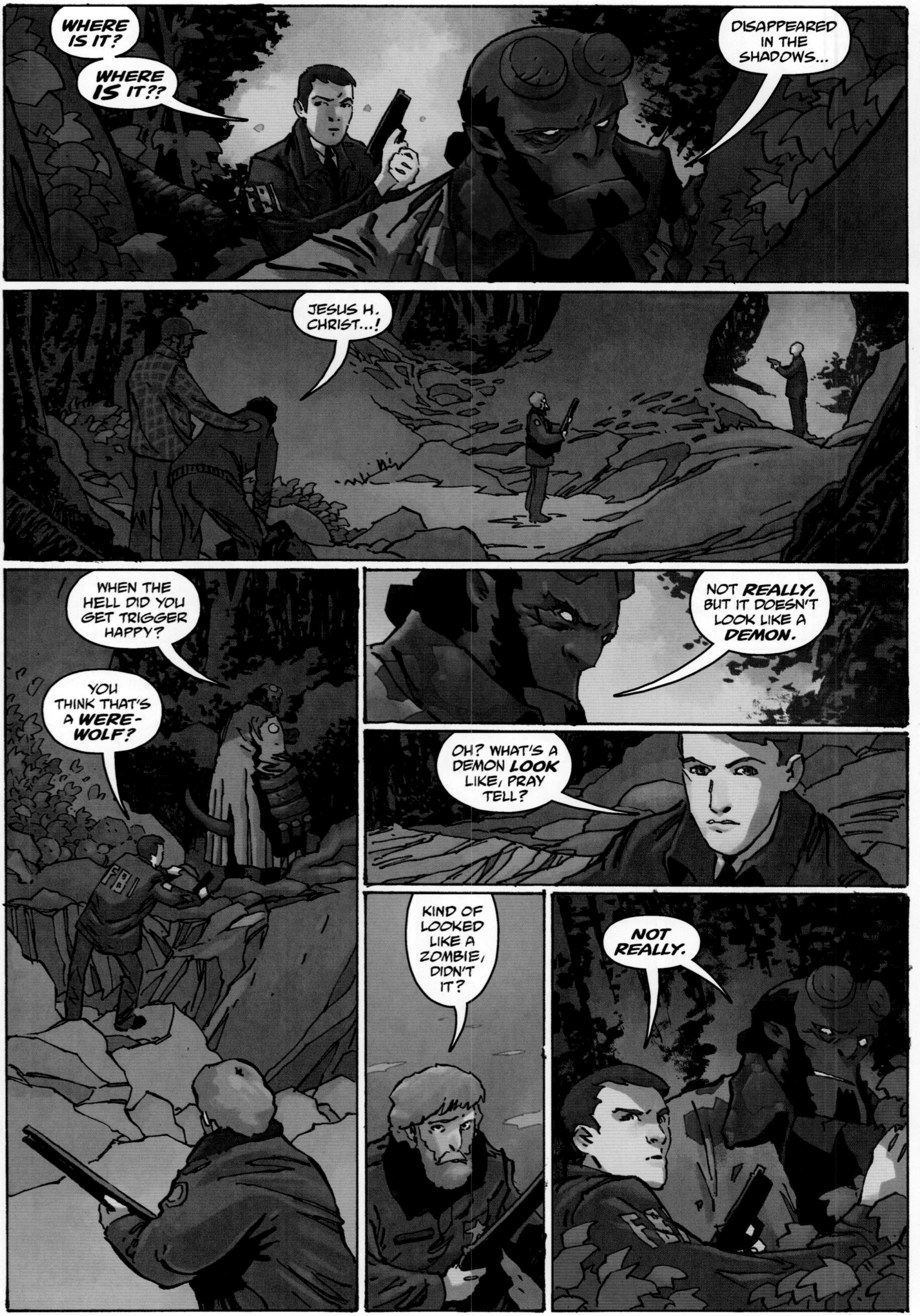

WHERE IS IT?
WHERE IS IT??
DISAPPEARED IN THE SHADOWS...
JESUS H. CHRIST...!
WHEN THE HELL DID YOU GET TRIGGER HAPPY?
YOU THINK THAT'S A WERE-WOLF?
NOT REALLY, BUT IT DOESN'T LOOK LIKE A DEMON.
OH? WHAT'S A DEMON LOOK LIKE, PRAY TELL?
KIND OF LOOKED LIKE A ZOMBIE, DIDN'T IT?
NOT REALLY.
FBI

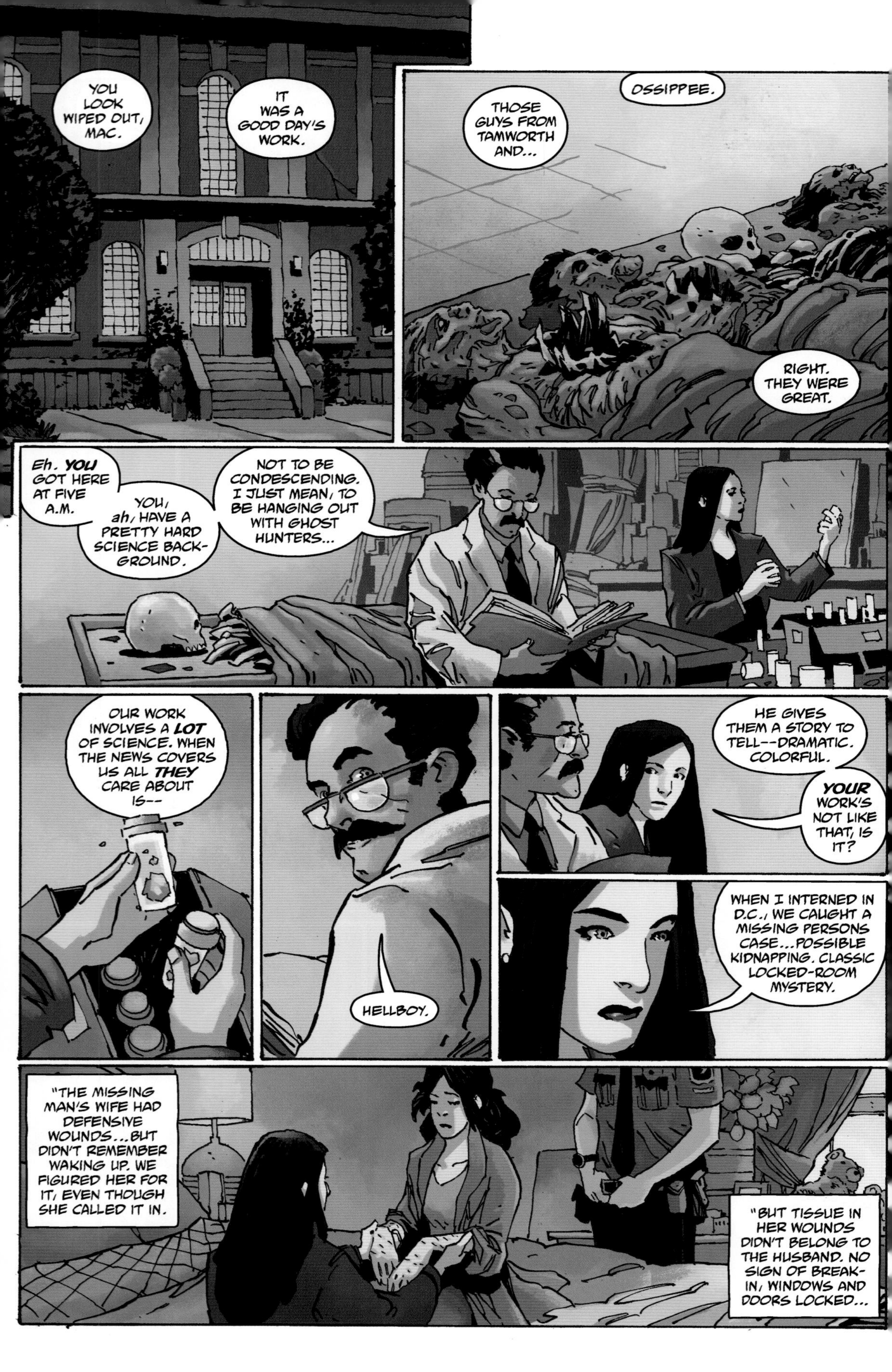

YOU LOOK WIPED OUT, MAC.
IT WAS A GOOD DAY'S WORK.
THOSE GUYS FROM TAMWORTH AND...
OSSIPPEE.
RIGHT. THEY WERE GREAT.
Eh. YOU GOT HERE AT FIVE A.M.
YOU, ah, HAVE A PRETTY HARD SCIENCE BACK-GROUND.
NOT TO BE CONDESCENDING. I JUST MEAN, TO BE HANGING OUT WITH GHOST HUNTERS...
OUR WORK INVOLVES A LOT OF SCIENCE. WHEN THE NEWS COVERS US ALL THEY CARE ABOUT IS--
HELLBOY.
HE GIVES THEM A STORY TO TELL--DRAMATIC. COLORFUL.
YOUR WORK'S NOT LIKE THAT, IS IT?
WHEN I INTERNED IN D.C., WE CAUGHT A MISSING PERSONS CASE...POSSIBLE KIDNAPPING. CLASSIC LOCKED-ROOM MYSTERY.
"THE MISSING MAN'S WIFE HAD DEFENSIVE WOUNDS...BUT DIDN'T REMEMBER WAKING UP. WE FIGURED HER FOR IT, EVEN THOUGH SHE CALLED IT IN.
"BUT TISSUE IN HER WOUNDS DIDN'T BELONG TO THE HUSBAND. NO SIGN OF BREAK-IN, WINDOWS AND DOORS LOCKED...

"THEY FOUND HIM IN MEXICO SEVEN MONTHS LATER...

"...DEAD SINCE THE NIGHT HE DISAPPEARED.

"I'D ANALYZED THE *DATA* FROM EVERY ANGLE..."

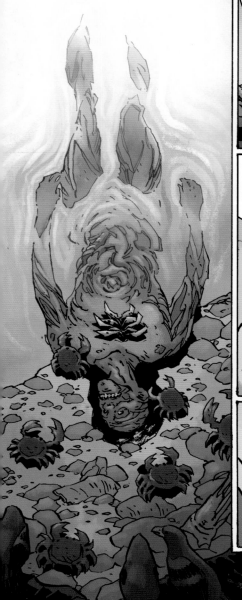

...AND IT GOT ME NO-WHERE.

"THERE ARE MORE THINGS IN HEAVEN AND EARTH, HORATIO, THAN ARE DREAMT OF IN YOUR PHILOSOPHIES..."

I'LL STICK WITH SCIENCE-- BUT YOUR HUNCH DID GIVE US A SHORT CUT.

EXCUSE ME?

YOU WORKED ON THE OLDEST REMAINS, WHILE MY GUYS HANDLED THE EASIER TO *I.D.* ...

WE CLOSED FIVE OF THE SIX OLDEST COLD CASES.

YES YOU DID.

SO WHO'S LEFT?

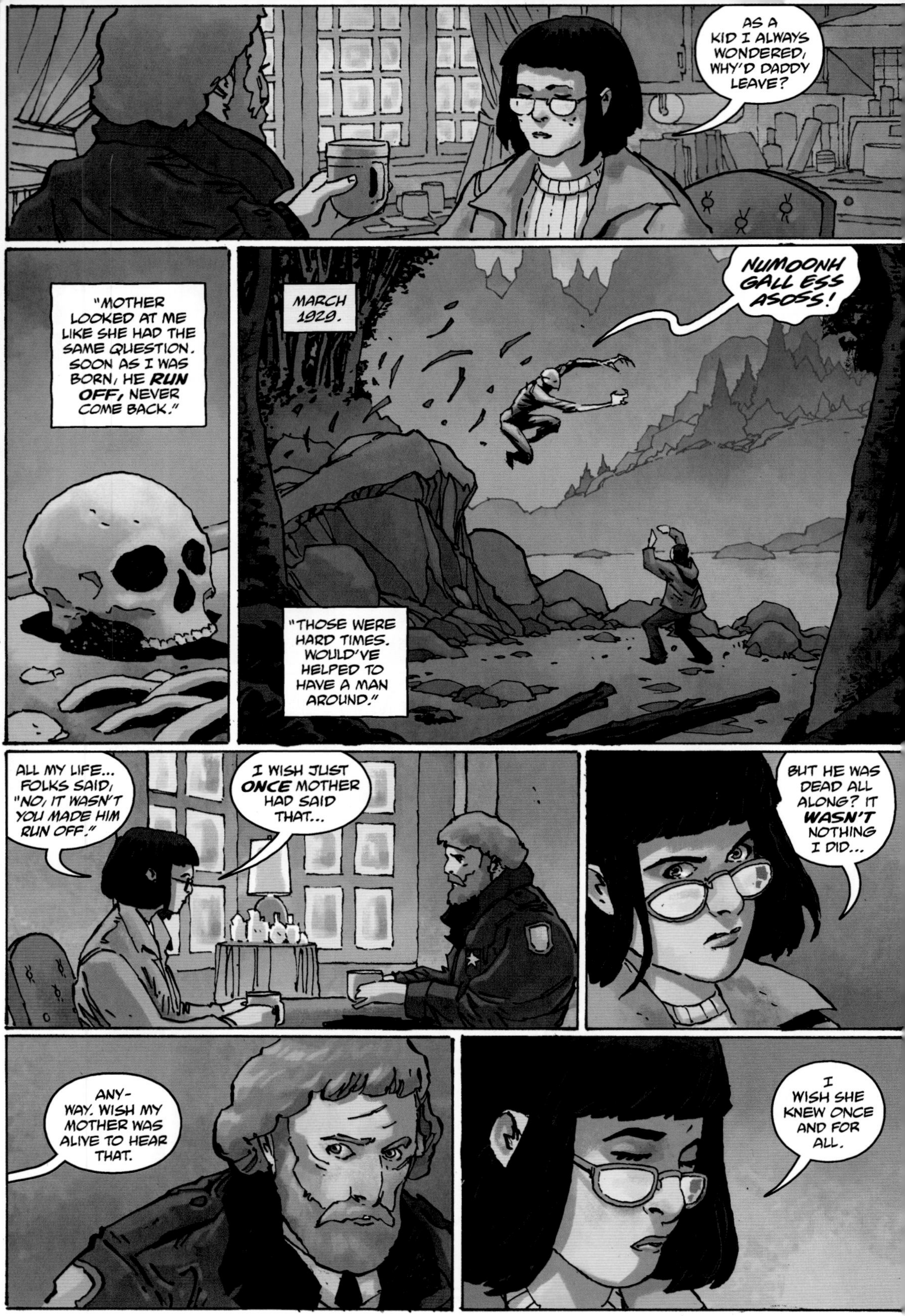
AS A KID I ALWAYS WONDERED, WHY'D DADDY LEAVE?
"MOTHER LOOKED AT ME LIKE SHE HAD THE SAME QUESTION. SOON AS I WAS BORN, HE RUN OFF, NEVER COME BACK."
MARCH 1929.
NUMOONH GALL ESS ASOSS!
"THOSE WERE HARD TIMES. WOULD'VE HELPED TO HAVE A MAN AROUND."
ALL MY LIFE... FOLKS SAID, "NO, IT WASN'T YOU MADE HIM RUN OFF."
I WISH JUST ONCE MOTHER HAD SAID THAT...
BUT HE WAS DEAD ALL ALONG? IT WASN'T NOTHING I DID...
ANY-WAY. WISH MY MOTHER WAS ALIVE TO HEAR THAT.
I WISH SHE KNEW ONCE AND FOR ALL.

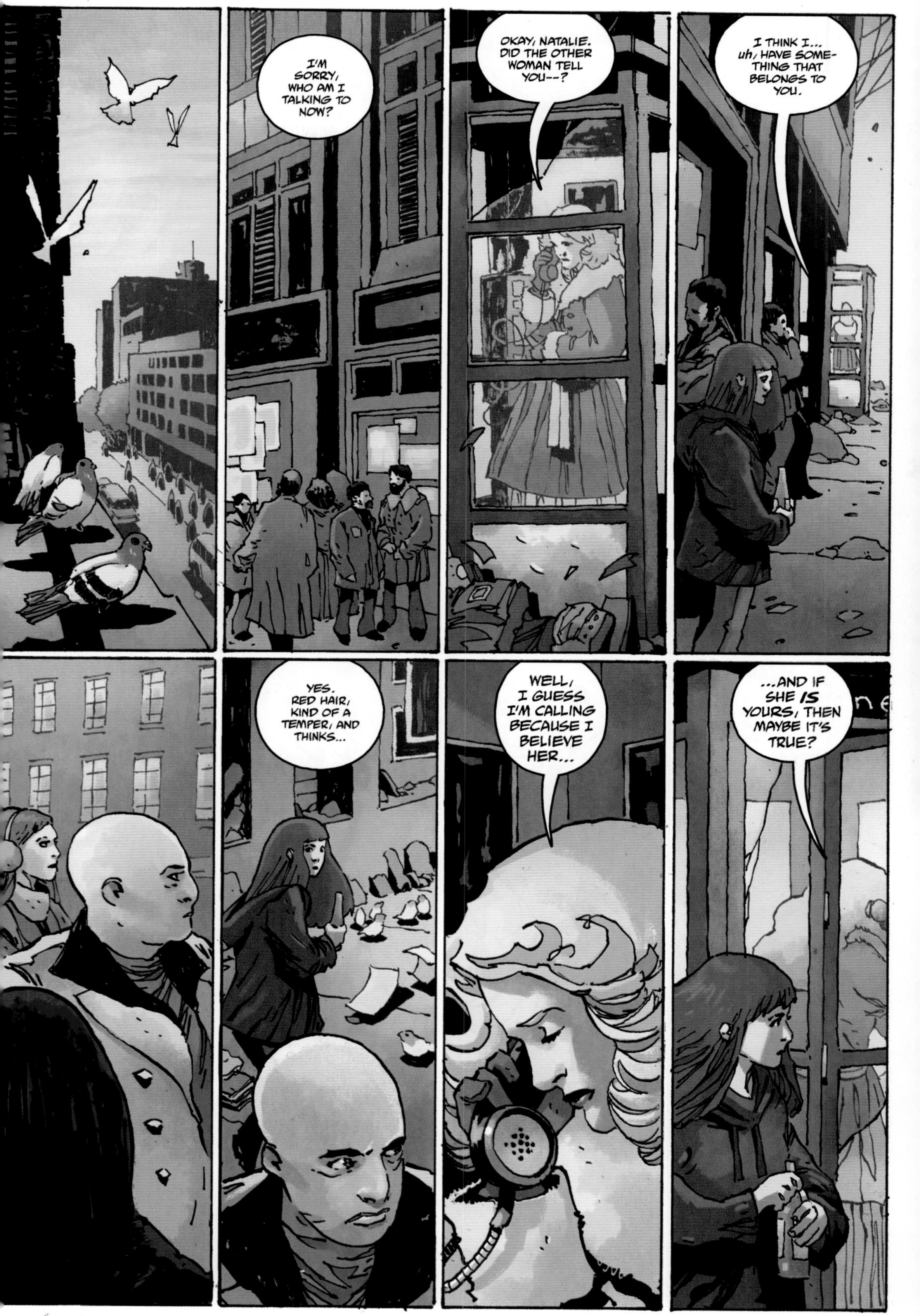
I'M SORRY, WHO AM I TALKING TO NOW?
OKAY, NATALIE. DID THE OTHER WOMAN TELL YOU--?
I THINK I... uh, HAVE SOMETHING THAT BELONGS TO YOU.
YES. RED HAIR, KIND OF A TEMPER, AND THINKS...
WELL, I GUESS I'M CALLING BECAUSE I BELIEVE HER...
...AND IF SHE IS YOURS, THEN MAYBE IT'S TRUE?

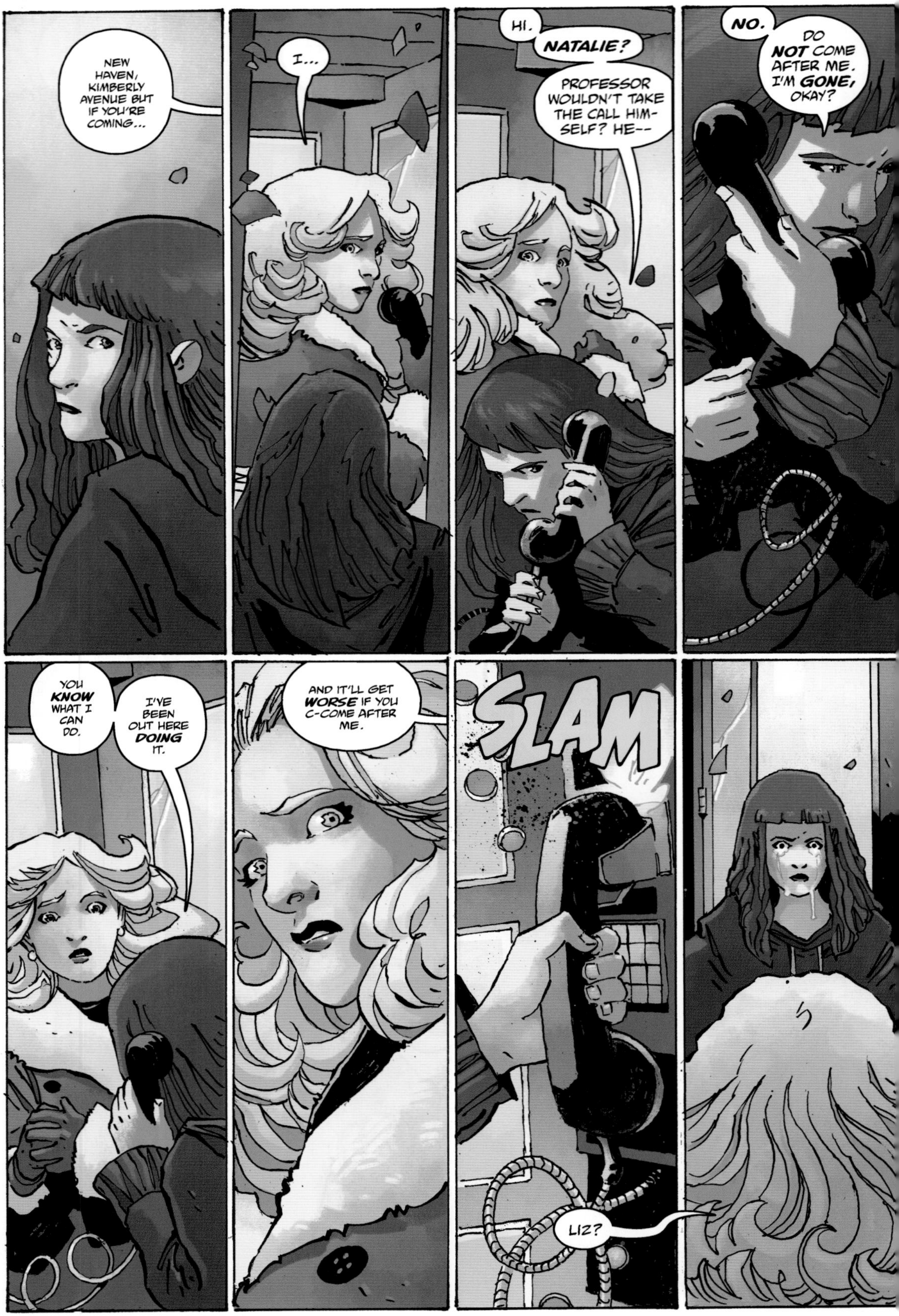
NEW HAVEN, KIMBERLY AVENUE BUT IF YOU'RE COMING...
I...
HI.
NATALIE?
PROFESSOR WOULDN'T TAKE THE CALL HIM-SELF? HE--
NO.
DO NOT COME AFTER ME. I'M GONE, OKAY?
YOU KNOW WHAT I CAN DO.
I'VE BEEN OUT HERE DOING IT.
AND IT'LL GET WORSE IF YOU C-COME AFTER ME.
SLAM
LIZ?

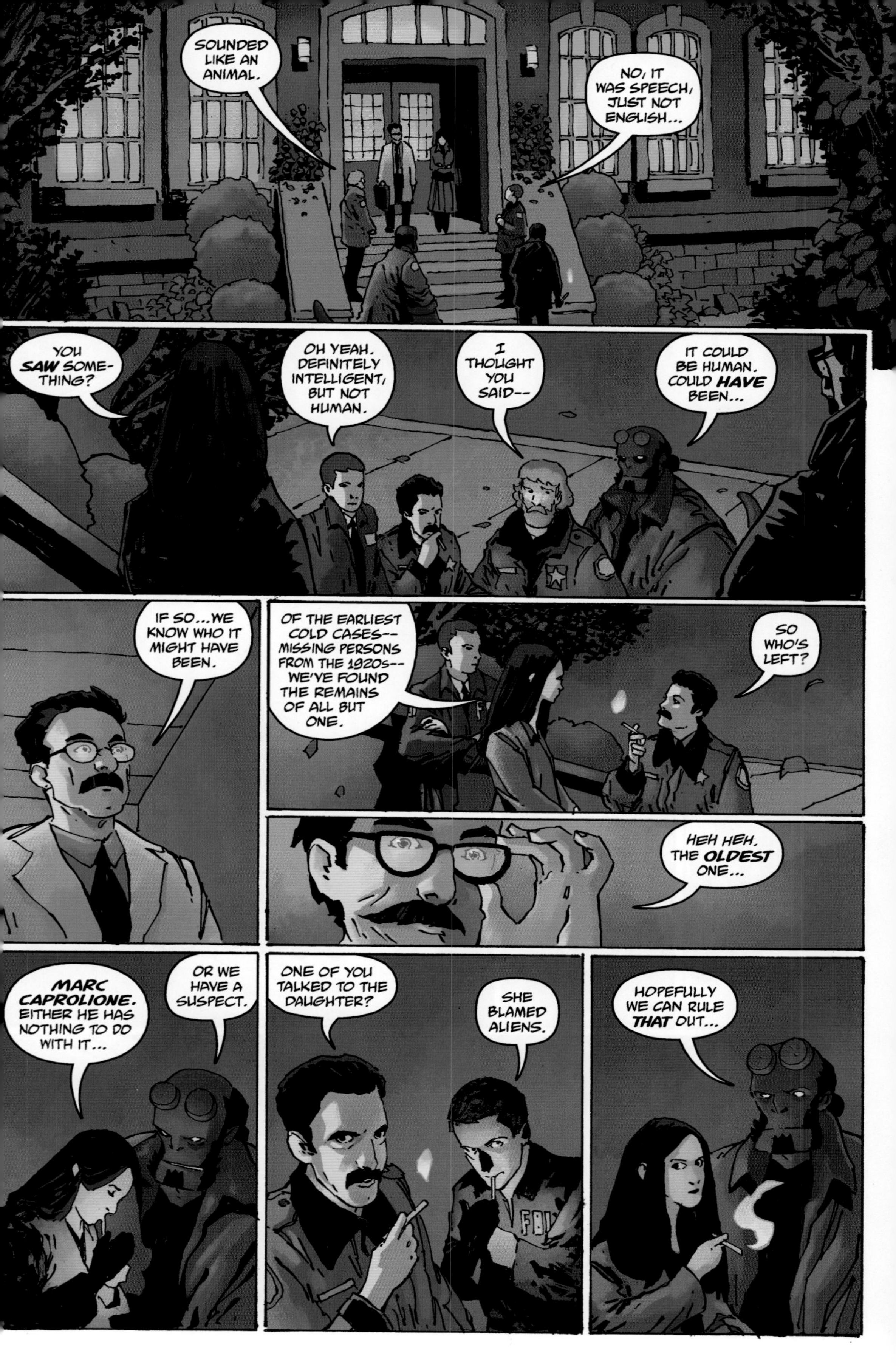
SOUNDED LIKE AN ANIMAL.
NO, IT WAS SPEECH, JUST NOT ENGLISH...
YOU SAW SOMETHING?
OH YEAH. DEFINITELY INTELLIGENT, BUT NOT HUMAN.
I THOUGHT YOU SAID--
IT COULD BE HUMAN. COULD HAVE BEEN...
IF SO...WE KNOW WHO IT MIGHT HAVE BEEN.
OF THE EARLIEST COLD CASES-- MISSING PERSONS FROM THE 1920s-- WE'VE FOUND THE REMAINS OF ALL BUT ONE.
SO WHO'S LEFT?
HEH HEH. THE OLDEST ONE...
MARC CAPROLIONE. EITHER HE HAS NOTHING TO DO WITH IT...
OR WE HAVE A SUSPECT.
ONE OF YOU TALKED TO THE DAUGHTER?
SHE BLAMED ALIENS.
HOPEFULLY WE CAN RULE THAT OUT...

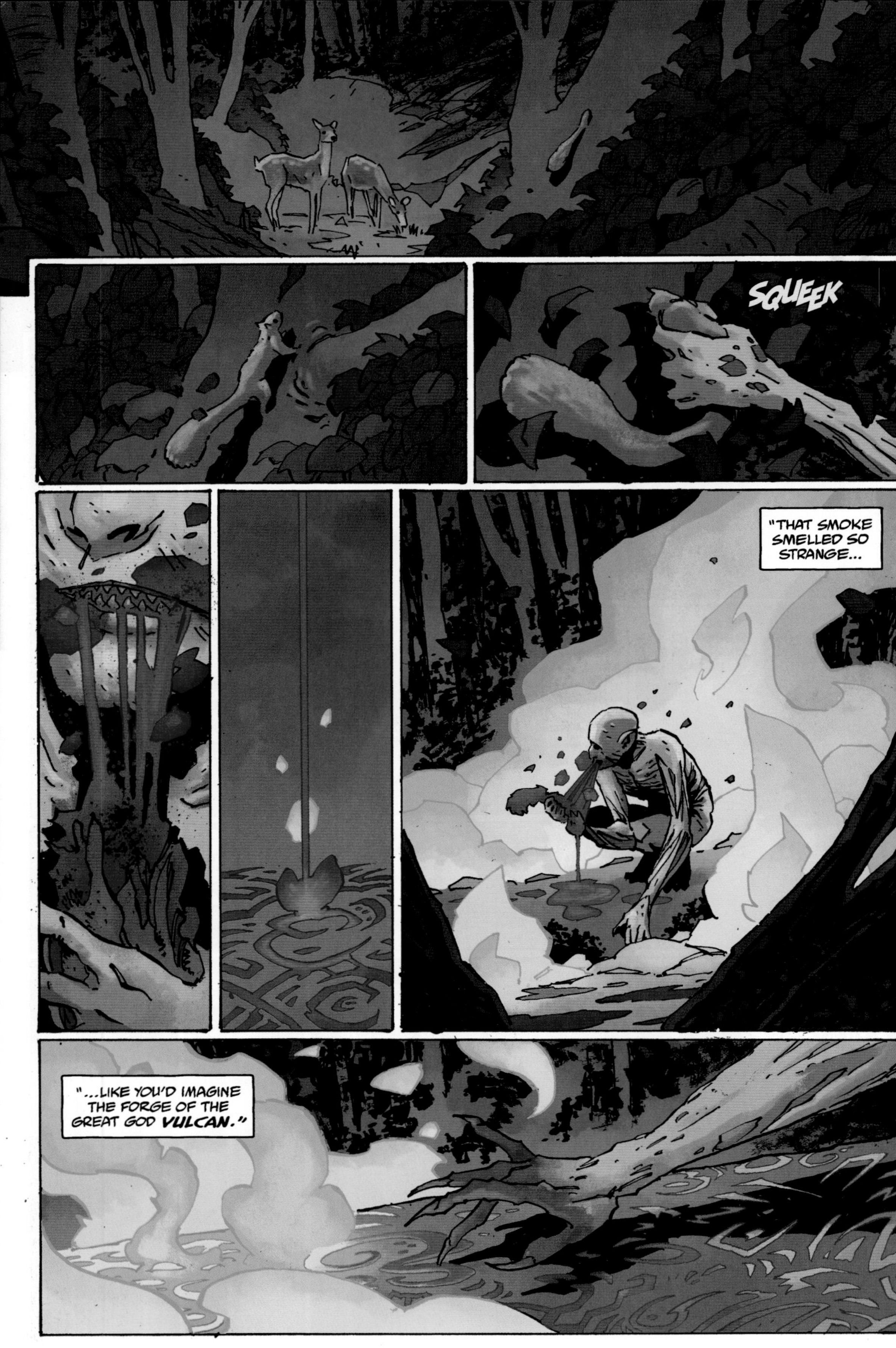
SQUEEK
"THAT SMOKE SMELLED SO STRANGE...
"...LIKE YOU'D IMAGINE THE FORGE OF THE GREAT GOD VULCAN."

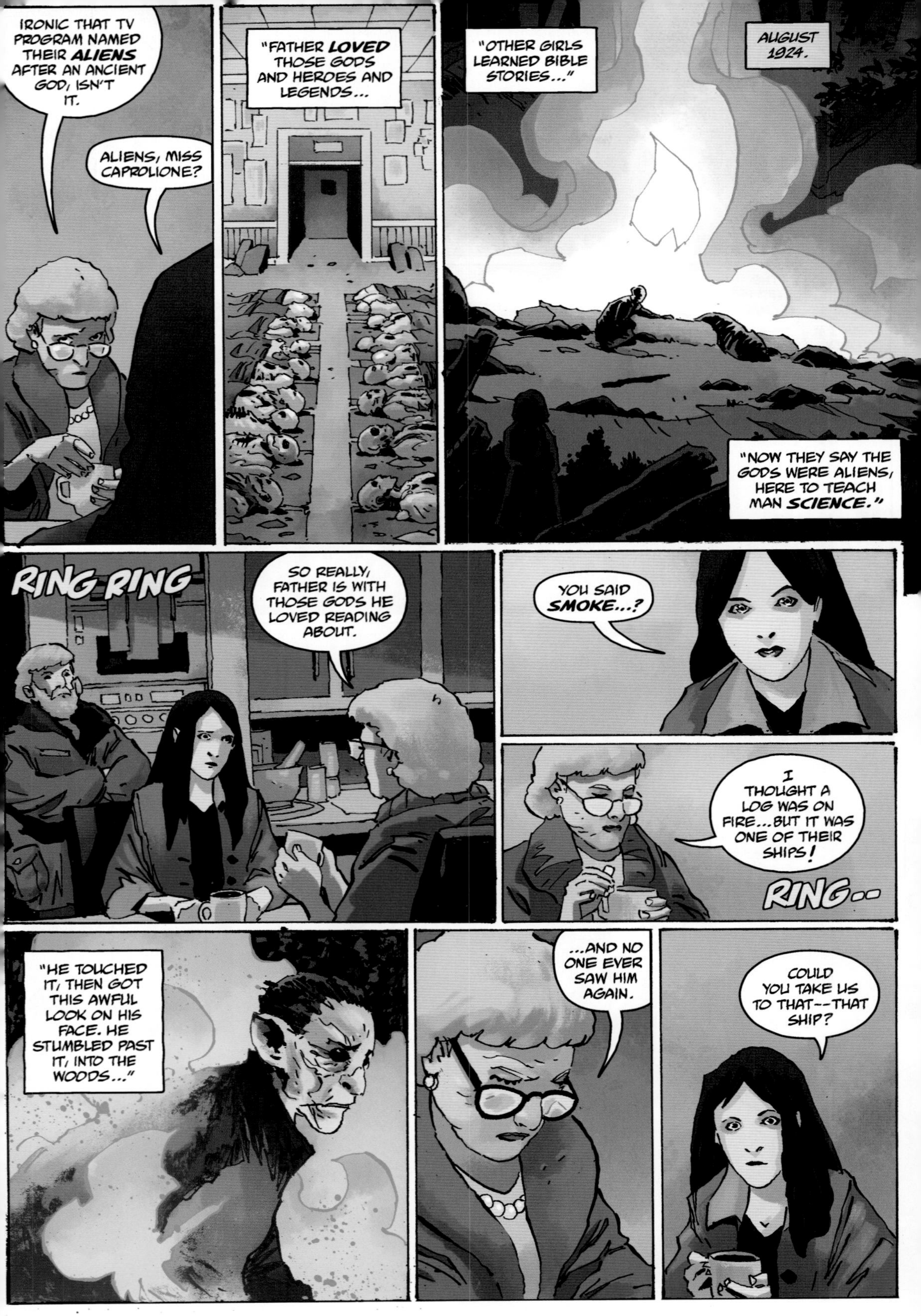
IRONIC THAT TV PROGRAM NAMED THEIR ALIENS AFTER AN ANCIENT GOD, ISN'T IT.
ALIENS, MISS CAPROLIONE?
"FATHER LOVED THOSE GODS AND HEROES AND LEGENDS...
"OTHER GIRLS LEARNED BIBLE STORIES..."
AUGUST 1924.
"NOW THEY SAY THE GODS WERE ALIENS, HERE TO TEACH MAN SCIENCE."
RING RING
SO REALLY, FATHER IS WITH THOSE GODS HE LOVED READING ABOUT.
YOU SAID SMOKE...?
I THOUGHT A LOG WAS ON FIRE...BUT IT WAS ONE OF THEIR SHIPS!
RING..
"HE TOUCHED IT, THEN GOT THIS AWFUL LOOK ON HIS FACE. HE STUMBLED PAST IT, INTO THE WOODS..."
...AND NO ONE EVER SAW HIM AGAIN.
COULD YOU TAKE US TO THAT--THAT SHIP?

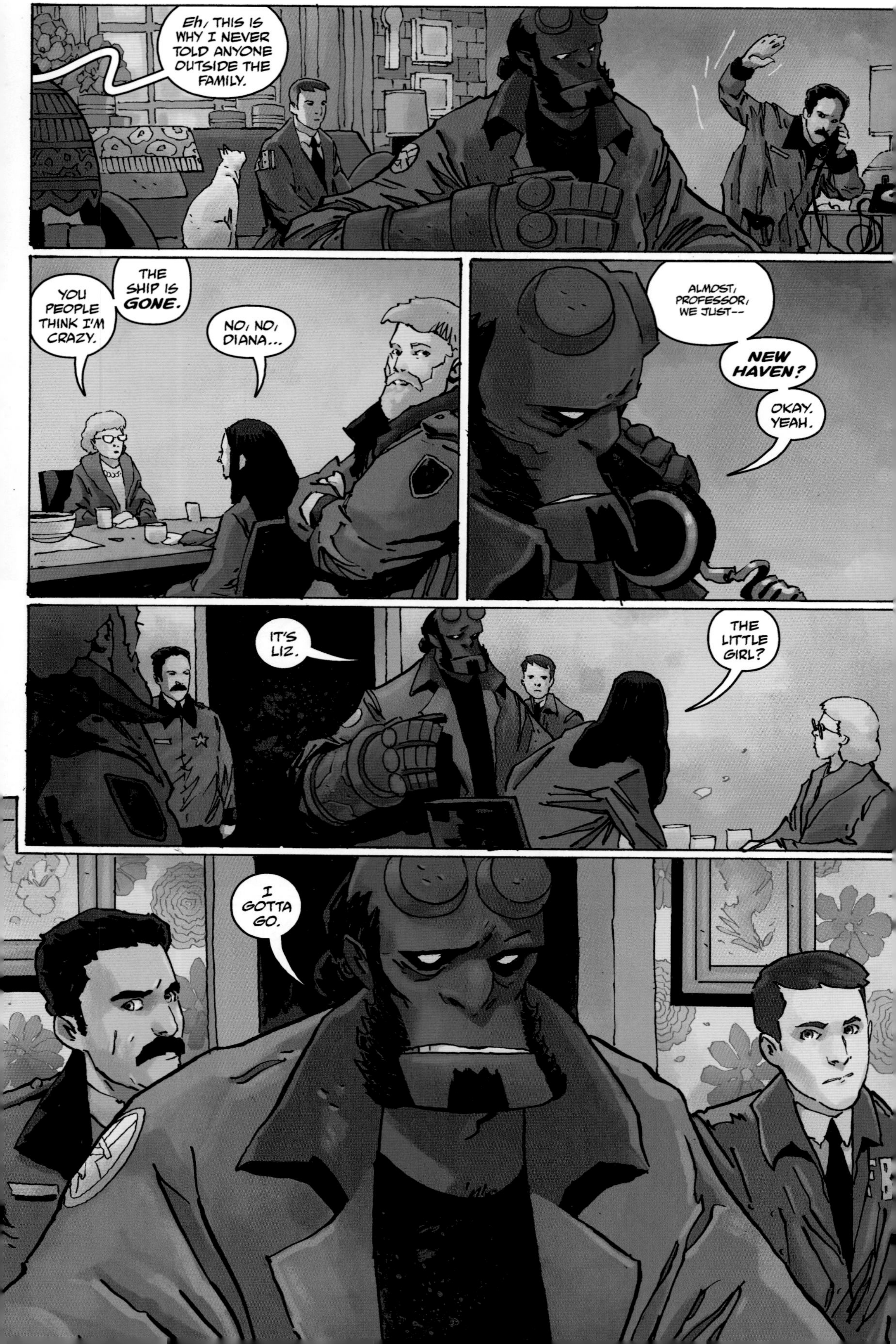
Eh, THIS IS WHY I NEVER TOLD ANYONE OUTSIDE THE FAMILY.
YOU PEOPLE THINK I'M CRAZY.
THE SHIP IS GONE.
NO, NO, DIANA...
ALMOST, PROFESSOR, WE JUST--
NEW HAVEN?
OKAY. YEAH.
IT'S LIZ.
THE LITTLE GIRL?
I GOTTA GO.

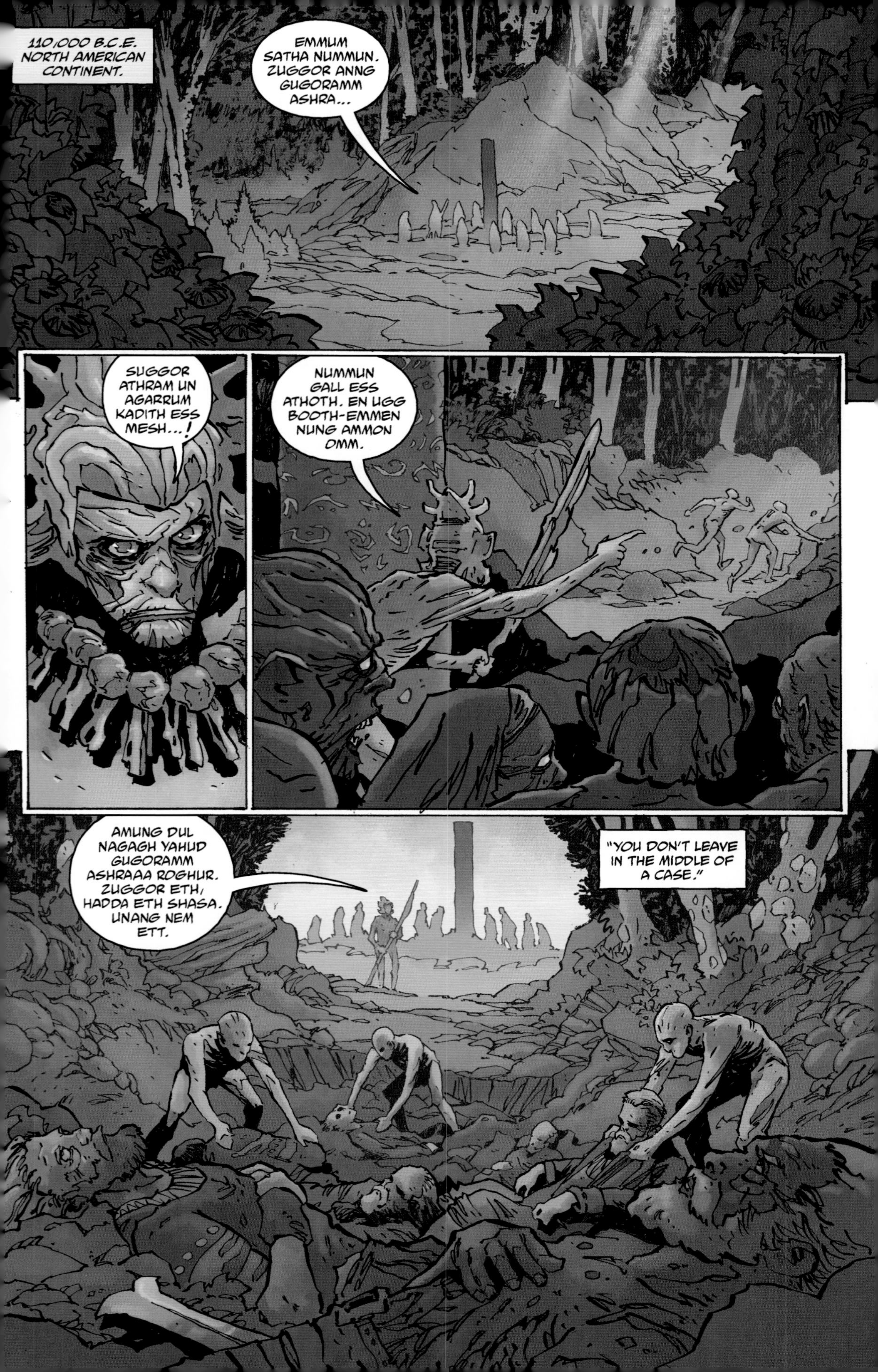
110,000 B.C.E. NORTH AMERICAN CONTINENT.
EMMUM SATHA NUMMUN. ZUGGOR ANNG GUGORAMM ASHRA...
SUGGOR ATHRAM UN AGARRUM KADITH ESS MESH...!
NUMMUN GALL ESS ATHOTH. EN UGG BOOTH-EMMEN NUNG AMMON OMM.
AMUNG DUL NAGAGH YAHUD GUGORAMM ASHRAAA ROGHUR. ZUGGOR ETH, HADDA ETH SHASA. UNANG NEM ETT.
"YOU DON'T LEAVE IN THE MIDDLE OF A CASE."

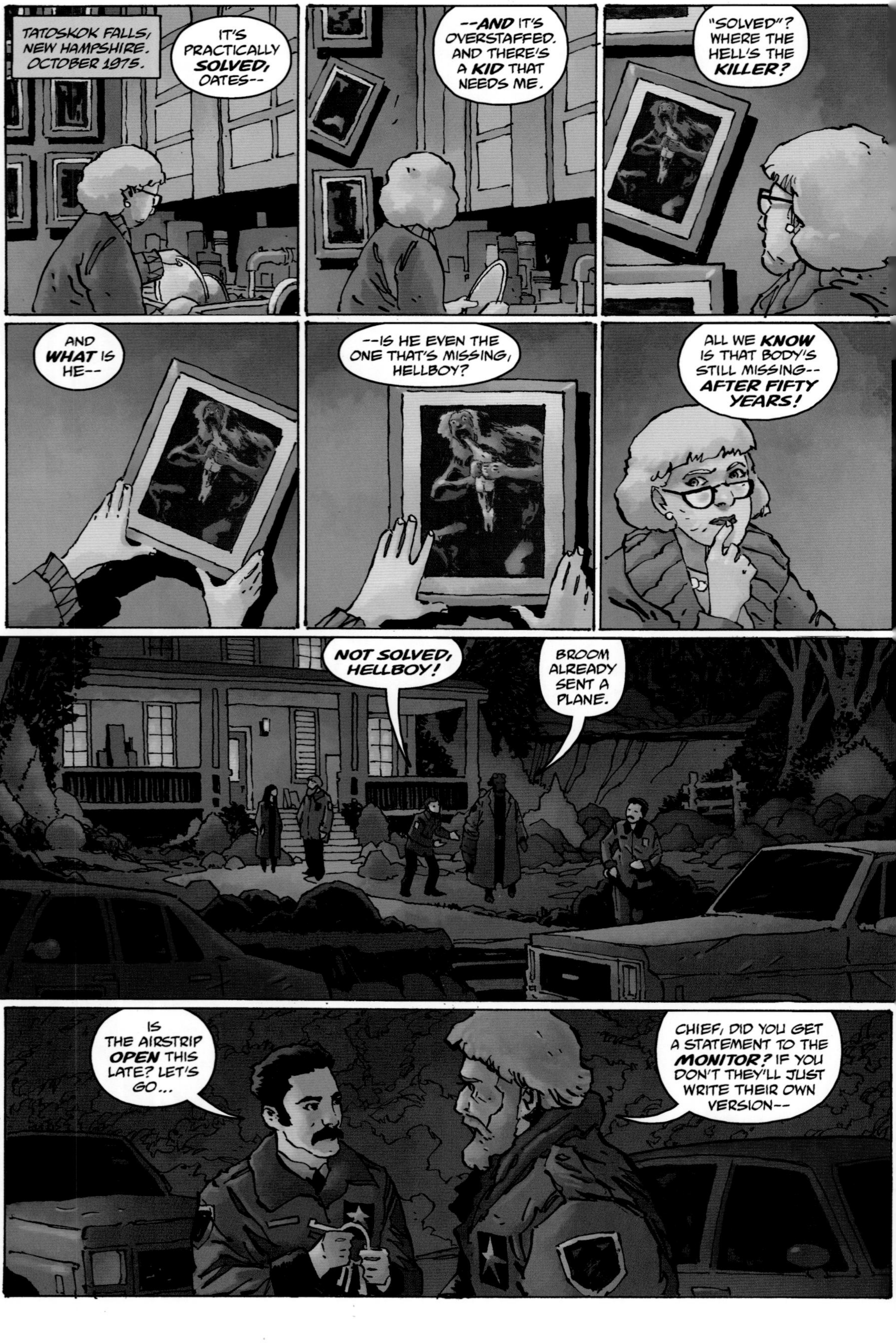
TATOSKOK FALLS, NEW HAMPSHIRE. OCTOBER 1975.
IT'S PRACTICALLY SOLVED, OATES--
--AND IT'S OVERSTAFFED. AND THERE'S A KID THAT NEEDS ME.
"SOLVED"? WHERE THE HELL'S THE KILLER?
AND WHAT IS HE--
--IS HE EVEN THE ONE THAT'S MISSING, HELLBOY?
ALL WE KNOW IS THAT BODY'S STILL MISSING-- AFTER FIFTY YEARS!
NOT SOLVED, HELLBOY!
BROOM ALREADY SENT A PLANE.
IS THE AIRSTRIP OPEN THIS LATE? LET'S GO...
CHIEF, DID YOU GET A STATEMENT TO THE MONITOR? IF YOU DON'T THEY'LL JUST WRITE THEIR OWN VERSION--

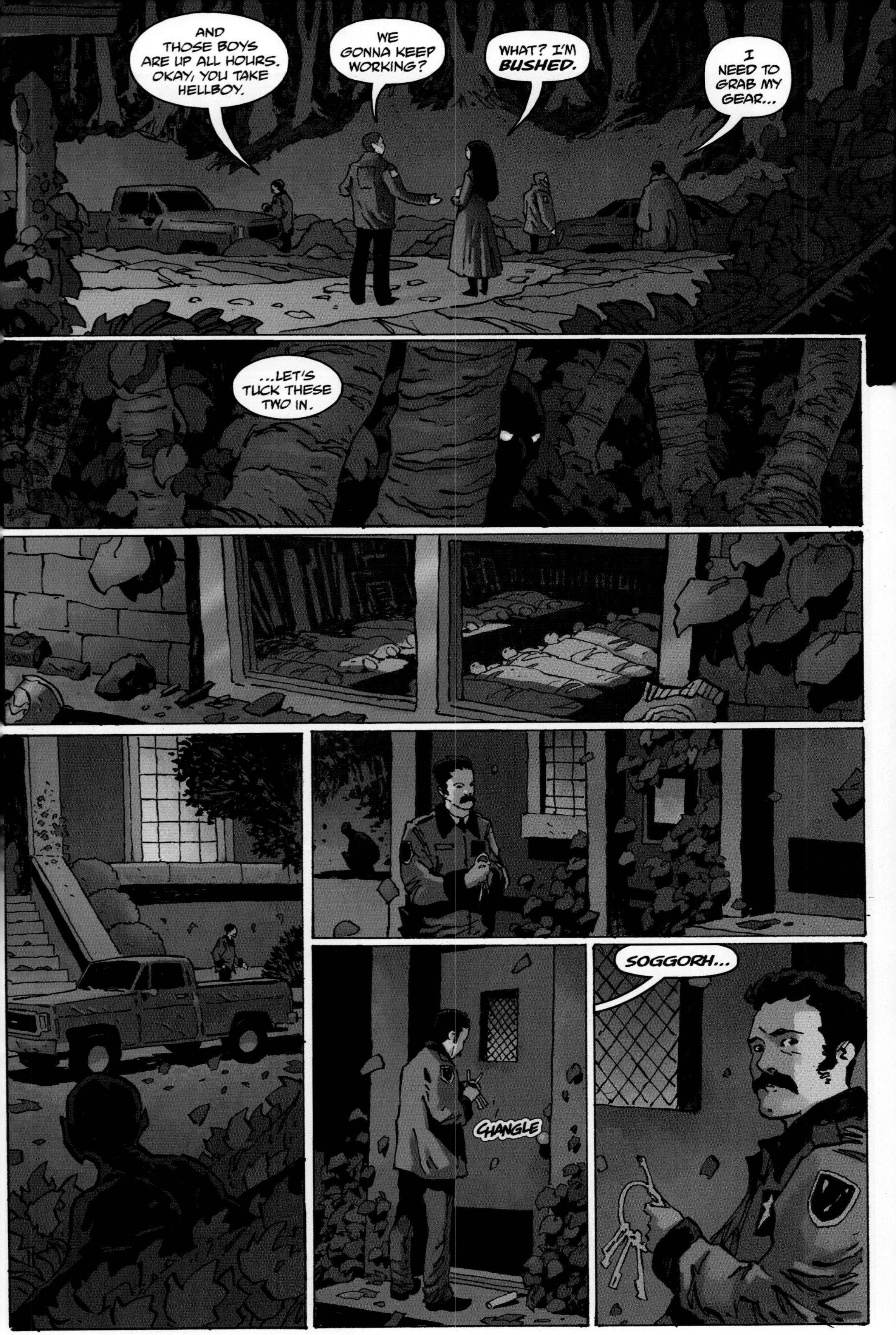
AND THOSE BOYS ARE UP ALL HOURS. OKAY, YOU TAKE HELLBOY.
WE GONNA KEEP WORKING?
WHAT? I'M **BUSHED.**
I NEED TO GRAB MY GEAR...
...LET'S TUCK THESE TWO IN.
CHANGLE
SOGGORH...

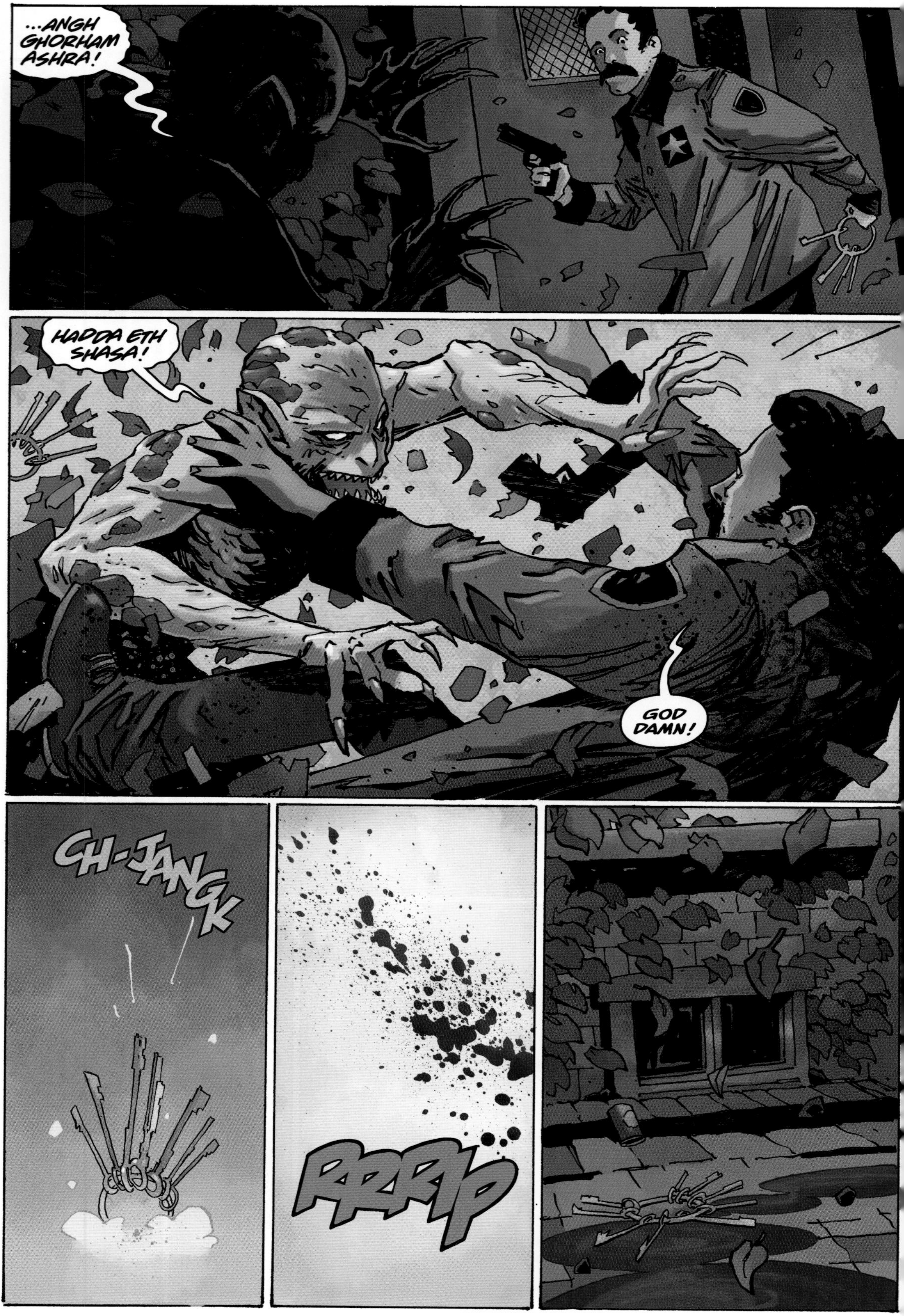
...ANGH GHORHAM ASHRA!
HADDA ETH SHASA!
GOD DAMN!
CH-JANGK
RRRIP

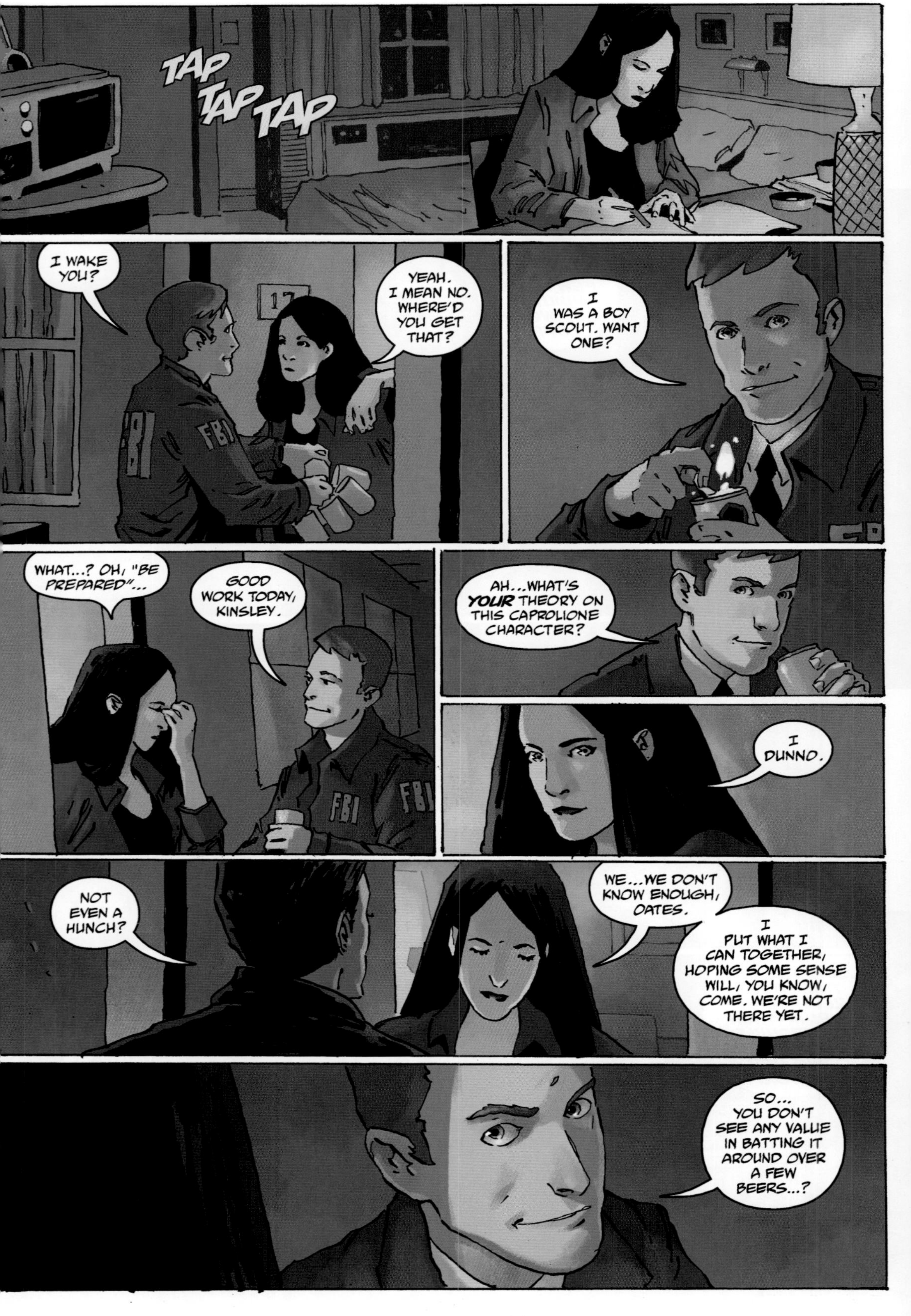
TAP
TAP TAP
I WAKE YOU?
YEAH. I MEAN NO. WHERE'D YOU GET THAT?
I WAS A BOY SCOUT. WANT ONE?
WHAT...? OH, "BE PREPARED"...
GOOD WORK TODAY, KINSLEY.
AH...WHAT'S YOUR THEORY ON THIS CAPROLIONE CHARACTER?
I DUNNO.
NOT EVEN A HUNCH?
WE...WE DON'T KNOW ENOUGH, OATES.
I PUT WHAT I CAN TOGETHER, HOPING SOME SENSE WILL, YOU KNOW, COME. WE'RE NOT THERE YET.
SO... YOU DON'T SEE ANY VALUE IN BATTING IT AROUND OVER A FEW BEERS...?

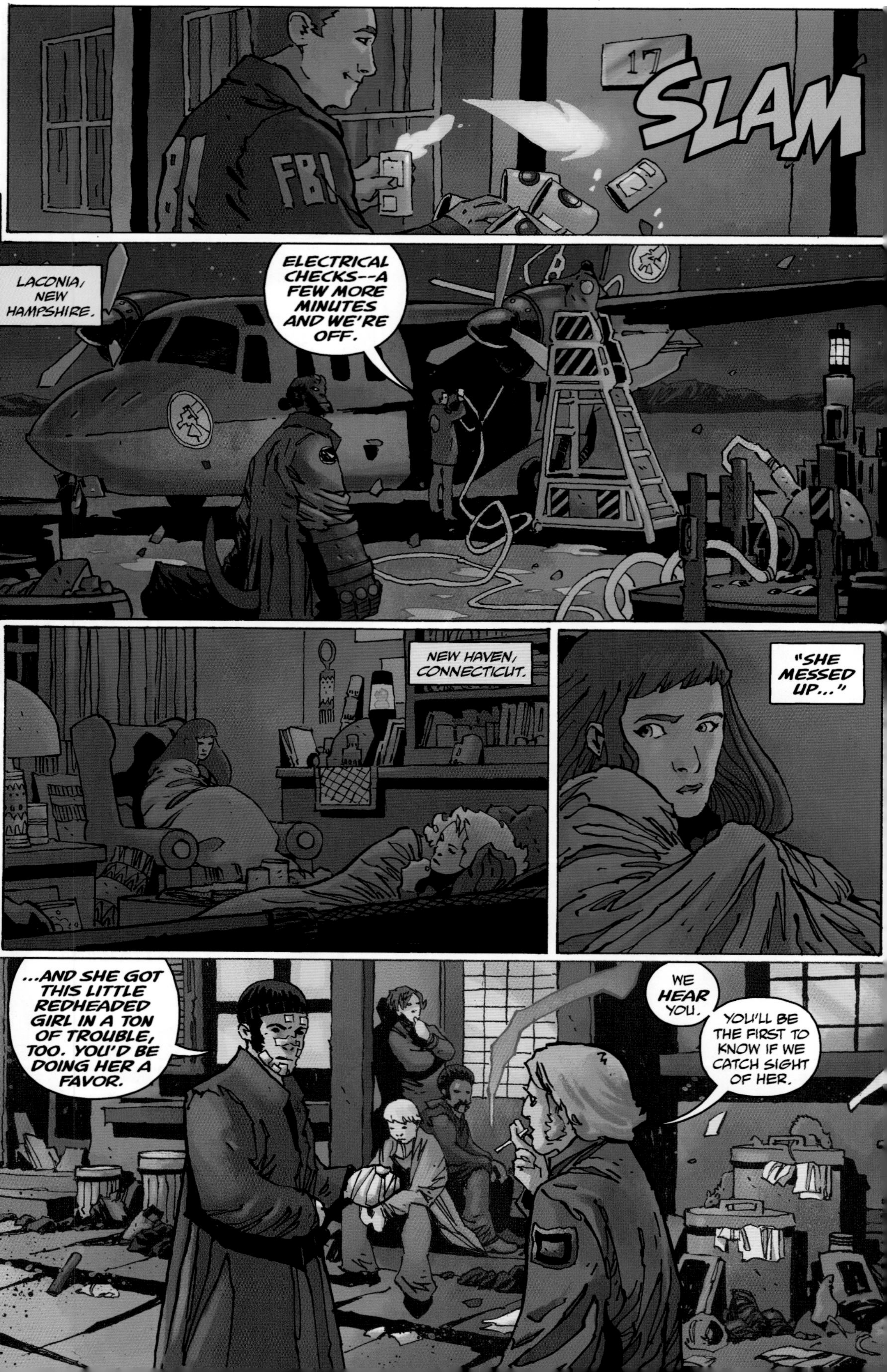
17
SLAM
LACONIA, NEW HAMPSHIRE.
ELECTRICAL CHECKS--A FEW MORE MINUTES AND WE'RE OFF.
NEW HAVEN, CONNECTICUT.
"SHE MESSED UP..."
...AND SHE GOT THIS LITTLE REDHEADED GIRL IN A TON OF TROUBLE, TOO. YOU'D BE DOING HER A FAVOR.
WE HEAR YOU.
YOU'LL BE THE FIRST TO KNOW IF WE CATCH SIGHT OF HER.

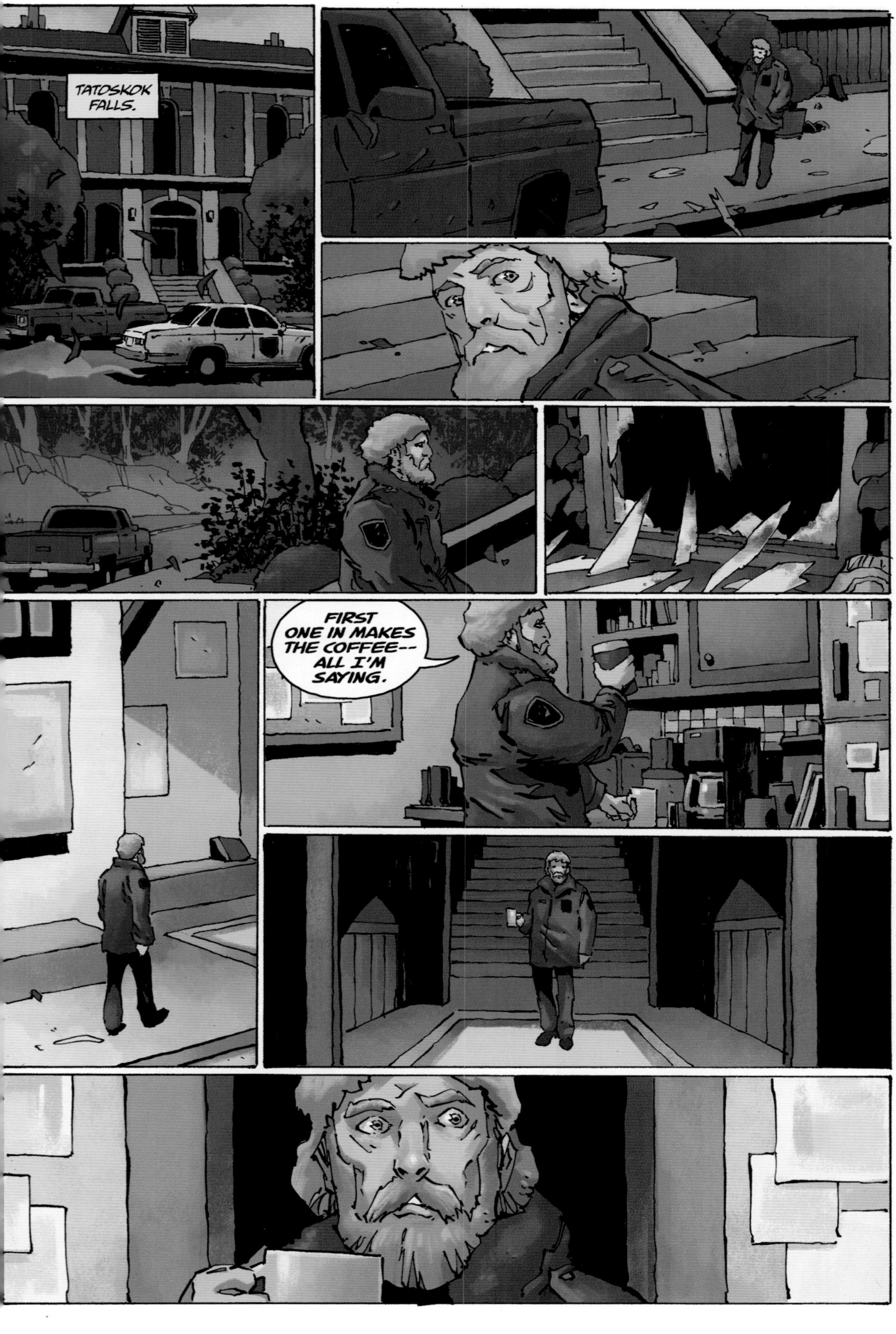
TATOSKOK FALLS.
FIRST ONE IN MAKES THE COFFEE-- ALL I'M SAYING.

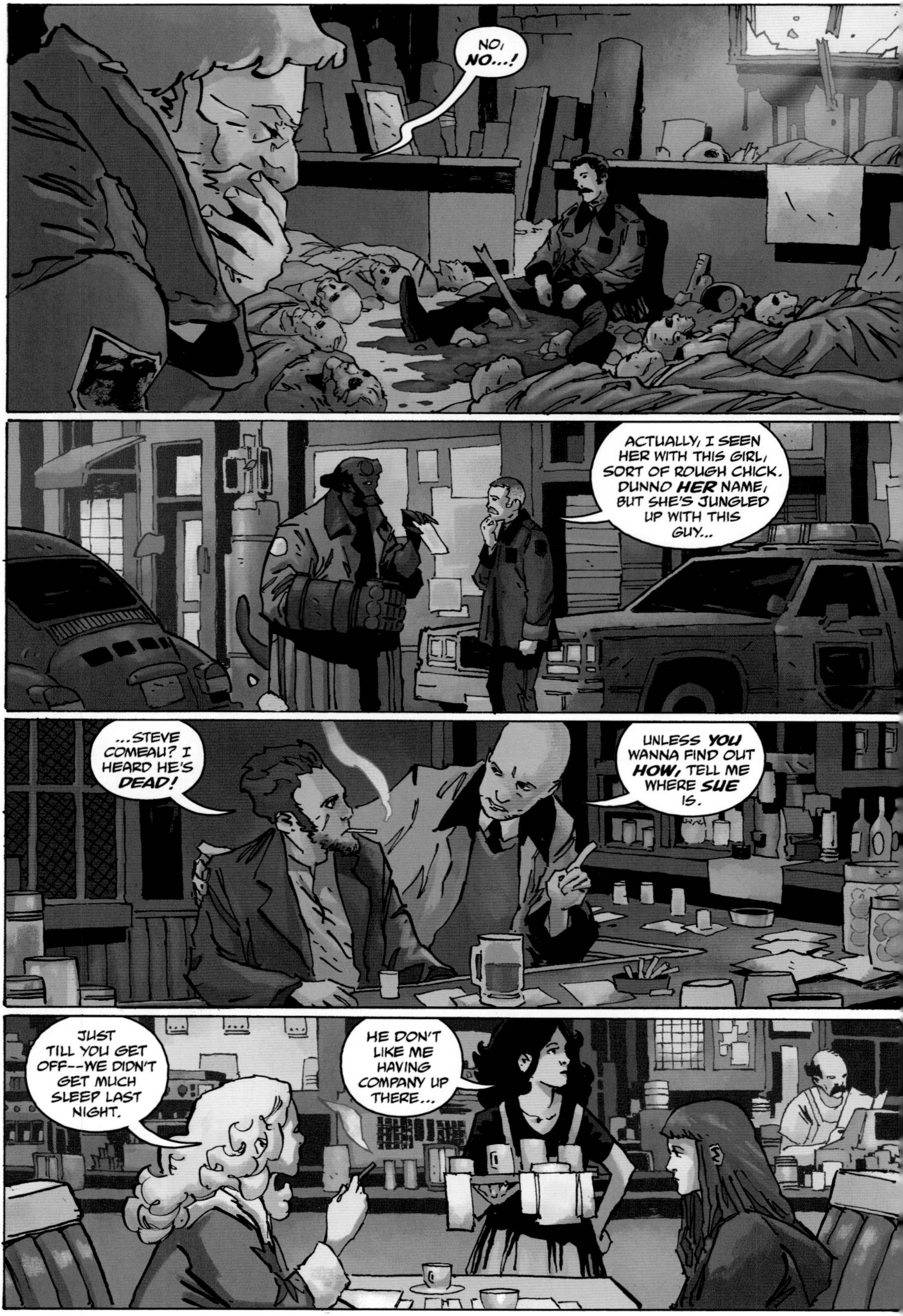
NO, NO...!
ACTUALLY, I SEEN HER WITH THIS GIRL, SORT OF ROUGH CHICK. DUNNO HER NAME, BUT SHE'S JUNGLED UP WITH THIS GUY...
...STEVE COMEAU? I HEARD HE'S DEAD!
UNLESS YOU WANNA FIND OUT HOW, TELL ME WHERE SUE IS.
JUST TILL YOU GET OFF--WE DIDN'T GET MUCH SLEEP LAST NIGHT.
HE DON'T LIKE ME HAVING COMPANY UP THERE...

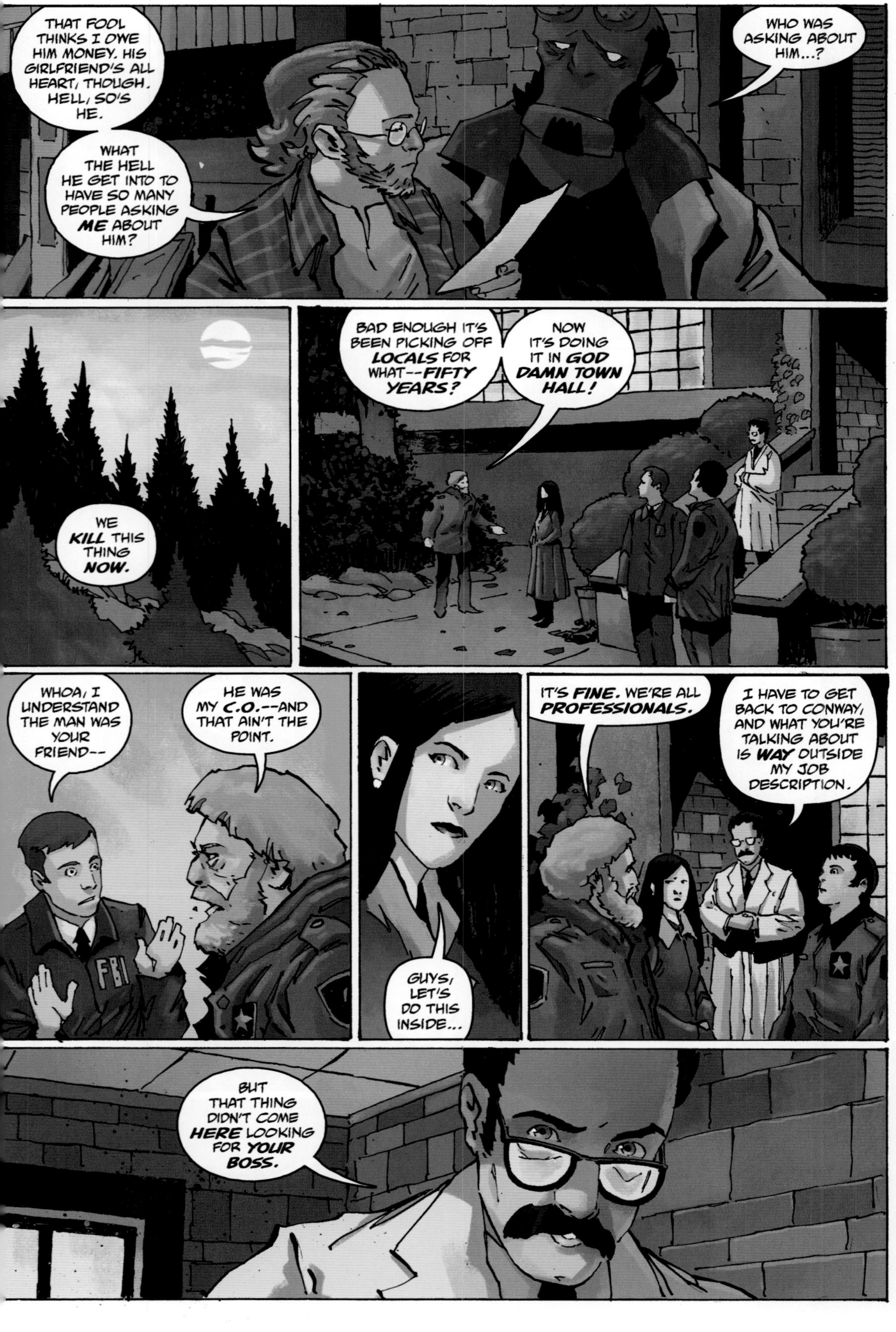
THAT FOOL THINKS I OWE HIM MONEY. HIS GIRLFRIEND'S ALL HEART, THOUGH. HELL, SO'S HE.
WHAT THE HELL HE GET INTO TO HAVE SO MANY PEOPLE ASKING ME ABOUT HIM?
WHO WAS ASKING ABOUT HIM...?
WE KILL THIS THING NOW.
BAD ENOUGH IT'S BEEN PICKING OFF LOCALS FOR WHAT--FIFTY YEARS?
NOW IT'S DOING IT IN GOD DAMN TOWN HALL!
WHOA, I UNDERSTAND THE MAN WAS YOUR FRIEND--
HE WAS MY C.O.--AND THAT AIN'T THE POINT.
GUYS, LET'S DO THIS INSIDE...
IT'S FINE. WE'RE ALL PROFESSIONALS.
I HAVE TO GET BACK TO CONWAY, AND WHAT YOU'RE TALKING ABOUT IS WAY OUTSIDE MY JOB DESCRIPTION.
BUT THAT THING DIDN'T COME HERE LOOKING FOR YOUR BOSS.

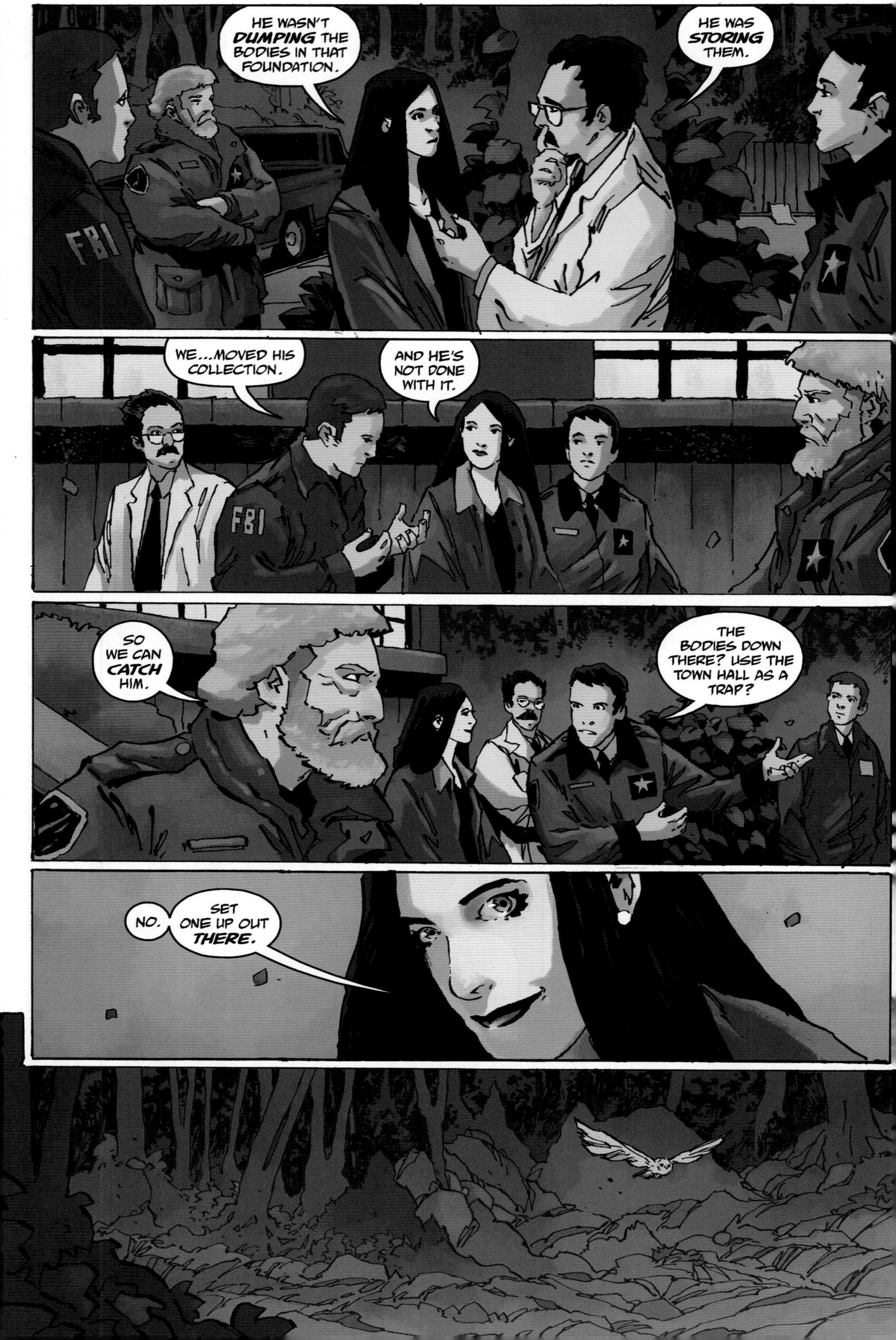
HE WASN'T DUMPING THE BODIES IN THAT FOUNDATION.
HE WAS STORING THEM.
FBI
WE...MOVED HIS COLLECTION.
AND HE'S NOT DONE WITH IT.
FBI
SO WE CAN CATCH HIM.
THE BODIES DOWN THERE? USE THE TOWN HALL AS A TRAP?
NO.
SET ONE UP OUT THERE.

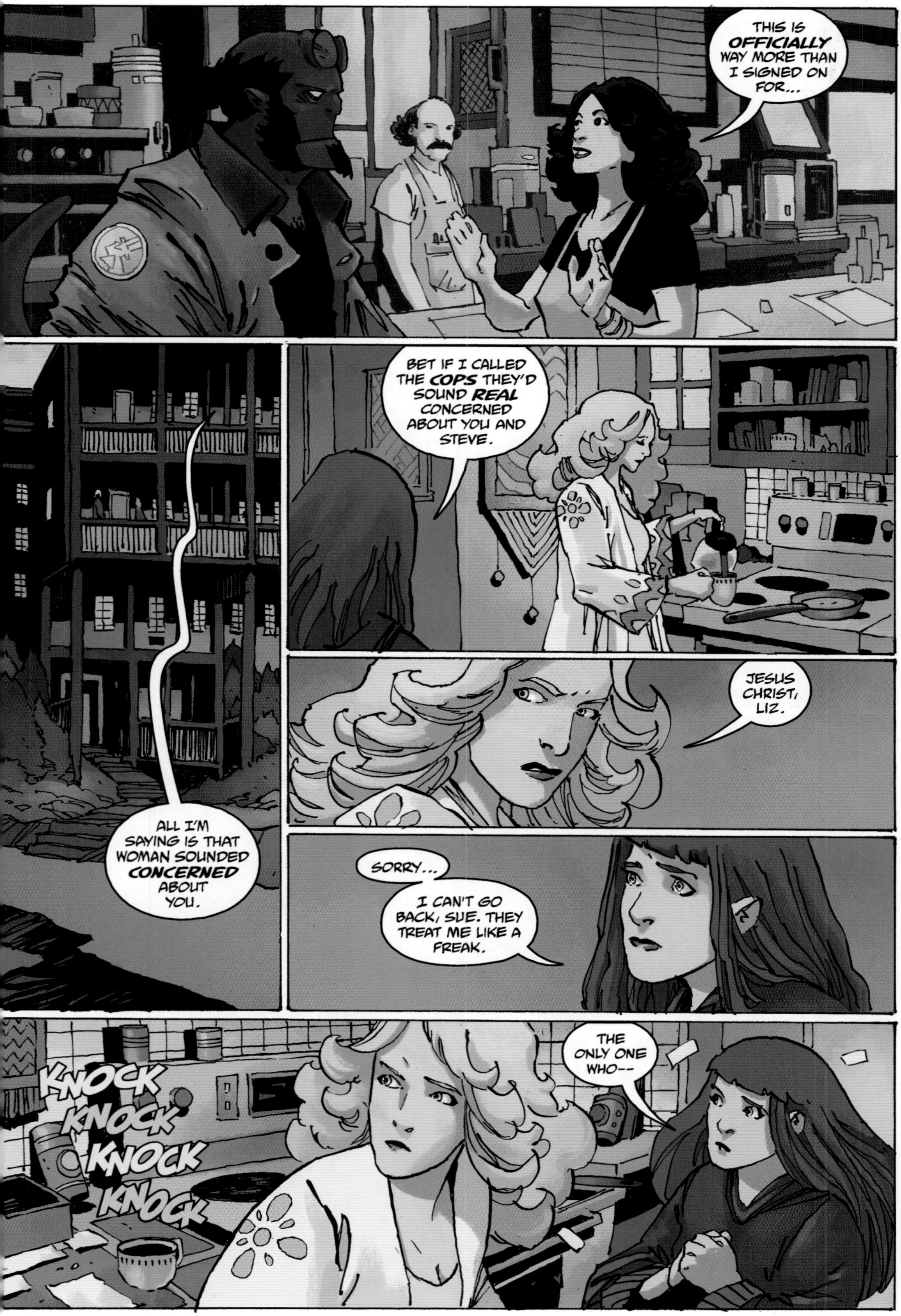

THIS IS *OFFICIALLY* WAY MORE THAN I SIGNED ON FOR...
BET IF I CALLED THE *COPS* THEY'D SOUND *REAL* CONCERNED ABOUT YOU AND STEVE.
ALL I'M SAYING IS THAT WOMAN SOUNDED *CONCERNED* ABOUT YOU.
JESUS CHRIST, LIZ.
SORRY...
I CAN'T GO BACK, SUE. THEY TREAT ME LIKE A FREAK.
THE ONLY ONE WHO--
KNOCK KNOCK KNOCK KNOCK

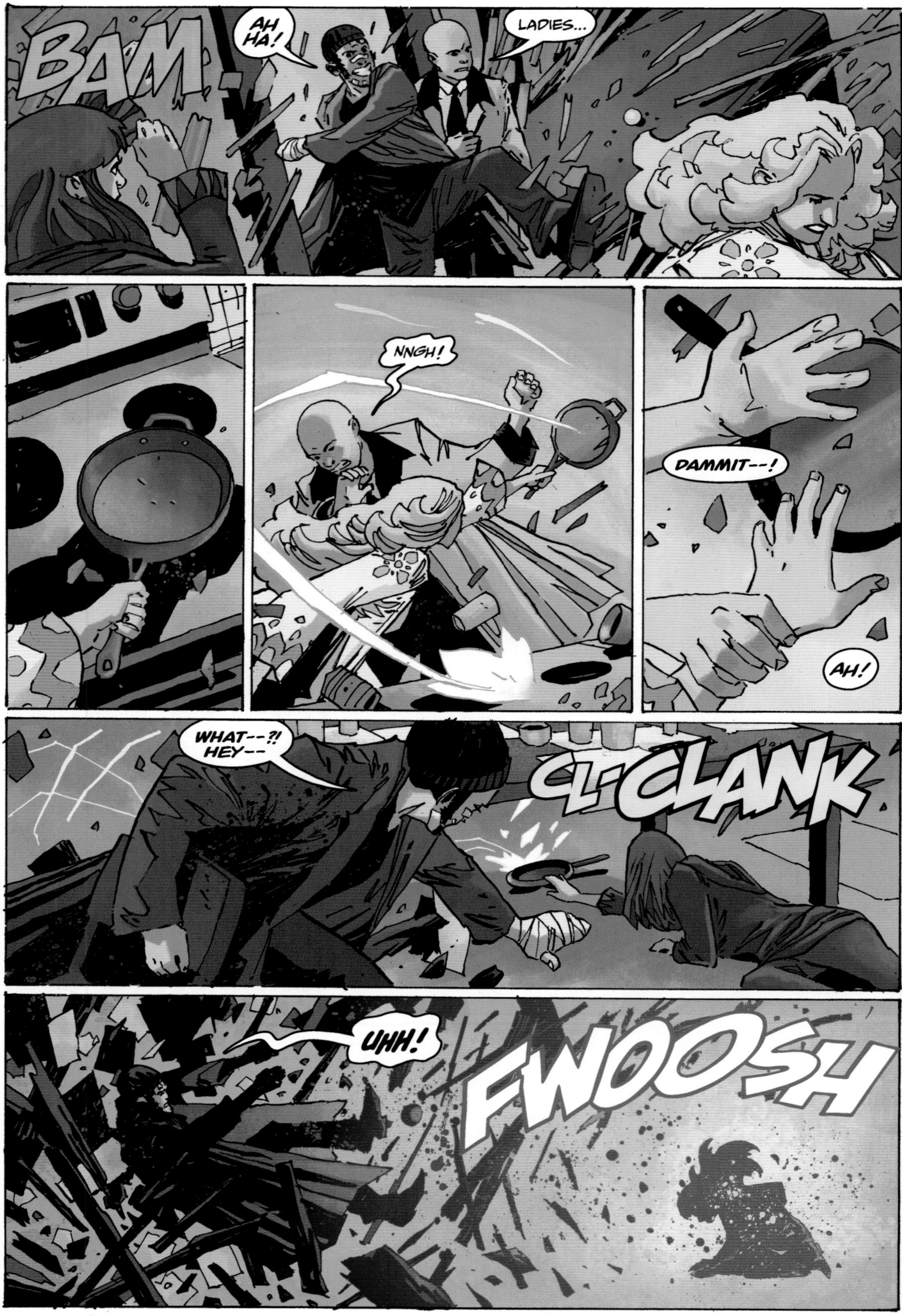
BAM
AH HA!
LADIES...
NNGH!
DAMMIT--!
AH!
WHAT--?! HEY--
CL-CLANK
UHH!
FWOOSH

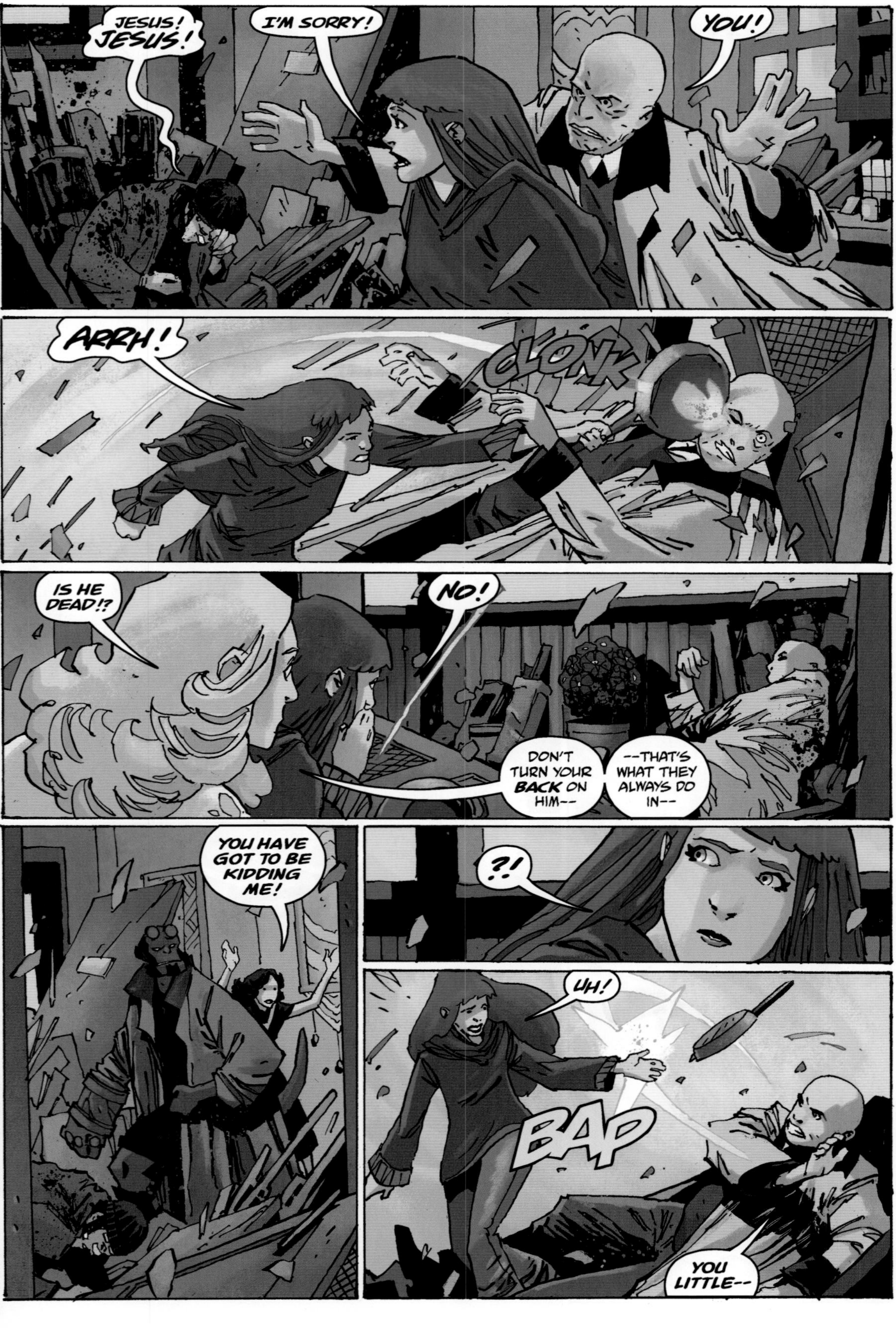
JESUS! JESUS!
I'M SORRY!
YOU!
ARRH!
CLONK
IS HE DEAD!?
NO!
DON'T TURN YOUR BACK ON HIM--
--THAT'S WHAT THEY ALWAYS DO IN--
YOU HAVE GOT TO BE KIDDING ME!
?!
UH!
BAP
YOU LITTLE--

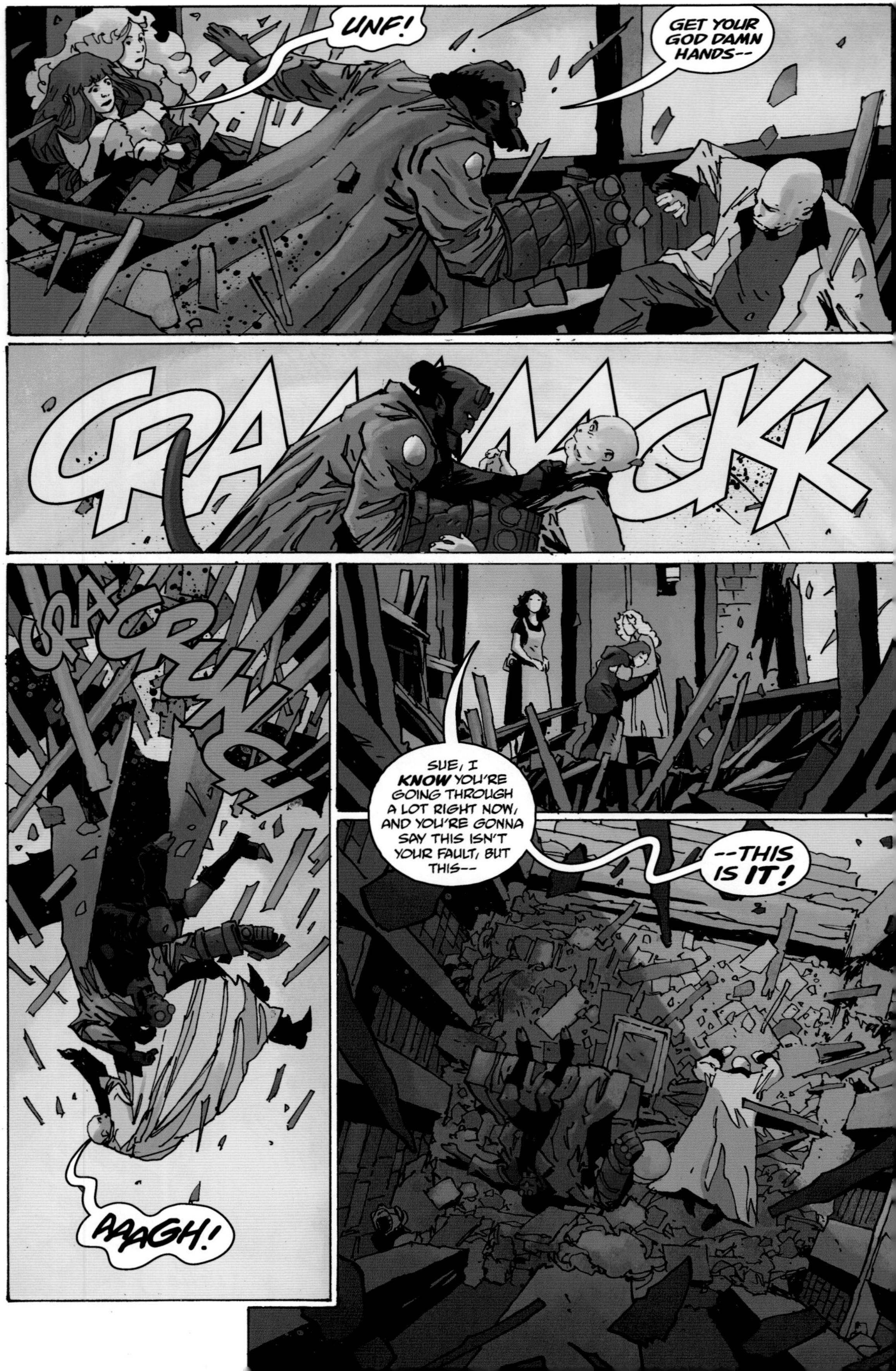

UNF!
GET YOUR GOD DAMN HANDS--
CRAAAACKK
CRA-CRUNCH
AAAGH!
SUE, I KNOW YOU'RE GOING THROUGH A LOT RIGHT NOW, AND YOU'RE GONNA SAY THIS ISN'T YOUR FAULT, BUT THIS--
--THIS IS IT!

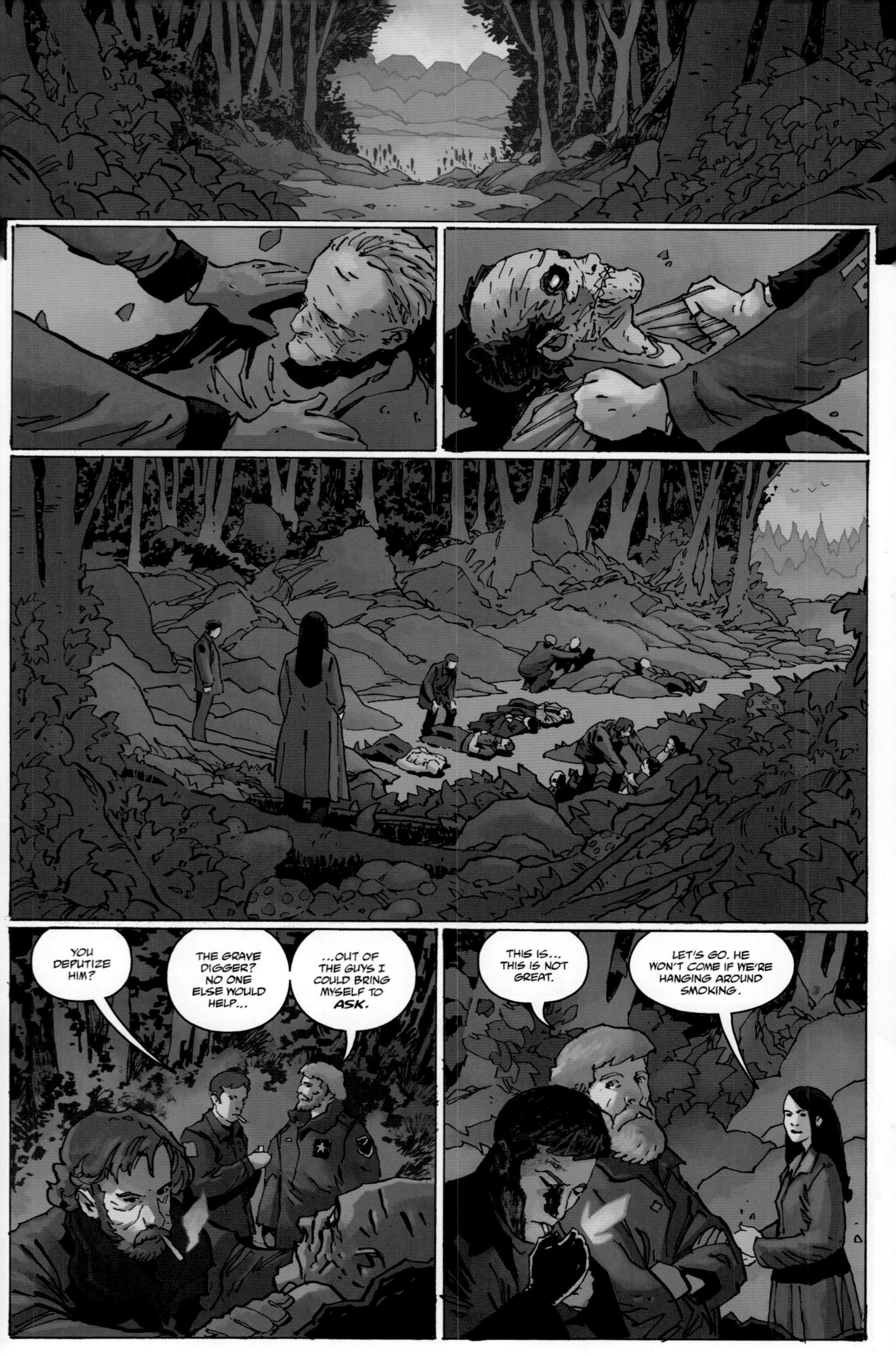
YOU DEPUTIZE HIM?
THE GRAVE DIGGER? NO ONE ELSE WOULD HELP...
...OUT OF THE GUYS I COULD BRING MYSELF TO ASK.
THIS IS... THIS IS NOT GREAT.
LET'S GO. HE WON'T COME IF WE'RE HANGING AROUND SMOKING.

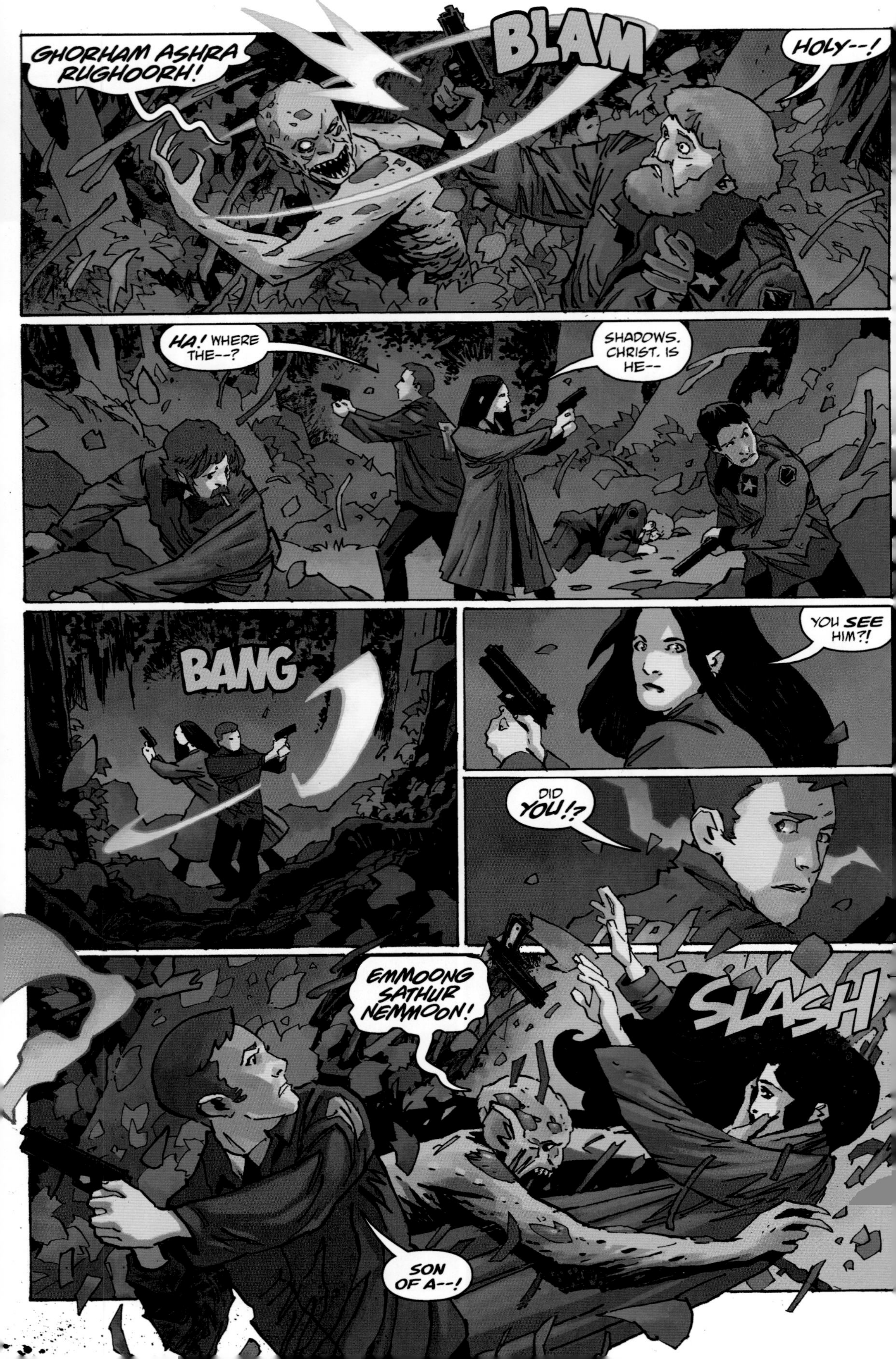
GHORHAM ASHRA RUGHOORH!
BLAM
HOLY--!
HA! WHERE THE--?
SHADOWS. CHRIST. IS HE--
BANG
YOU SEE HIM?!
DID YOU!?
EMMOONG SATHUR NEMMOON!
SLASH
SON OF A--!

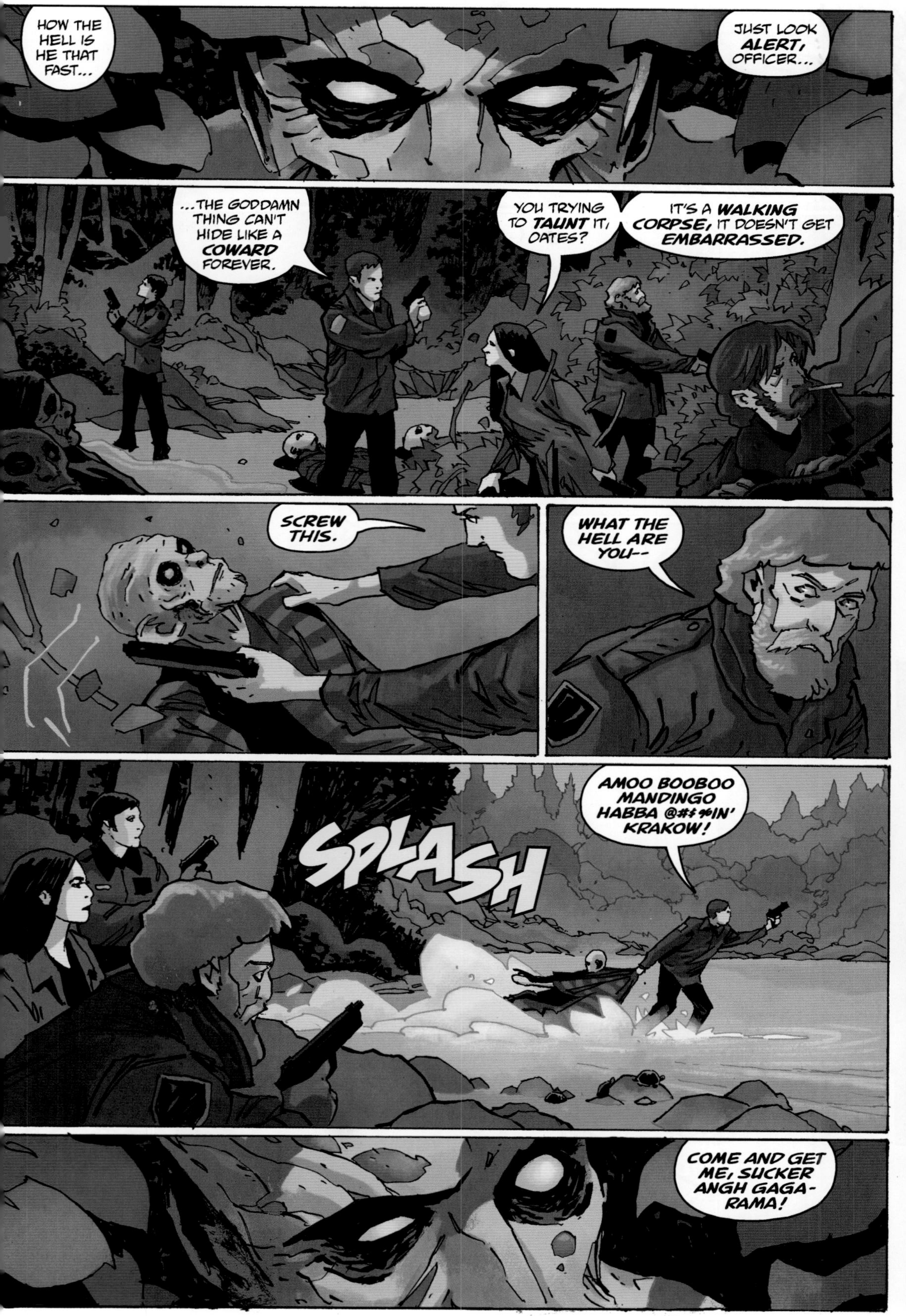

HOW THE HELL IS HE THAT FAST...
JUST LOOK ALERT, OFFICER...
...THE GODDAMN THING CAN'T HIDE LIKE A COWARD FOREVER.
YOU TRYING TO TAUNT IT, OATES?
IT'S A WALKING CORPSE, IT DOESN'T GET EMBARRASSED.
SCREW THIS.
WHAT THE HELL ARE YOU--
SPLASH
AMOO BOOBOO MANDINGO HABBA @#$%IN' KRAKOW!
COME AND GET ME, SUCKER ANGH GAGA-RAMA!

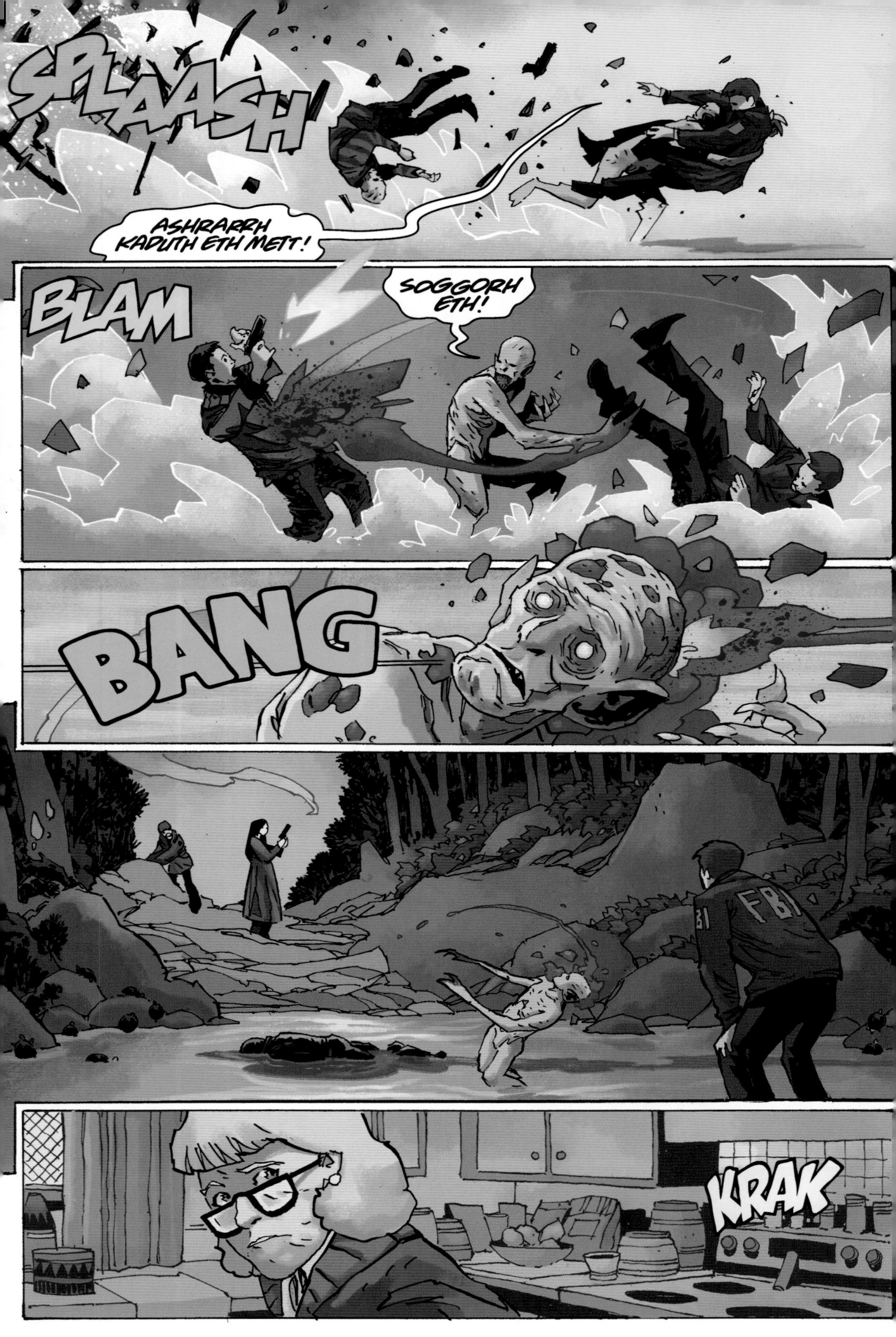
SPLAASH
ASHRARRH KADUTH ETH METT!
BLAM
SOGGORH ETH!
BANG
FBI
KRAK

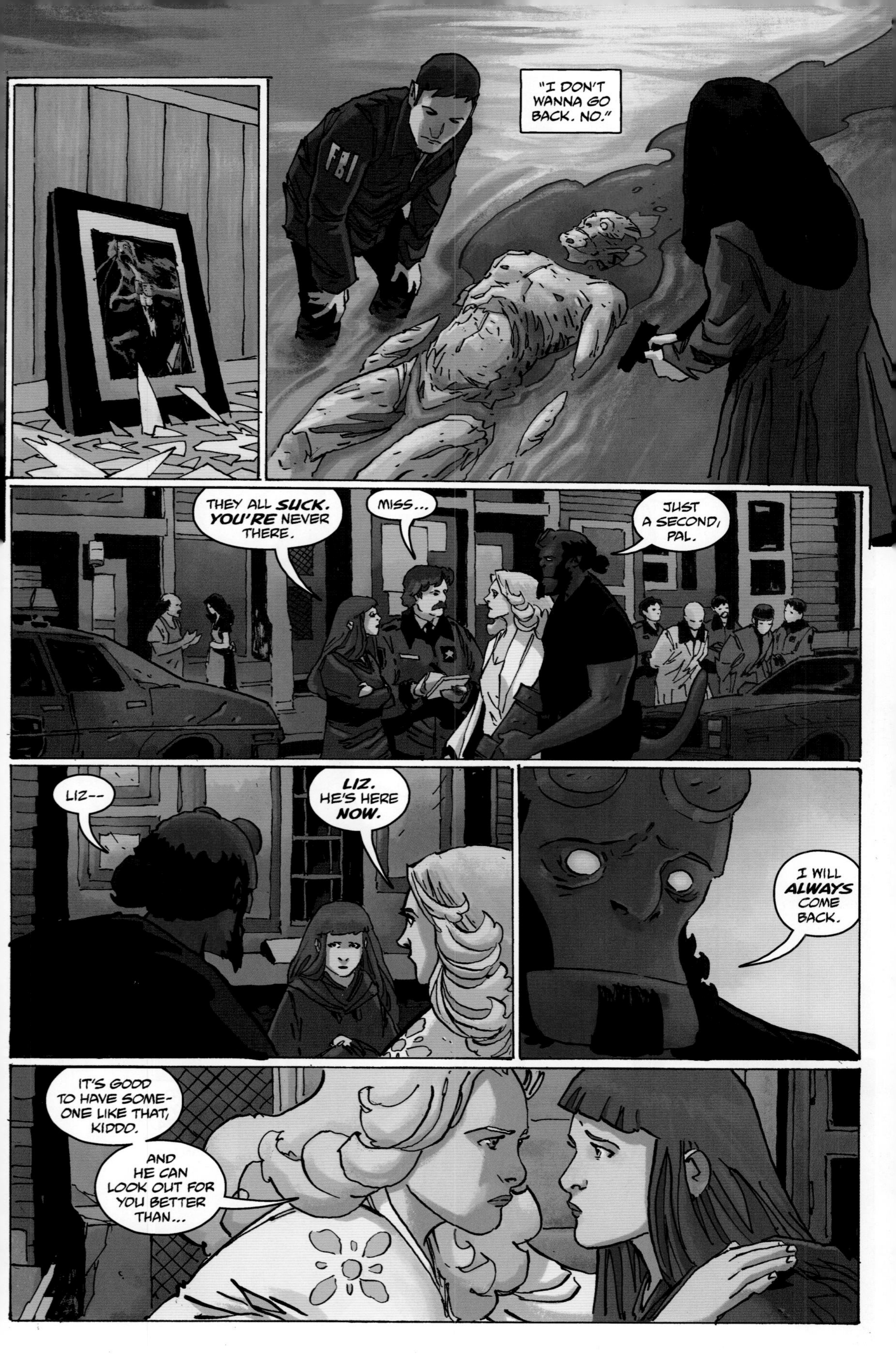
"I DON'T WANNA GO BACK. NO."
THEY ALL SUCK. YOU'RE NEVER THERE.
MISS...
JUST A SECOND, PAL.
LIZ--
LIZ. HE'S HERE NOW.
I WILL ALWAYS COME BACK.
IT'S GOOD TO HAVE SOMEONE LIKE THAT, KIDDO.
AND HE CAN LOOK OUT FOR YOU BETTER THAN...

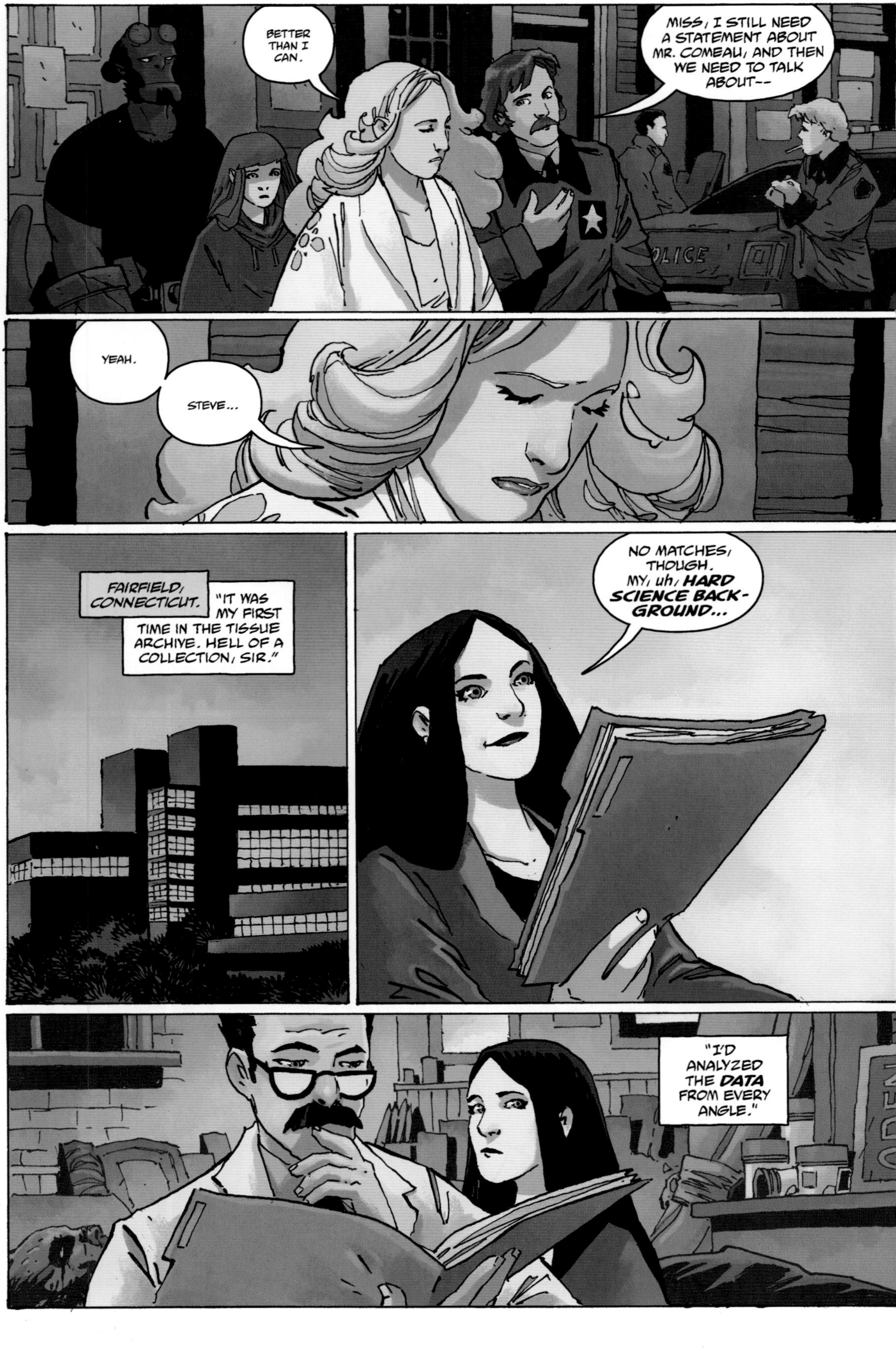
BETTER THAN I CAN.
MISS, I STILL NEED A STATEMENT ABOUT MR. COMEAU, AND THEN WE NEED TO TALK ABOUT--
POLICE
YEAH.
STEVE...
FAIRFIELD, CONNECTICUT.
"IT WAS MY FIRST TIME IN THE TISSUE ARCHIVE. HELL OF A COLLECTION, SIR."
NO MATCHES, THOUGH. MY, uh, HARD SCIENCE BACK-GROUND...
"I'D ANALYZED THE DATA FROM EVERY ANGLE."

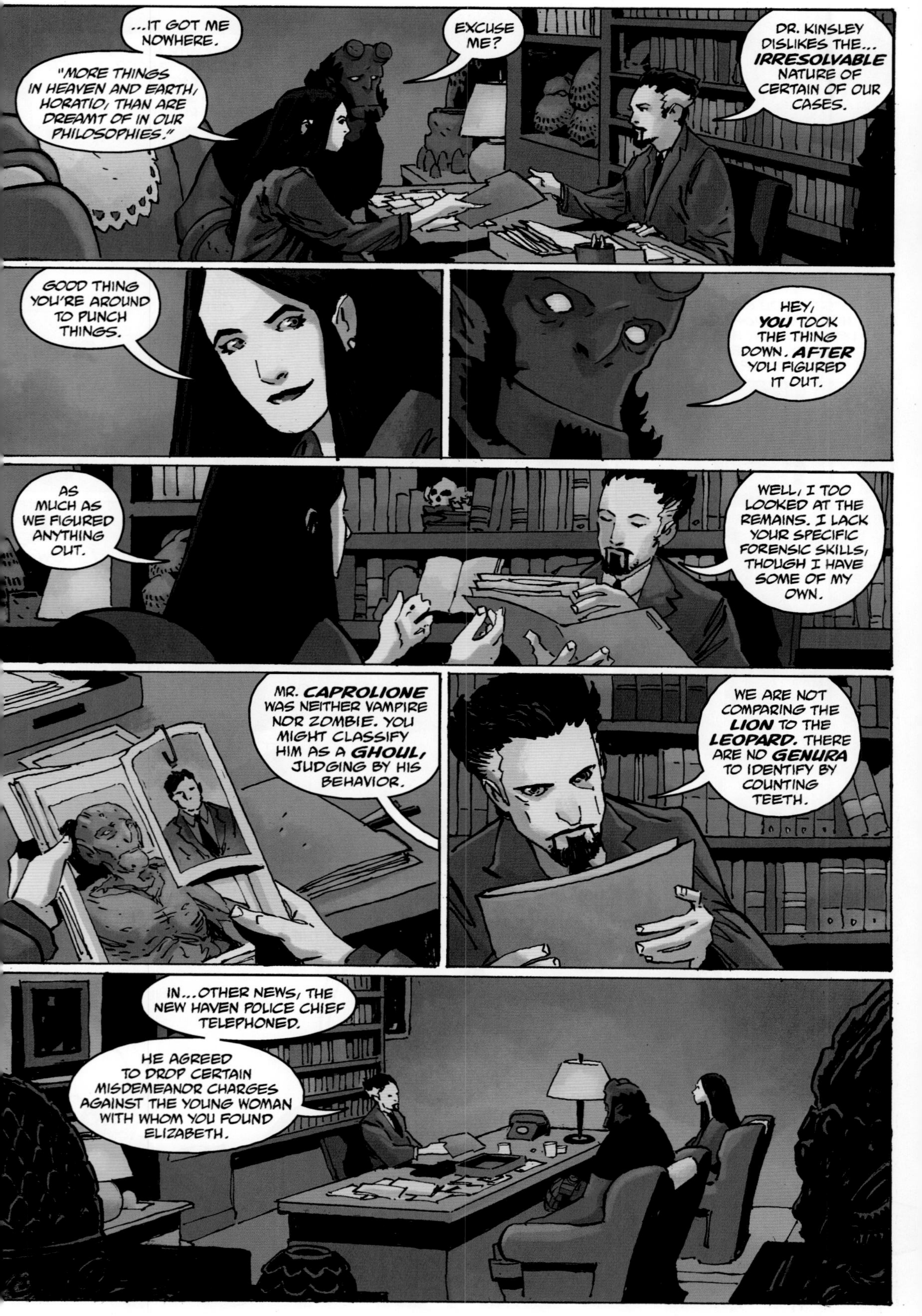
...IT GOT ME NOWHERE.
"MORE THINGS IN HEAVEN AND EARTH, HORATIO, THAN ARE DREAMT OF IN OUR PHILOSOPHIES."
EXCUSE ME?
DR. KINSLEY DISLIKES THE... IRRESOLVABLE NATURE OF CERTAIN OF OUR CASES.
GOOD THING YOU'RE AROUND TO PUNCH THINGS.
HEY, YOU TOOK THE THING DOWN. AFTER YOU FIGURED IT OUT.
AS MUCH AS WE FIGURED ANYTHING OUT.
WELL, I TOO LOOKED AT THE REMAINS. I LACK YOUR SPECIFIC FORENSIC SKILLS, THOUGH I HAVE SOME OF MY OWN.
MR. CAPROLIONE WAS NEITHER VAMPIRE NOR ZOMBIE. YOU MIGHT CLASSIFY HIM AS A GHOUL, JUDGING BY HIS BEHAVIOR.
WE ARE NOT COMPARING THE LION TO THE LEOPARD. THERE ARE NO GENURA TO IDENTIFY BY COUNTING TEETH.
IN...OTHER NEWS, THE NEW HAVEN POLICE CHIEF TELEPHONED.
HE AGREED TO DROP CERTAIN MISDEMEANOR CHARGES AGAINST THE YOUNG WOMAN WITH WHOM YOU FOUND ELIZABETH.

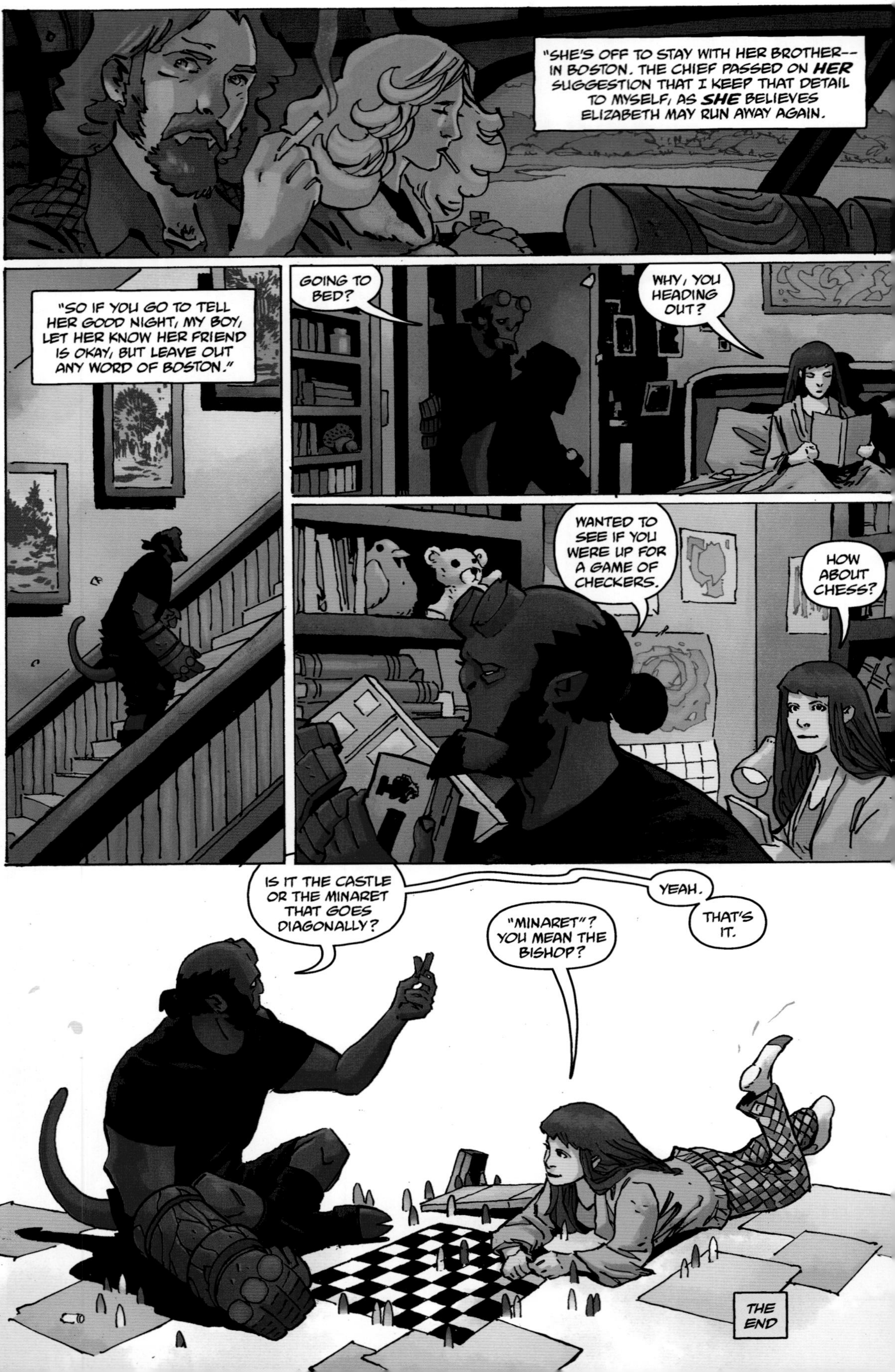
"SHE'S OFF TO STAY WITH HER BROTHER-- IN BOSTON. THE CHIEF PASSED ON HER SUGGESTION THAT I KEEP THAT DETAIL TO MYSELF, AS SHE BELIEVES ELIZABETH MAY RUN AWAY AGAIN.
"SO IF YOU GO TO TELL HER GOOD NIGHT, MY BOY, LET HER KNOW HER FRIEND IS OKAY, BUT LEAVE OUT ANY WORD OF BOSTON."
GOING TO BED?
WHY, YOU HEADING OUT?
WANTED TO SEE IF YOU WERE UP FOR A GAME OF CHECKERS.
HOW ABOUT CHESS?
IS IT THE CASTLE OR THE MINARET THAT GOES DIAGONALLY?
"MINARET"? YOU MEAN THE BISHOP?
YEAH.
THAT'S IT.
THE END

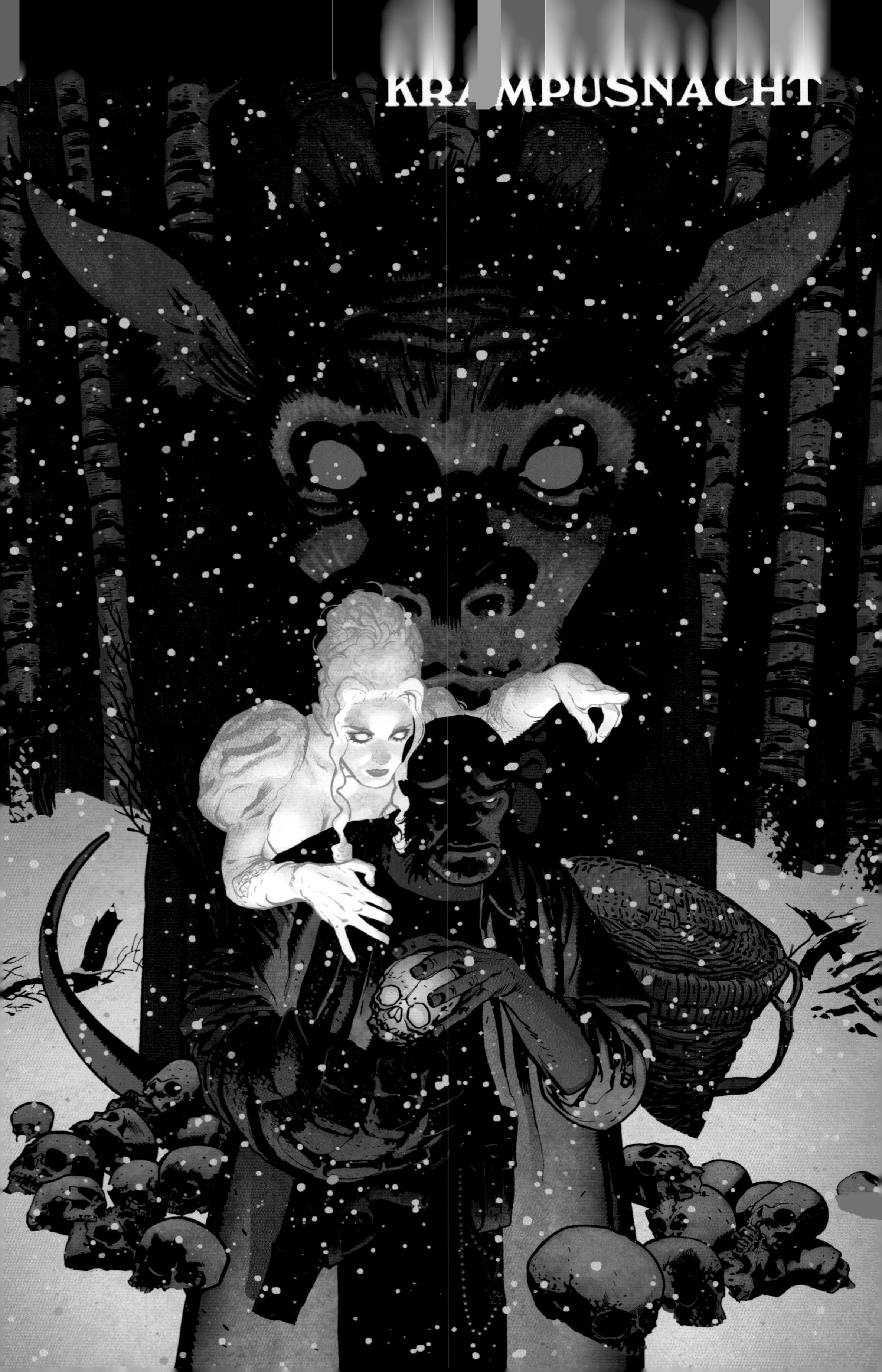
KRAMPUSNACHT

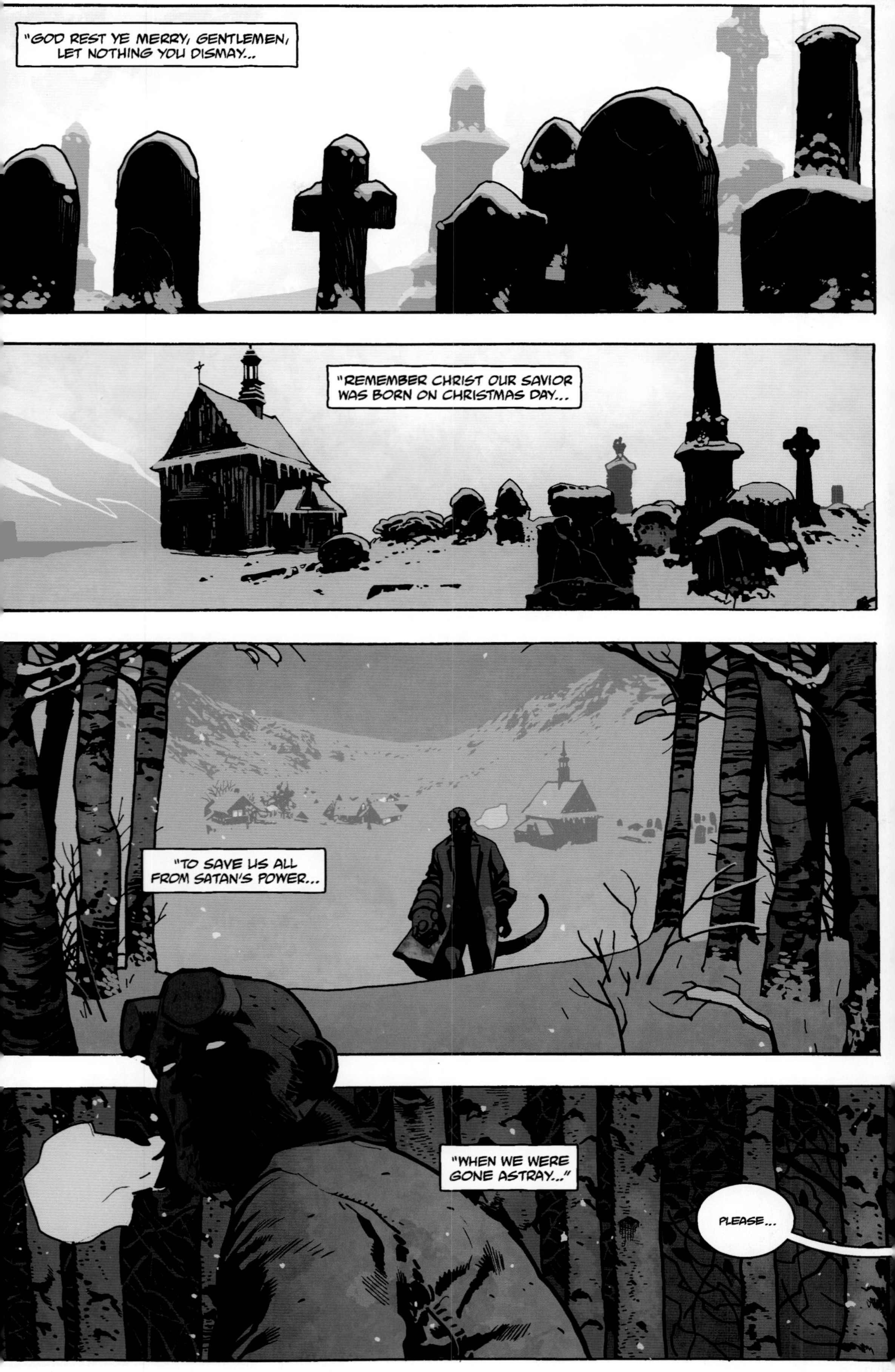
"GOD REST YE MERRY, GENTLEMEN, LET NOTHING YOU DISMAY...
"REMEMBER CHRIST OUR SAVIOR WAS BORN ON CHRISTMAS DAY...
"TO SAVE US ALL FROM SATAN'S POWER...
"WHEN WE WERE GONE ASTRAY..."
PLEASE...

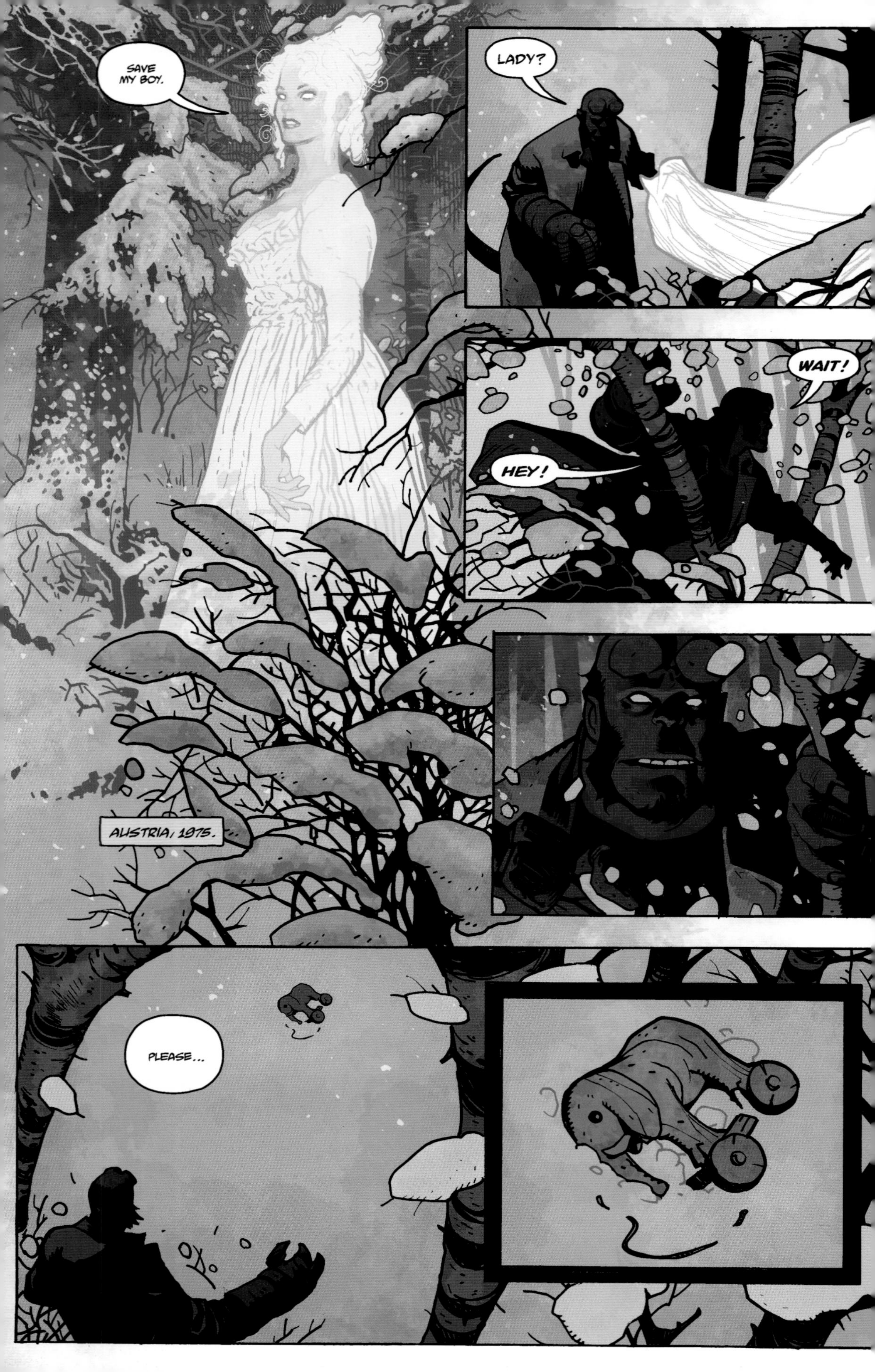
SAVE MY BOY.
LADY?
WAIT!
HEY!
AUSTRIA, 1975.
PLEASE...

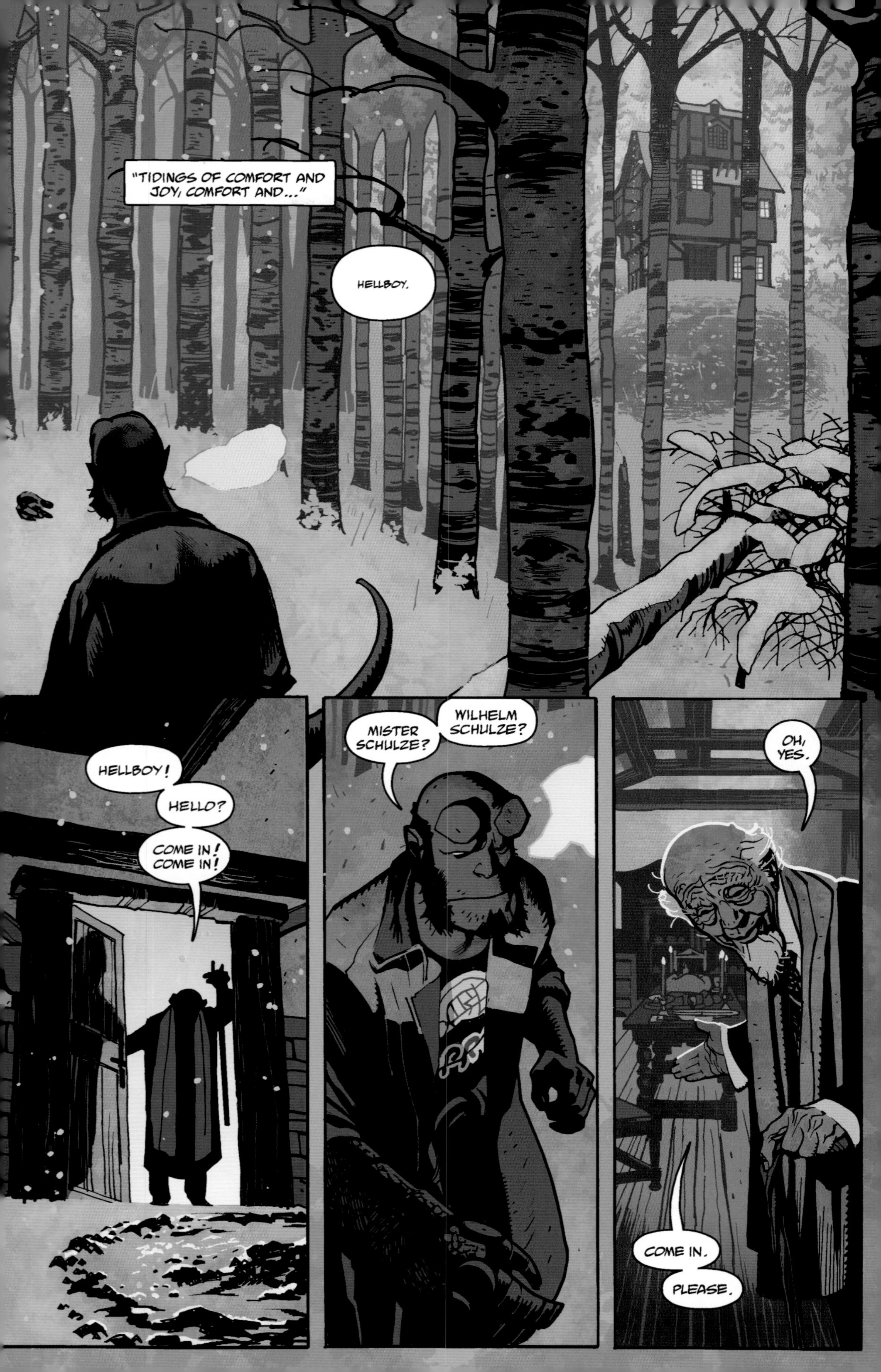
"TIDINGS OF COMFORT AND JOY, COMFORT AND..."
HELLBOY.
HELLBOY!
HELLO?
COME IN! COME IN!
MISTER SCHULZE?
WILHELM SCHULZE?
OH, YES.
COME IN.
PLEASE.

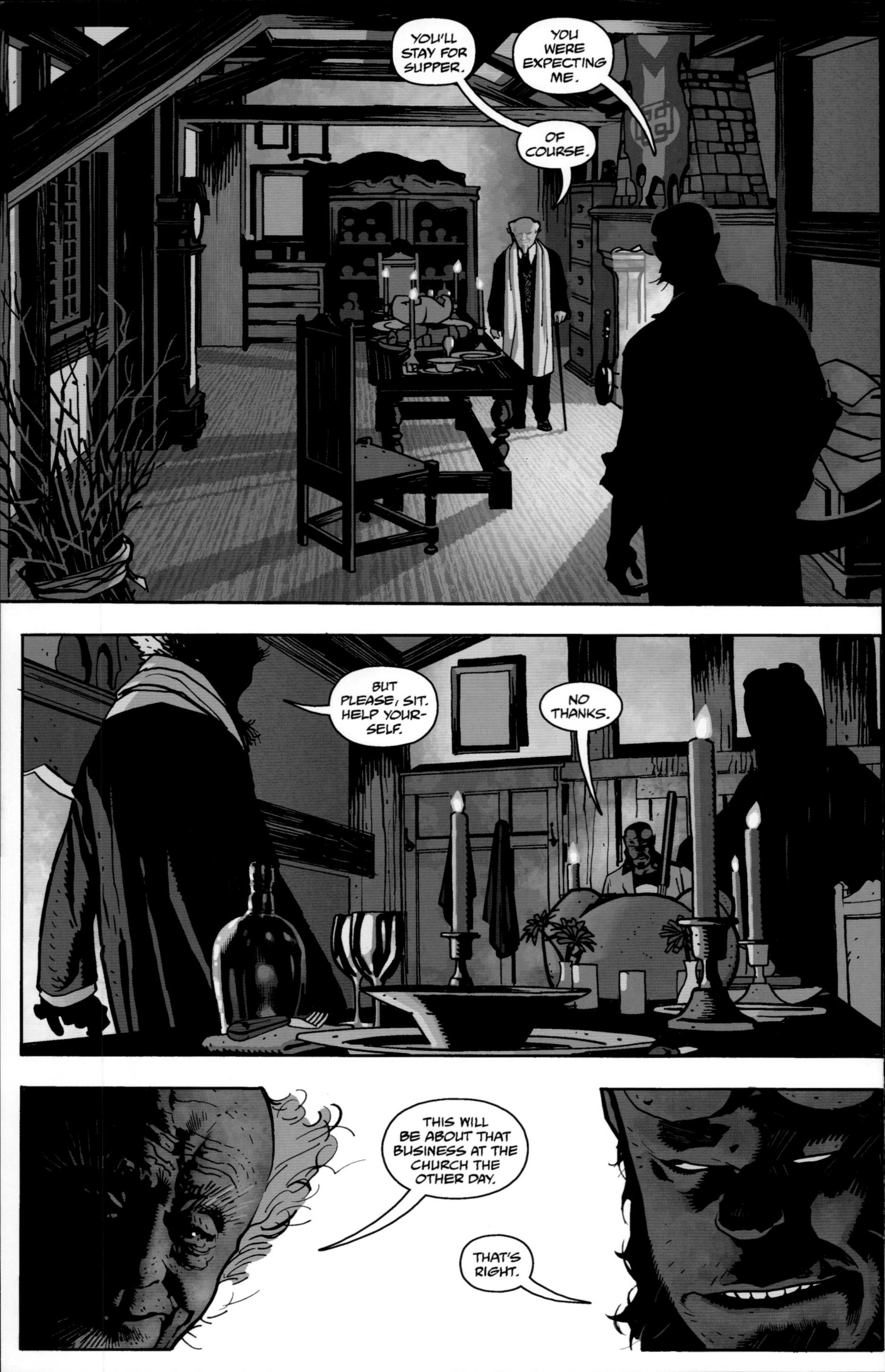
YOU WERE EXPECTING ME.
OF COURSE.
YOU'LL STAY FOR SUPPER.
BUT PLEASE, SIT. HELP YOUR-SELF.
NO THANKS.
THIS WILL BE ABOUT THAT BUSINESS AT THE CHURCH THE OTHER DAY.
THAT'S RIGHT.

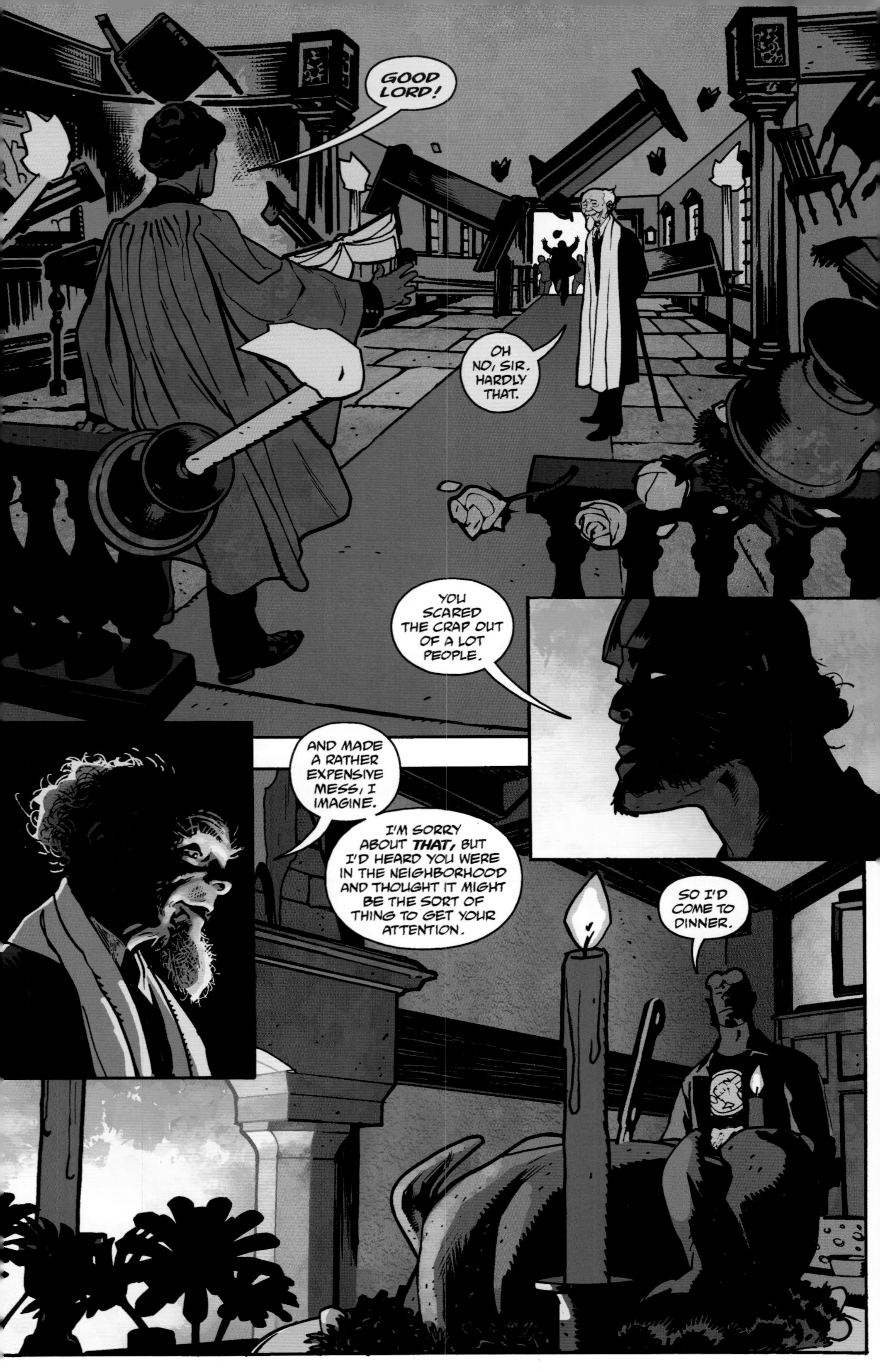
GOOD LORD!
OH NO, SIR. HARDLY THAT.
YOU SCARED THE CRAP OUT OF A LOT PEOPLE.
AND MADE A RATHER EXPENSIVE MESS, I IMAGINE.
I'M SORRY ABOUT THAT, BUT I'D HEARD YOU WERE IN THE NEIGHBORHOOD AND THOUGHT IT MIGHT BE THE SORT OF THING TO GET YOUR ATTENTION.
SO I'D COME TO DINNER.

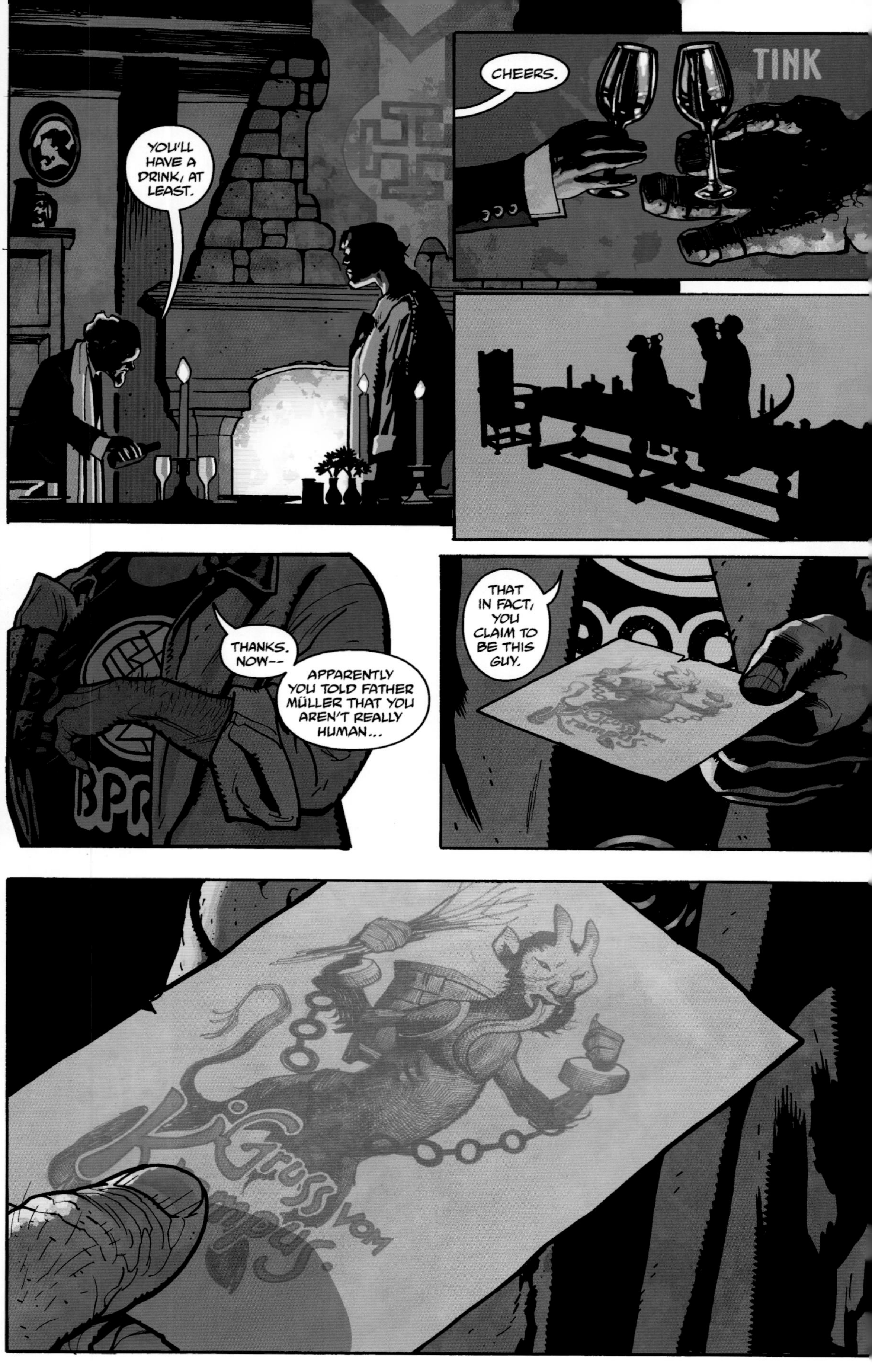
YOU'LL HAVE A DRINK, AT LEAST.
CHEERS.
TINK
THANKS. NOW--
APPARENTLY YOU TOLD FATHER MÜLLER THAT YOU AREN'T REALLY HUMAN...
THAT IN FACT, YOU CLAIM TO BE THIS GUY.
Gruss vom Krampus.

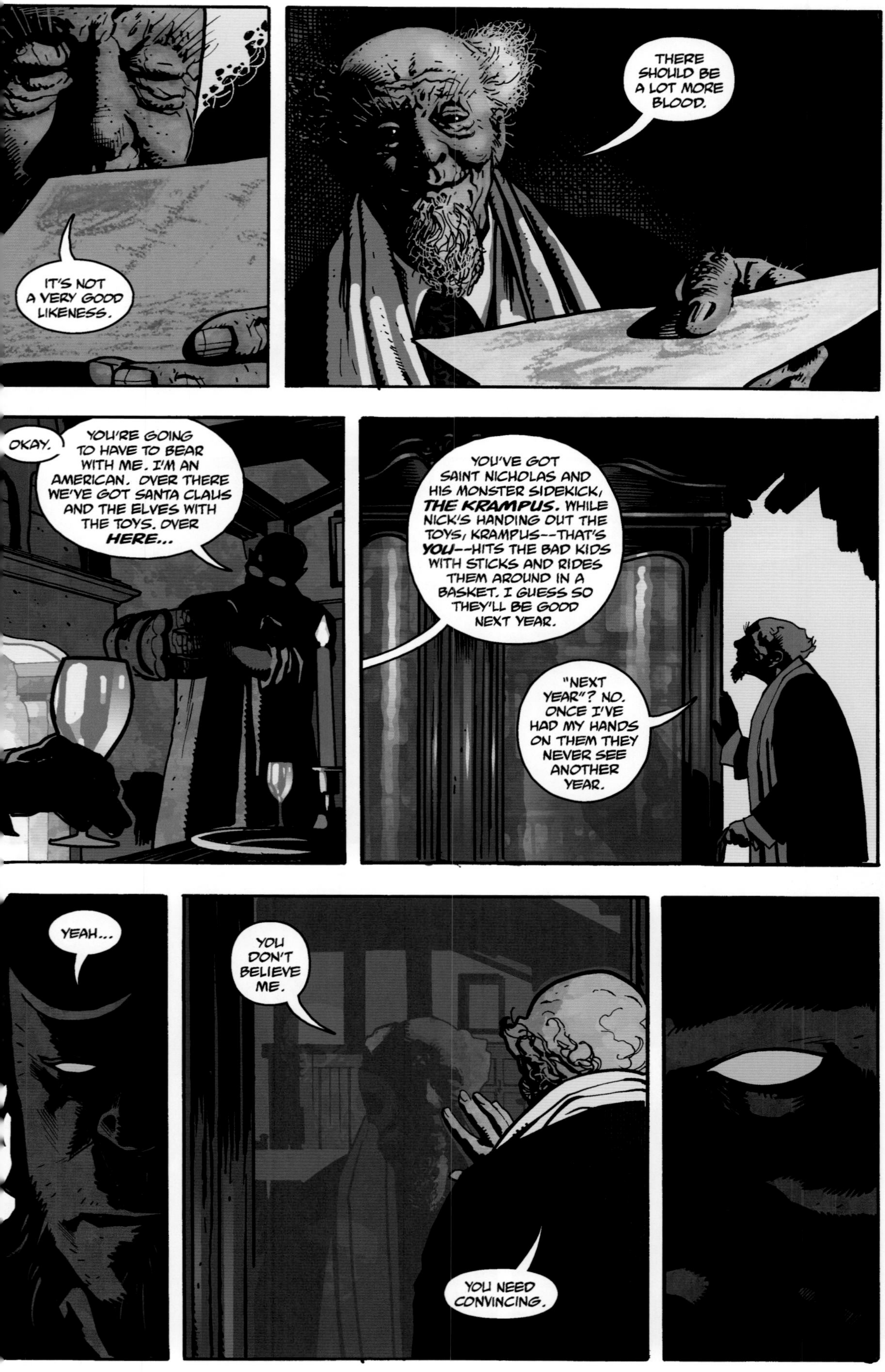
IT'S NOT A VERY GOOD LIKENESS.
THERE SHOULD BE A LOT MORE BLOOD.
OKAY.
YOU'RE GOING TO HAVE TO BEAR WITH ME. I'M AN AMERICAN. OVER THERE WE'VE GOT SANTA CLAUS AND THE ELVES WITH THE TOYS. OVER HERE...
YOU'VE GOT SAINT NICHOLAS AND HIS MONSTER SIDEKICK, THE KRAMPUS. WHILE NICK'S HANDING OUT THE TOYS, KRAMPUS--THAT'S YOU--HITS THE BAD KIDS WITH STICKS AND RIDES THEM AROUND IN A BASKET. I GUESS SO THEY'LL BE GOOD NEXT YEAR.
"NEXT YEAR"? NO. ONCE I'VE HAD MY HANDS ON THEM THEY NEVER SEE ANOTHER YEAR.
YEAH...
YOU DON'T BELIEVE ME.
YOU NEED CONVINCING.

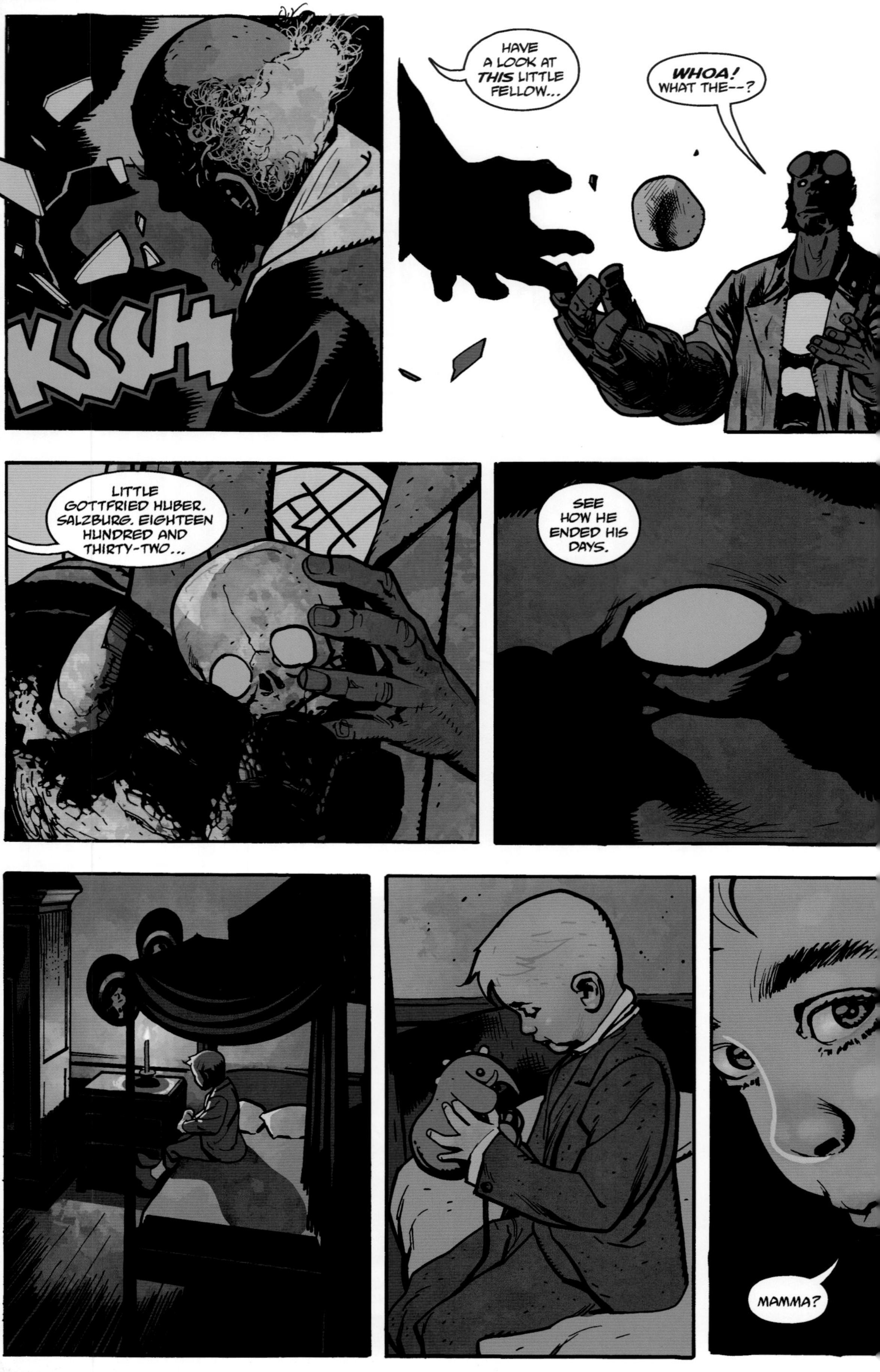
KSSH
HAVE A LOOK AT THIS LITTLE FELLOW...
WHOA! WHAT THE--?
LITTLE GOTTFRIED HUBER. SALZBURG. EIGHTEEN HUNDRED AND THIRTY-TWO...
SEE HOW HE ENDED HIS DAYS.
MAMMA?

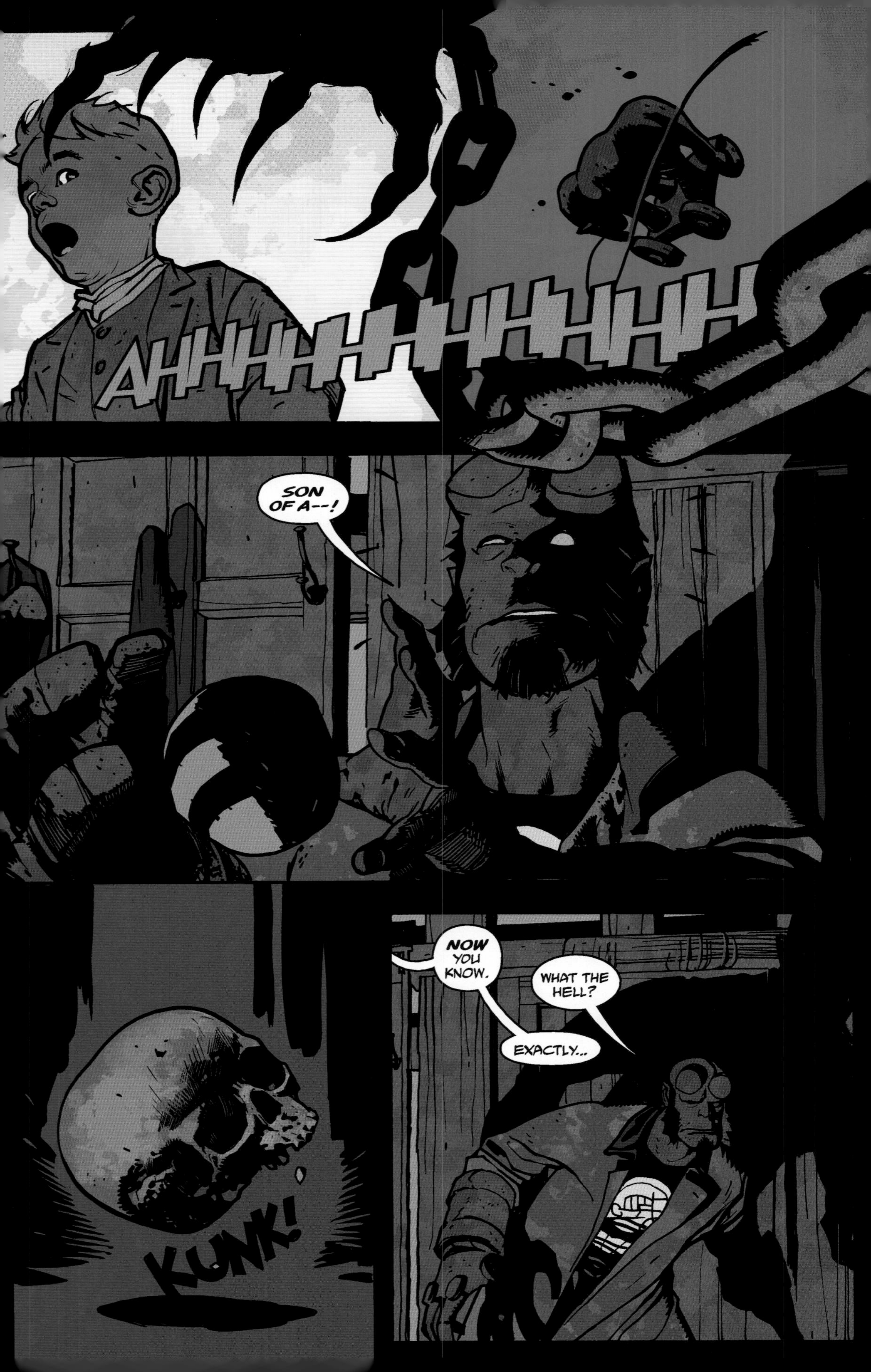
AHHHHHHHHHHHHHHH
SON OF A--!
KUNK!
NOW YOU KNOW.
WHAT THE HELL?
EXACTLY...

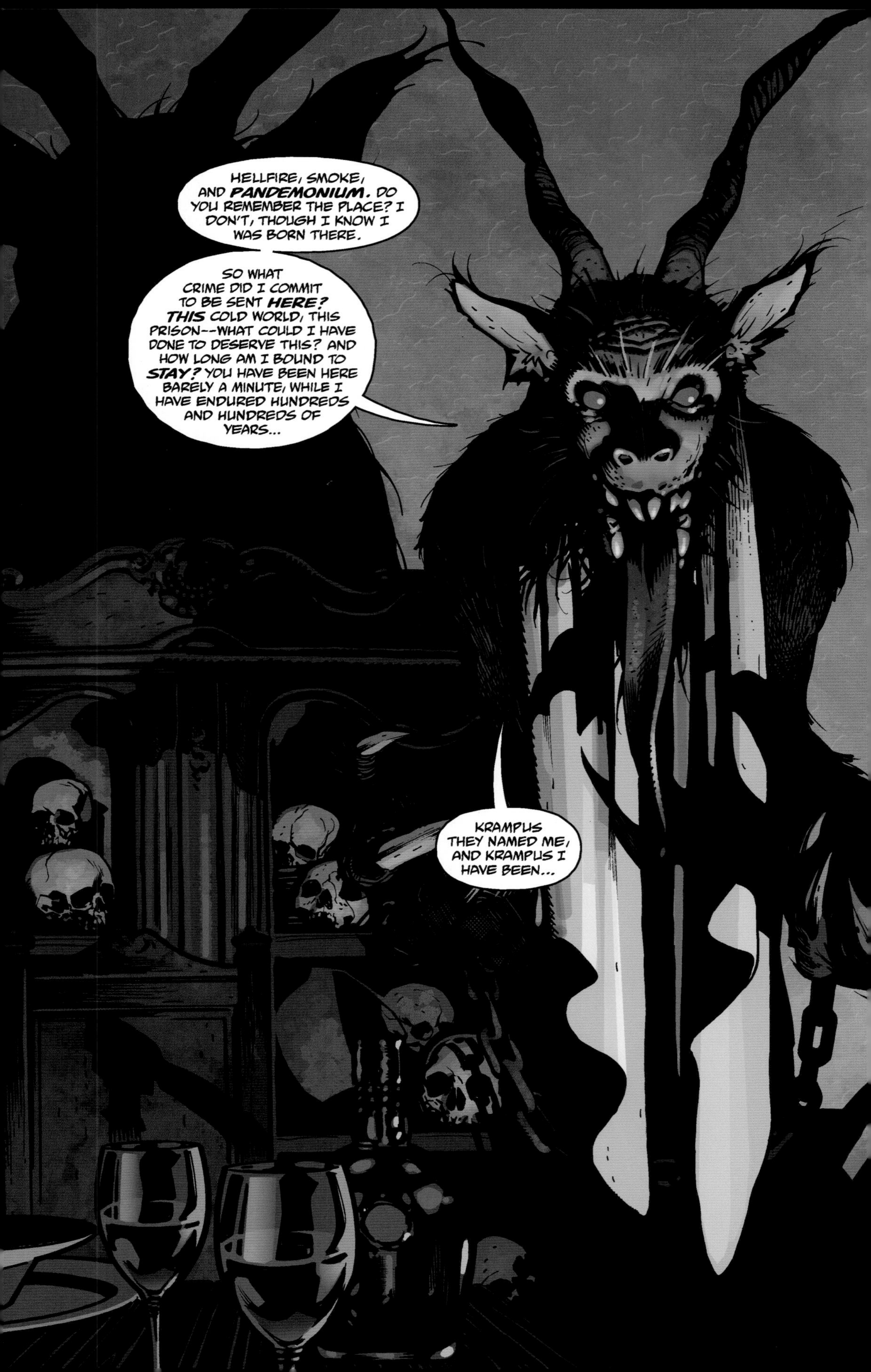
HELLFIRE, SMOKE, AND PANDEMONIUM. DO YOU REMEMBER THE PLACE? I DON'T, THOUGH I KNOW I WAS BORN THERE.
SO WHAT CRIME DID I COMMIT TO BE SENT HERE? THIS COLD WORLD, THIS PRISON--WHAT COULD I HAVE DONE TO DESERVE THIS? AND HOW LONG AM I BOUND TO STAY? YOU HAVE BEEN HERE BARELY A MINUTE, WHILE I HAVE ENDURED HUNDREDS AND HUNDREDS OF YEARS...
KRAMPUS THEY NAMED ME, AND KRAMPUS I HAVE BEEN...

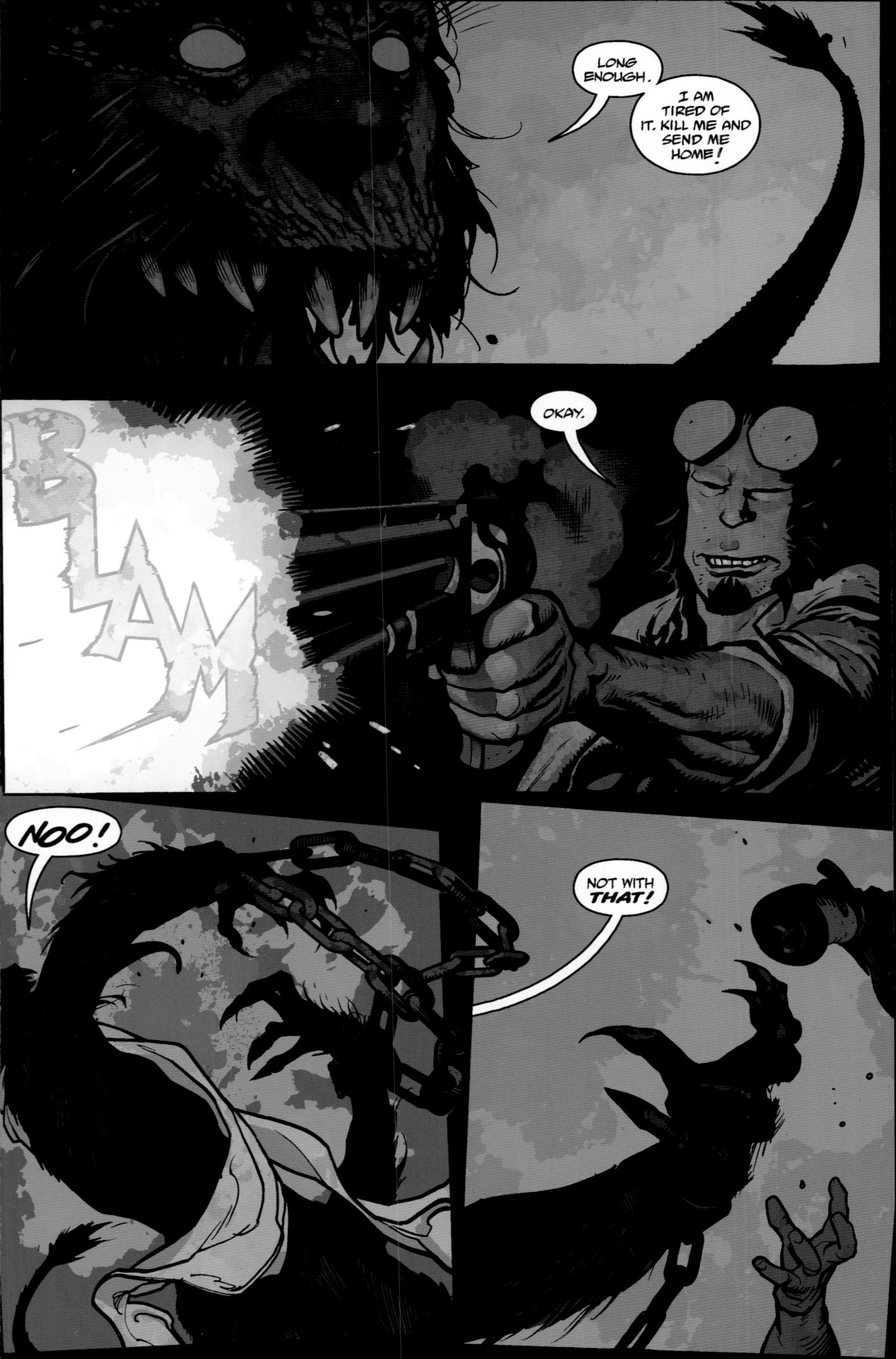
LONG ENOUGH.
I AM TIRED OF IT. KILL ME AND SEND ME HOME!
OKAY.
BLAM
NOO!
NOT WITH THAT!

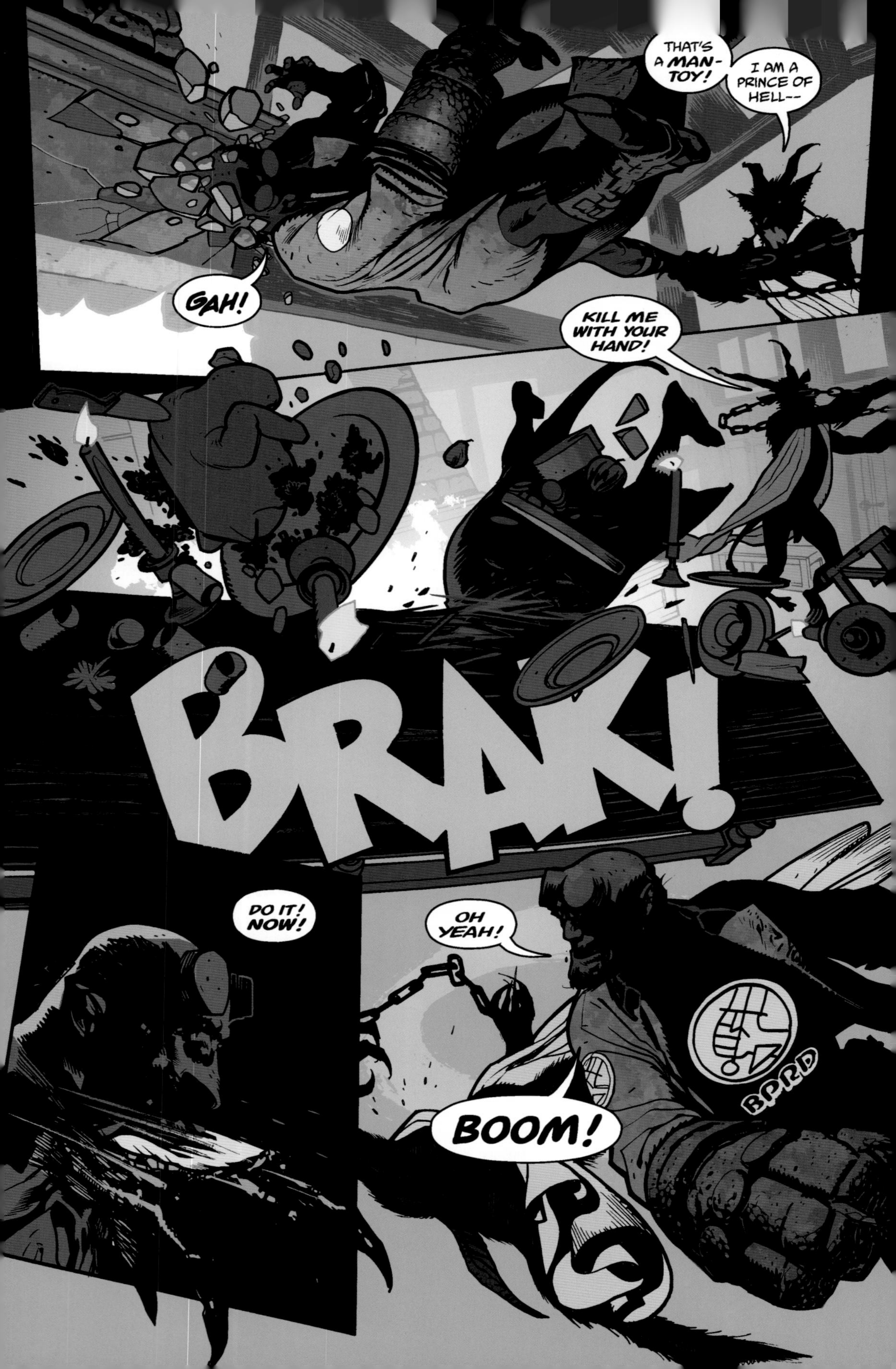
THAT'S A MAN-TOY!
I AM A PRINCE OF HELL--
GAH!
KILL ME WITH YOUR HAND!
BRAK!
DO IT! NOW!
OH YEAH!
BPRD
BOOM!

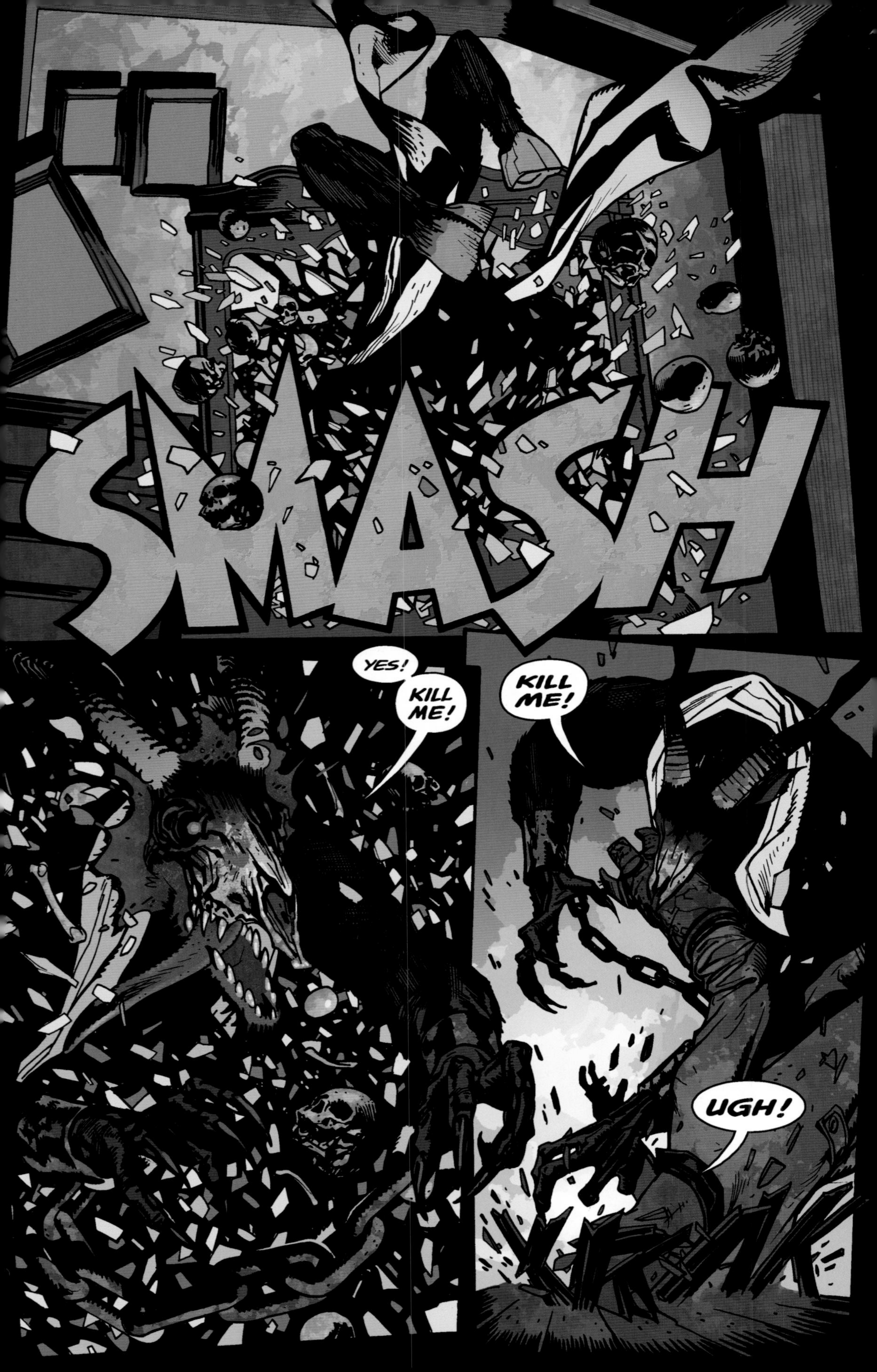
SMASH
YES!
KILL ME!
KILL ME!
UGH!

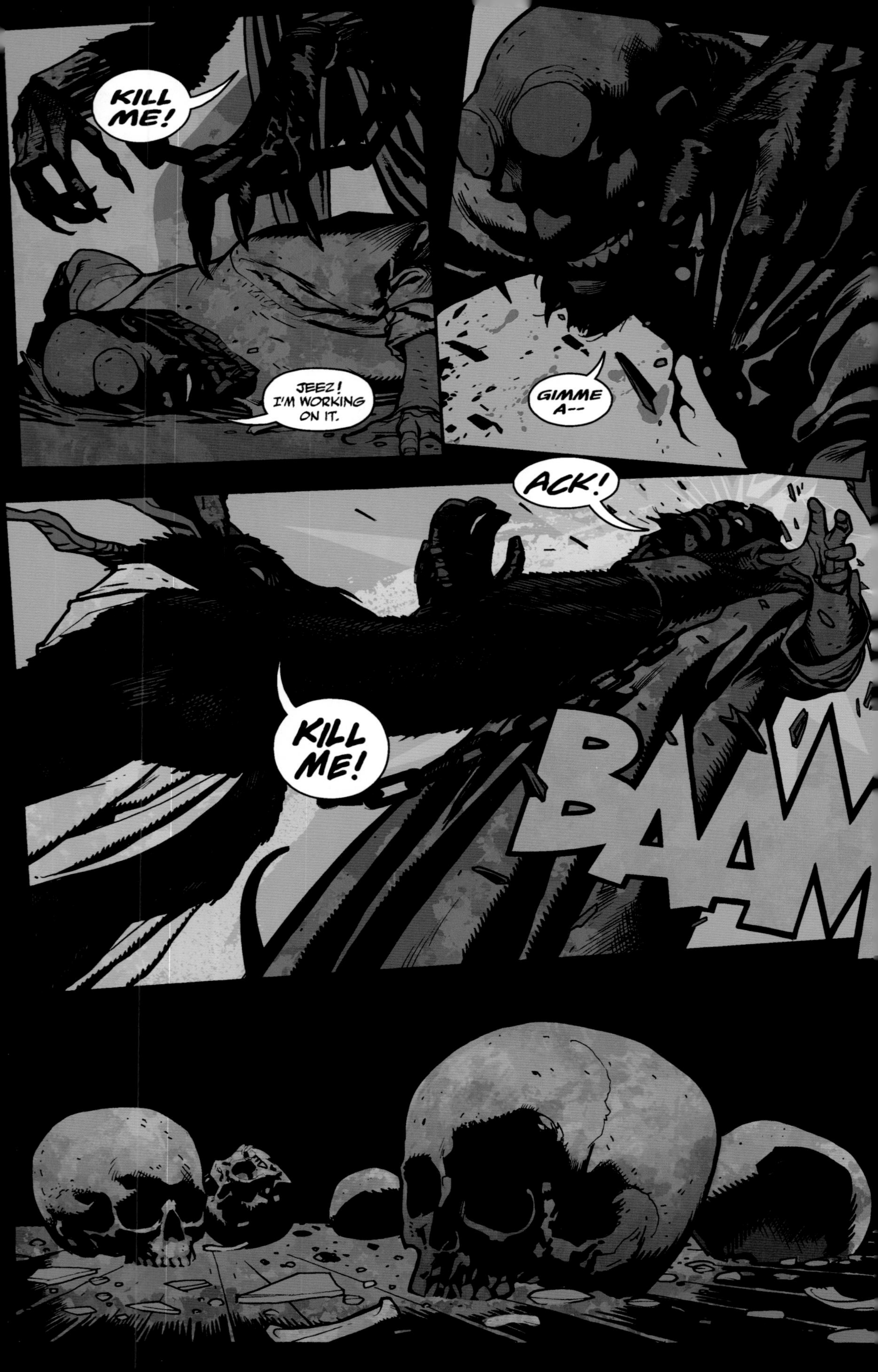
KILL ME!
JEEZ! I'M WORKING ON IT.
GIMME A--
ACK!
KILL ME!
BAAM

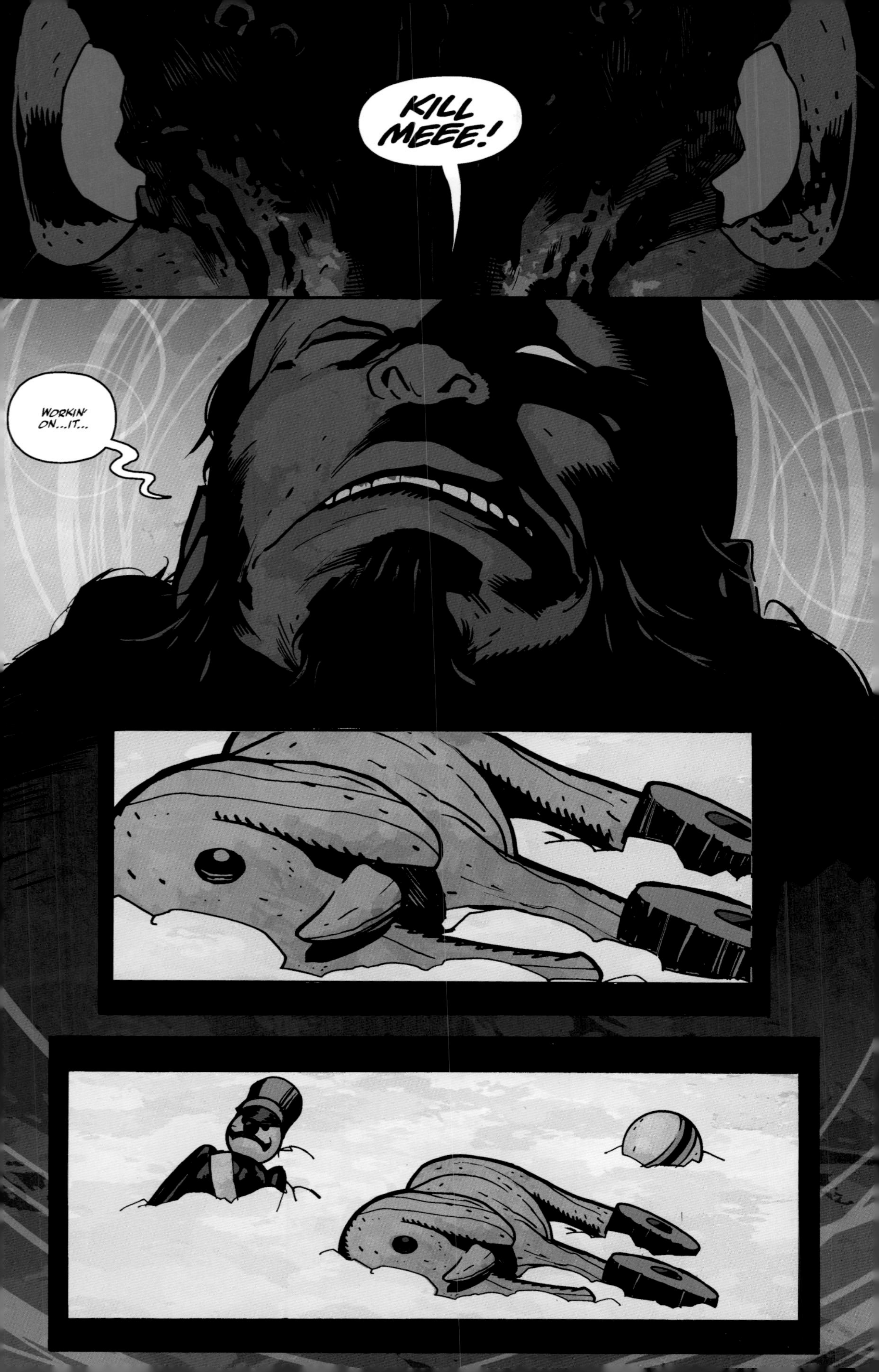
KILL MEEE!
WORKIN' ON...IT...

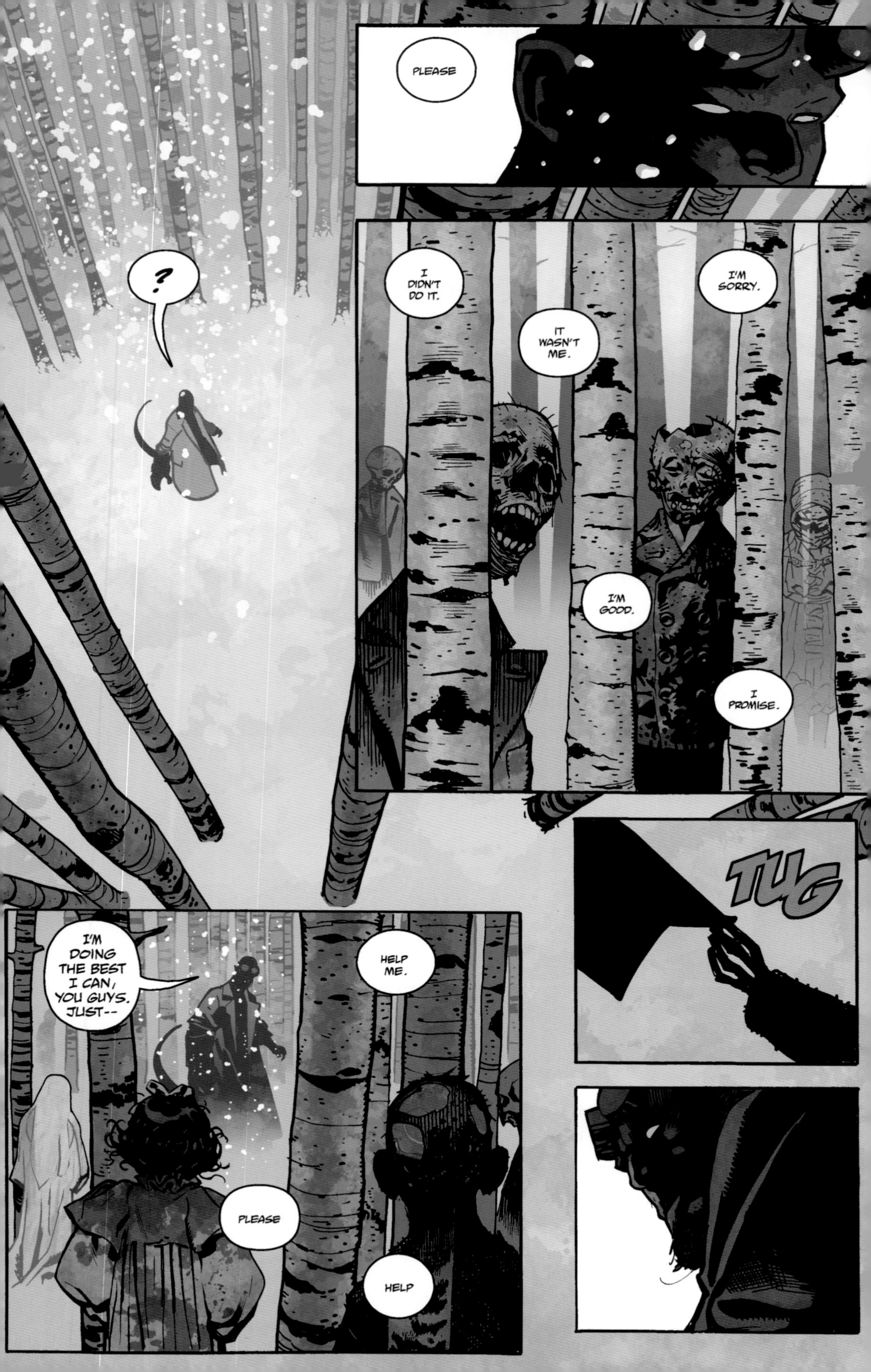
PLEASE
?
I DIDN'T DO IT.
IT WASN'T ME.
I'M SORRY.
I'M GOOD.
I PROMISE.
TUG
I'M DOING THE BEST I CAN, YOU GUYS. JUST--
HELP ME.
PLEASE
HELP

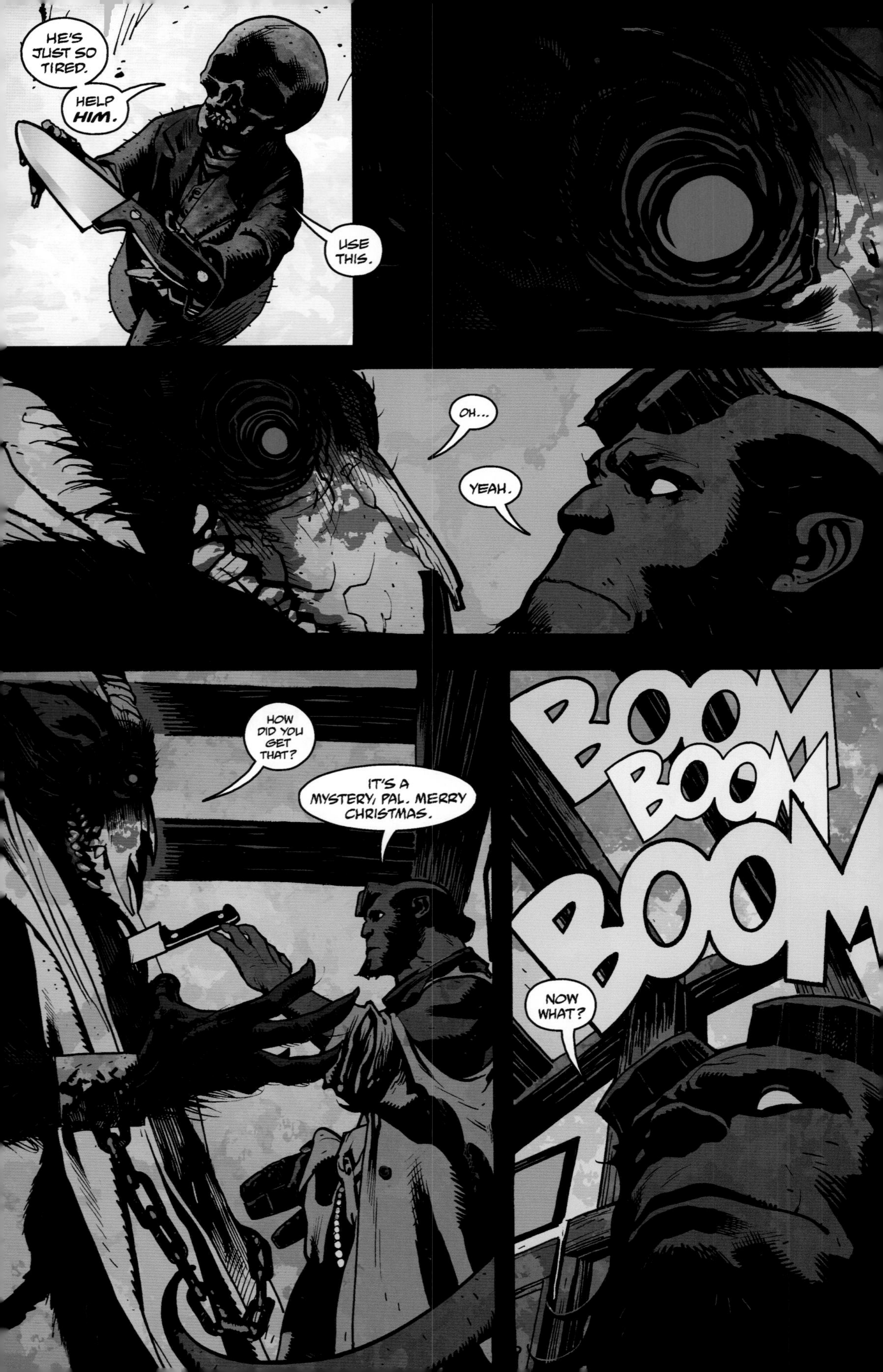
HE'S JUST SO TIRED.
HELP *HIM.*
USE THIS.
OH...
YEAH.
HOW DID YOU GET THAT?
IT'S A MYSTERY, PAL. MERRY CHRISTMAS.
BOOM BOOM BOOM
NOW WHAT?

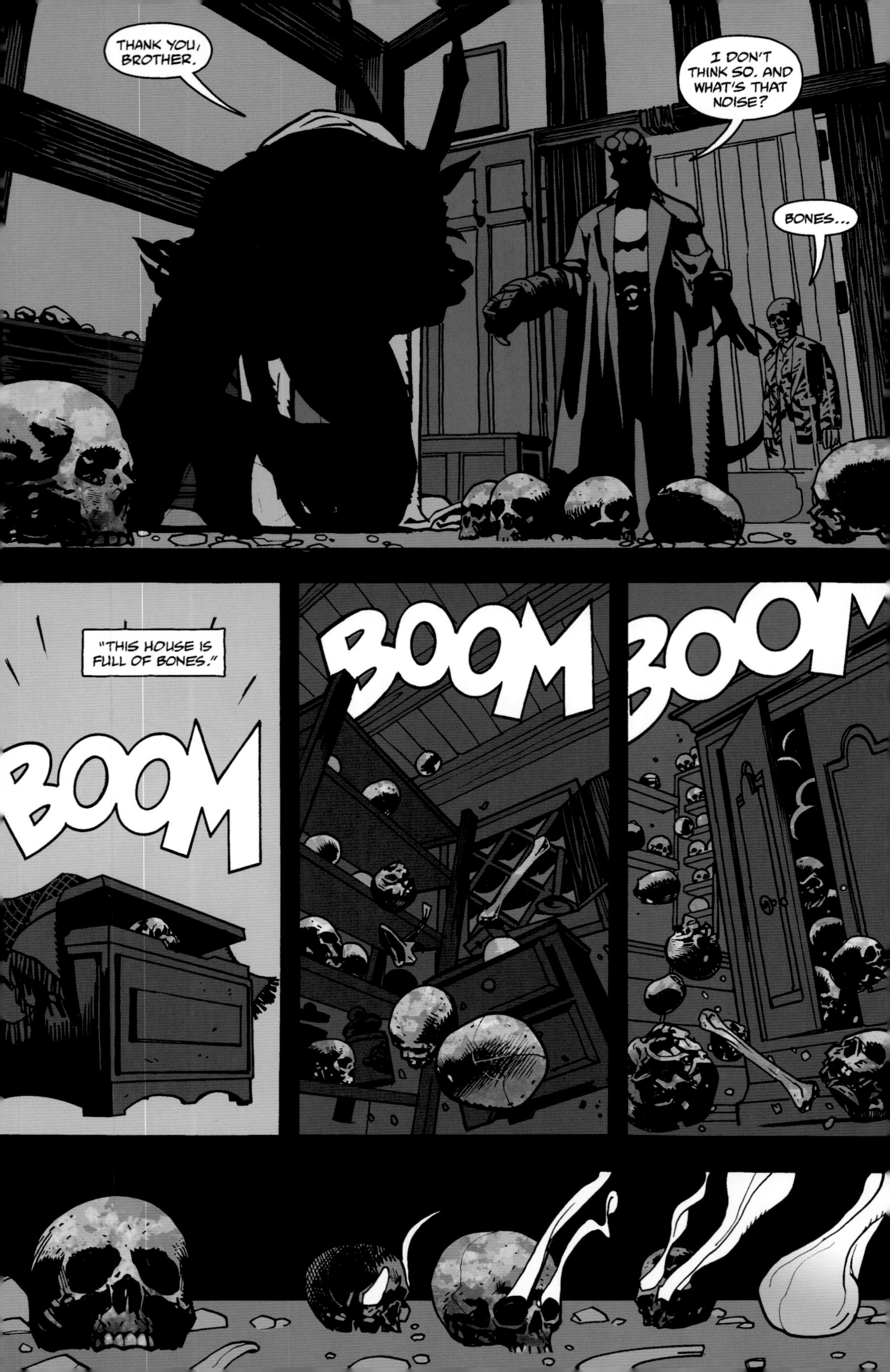
THANK YOU, BROTHER.
I DON'T THINK SO. AND WHAT'S THAT NOISE?
BONES...
"THIS HOUSE IS FULL OF BONES."
BOOM
BOOM
BOOM

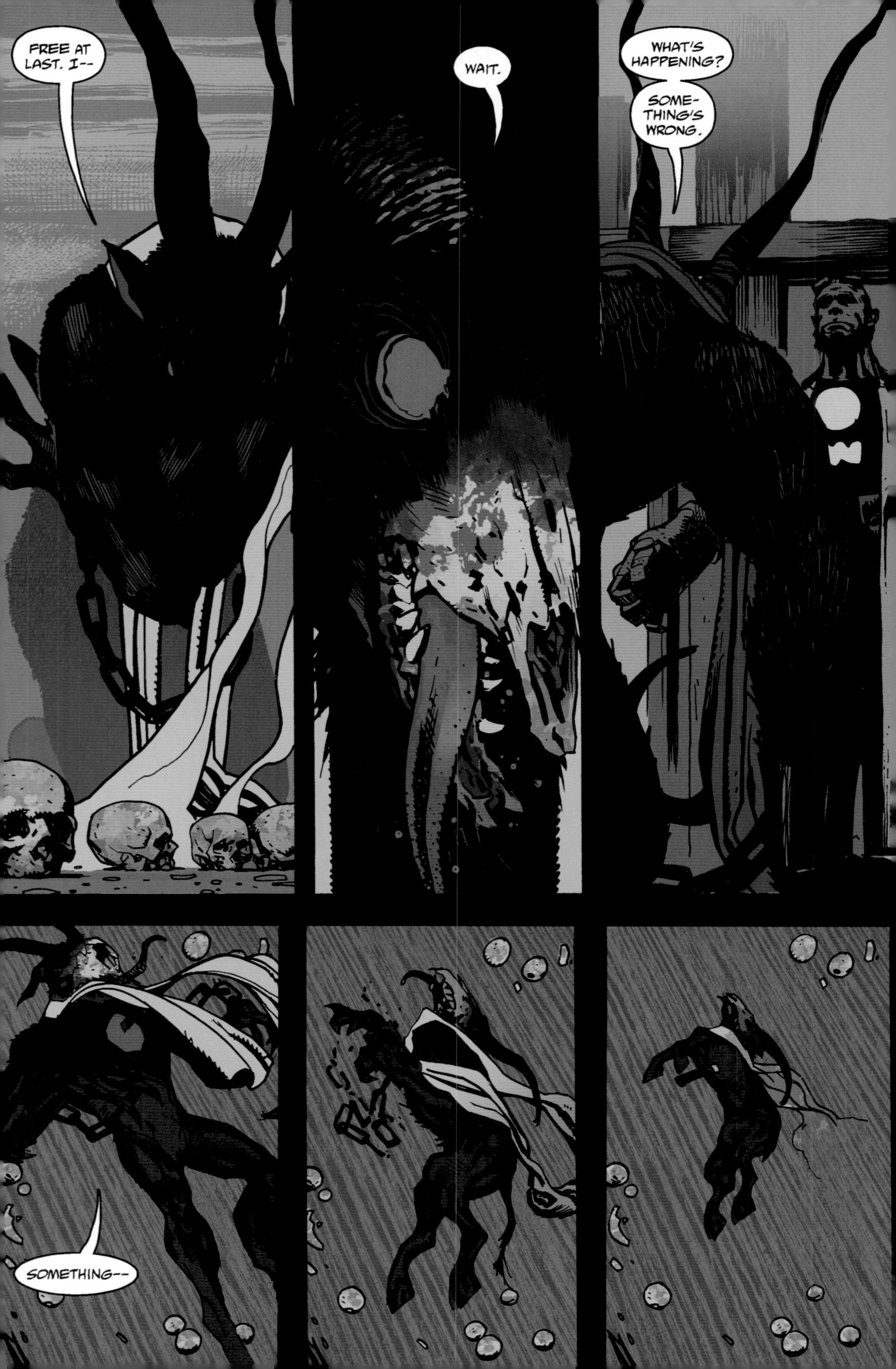
FREE AT LAST. I--
WAIT.
WHAT'S HAPPENING?
SOME-THING'S WRONG.
SOMETHING--

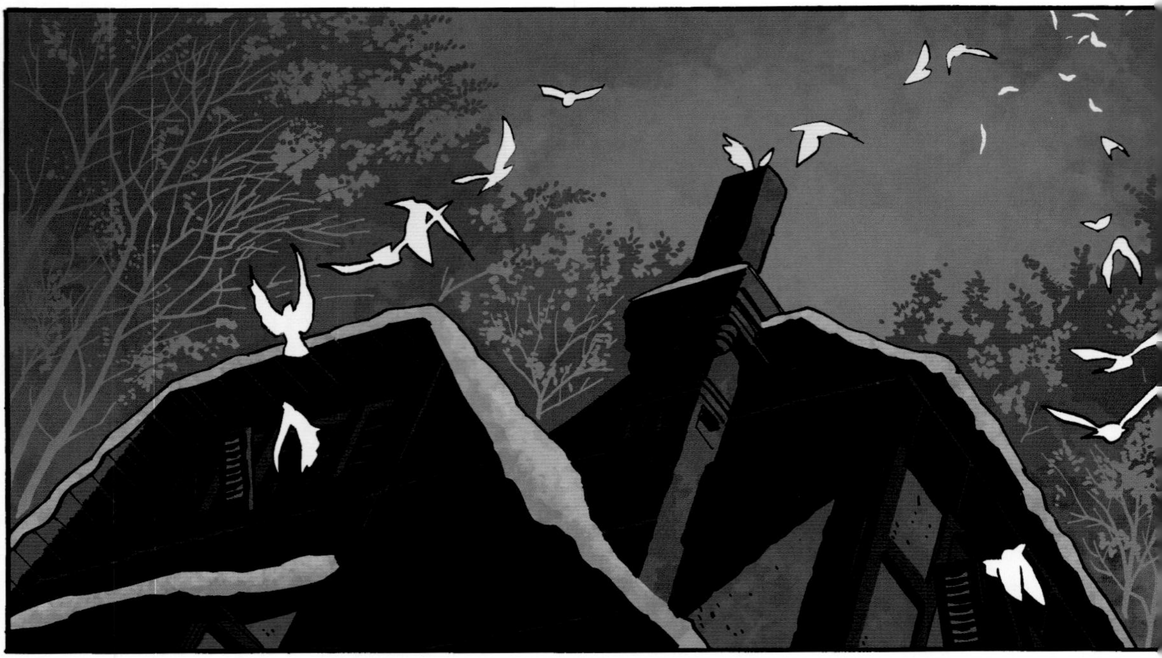

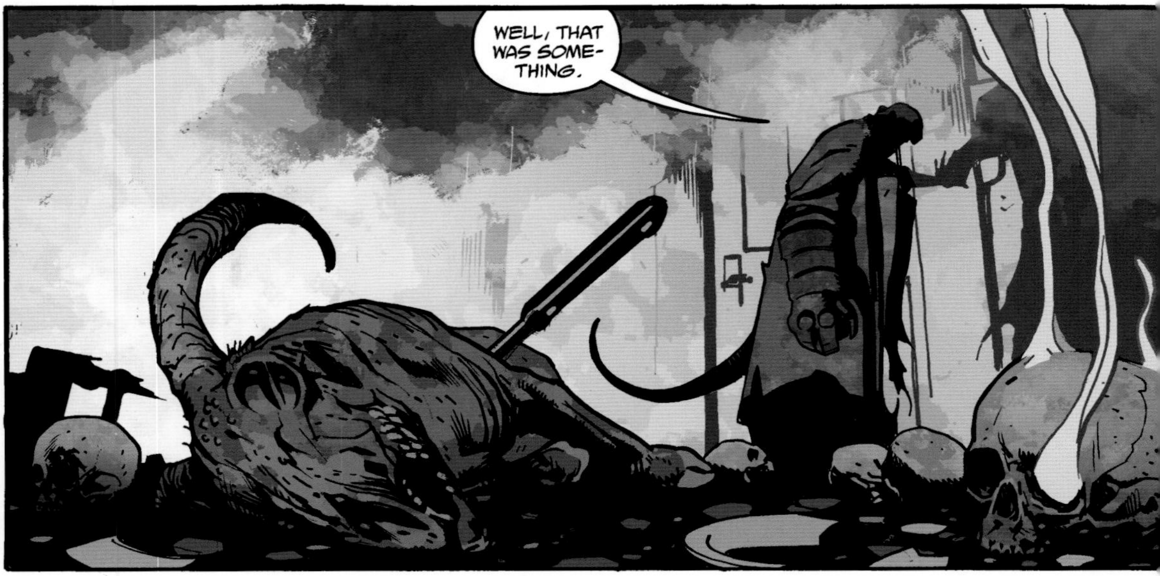
WELL, THAT WAS SOME-THING.

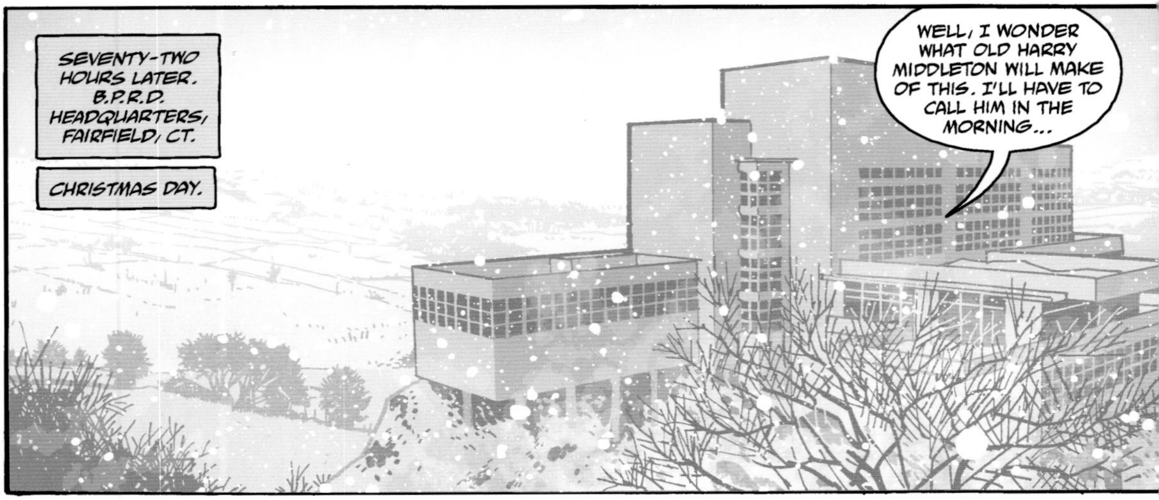
SEVENTY-TWO HOURS LATER. B.P.R.D. HEADQUARTERS, FAIRFIELD, CT.
CHRISTMAS DAY.
WELL, I WONDER WHAT OLD HARRY MIDDLETON WILL MAKE OF THIS. I'LL HAVE TO CALL HIM IN THE MORNING...

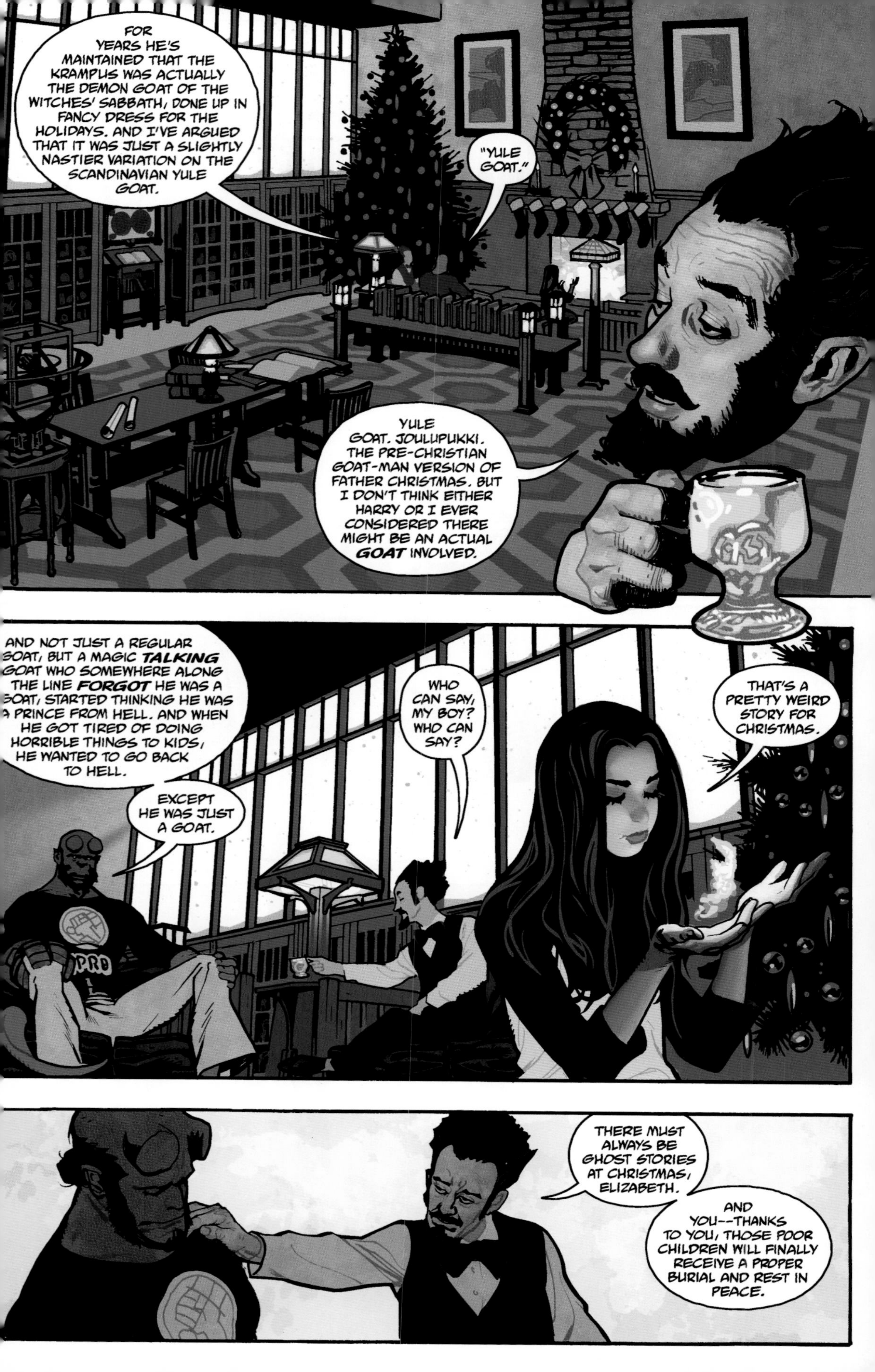
FOR YEARS HE'S MAINTAINED THAT THE KRAMPUS WAS ACTUALLY THE DEMON GOAT OF THE WITCHES' SABBATH, DONE UP IN FANCY DRESS FOR THE HOLIDAYS. AND I'VE ARGUED THAT IT WAS JUST A SLIGHTLY NASTIER VARIATION ON THE SCANDINAVIAN YULE GOAT.
"YULE GOAT."
YULE GOAT. JOULUPUKKI. THE PRE-CHRISTIAN GOAT-MAN VERSION OF FATHER CHRISTMAS. BUT I DON'T THINK EITHER HARRY OR I EVER CONSIDERED THERE MIGHT BE AN ACTUAL GOAT INVOLVED.
AND NOT JUST A REGULAR GOAT, BUT A MAGIC TALKING GOAT WHO SOMEWHERE ALONG THE LINE FORGOT HE WAS A GOAT, STARTED THINKING HE WAS A PRINCE FROM HELL. AND WHEN HE GOT TIRED OF DOING HORRIBLE THINGS TO KIDS, HE WANTED TO GO BACK TO HELL.
EXCEPT HE WAS JUST A GOAT.
WHO CAN SAY, MY BOY? WHO CAN SAY?
THAT'S A PRETTY WEIRD STORY FOR CHRISTMAS.
THERE MUST ALWAYS BE GHOST STORIES AT CHRISTMAS, ELIZABETH.
AND YOU--THANKS TO YOU, THOSE POOR CHILDREN WILL FINALLY RECEIVE A PROPER BURIAL AND REST IN PEACE.
PRO

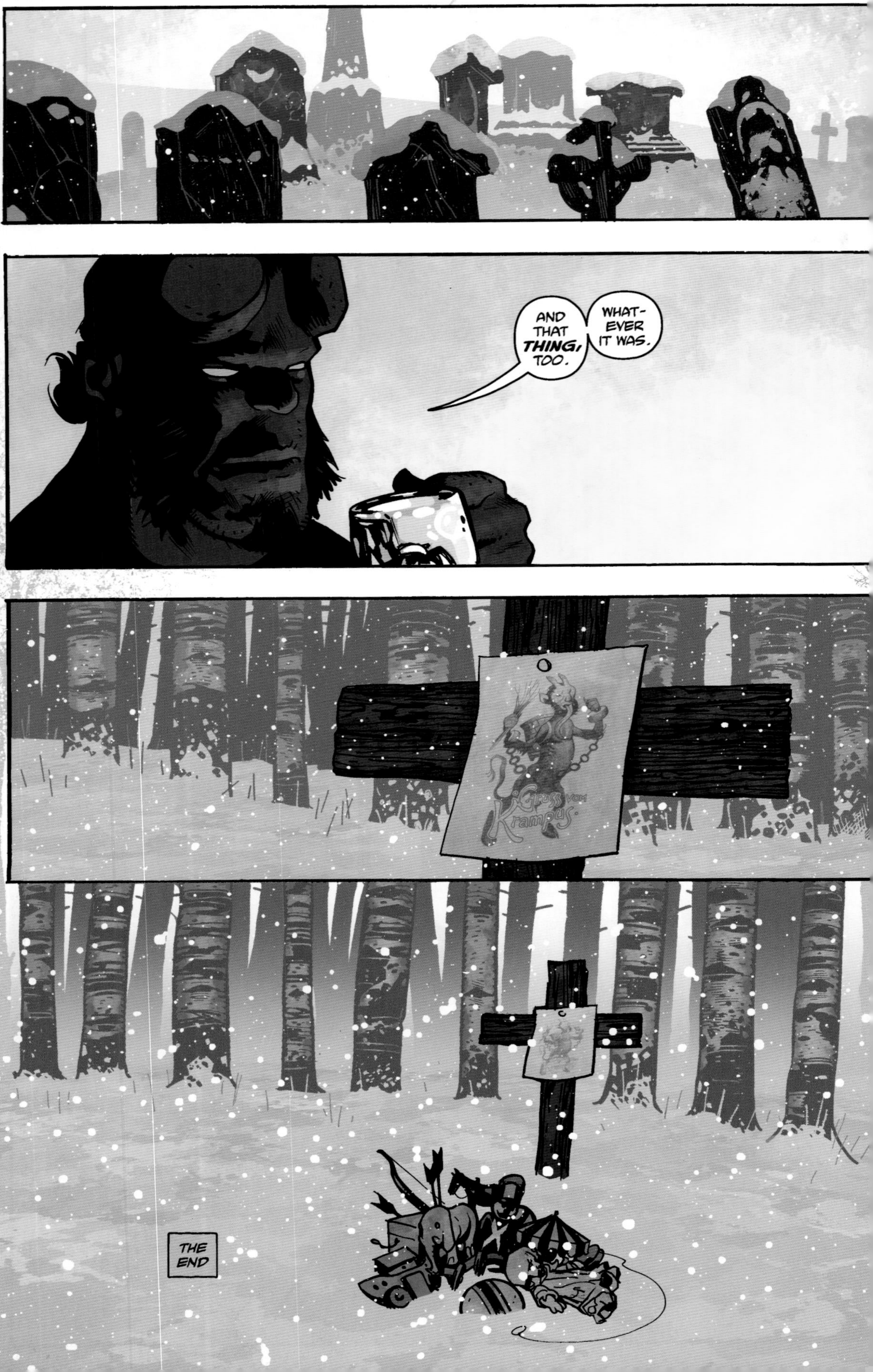
AND THAT THING, TOO.
WHAT-EVER IT WAS.
Gruss vom Krampus
THE END

RETURN OF THE LAMBTON WORM

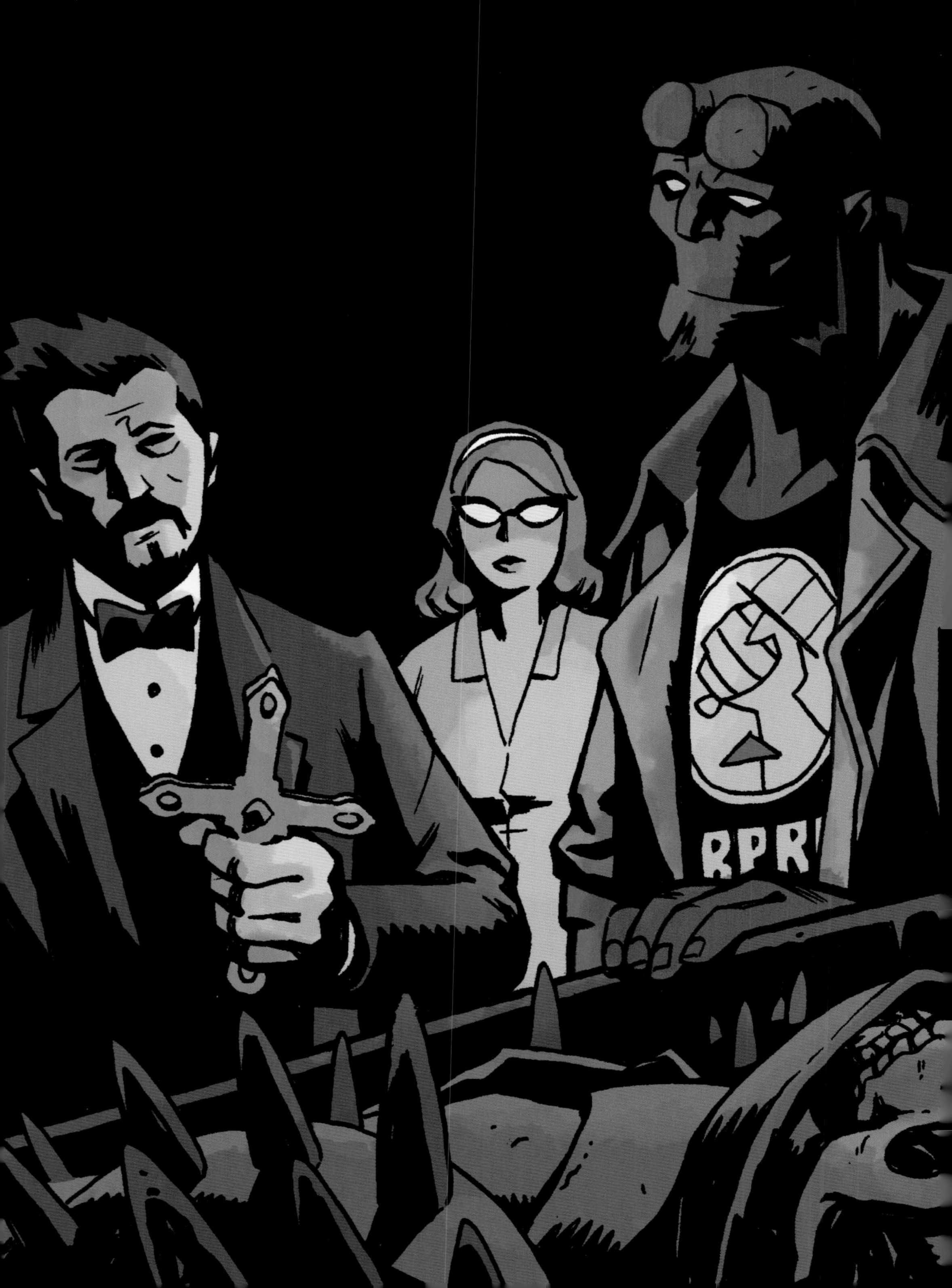
BPR

Hellboy: Return of the Lambton Worm

STORY:
MIKE MIGNOLA

ART:
BEN STENBECK

COLOR:
DAVE STEWART

LETTERS:
CLEM ROBINS

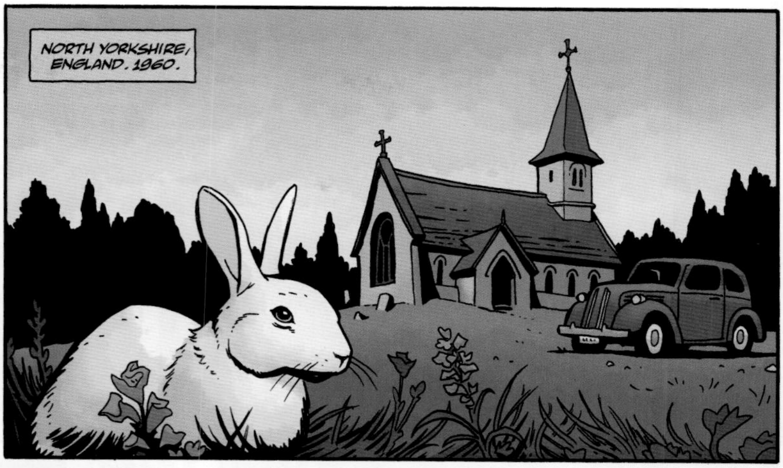

NORTH YORKSHIRE, ENGLAND. 1960.

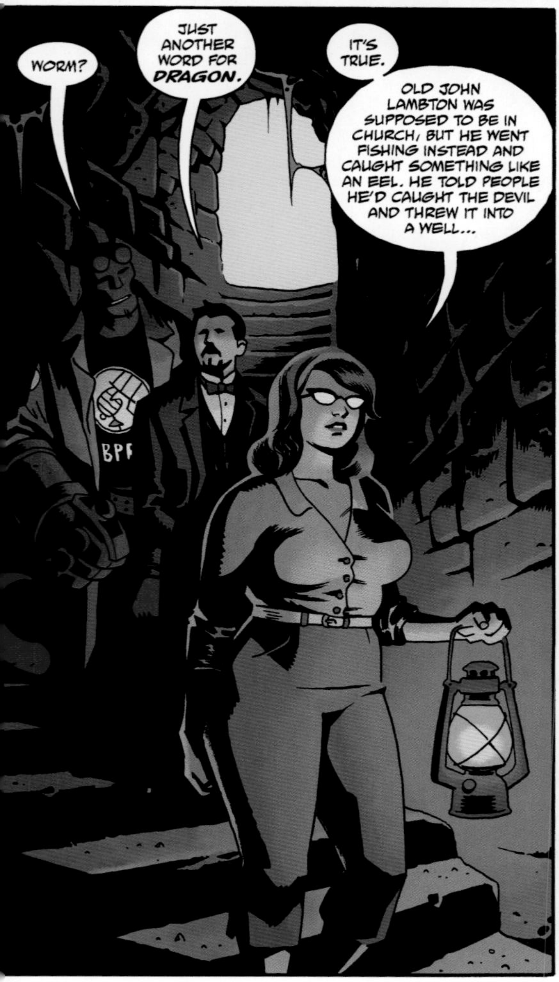

WORM?
JUST ANOTHER WORD FOR DRAGON.
IT'S TRUE.
OLD JOHN LAMBTON WAS SUPPOSED TO BE IN CHURCH, BUT HE WENT FISHING INSTEAD AND CAUGHT SOMETHING LIKE AN EEL. HE TOLD PEOPLE HE'D CAUGHT THE DEVIL AND THREW IT INTO A WELL...
BPR

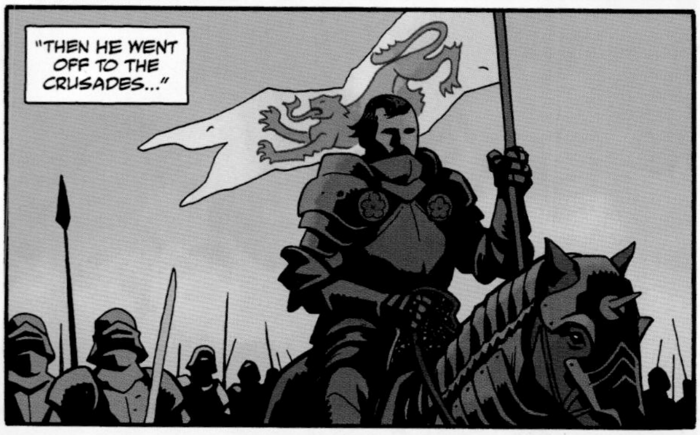

"THEN HE WENT OFF TO THE CRUSADES..."

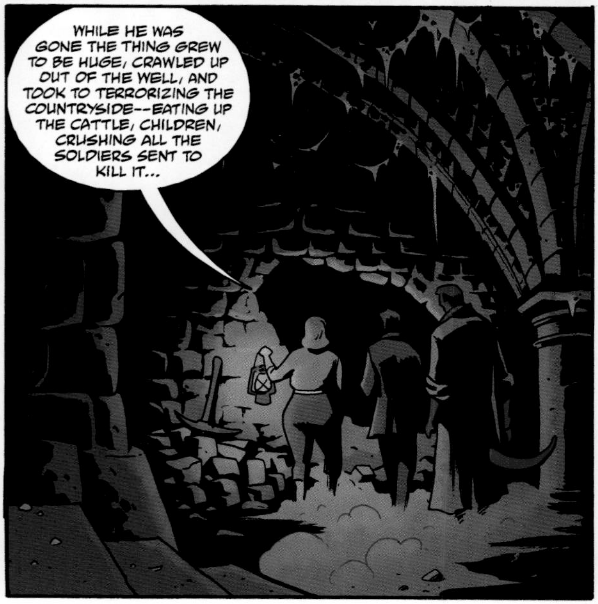

WHILE HE WAS GONE THE THING GREW TO BE HUGE, CRAWLED UP OUT OF THE WELL, AND TOOK TO TERRORIZING THE COUNTRYSIDE--EATING UP THE CATTLE, CHILDREN, CRUSHING ALL THE SOLDIERS SENT TO KILL IT...

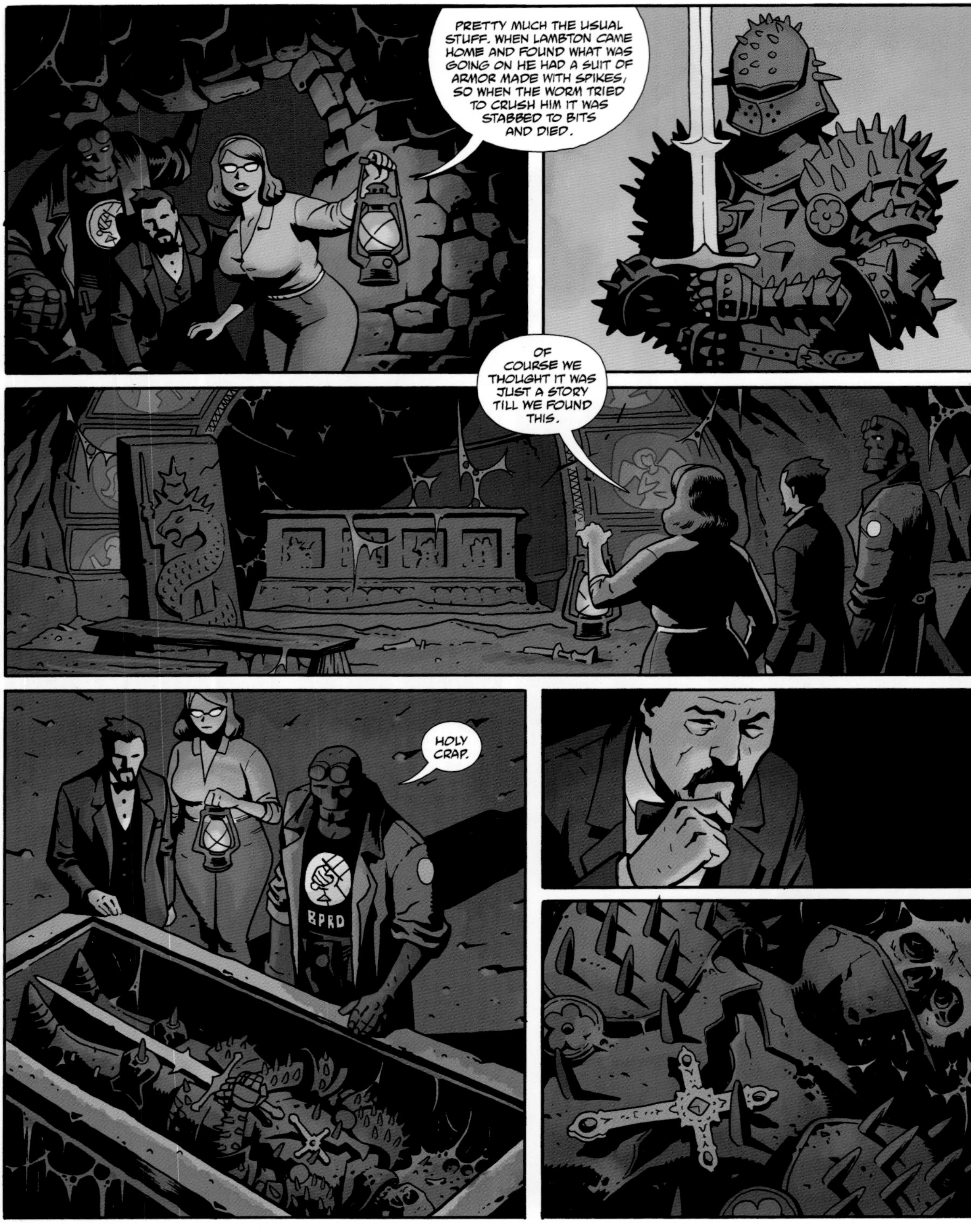
PRETTY MUCH THE USUAL STUFF. WHEN LAMBTON CAME HOME AND FOUND WHAT WAS GOING ON HE HAD A SUIT OF ARMOR MADE WITH SPIKES, SO WHEN THE WORM TRIED TO CRUSH HIM IT WAS STABBED TO BITS AND DIED.
OF COURSE WE THOUGHT IT WAS JUST A STORY TILL WE FOUND THIS.
HOLY CRAP.

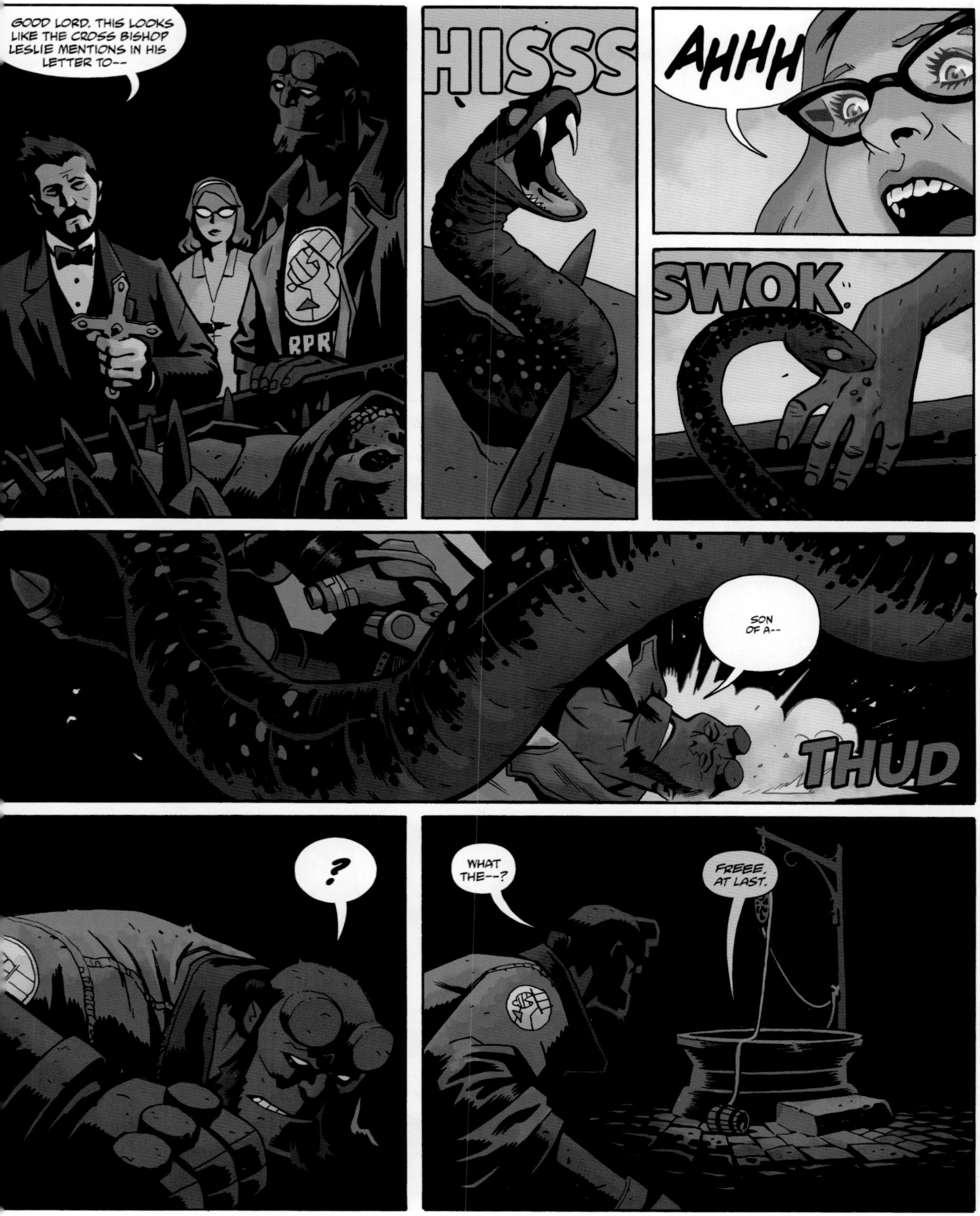
GOOD LORD. THIS LOOKS LIKE THE CROSS BISHOP LESLIE MENTIONS IN HIS LETTER TO--
HISSS
AHHH
SWOK
SON OF A--
THUD
?
WHAT THE--?
FREEE, AT LAST.

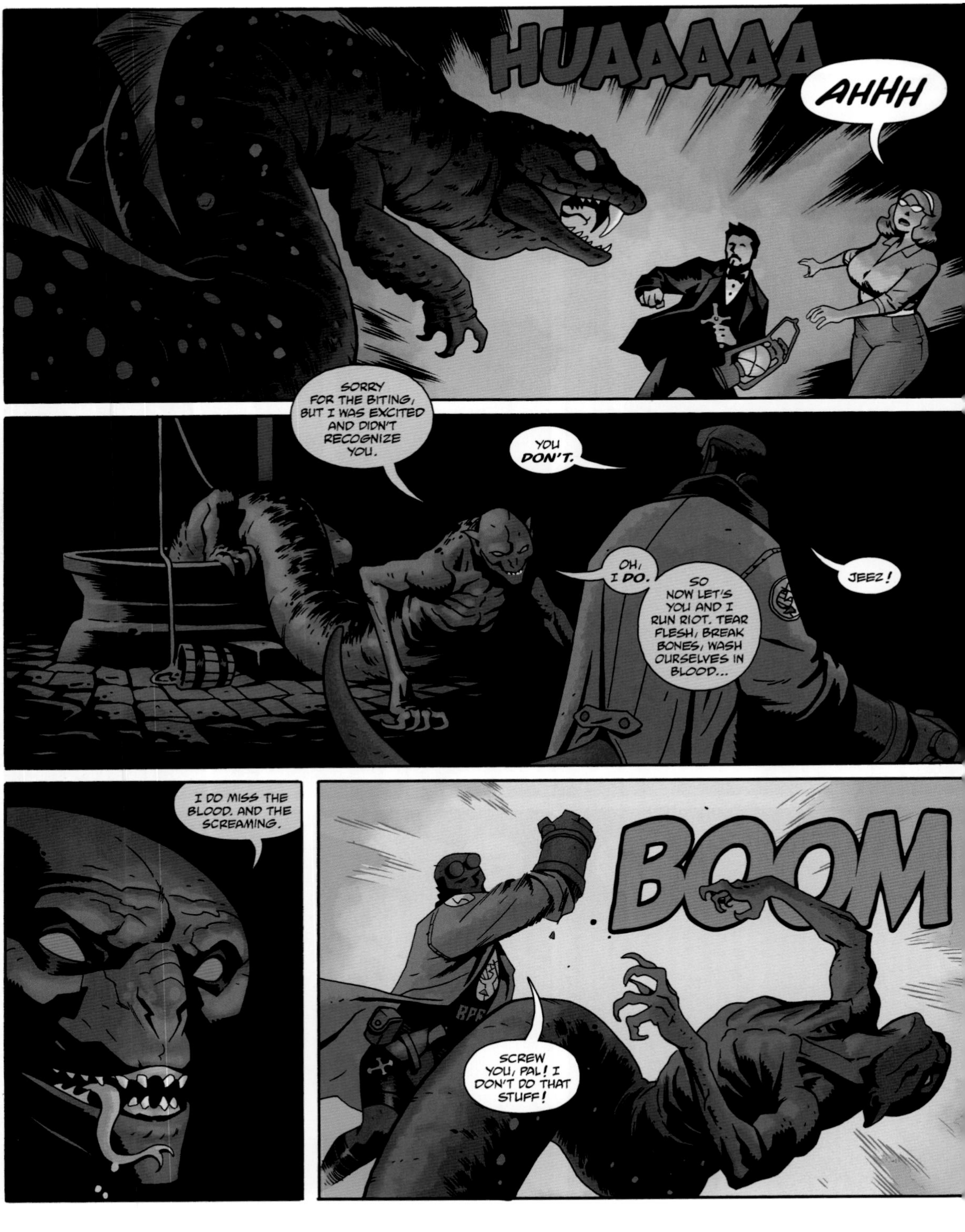
HUAAAAA
AHHH
SORRY FOR THE BITING, BUT I WAS EXCITED AND DIDN'T RECOGNIZE YOU.
YOU DON'T.
OH, I DO.
SO NOW LET'S YOU AND I RUN RIOT. TEAR FLESH, BREAK BONES, WASH OURSELVES IN BLOOD...
JEEZ!
I DO MISS THE BLOOD. AND THE SCREAMING.
BOOM
SCREW YOU, PAL! I DON'T DO THAT STUFF!

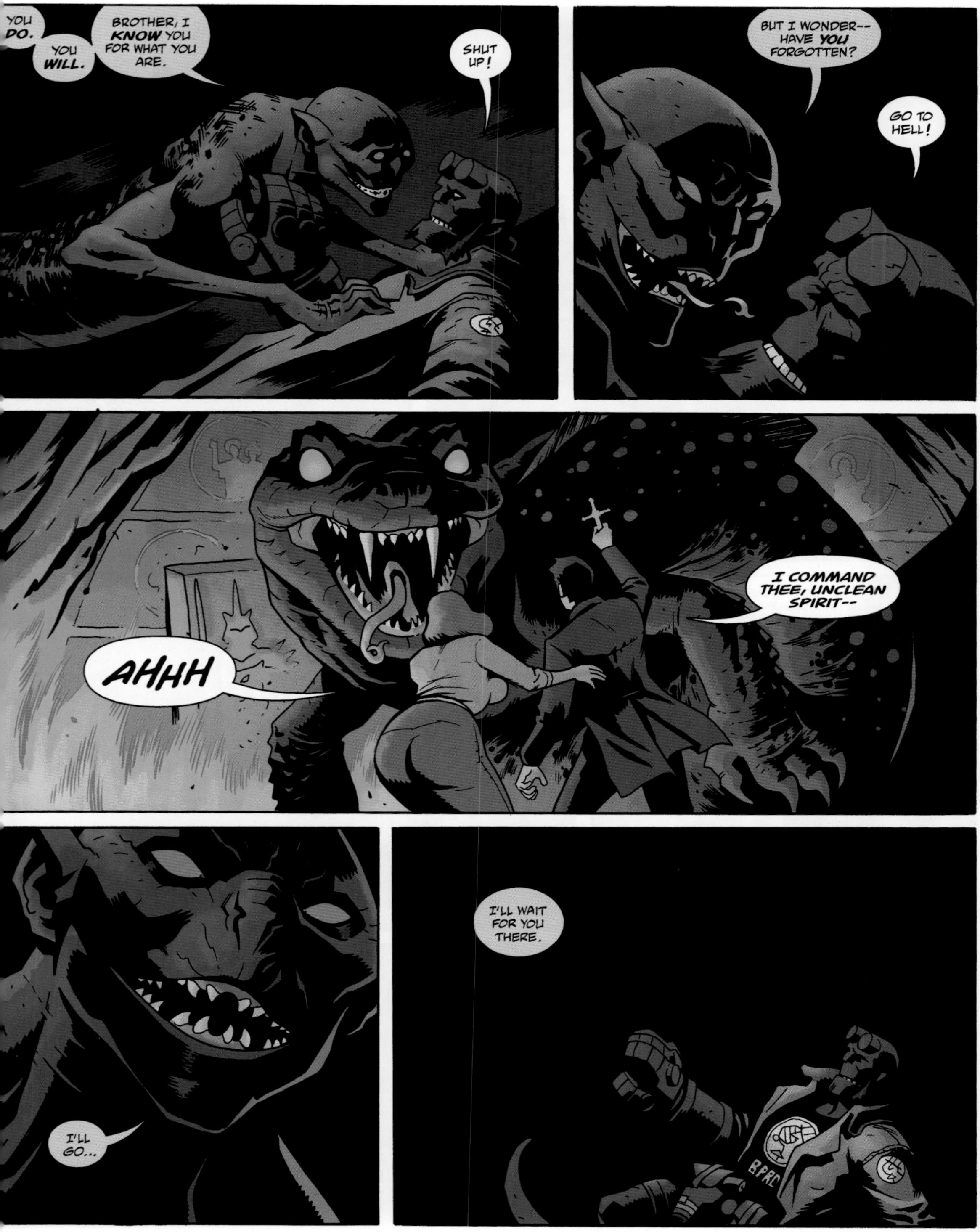
YOU DO.
YOU WILL.
BROTHER, I KNOW YOU FOR WHAT YOU ARE.
SHUT UP!
BUT I WONDER-- HAVE YOU FORGOTTEN?
GO TO HELL!
I COMMAND THEE, UNCLEAN SPIRIT--
AHHH
I'LL GO...
I'LL WAIT FOR YOU THERE.
BPRD

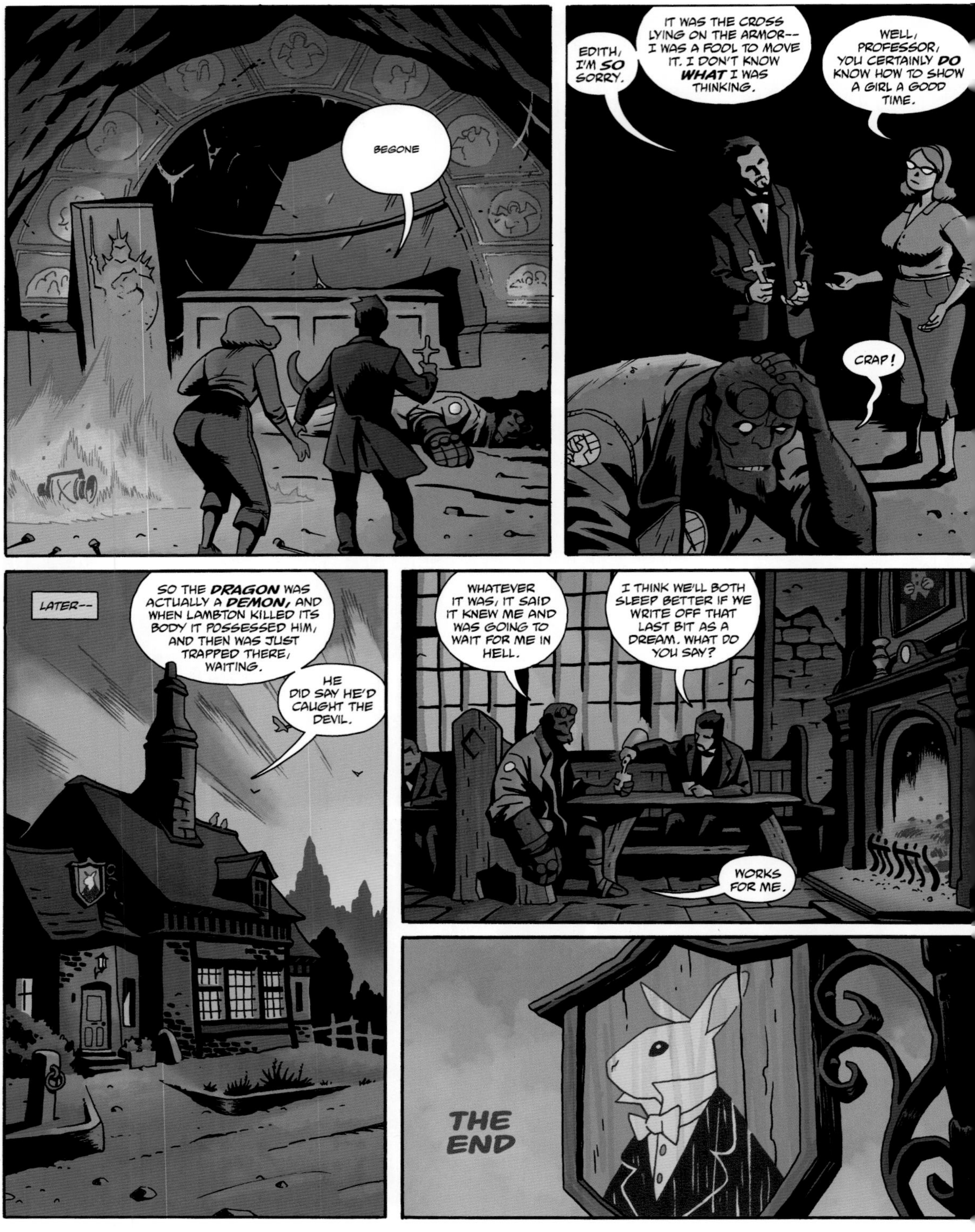
BEGONE
EDITH, I'M SO SORRY.
IT WAS THE CROSS LYING ON THE ARMOR-- I WAS A FOOL TO MOVE IT. I DON'T KNOW WHAT I WAS THINKING.
WELL, PROFESSOR, YOU CERTAINLY DO KNOW HOW TO SHOW A GIRL A GOOD TIME.
CRAP!
LATER--
SO THE DRAGON WAS ACTUALLY A DEMON, AND WHEN LAMBTON KILLED ITS BODY IT POSSESSED HIM, AND THEN WAS JUST TRAPPED THERE, WAITING.
HE DID SAY HE'D CAUGHT THE DEVIL.
WHATEVER IT WAS, IT SAID IT KNEW ME AND WAS GOING TO WAIT FOR ME IN HELL.
I THINK WE'LL BOTH SLEEP BETTER IF WE WRITE OFF THAT LAST BIT AS A DREAM. WHAT DO YOU SAY?
WORKS FOR ME.
THE END

HELLBOY™ AND THE B.P.R.D. SKETCHBOOK

Notes by Katii O'Brien

THE BEAST OF VARGU

Duncan's sketches for our mother and daughter characters.

Following four pages: Pencils for story pages 15–18.

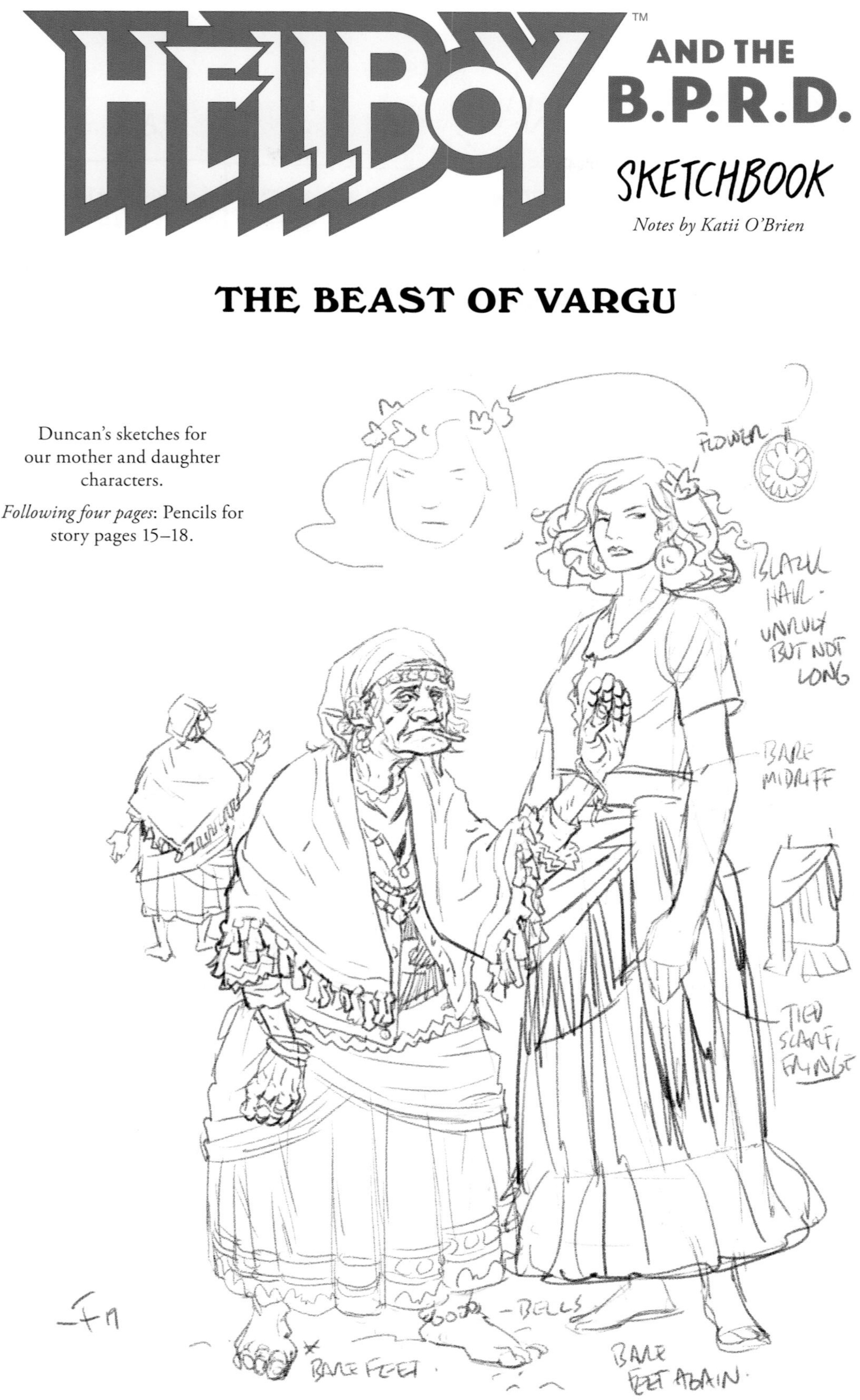
FLOWER
BLACK HAIR - UNRULY BUT NOT LONG
BARE MIDRIFF
TIED SCARF, FRINGE
BELLS
BARE FEET
BARE FEET AGAIN.
-FM

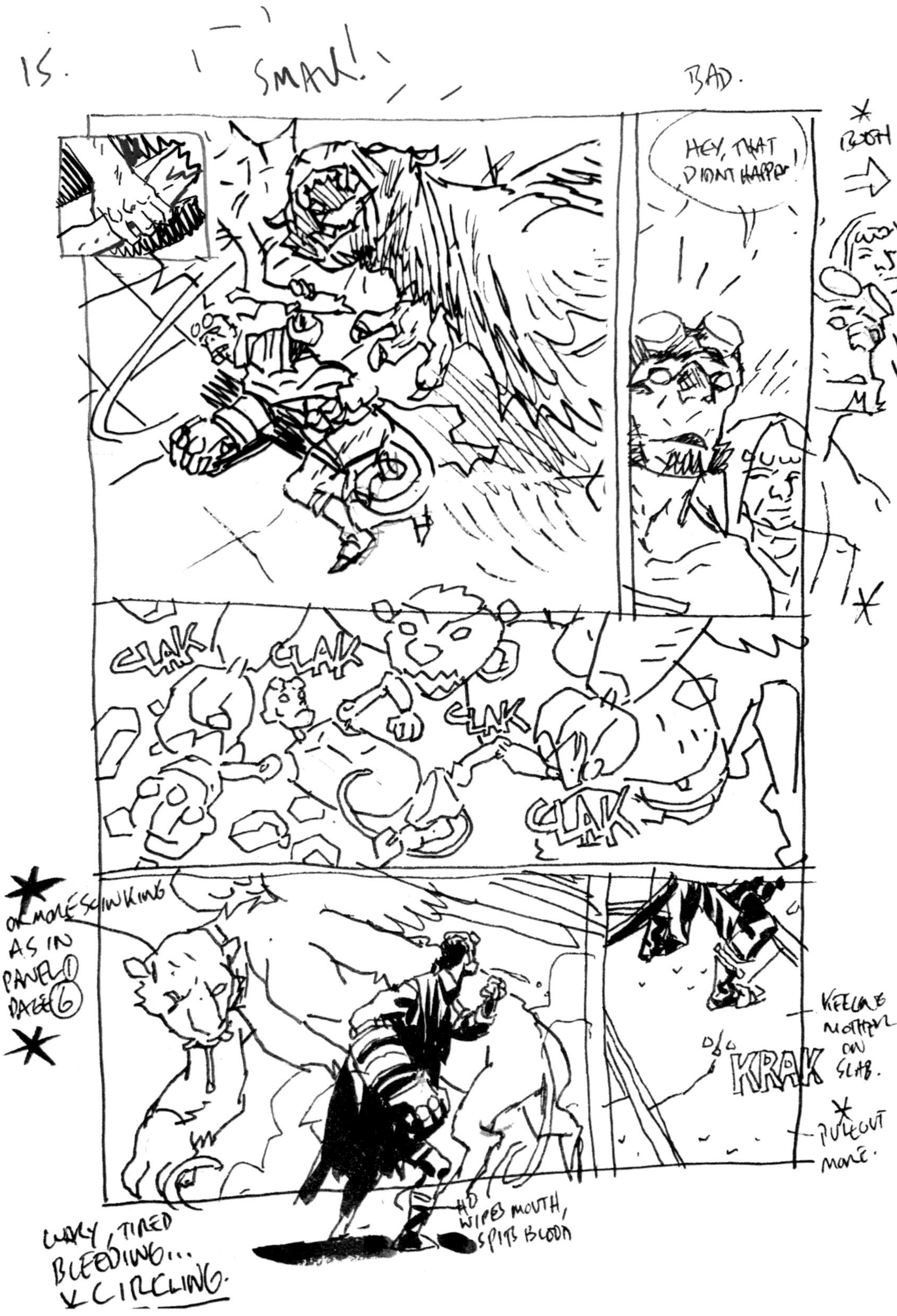
15.
SMAK!
BAD.
HEY, THAT DIDN'T HAPPEN!
BOTH
CLAK
CLAK
CLAK
CLAK
OR MORE SCHWINKING AS IN PANEL 1 PAGE 6
KRAK
KEELING MOTHER ON SLAB.
PULL OUT MORE.
HB WIPES MOUTH, SPITS BLOOD
WARY, TIRED BLEEDING... & CIRCLING.

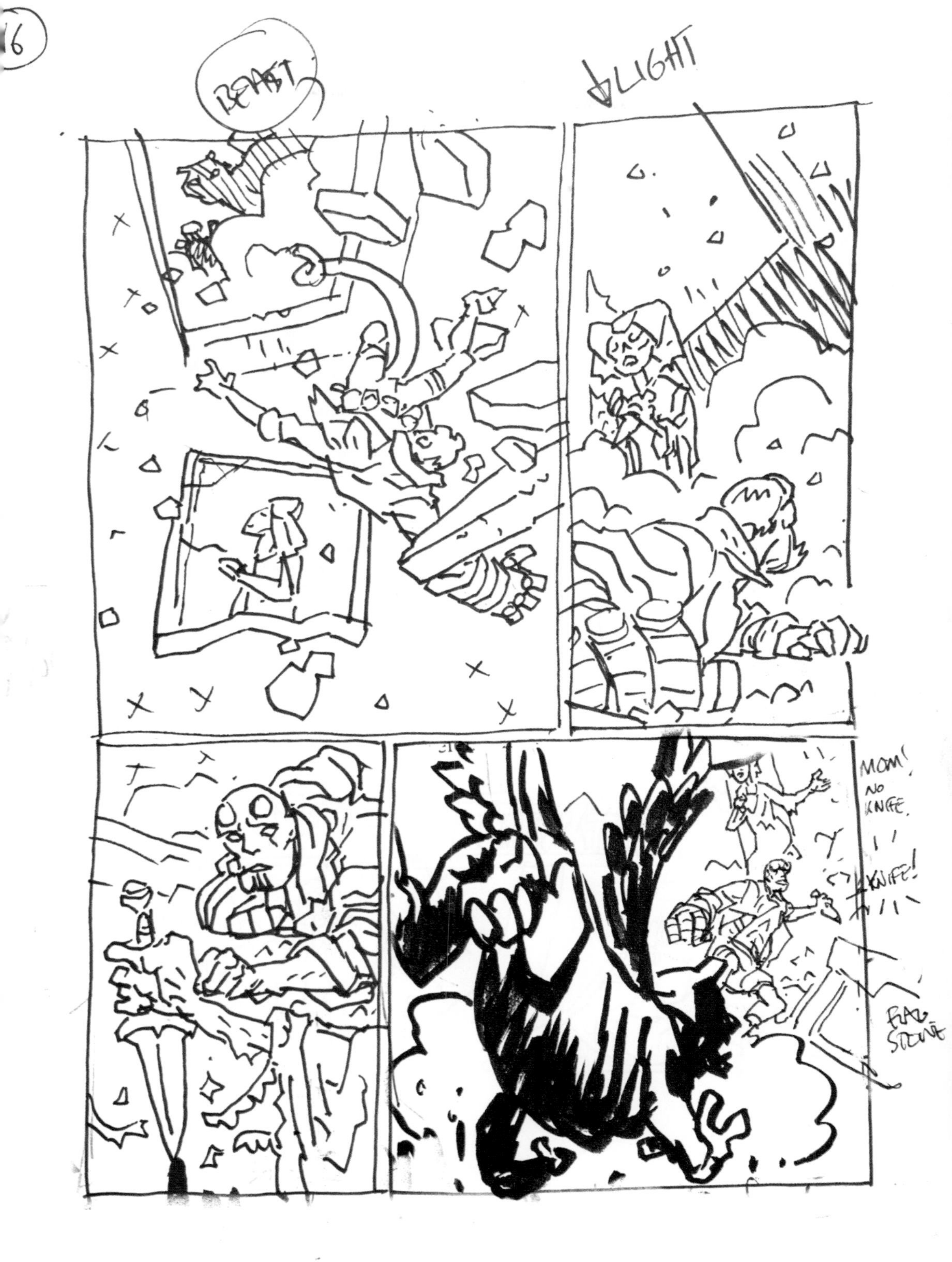
6
BEAST
LIGHT
MOM!
NO KNIFE.
KNIFE!
FLAG STONE

17

SHRD.

SHRD.

PANEL 2...
CURTAINS
ALREADY CLOSI

PSY
NAILED

18

REVERSE OF CASTLE RUINS — SUN COMING UP.

DOORFRAME

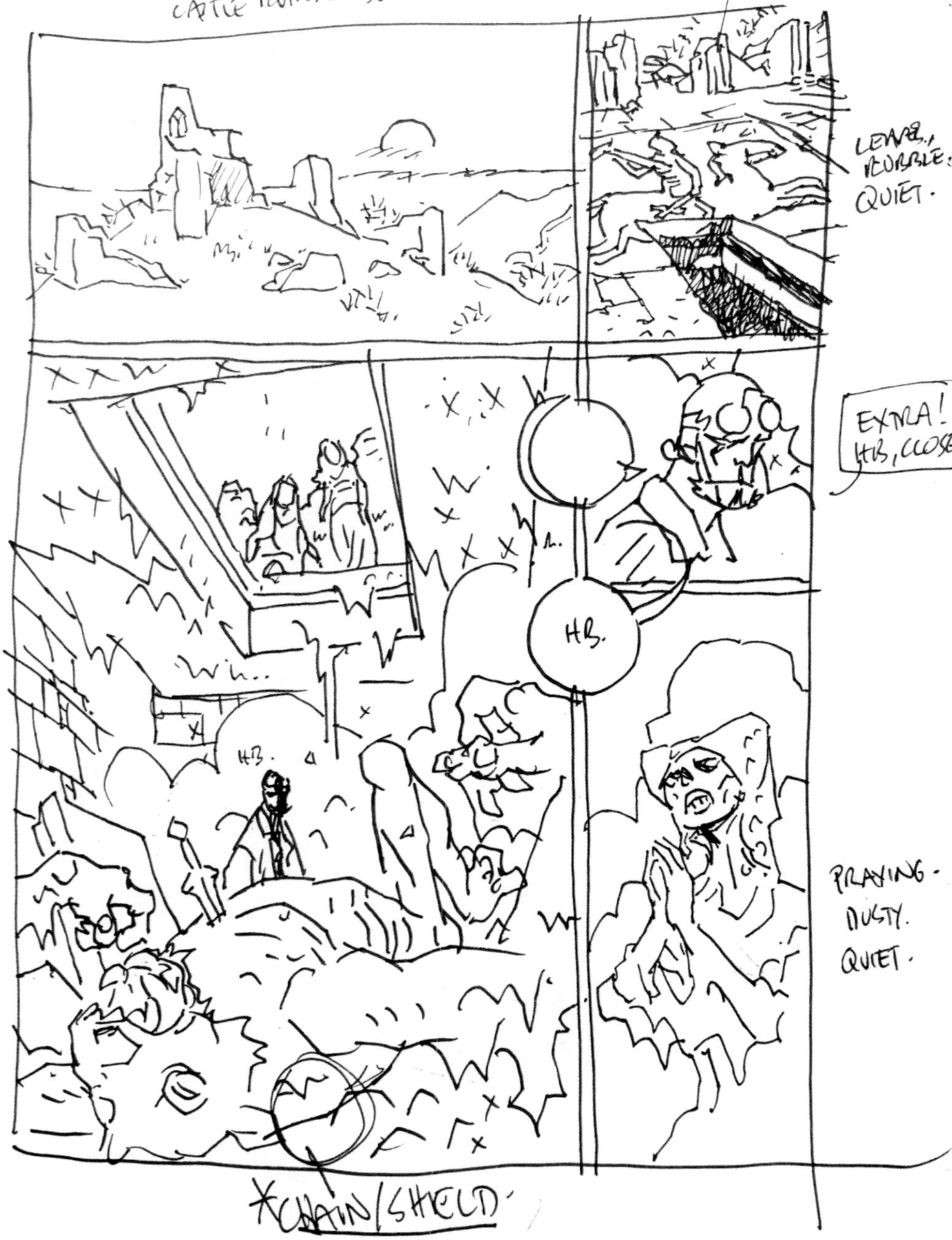
HB.
HB.

LEAVES, RUBBLE. QUIET.

EXTRA! HB, CLOSE

DUSTY. DRIED OUT.

PRAYING. DUSTY. QUIET.

*CHAIN/SHIELD

* HB ON TOP OF BODY, OR BEHIND?

HB—TALLER—CRUTCH

ROPE INTO CRYPT.

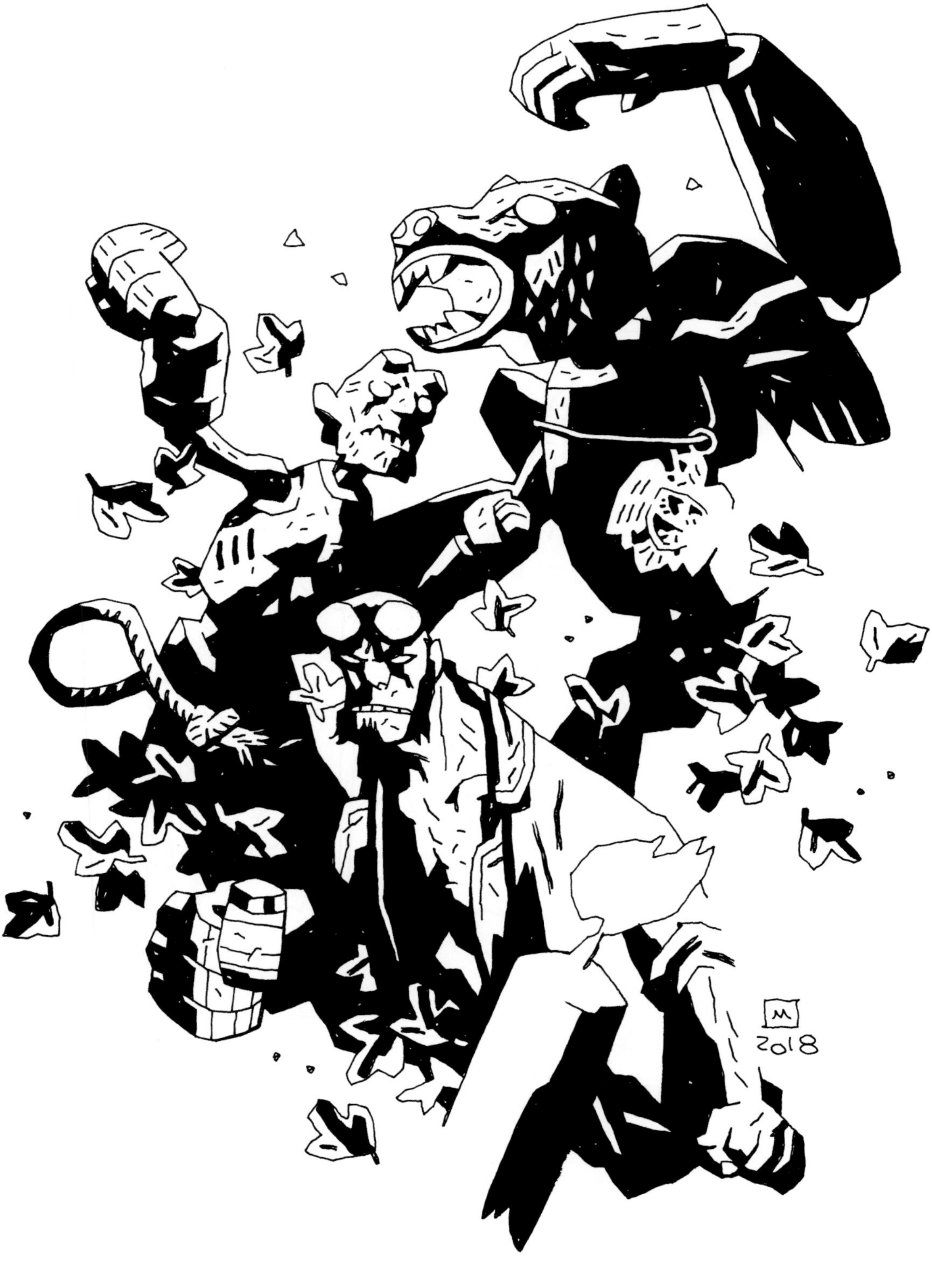
M
2018

SATURN RETURNS

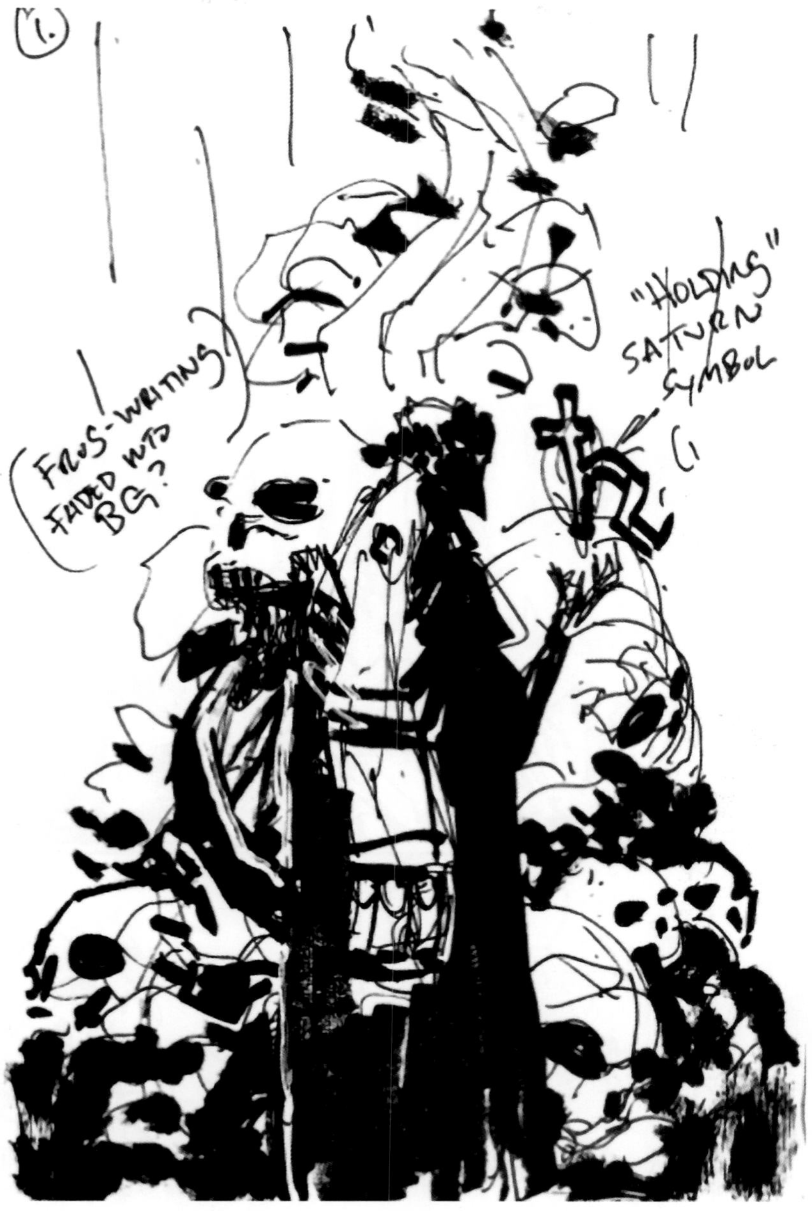

1.
FROG-WRITING FADED INTO BG?
"HOLDING" SATURN SYMBOL

Chris Mitten's unused second sketch for the first issue of *Saturn Returns*.

Following pages: Chris's layouts and pencils for the double-page spread revealing our basement full of corpses. These are story pages 2–3 of *Saturn Returns* #1.

Facing: Mignola's first attempt at the variant cover for *The Beast of Vargu*.

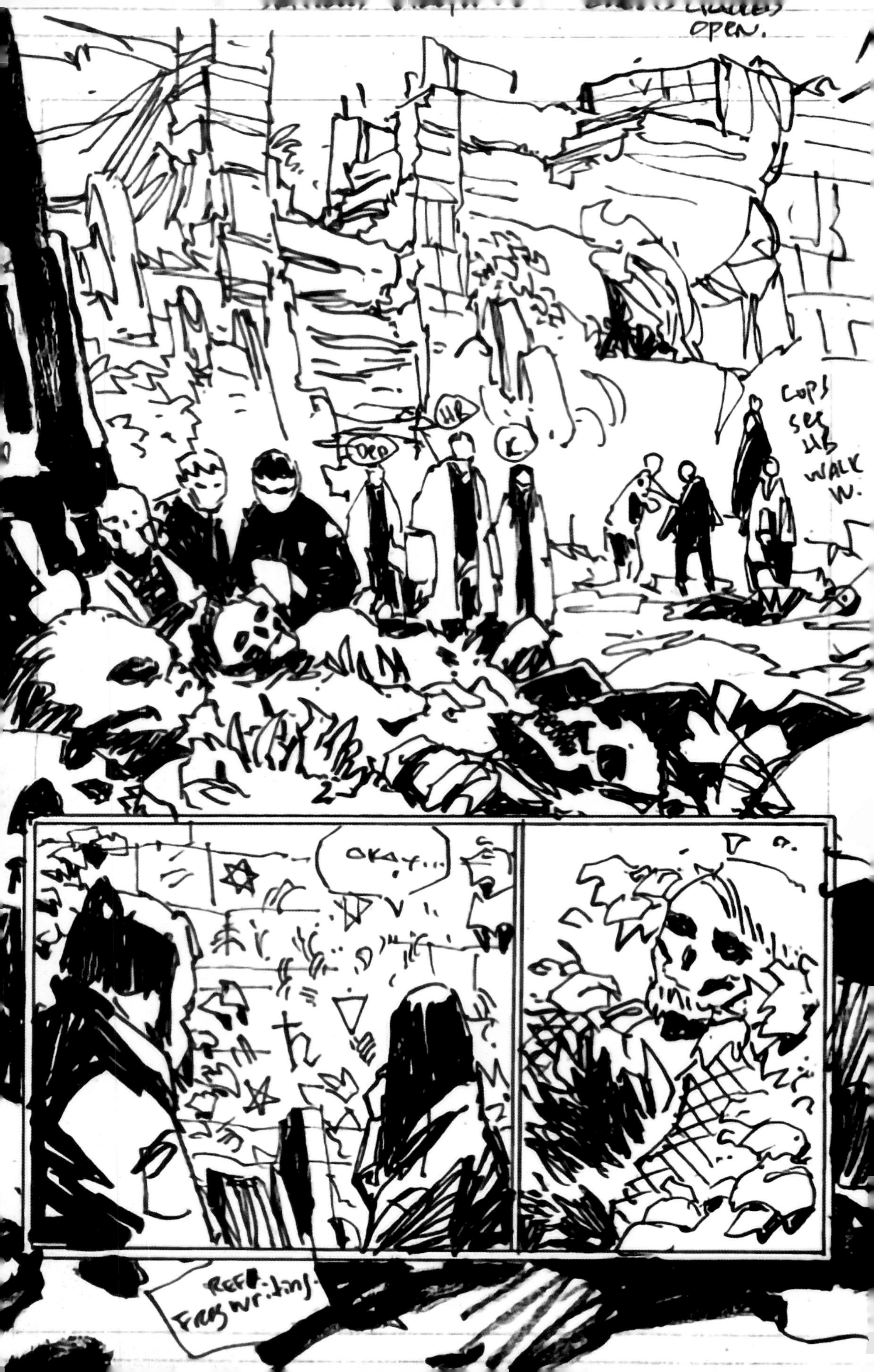
OPEN.
HB
DEP
K
COPS SEE HB WALK W.
OKAY...

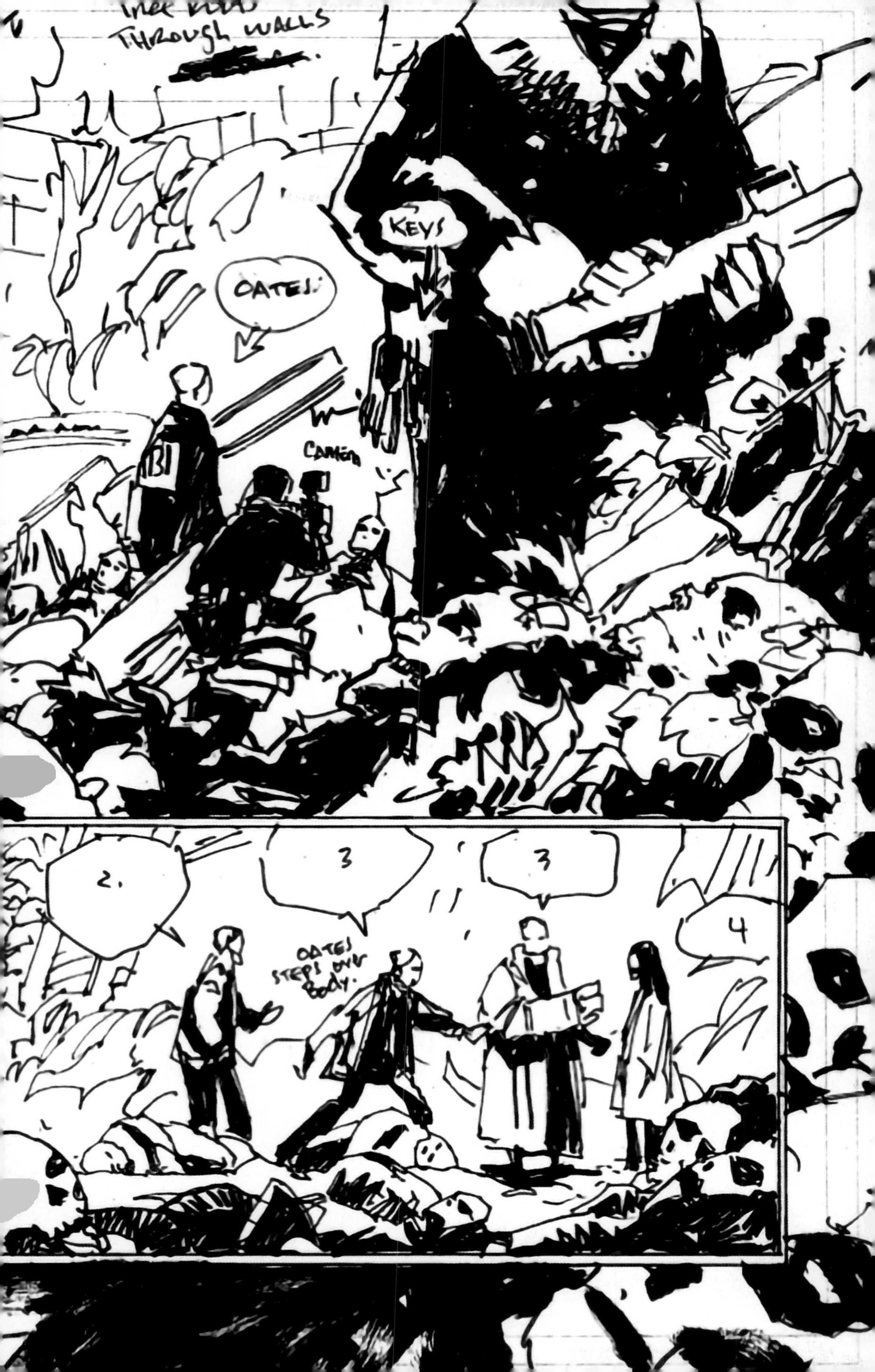

THROUGH WALLS
KEYS
OATES!
Camera
2.
3
3
4
OATES STEPS OVER BODY.

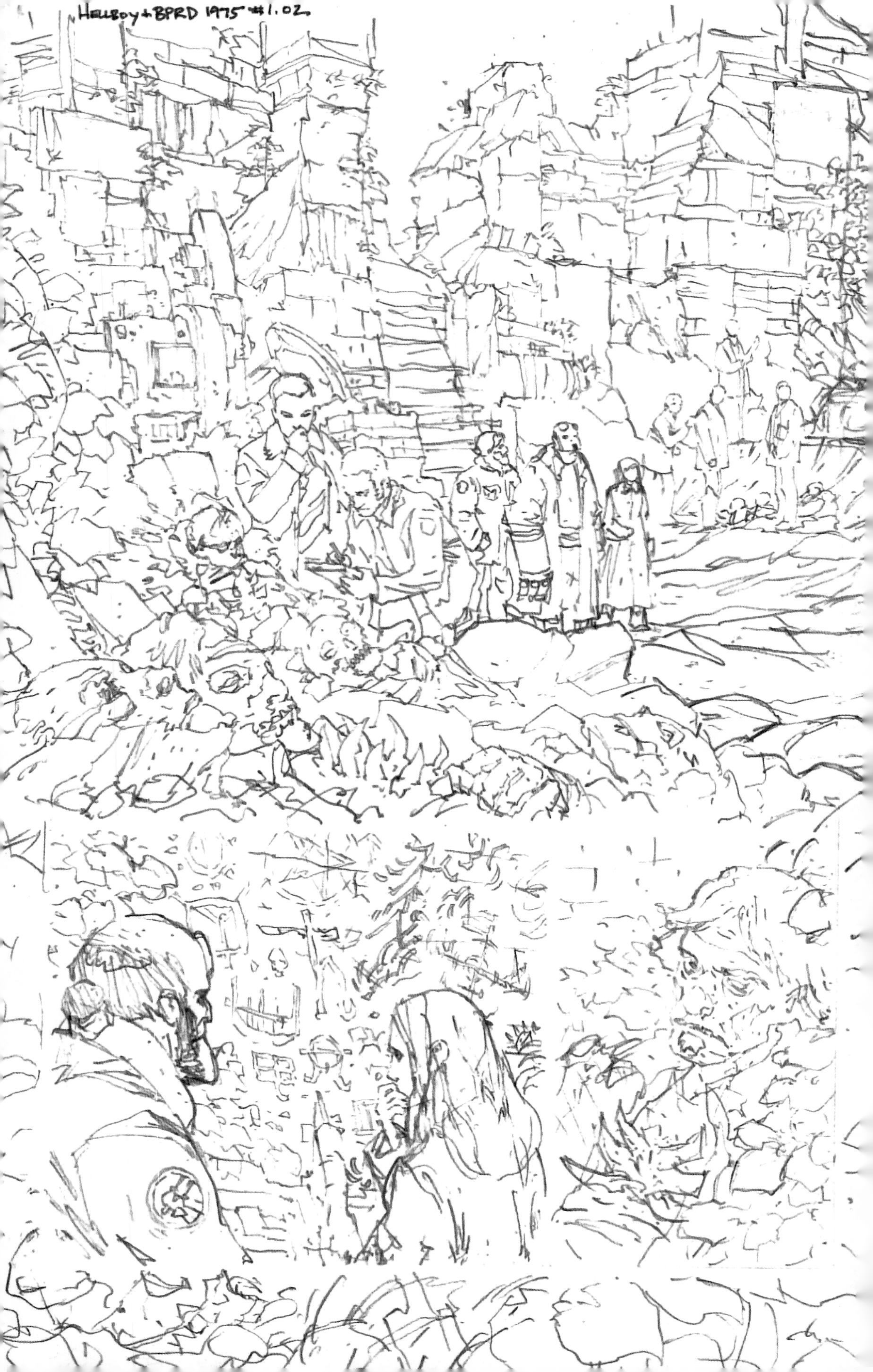
HELLBOY + BPRD 1975 #1.02

HELLBOY + BPRD 1975 #1.03

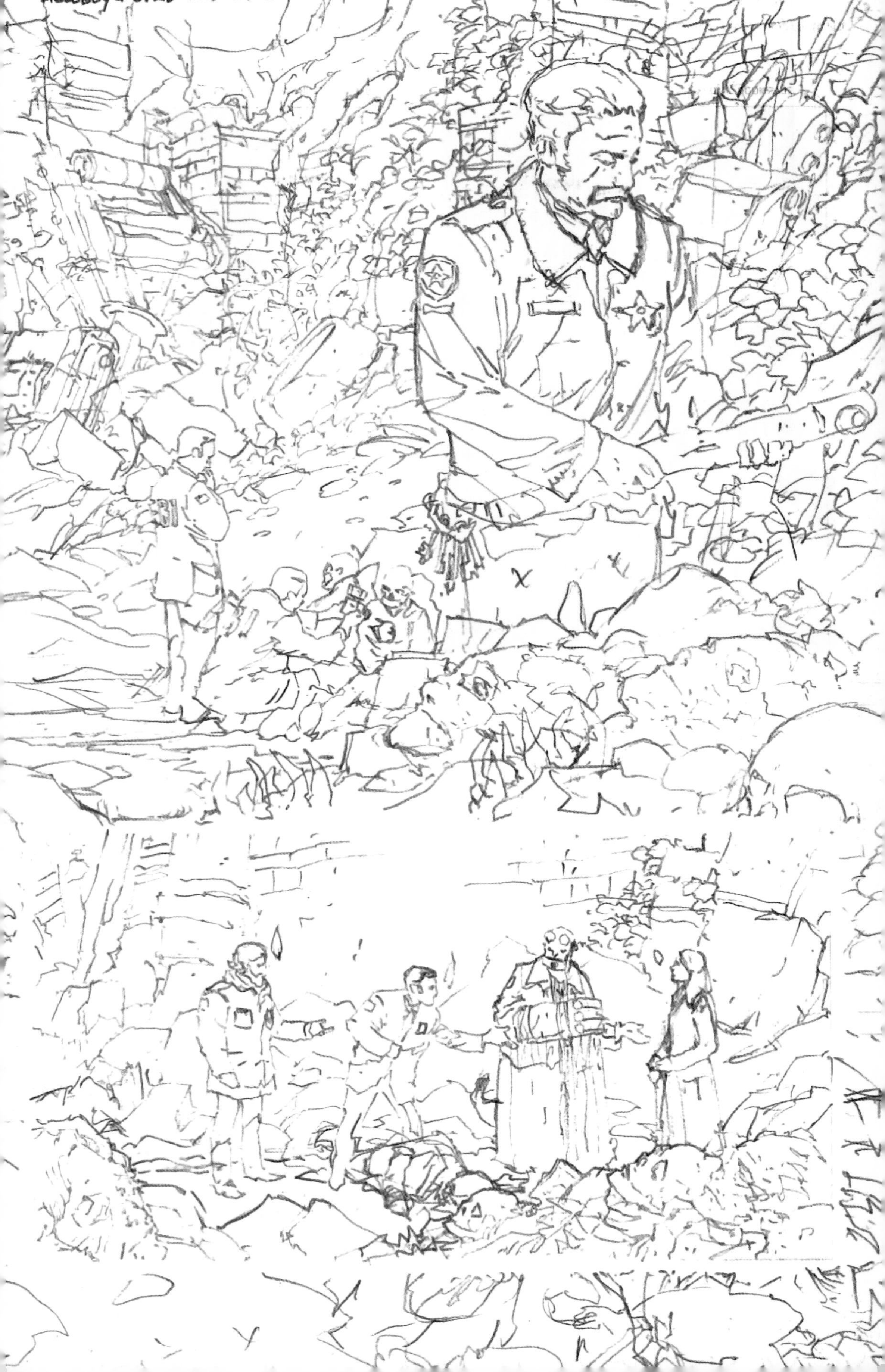

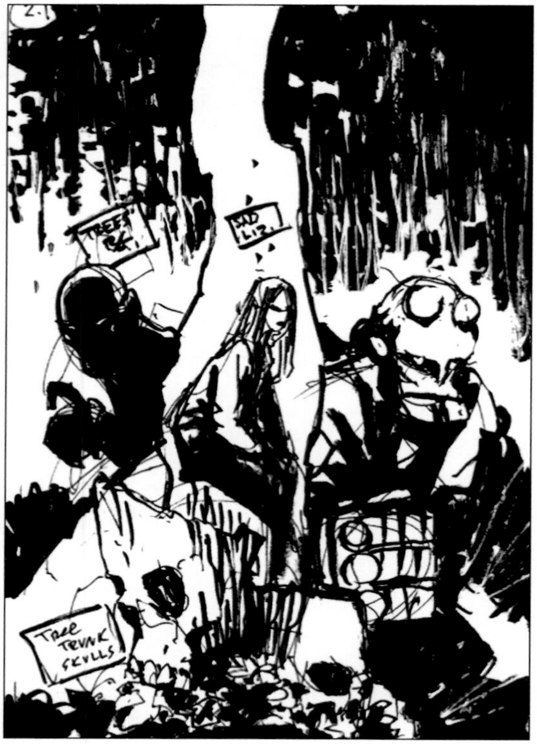
2.1
TREES BG.
MAD LIZ.
TREE TRUNK SKULLS

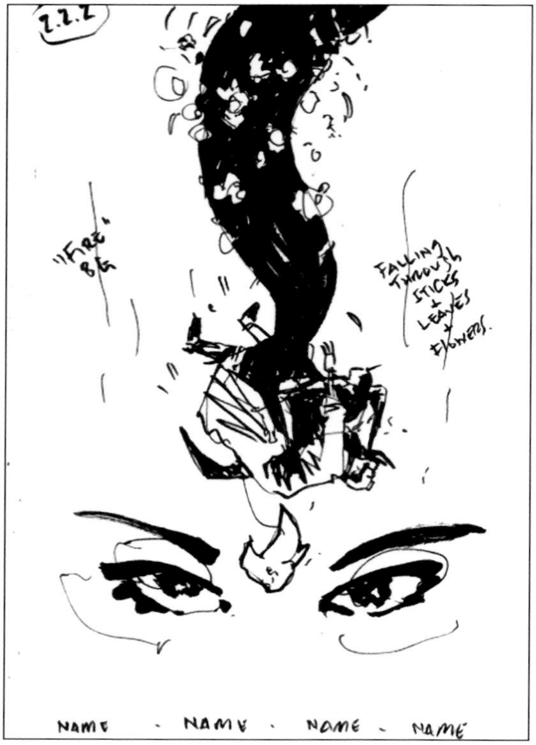
2.2.2
"FIRE" BG
FALLING THROUGH STICKS + LEAVES + FLOWERS.
NAME - NAME - NAME - NAME

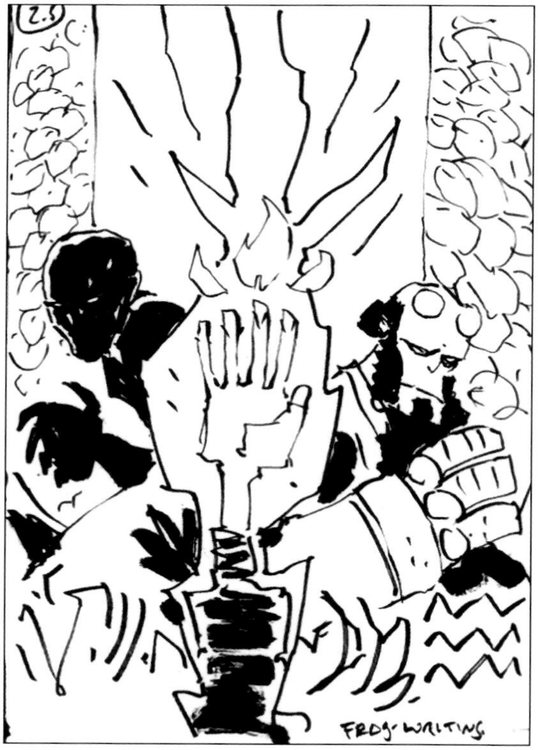
FROG-WRITING

This page: Unused cover sketches for #2.

Facing: The final cover for #2.

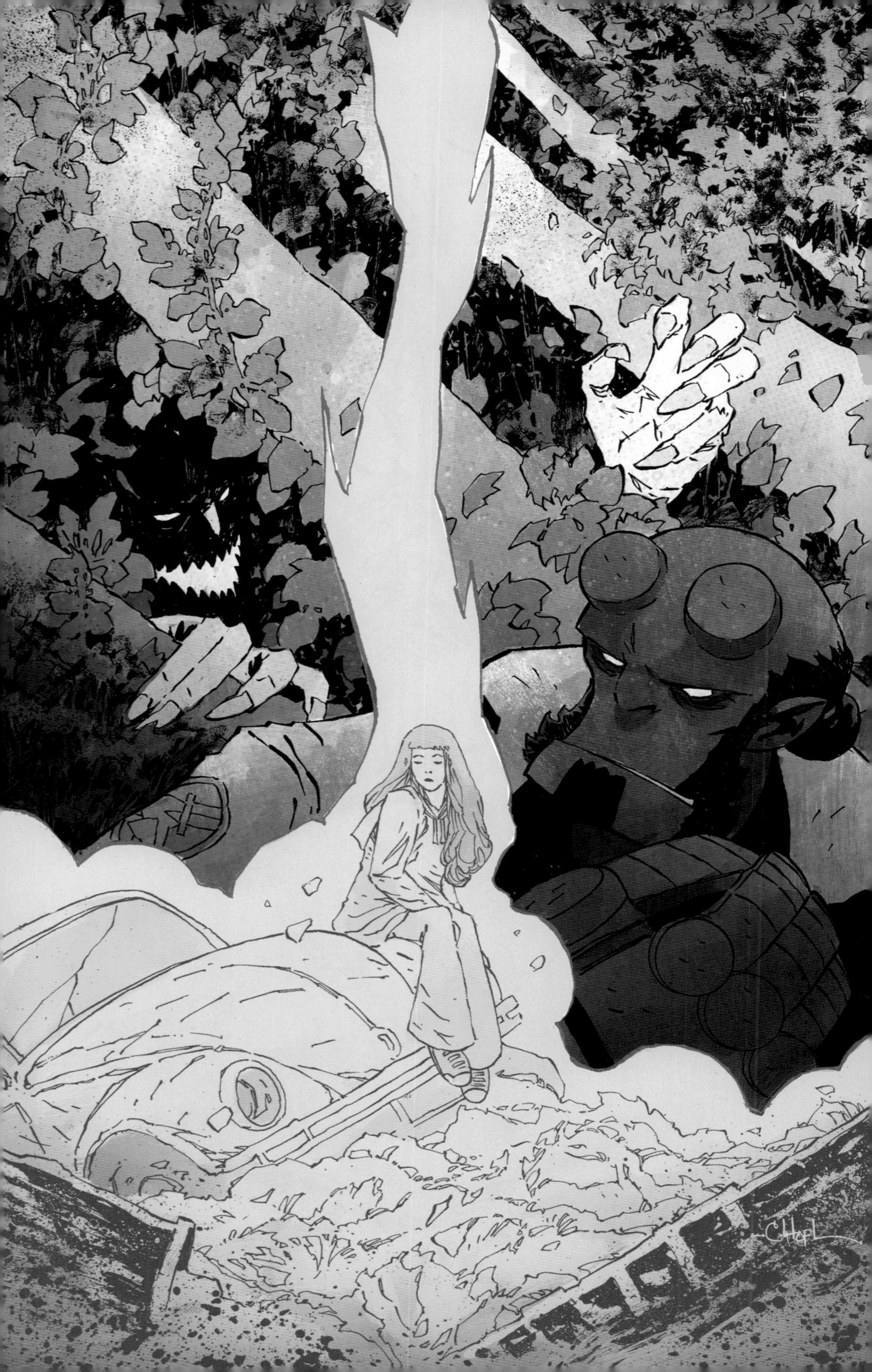

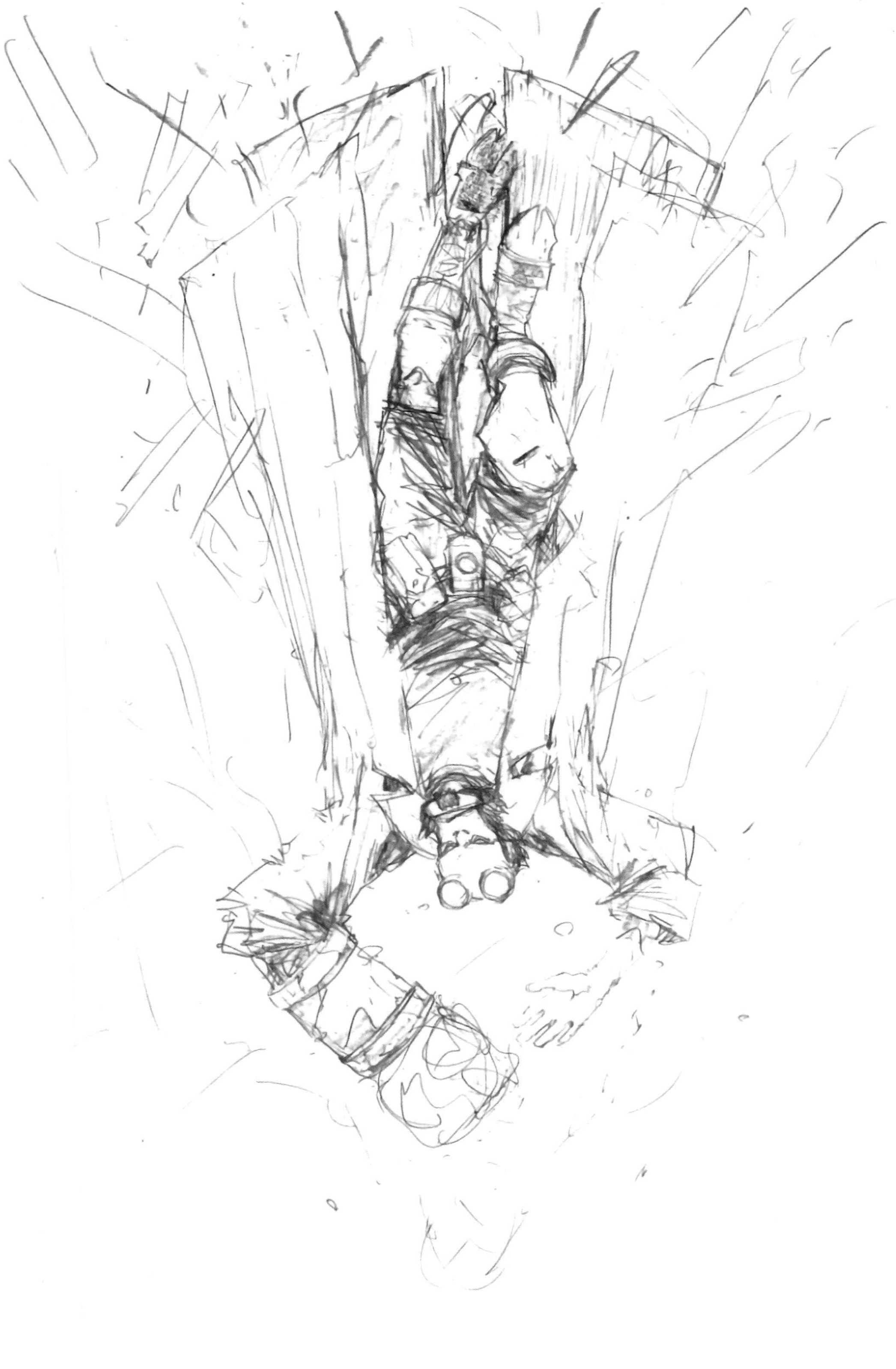

This page: Chris's in-progress pencils for #3.

Facing: The final cover for #3.

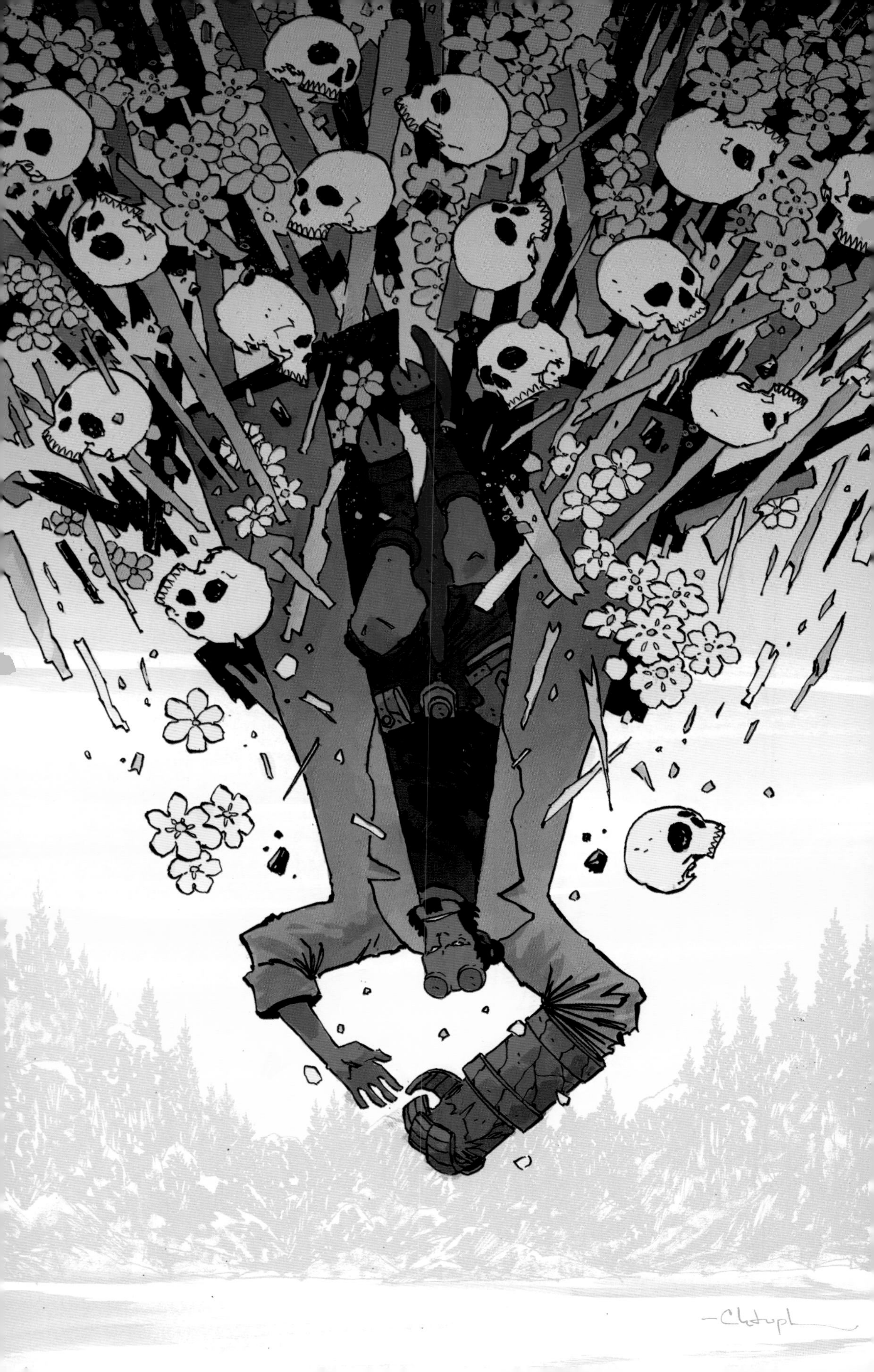

KRAMPUSNACHT

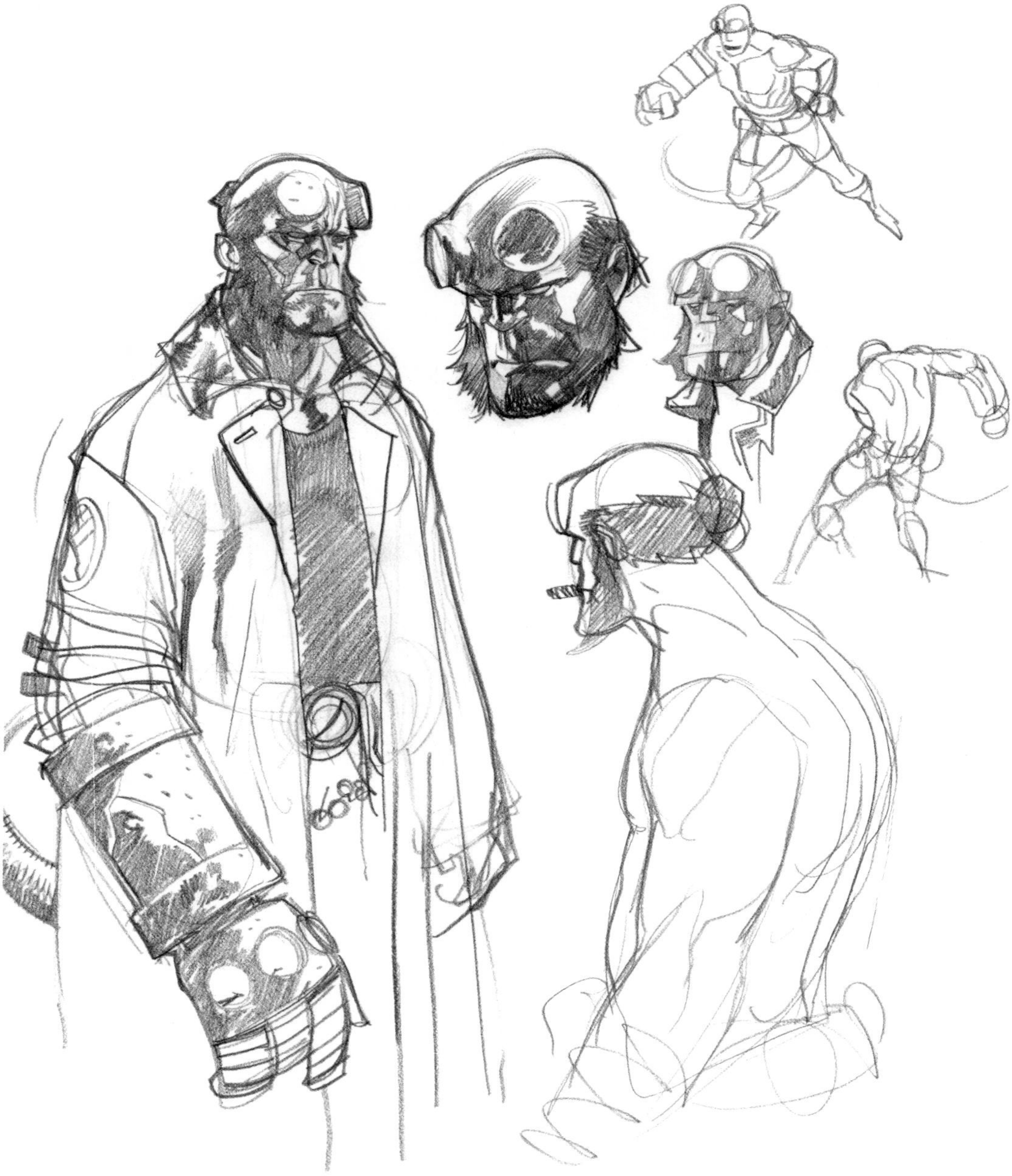

Some of Adam's early sketches to get the feel of Hellboy, in both design and movement.

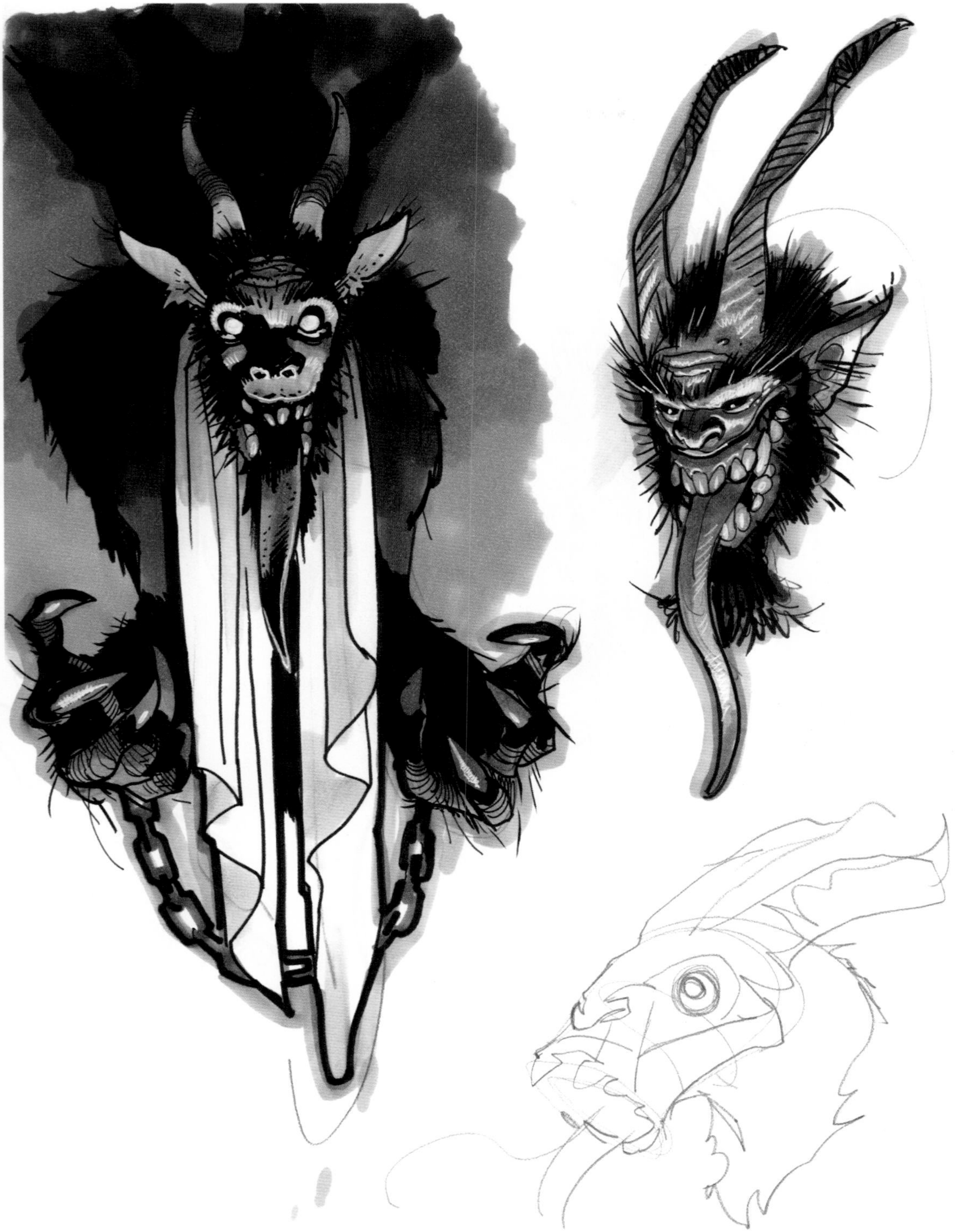

Adam's ideas for Krampus. Mike was the one to suggest that Krampus's head could transform throughout the fight scene, from his first monstrous appearance with the traditional goat face, to the more skeletal face at the end.

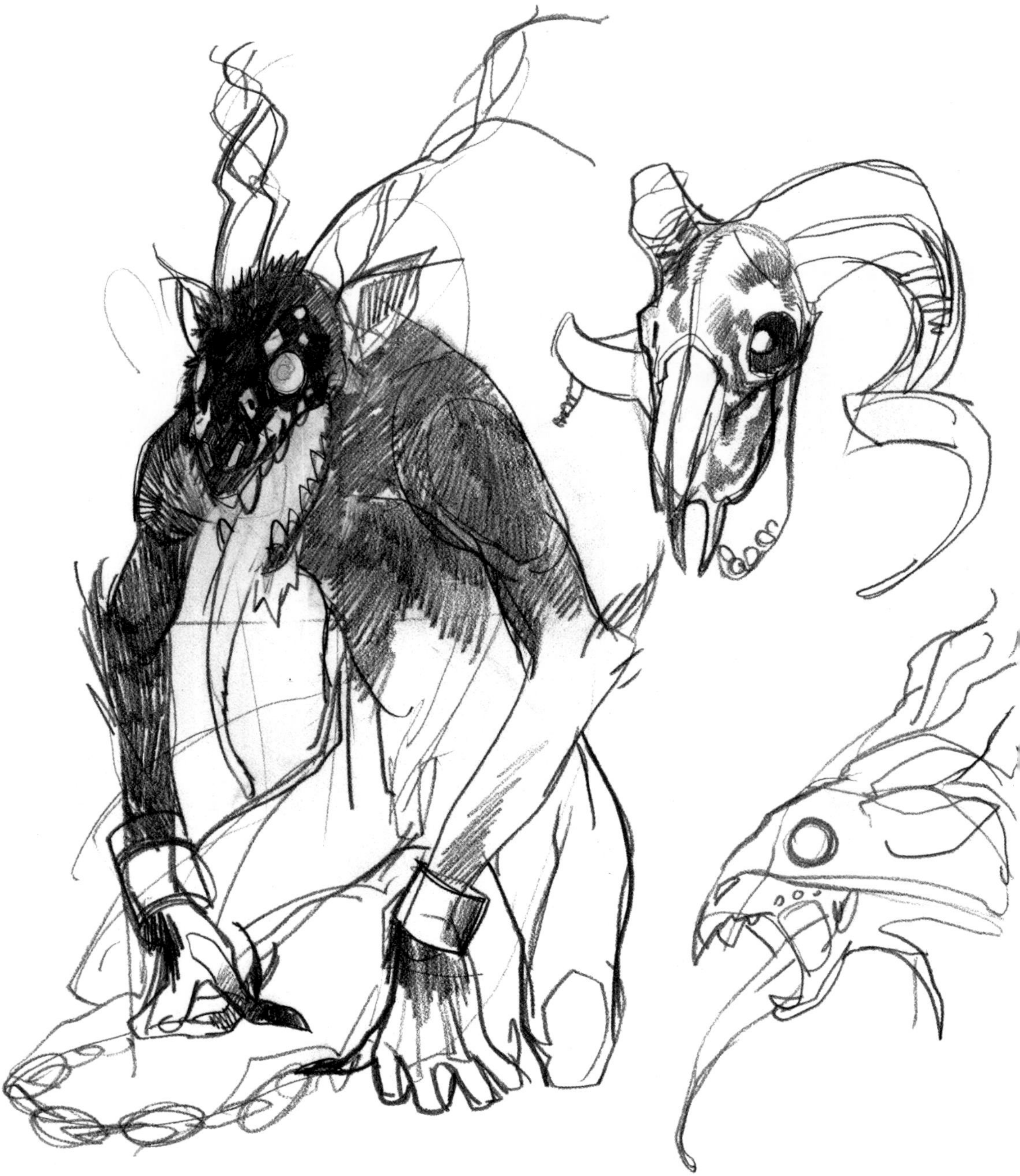

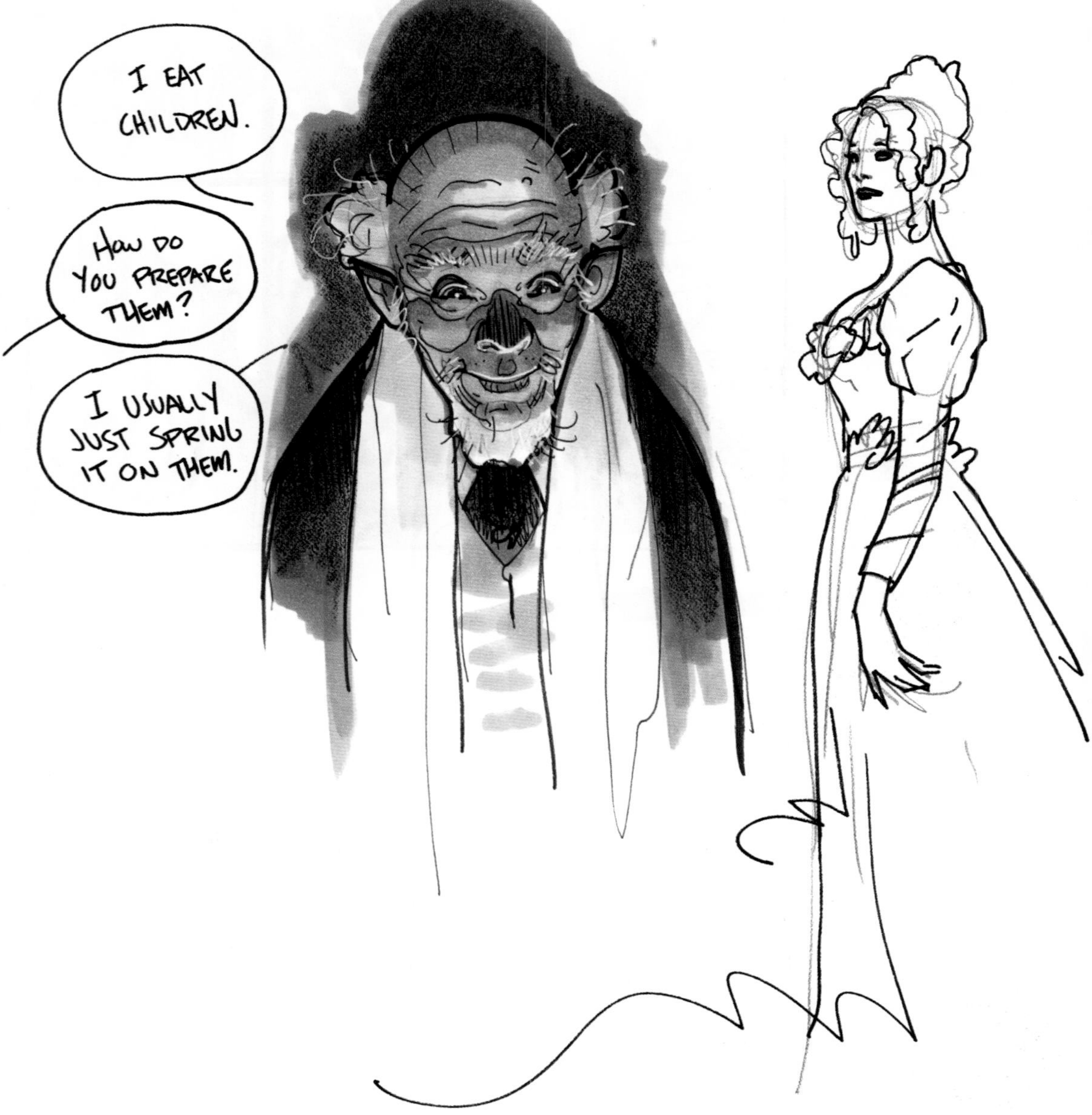
I EAT CHILDREN.
HOW DO YOU PREPARE THEM?
I USUALLY JUST SPRING IT ON THEM.

Krampus in his human form, or "Grampus" as Adam called him, and the ghostly woman who leads Hellboy through the woods to Krampus's house.

PISSED!
THROWS TABLE!
GUT PUNCH!
SMASH!
WHAM!

BRAK!
BPRD

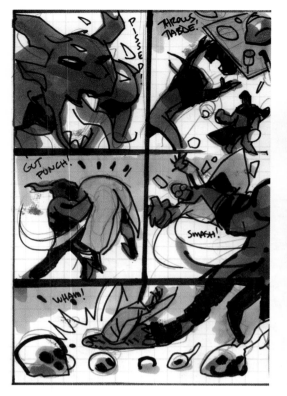

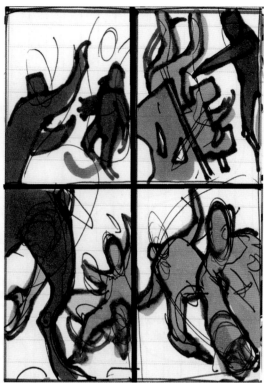

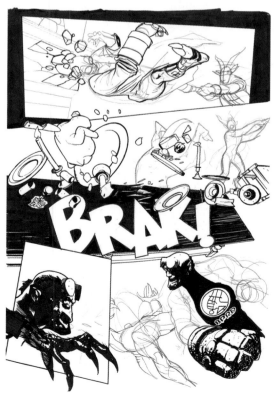

The evolution of page 12, including the initial layout (*top left*), revised layout (*top right*), and partially inked pencils (*bottom left*).

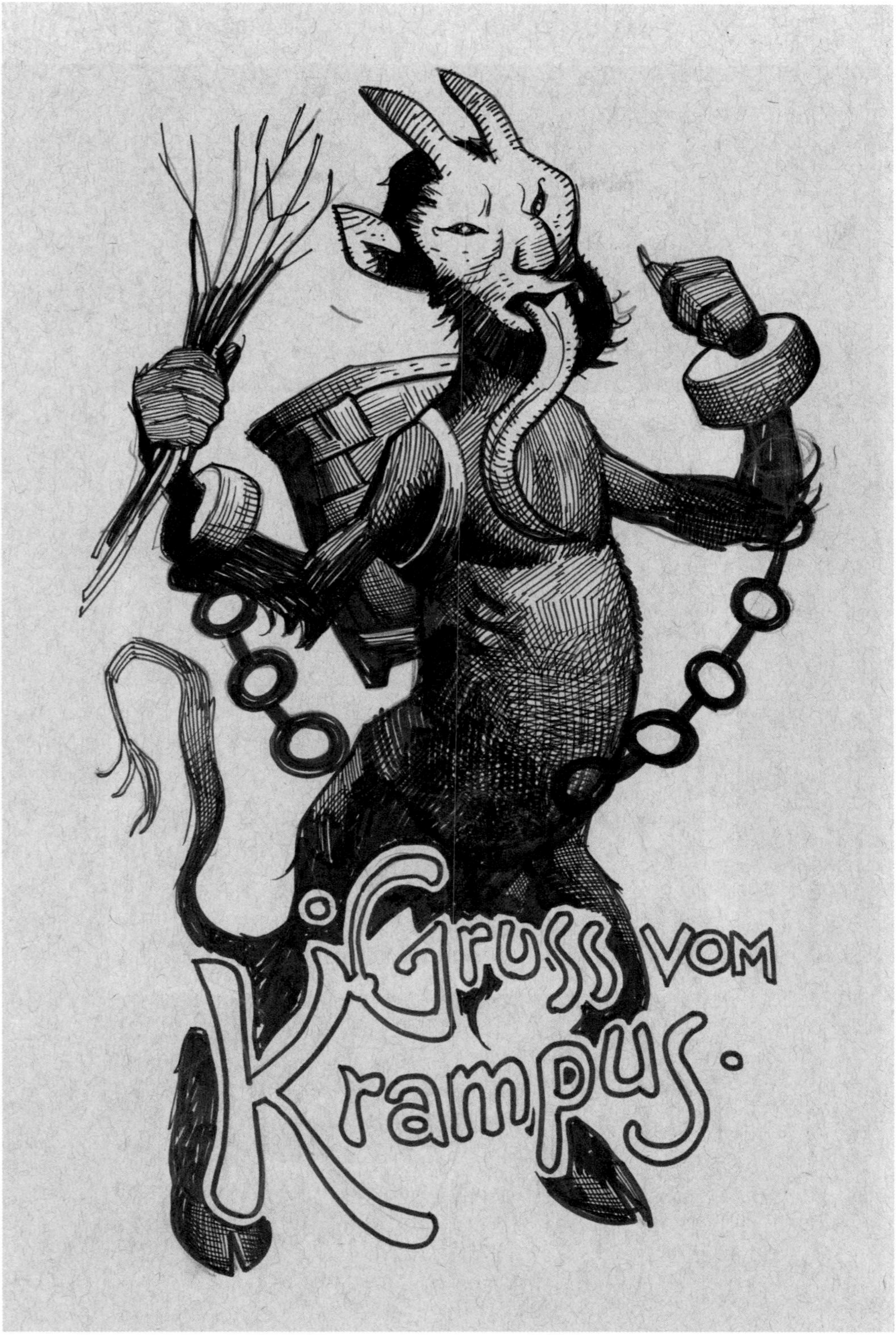
Gruss vom
Krampus.

A close-up on the Krampus drawing from the story, a more folkloric take on the real Krampus Hellboy meets.

Following pages: Adam's three pinups for the "Christmas Memories" section in the comic, followed by his line-art variant and Mike's variant covers.

Christmas, 1946
I got a Lobster Johnson
decoder ring!

Christmas, 1995
The year Abe got drunk!

Alice.

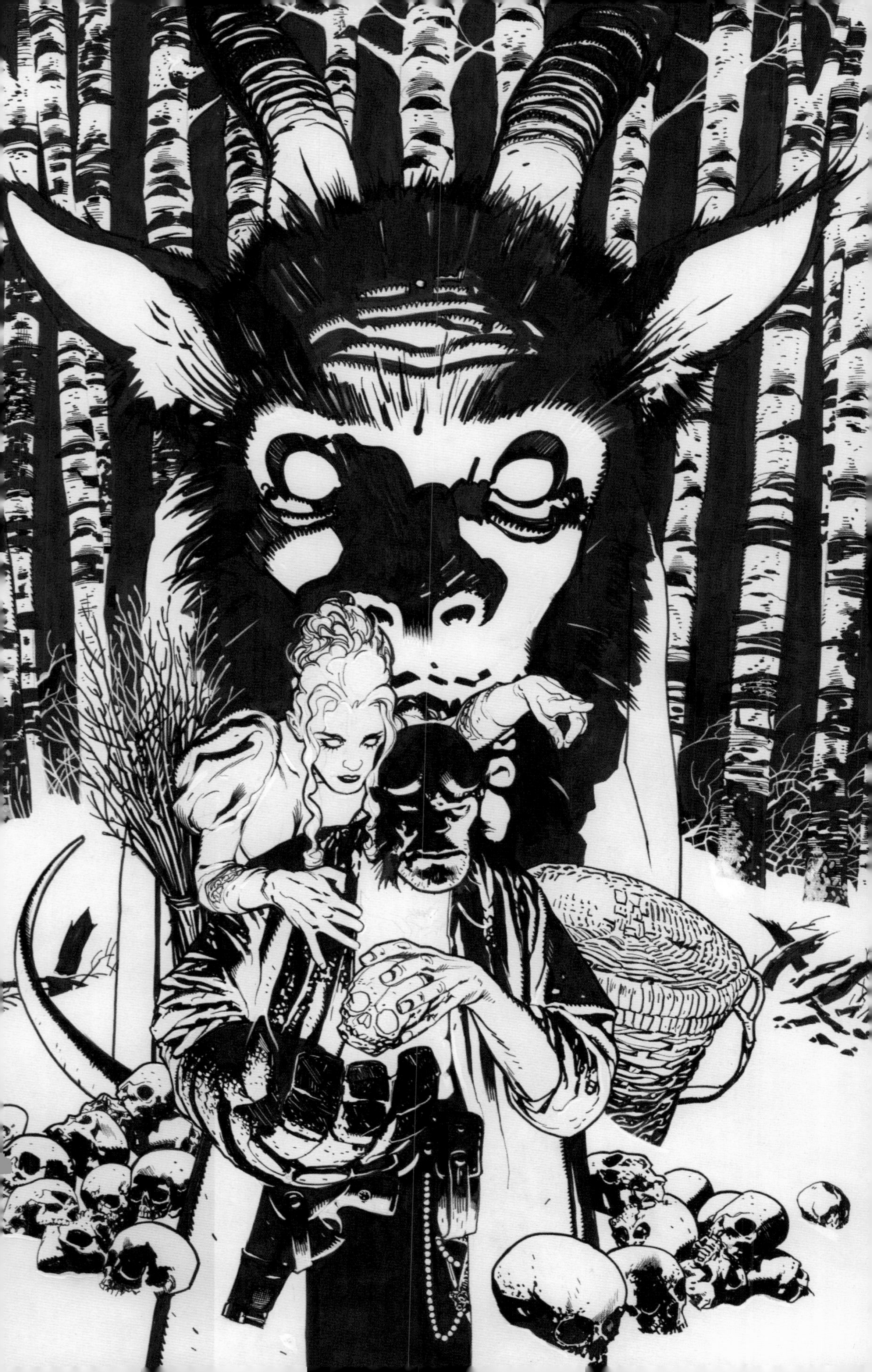

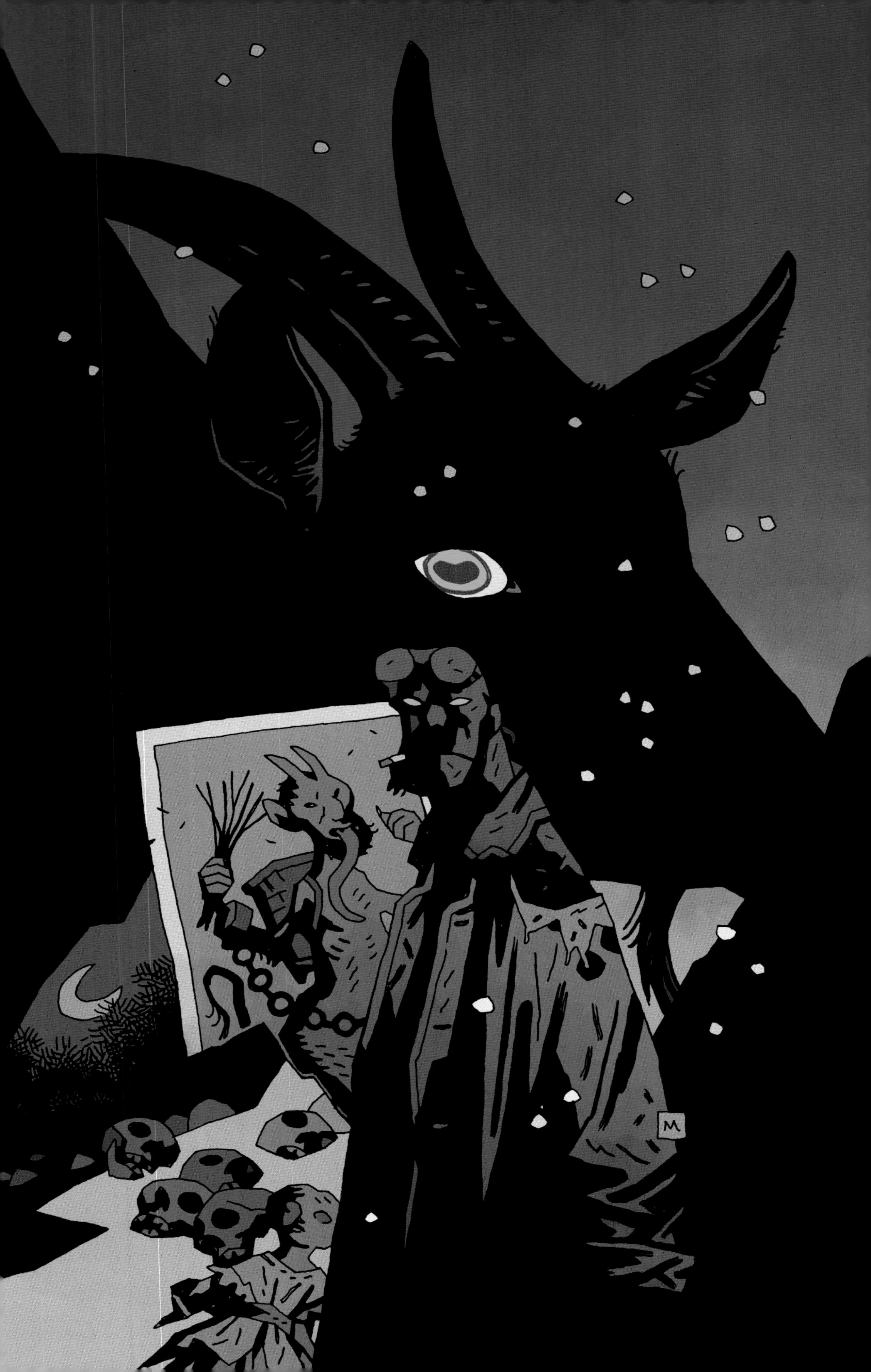

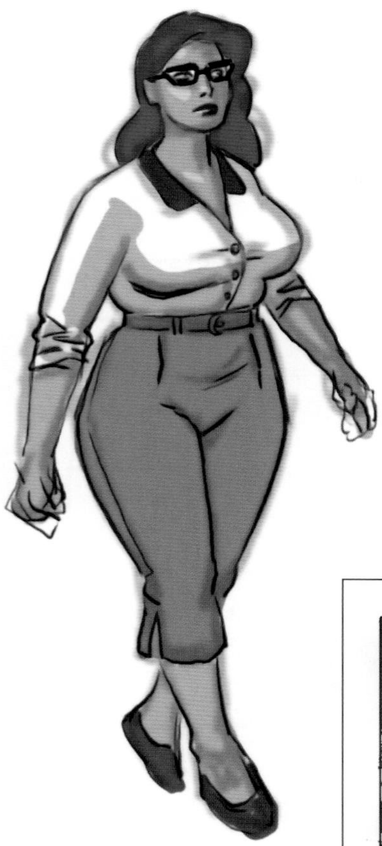

RETURN OF THE LAMBTON WORM

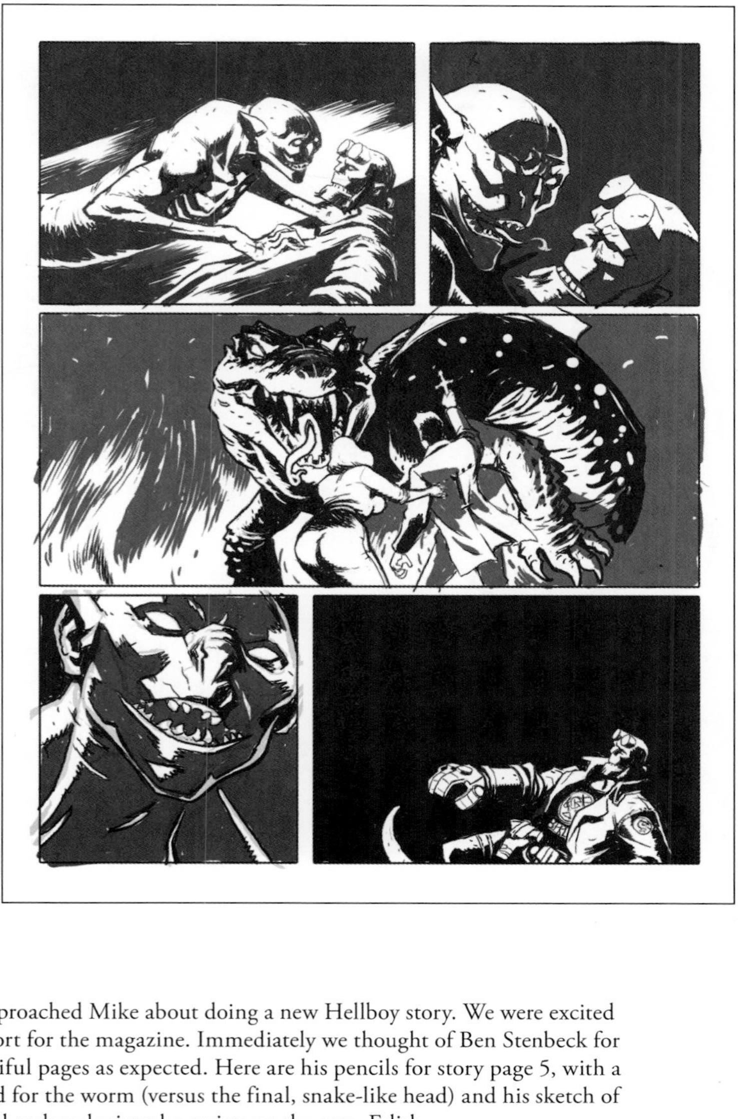

In late 2017, *Playboy* approached Mike about doing a new Hellboy story. We were excited at the chance to do a short for the magazine. Immediately we thought of Ben Stenbeck for art, who delivered beautiful pages as expected. Here are his pencils for story page 5, with a more crocodile-like head for the worm (versus the final, snake-like head) and his sketch of local archaeologist who assists on the case, Edith.

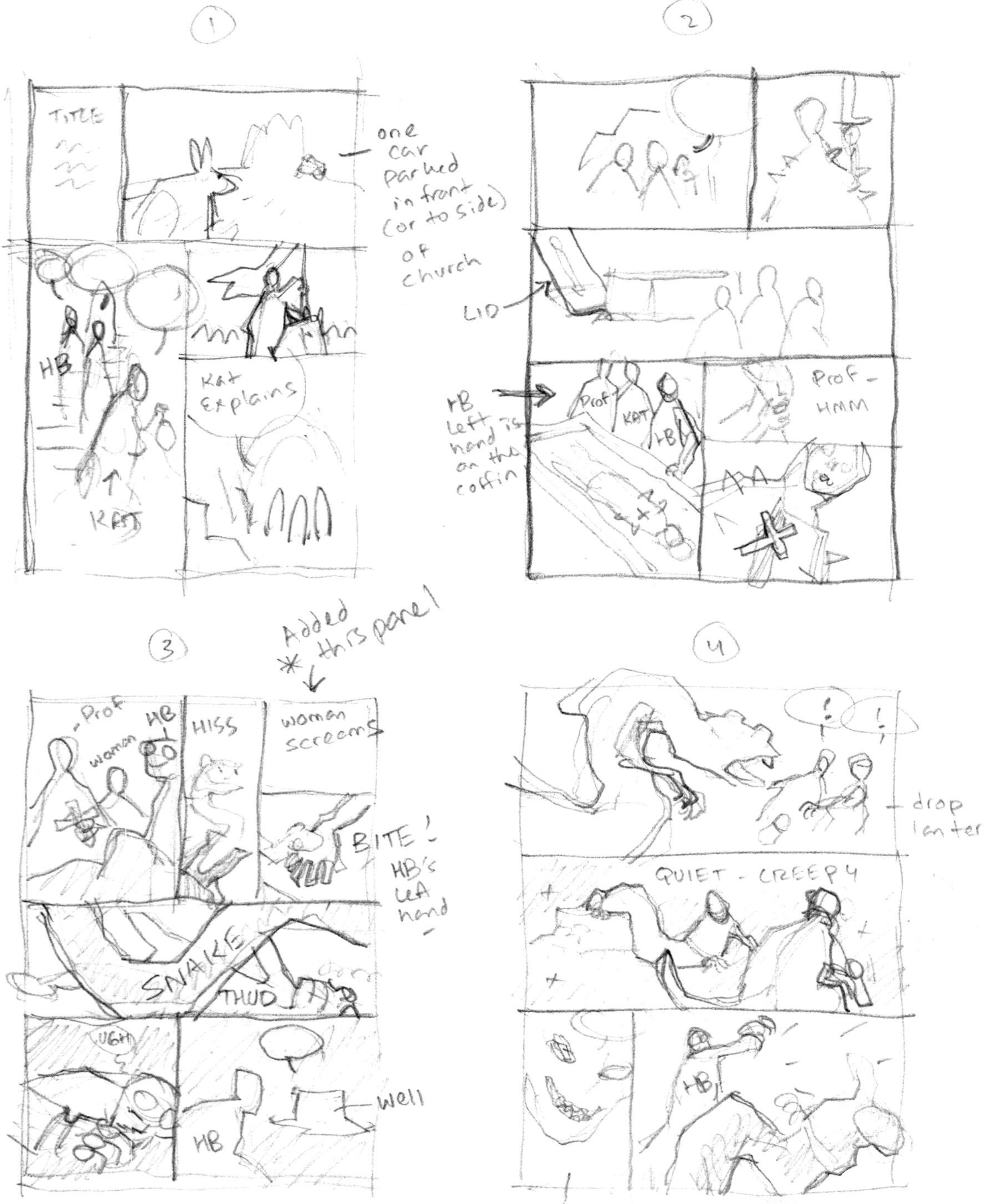
1
TITLE
one car parked in front (or to side) of church
HB
Kat Explains
KAT
2
LID
HB left hand is on the coffin
Prof
KAT
HB
Prof - HMM
3
Added this panel
Prof
woman
HB
HISS
woman screams
BITE!
HB's left hand
SNAKE
THUD
UGH
HB
well
4
drop lanter
QUIET - CREEPY
HB
Added panel demon close up

Mike's thumbails for all six pages.

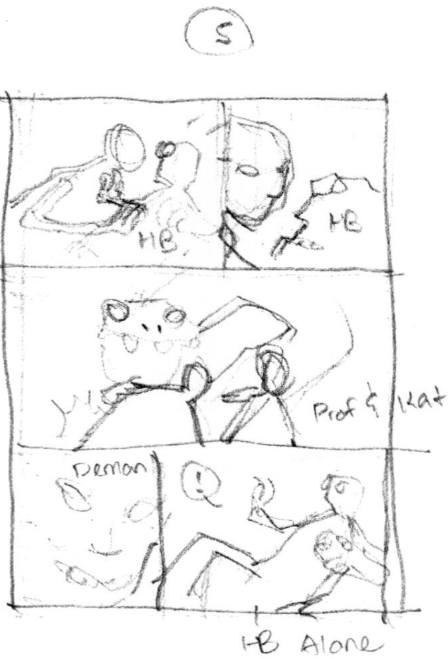
5
HB
HB
Prof & Kat
Demon
HB Alone

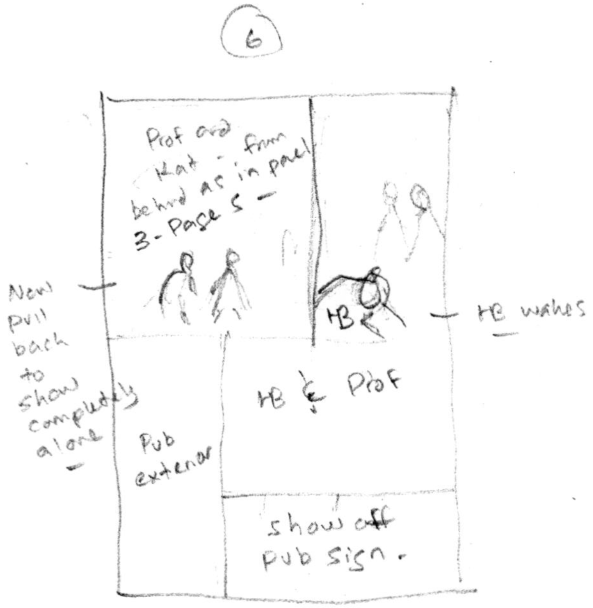
6
Prof and Kat - from behind as in panel 3 - Page 5 -
New pull back to show completely alone -
HB wakes
HB & Prof
Pub exterior
show off pub sign.

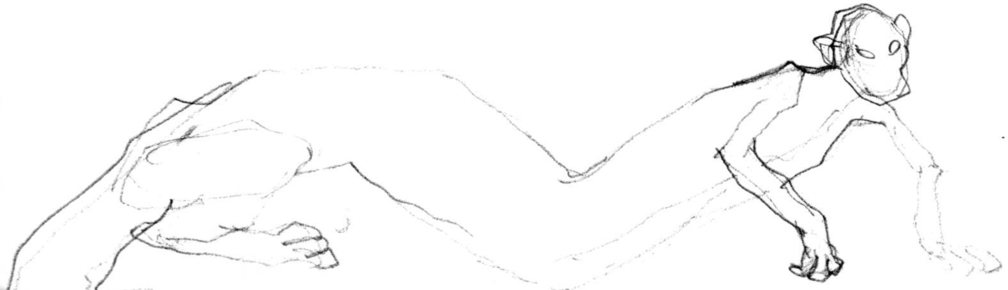

Demon in HB's dream - more human/Demon-like head and torso -- Noble but evil -

Demon that Prof and Kat face in the crypt is more serpent like - Non-human - Something along the lines of the Dragon in "Nature of the Beast" - Cross between snake and salamander/lizard -- Very big and scary.

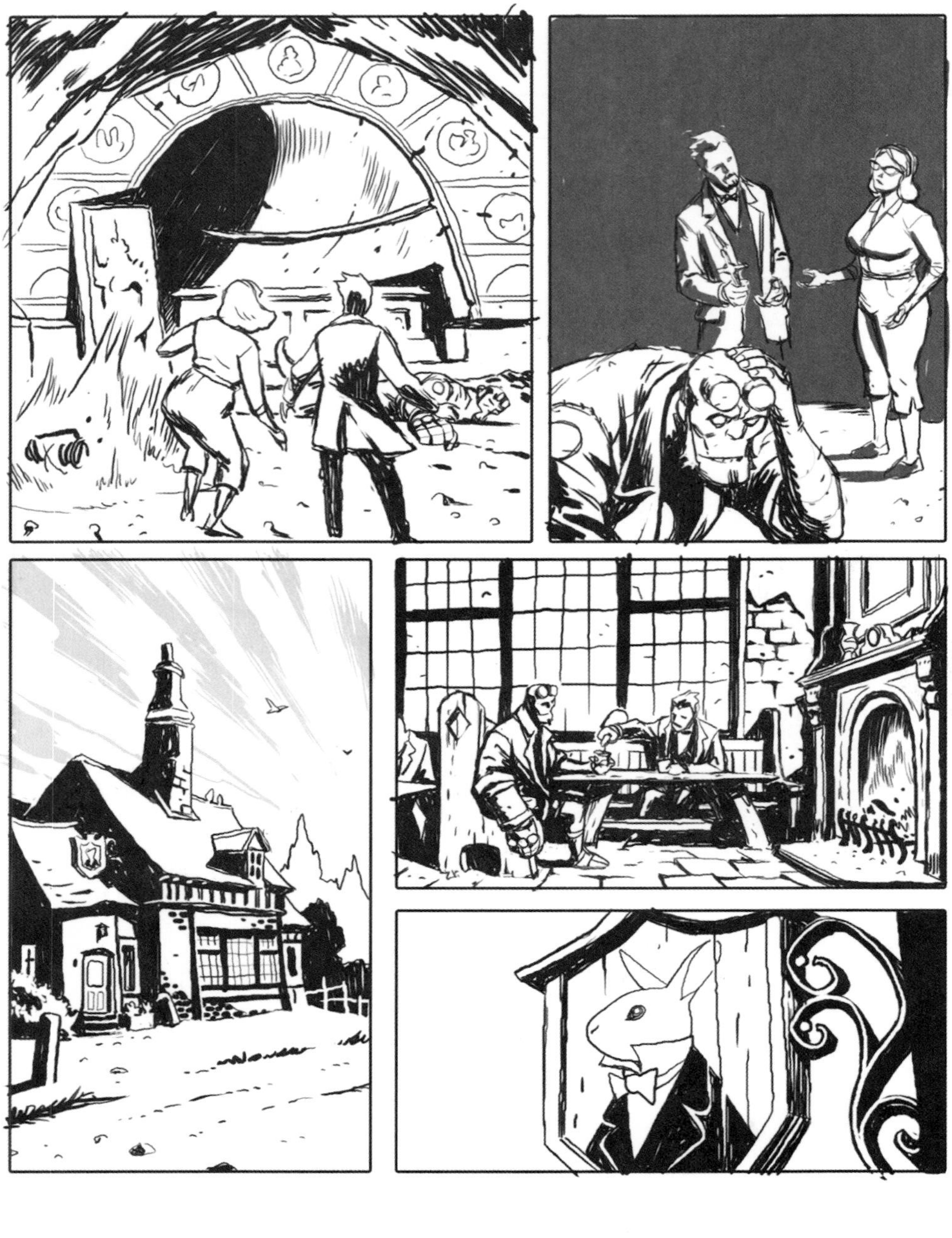

Ben's pencils for the final page, with one of two bunnies we snuck into the issue.

HELLBOY™

by MIKE MIGNOLA

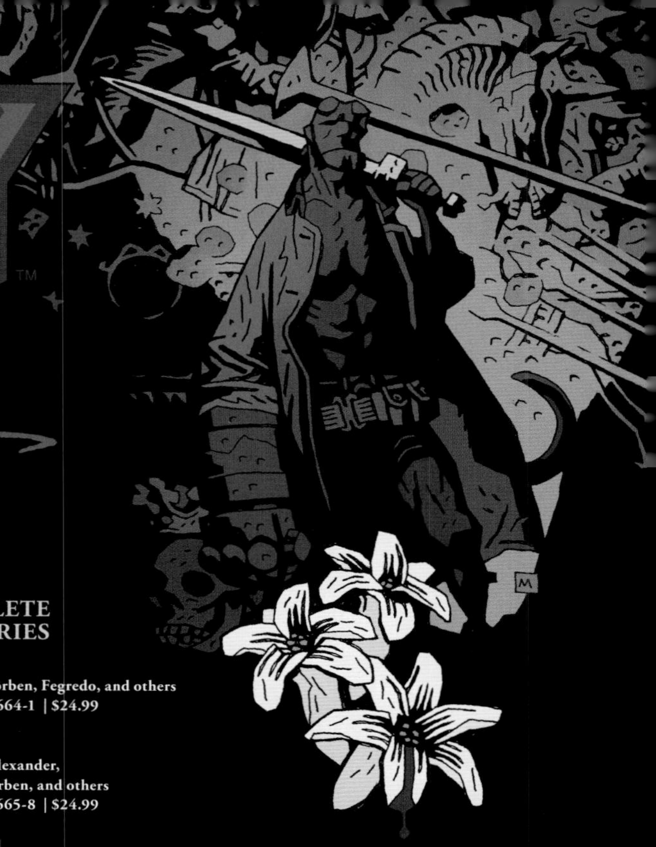

HELLBOY LIBRARY EDITION

VOLUME 1: Seed of Destruction and Wake the Devil
ISBN 978-1-59307-910-9 | $49.99

VOLUME 2: The Chained Coffin and The Right Hand of Doom
ISBN 978-1-59307-989-5 | $49.99

VOLUME 3: Conqueror Worm and Strange Places
ISBN 978-1-59582-352-6 | $49.99

VOLUME 4: The Crooked Man and The Troll Witch
with Richard Corben and others
ISBN 978-1-59582-658-9 | $49.99

VOLUME 5: Darkness Calls and The Wild Hunt
with Duncan Fegredo
ISBN 978-1-59582-886-6 | $49.99

VOLUME 6: The Storm and the Fury and The Bride of Hell
with Duncan Fegredo, Richard Corben, Kevin Nowlan, and Scott Hampton
ISBN 978-1-61655-133-9 | $49.99

HELLBOY IN HELL
ISBN 978-1-50670-363-3 | $49.99

HELLBOY OMNIBUS

VOLUME 1: Seed of Destruction
with John Byrne
ISBN 978-1-50670-666-5 | $24.99

VOLUME 2: Strange Places
with John Byrne
ISBN 978-1-50670-667-2 | $24.99

VOLUME 3: The Wild Hunt
with Duncan Fegredo
ISBN 978-1-50670-668-9 | $24.99

VOLUME 4: Hellboy In Hell
with Richard Corben and Gary Gianni
ISBN 978-1-50670-749-5 | $24.99

HELLBOY: THE COMPLETE SHORT STORIES

VOLUME 1
with John Byrne, Corben, Fegredo, and others
ISBN 978-1-50670-664-1 | $24.99

VOLUME 2
with Jason Shawn Alexander, P. Craig Russell, Corben, and others
ISBN 978-1-50670-665-8 | $24.99

HELLBOY: 25 YEARS OF COVERS
ISBN 978-1-50671-455-4 | $34.99

INTO THE SILENT SEA
with Gary Gianni
ISBN 978-1-50670-143-1 | $14.99

HELLBOY IN MEXICO
with Richard Corben, Fábio Moon, Gabriel Bá, and others
ISBN 978-1-61655-897-0 | $19.99

HELLBOY: THE FIRST 20 YEARS
ISBN 978-1-61655-353-1 | $19.99

GARY GIANNI'S MONSTERMEN AND OTHER SCARY STORIES
by Gary Gianni
ISBN 978-1-59582-829-3 | $24.99

HELLBOY: WEIRD TALES
ISBN 978-1-61655-510-8 | $24.99

HELLBOY: MASKS AND MONSTERS
with James Robinson and Scott Benefiel
ISBN 978-1-59582-567-4 | $17.99

HELLBOY: AN ASSORTMENT OF HORRORS
ISBN 978-1-50670-343-5 | $14.99

HELLBOY AND THE B.P.R.D.: 1952
with John Arcudi and Alex Maleev
ISBN 978-1-61655-660-0 | $19.99

HELLBOY AND THE B.P.R.D.: 1953
with Chris Roberson, Ben Stenbeck, Paolo Rivera, and Joe Rivera
ISBN 978-1-61655-967-0 | $19.99

HELLBOY AND THE B.P.R.D.: 1954
with Roberson, Corben, Churilla, and others
ISBN 978-1-50670-207-0 | $19.99

HELLBOY AND THE B.P.R.D.: 1955
with Roberson, Churilla, Rivera, and Shawn Martinbrough
ISBN 978-1-50670-531-6 | $19.99

HELLBOY AND THE B.P.R.D.: 1956
with Roberson, Mike Norton, Yishan Li, Michael Avon Oeming, and Paul Grist
ISBN 978-1-50671-105-8 | $19.99

THE HELLBOY 100 PROJECT
TPB: ISBN 978-1-61655-932-8 | $12.99
HC: ISBN 978-1-61655-933-5 | $24.99

NOVELS

HELLBOY: EMERALD HELL
by Tom Piccirilli
ISBN 978-1-59582-141-6 | $12.99

HELLBOY: THE ALL-SEEING EYE
by Mark Morris
ISBN 978-1-59582-142-3 | $12.99

HELLBOY: THE FIRE WOLVES
by Tim Lebbon
ISBN 978-1-59582-204-8 | $12.99

HELLBOY: THE ICE WOLVES
by Mark Chadbourn
ISBN 978-1-59582-205-5 | $12.99

AVAILABLE AT YOUR LOCAL COMICS SHOP OR BOOKSTORE! • To find a comics shop in your area, visit comicshoplocator.com.
For more information or to order direct, visit DarkHorse.com. Prices and availability subject to change without notice.

DARK HORSE BOOKS
DarkHorse.com

Also by MIKE MIGNOLA

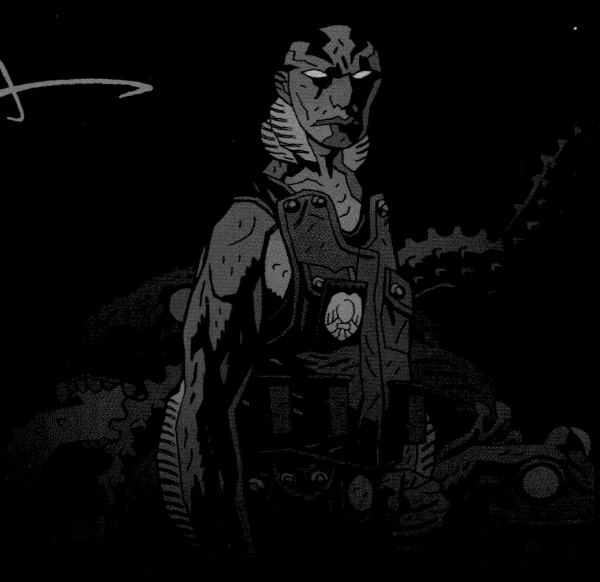

B.P.R.D. PLAGUE OF FROGS

VOLUME 1
with John Arcudi, Guy Davis, and others
TPB: ISBN 978-1-59582-675-6 | $19.99

VOLUME 2
ISBN 978-1-59582-676-3 | $24.99

VOLUME 3
ISBN 978-1-61655-622-8 | $24.99

VOLUME 4
ISBN 978-1-61655-641-9 | $24.99

1946–1948
with Joshua Dysart, Paul Azaceta, Fábio Moon, Gabriel Bá, Max Fiumara, and Arcudi
ISBN 978-1-50671-433-2 | $24.99

BEING HUMAN
with Scott Allie, Arcudi, Davis, and others
ISBN 978-1-59582-756-2 | $17.99

BPRD: VAMPIRE Second Edition
with Moon and Bá
ISBN 978-1-50671-189-8 | $19.99

B.P.R.D. HELL ON EARTH

VOLUME 1
with Allie, Arcudi, Davis, Tyler Crook, and others
ISBN 978-1-50670-360-2 | $34.99

VOLUME 2
ISBN 978-1-50670-388-6 | $34.99

VOLUME 3
ISBN 978-1-50670-490-6 | $34.99

VOLUME 4
ISBN 978-1-50670-654-2 | $34.99

VOLUME 5
ISBN 978-1-50670-815-7 | $34.99

B.P.R.D. THE DEVIL YOU KNOW

VOLUME 1: MESSIAH
ISBN 978-1-50670-196-7 | $19.99

VOLUME 2: PANDEMONIUM
ISBN 978-1-50670-653-5 | $19.99

VOLUME 3: RAGNA ROK
ISBN 978-1-50670-814-0 | $19.99

ABE SAPIEN

DARK AND TERRIBLE
VOLUME 1
with Allie, S. Fiumara, and M. Fiumara
ISBN 978-1-50670-538-5 | $34.99

VOLUME 2
ISBN 978-1-50670-385-5 | $34.99

LOST LIVES
AND OTHER STORIES
with Allie, Arcudi, Michael Avon Oeming, and others
ISBN 978-1-50670-220-9 | $19.99

LOBSTER JOHNSON

THE IRON PROMETHEUS
with Arcudi, Tonci Zonjic, and others
ISBN 978-1-59307-975-8 | $17.99

THE BURNING HAND
ISBN 978-1-61655-031-8 | $17.99

SATAN SMELLS A RAT
ISBN 978-1-61655-203-9 | $18.99

GET THE LOBSTER
ISBN 978-1-61655-505-4 | $19.99

THE PIRATE'S GHOST AND METAL MONSTERS OF MIDTOWN
ISBN 978-1-50670-206-3 | $19.99

A CHAIN FORGED IN LIFE
ISBN 978-1-50670-178-3 | $19.99

WITCHFINDER

OMNIBUS VOLUME 1
With Ben Stenbeck, John Arcudi, Tyler Crook, and others
ISBN 978-1-50671-442-4 | $34.99

CITY OF THE DEAD
with Roberson and Stenbeck
ISBN 978-1-50670-166-0 | $19.99

THE GATES OF HEAVEN
with Roberson, D'Israeli, and Clem Robins
ISBN 978-1-50670-683-2 | $19.99

RISE OF THE BLACK FLAME

with Roberson and Christopher Mitten
ISBN 978-1-50670-155-4 | $19.99

THE VISITOR: HOW AND WHY HE STAYED

with Roberson, Paul Grist, and Bill Crabtree
ISBN 978-1-50670-345-9 | $19.99

FRANKENSTEIN UNDERGROUND

with Stenbeck
ISBN 978-1-61655-782-9 | $19.99

RASPUTIN: THE VOICE OF THE DRAGON

with Roberson and Mitten
ISBN 978-1-50670-498-2 | $19.99

KOSHCHEI THE DEATHLESS

with Ben Stenbeck
ISBN 978-1-50670-672-6 | $19.99

CRIMSON LOTUS

John Arcudi and Mindy Lee
ISBN 978-1-50670-822-5 | $19.99

JOE GOLEM: OCCULT DETECTIVE—

THE RAT CATCHER & THE SUNKEN DEAD
with Christopher Golden and Patric Reynolds
ISBN 978-1-61655-964-9 | $24.99

THE OUTER DARK
with Golden and Reynolds
ISBN 978-1-50670-395-4 | $24.99

THE DROWNING CITY
with Golden and Bergting
ISBN 978-1-50670-945-1 | $24.99

THE CONJURORS
With Golden and Bergting
ISBN 978-1-50671-413-4 | $24.99

BALTIMORE

OMNIBUS VOLUME 1
With Golden, Stenbeck, and Peter Bergting
ISBN 978-1-50671-246-8 | $34.99

OMNIBUS VOLUME 2
ISBN 978-1-50671-247-5 | $34.99

NOVELS

LOBSTER JOHNSON: THE SATAN FACTORY
with Thomas E. Sniegoski
ISBN 978-1-59582-203-1 | $12.95

JOE GOLEM AND THE DROWNING CITY
with Golden
ISBN 978-1-59582-971-9 | $99.99

BALTIMORE; OR, THE STEADFAST TIN SOLDIER & THE VAMPIRE
with Golden
ISBN 978-1-61655-803-1 | $12.99
